THE CLONING OF
JOANNA MAY

AFFLICTION

FAY WELDON

THE CLONING OF
JOANNA MAY

AFFLICTION

HarperCollins*Publishers*

This omnibus edition published in 1999 by HarperCollins*Publishers*

HarperCollins*Publishers*
77-85 Fulham Palace Road,
Hammersmith, London W6 8JB

ISBN 0 261 67225 8

Printed and bound in Great Britain by
Caledonian International Book Manufacturing Ltd, Glasgow

The Cloning of
Joanna May

1

This has been a year of strange events: some wonderful, some terrible.

In the autumn a great wind swept through my garden one night, and toppled two oaks, three maples and a chestnut tree, all top-heavy with wet leaves, rooted in sodden earth. Had the gale come a week later the leaves would have been gone and the trees no doubt survived: a week earlier and the earth would have been dry and the roots steadier, and all would have been well. As it was, the chestnut crashed through the conservatory and set off all the alarms, which joined with the sound of the gale to frighten me out of my wits, so that I would have telephoned Carl, my ex-husband, and forthwith begged for his forgiveness and the restoration of his protection, but as the chestnut had brought down the wires I couldn't. By the morning the wind had died down and I, Joanna May, was my proper self again, or thought I was.

I went out into the garden and studied the sorry fallen giants, their earthy boles pointing unnaturally skyward, their scuttling insect population stricken by sudden cold and light: and wondered if there was any way of yanking them to their feet again, resettling them in the soil, making good what had been spoiled, but Oliver, my gardener and lover, told me there was not. The truth had to be faced – the trees were finished. That was the end of them: now all they could do was slowly die. I found myself weeping and that was very strange, and wonderful.

And that evening when preparing for bed I looked into my mirror and saw the face of an old woman looking back at me, and that was very strange and terrible. I attended to this apparition at once with astringent masks, moisturizing creams and make-up, and by the time Oliver padded into my bedroom on bare young feet with earthy nails, I, Joanna May, looked almost myself again; but there is no avoiding this truth either – that the task of rehabilitation will get more difficult year by year. Most things get easier the more they are done – but not this. The passage of time makes fools of us all.

I said as much to Oliver and he replied, 'Well, you're sixty, and should be used to it by now,' which is easy enough to say when you are twenty-eight, as he was. Personally I had expected to live for ever, frozen in time at the age of, say, thirty. 'I don't mind how old you are,' said Oliver that night, 'let alone how old you look. It's you I love.'

'Love' I could understand, but what did he mean by this 'you'? Small children (so I'm told) start out by confusing 'me' with 'you'. Addressed so frequently as 'you', their clever little minds work out that this must be their name. 'You cold,' they say, shivering, as the wind blows through the window. 'Not you,' comes the response, 'me.' 'Me cold,' says the child, obligingly. Presently the little thing progresses to the gracious 'I am cold.' But is the 'me', the 'I', really the same as that initial 'you' with which we all begin; the sudden bright consciousness of the self as something defined by others? Perhaps we did better in our initial belief, that the shivering cold is jointly experienced, something shared. I wonder.

Well, well, we will see. And as so often happens, the events that ensued ensured that I did see. Any enquiry, however primitive, this 'you' of ours manages to formulate in its mind as to the nature of reality, is met at once by such an eager response from that reality, such a convulsion of events, as to suggest that its only function is to provide us with examples, illustrations, of propositions that occur to the mind. Like Directory Enquiries, existing only to be asked, there to be consulted.

By the end of that year of strange events, I can tell you, when I looked in a mirror, I saw a face that would need a great deal more than a jar of wrinkle-cream and some exfoliator to bring it back to order. I was indeed old. Having children makes you old. It is the price we pay for immortality. God's last laugh, imposing this extra penalty on mankind before he flew off, leaving time the murderer behind, just waiting.

2

The great October wind frightened Jane Jarvis, aged thirty. It howled and raged outside her attic window, and quivered the panes until one of them actually cracked and shattered; then it swept in and around the room, bringing wet and cold with it. Rain spattered the TV screenplay she was sitting up late to read for Home Box-Office, and the wind somehow pried the sheets loose from their binder and swept them into the air and fluttered them round the room. Jane Jarvis thought the wind was alive: that it was some kind of vengeful spirit: that it whined and whinnied like the ghost of her aborted baby, long ago. She went into her bedroom and shut the door on the wind and the manuscript — not one she would recommend, in any case — and tried to sleep, but could not. She considered the temporary nature of all things, including her own life, and panicked, and rang her live-out lover Tom when she heard the clock strike three to say she'd changed her mind, he could be a live-in lover, they'd have a baby, but no one answered and by the morning prudence and courage had re-established themselves in her head and heart. She tacked strong polythene over the broken window; there would be a long wait for a glazier. The streets of London glittered with slivers of broken glass.

'You don't need me at all,' said Tom. 'You're self-sufficient.'

'I need you for some things,' she said, in the lingering sensuous voice that came so oddly from her rather thin, ladylike lips, 'of course I do. It's just I'd be mad to give all this up.' By which she meant freedom, independence, control over her own life.

'You're cold,' he said. 'Cold and over-educated and selfish.'

'Just rational,' she said, but Jane Jarvis was hurt. She took care not to show it. She had her pride. She did not want him; she did not want to lose him. She did not know what she wanted

7

– except her career. Soon, if she played her cards right, she would be head of the London office of HBO.

'Where were you last night at three in the morning?' she asked.

'That has nothing to do with you,' he said. 'How can it?'

The wind lobbed someone else's chimney through the neat suburban roof of the home of Julie Rainer, aged thirty, and spoiled its perfection in many ways, and broke the round fish-bowl in which Samson the goldfish spent his timeless, circling days, and Samson died on the wet thick pile of the carpet. Julie was frightened and wept and in the morning rang the vet and asked him, in her lingering bedroom voice, why she brought death to so many small lives and he said they died in the glare of her perfection; and she puzzled over the answer for days. When he rang her the following week and asked her out to dinner she accepted the invitation. She liked the smell of antiseptic on his fingernails and her husband was away.

The wind not only frightened Gina Herriot and Gina's three children Ben, Sue and Anthony (ages twelve, nine and two) but crashed an oak tree through the bonnet of the car in which they were sleeping. None was hurt, but the frame was bent and the doors were jammed and had to be opened up by the iron claws of the emergency services, as if it were a can of beans and they the can-opener. The car was parked in the road outside the house where the Herriots lived. The children's father, Cliff Herriot, had been drinking, and it was sometimes easier, as Gina explained to the social worker in her gentle, sexy voice and using language of a violence which issued oddly from her rather thin, ladylike lips, to lock him in than lock him out. Gina seldom confided so much of the detail of her situation to anyone, having her pride, indeed too much of it, but the violence of the wind had frightened her, more than her husband ever did. Fortunately the report went missing, since it was made out at the time the contents of all Social Service file cards were being transferred to disc: or perhaps because fate has a propensity to behave in the same way to people of similar nature. Events fall out, this way

8

or that, beyond our apparent control, yet in keeping with our expectations.

Gina was thirty, but born seven weeks prematurely, and this initial misfortune, this first hard, grating sharpening of the knives of fate, echoed like a sound, a siren song, through her life. 'Trust Gina', her neighbours said to each other, 'to be in the car when the tree fell,' but they didn't say it to her face. They feared her calm, quick look of disapproval: she did not like personal comments or appreciate advice. Her nose was broken but she remained chilly in her beauty: like Grace Kelly, they said, in that old film. 'Why doesn't she leave Cliff?' they asked. 'The brute!' But they didn't ask her to her face. Anyway, they knew the answer. She loved him.

——— ❧ ———

As for Alice Morthampton, aged thirty, in the womb a week longer than her mother-apparent had expected, the great wind bypassed her: of course it did. Alice was smiled upon by different stars than were Jane, Julie and Gina. The storm cut a swathe through southern England, passing from east to west, taking in London on its way, but Alice was not in London at the time, but in Liverpool, where she was engaged in a photo session: smart clothes against demolished warehouses.

'Smile, damn you, smile!' Angus the photographer had implored her during the day, but Alice Morthampton would not, saying in her languid, croaking voice that she knew better than he; she had surely been employed to actively not-smile, since that was her speciality. She spent the night in bed with him, however. 'You don't care about me,' he complained. 'You only do this for the sake of your career.' And she sighed and said she wasn't sure why she did it, she certainly didn't enjoy it: her career would get on well enough without him, probably better – and as she felt his assault upon her, as it were, weaken and tremble within her at least had the decency to apologize for her habit of speaking the truth, even when least welcomed, so he felt man enough to continue.

'I love you,' he said.

'Whatever that means,' she said, apparently unmoved by either desire or emotion, or perhaps too proud to show either. The storm caused a short delay on landing at Heathrow the following morning, true: aircraft were slewed across the runways and took time to move: but on the whole the fates were on Alice's side.

Jane, Julie, Gina, Alice: these were the clones of Joanna May.

3

After Carl May divorced his much-loved wife, Joanna May, for infidelity and had her lover killed, he lived celibate for several years (as did she) concentrating upon his business interests, which were many and various. But nature abhors a vacuum, in particular one to do with sex, and presently a Mr Hughie Scotland, aged forty-five, a TV and newspaper magnate, fleshy, vigorous and wilful, reached for his address book and ran his finger down the M's. Then he called Carl May on his personal number, not even leaving it to his secretary to do. She was crying anyway. His staff often did: tears dropped into the word processors, doing them no good at all. But Hughie Scotland was rich enough not to worry.

'Let me be blunt and to the point,' he said.

'You always are,' said Carl.

'I'm in a fix,' said Scotland. 'My wife is screaming at me all hours of the day and night –'

'I thought she was in Iceland,' said Carl. Susan Scotland, born in Alabama, had recently been appointed US Lady Ambassador to that chilly, prosperous country.

'She is,' said Scotland. 'I don't mind her screaming in person, but she screams over the international telephone system, and causes me embarrassment, for nothing is private to a man in communications who has enemies; you have no idea the language she uses. I don't want it to get about, for her sake.'

'I have to be at a meeting in ten minutes,' said Carl, 'or I'll have enemies.'

'I'll be brief,' said Scotland. 'I want you to take this bimbo of mine off my hands. These girls topple presidents and bishops, and I don't want this one toppling me; she could be on the phone to the gutter press day and night; she'd upset my wife.'

11

'Hughie,' said Carl, 'you *are* the gutter press,' but Hughie took no notice. Susan Scotland's recent distress had been caused by press photographs of her husband and a young woman named Bethany bathing and sporting naked in the waters of a trout farm: they had been published not only in rival newspapers but throughout his own extensive syndicate. 'You'll shit in your own nest for a profit,' she'd wept down the line from Reykjavik, thus shocking and alarming her husband.

'Hughie,' said Carl, 'I don't need a bimbo. I am a serious person. I am not like you: I am not in the habit of splashing about naked in trout tanks.'

Hughie said, 'Carl, those were free-range trout, it was a pool, not a tank, and a hot day, and a man can surely do as he wishes on his own property. You know I've diversified into fish farms? If my wife wants to see more of me let her come back from Iceland.'

'I'm sorry,' said Carl, 'but no. Pay the girl off. Isn't that what people do? What's the worry?'

'You're a dry old stick,' said Hughie, 'and getting worse since your wife left.'

And Carl went to his meeting. But presently he was tempted out to lunch by Hughie: few people can resist the lure of an inside story. Even Carl May could be affected in this way. Hughie, rather disappointingly, chose an obscure restaurant.

'I can cope with governments,' said Hughie, 'and monstrous taxes and creeping socialism but I cannot cope with women. Take this bimbo off my hands. She keeps crying. Why do women spend so much time in tears?'

'Why me?' asked Carl, picking at a lemon sole. He ate little, and drank less. He preferred his fish unfilleted.

'These girls have to move upwards,' said Hughie, 'or they get offended, and that's when the trouble starts. And you have class. I have style but you have class.'

'Me?' asked Carl, surprised. 'Me? Class?'

'How many women have you slept with in your life?' asked Hughie.

'One,' said Carl. 'My wife.'

'That's class,' said Hughie. 'Why don't you leave that fish

12

alone? It comes from the North Sea; it will have died of pollution, caused by your outfall.' Carl May was Chief Executive of Britnuc, a corporation which had become involved with the rehabilitation of the old Magnox nuclear power stations, two of them sited on North Sea shores. 'Freshwater fish are the meat of the future. Do me a favour, I'll do you a favour.'

'What?' asked Carl.

'I'll hold the story on the plutonium leak last March at Britnuc A. No one else has got it.'

'They haven't got it,' said Carl, 'because there wasn't one.'

'The public's too sanguine about nuclear power,' said Hughie. (How was he to know Chernobyl was to blow?) 'They need stirring up. So do you. Bethany's the girl to do it. Those press photos didn't do her justice.'

'I only read the financial papers,' said Carl.

'Out of touch,' said Hughie. 'You don't want to lose your touch. What you need, mate, is a bit of pain to stir things up again. You're slipping.'

It seemed to Carl that he would use less energy obliging Hughie Scotland than disobliging him, and so he agreed to take the girl Bethany on to his personal staff, Scotland paying her wages. The rich stay rich by staying mean. Fish with the bones in cost less than fish with the bones removed.

4

'I dreamt that I dwelt in marble halls,' Carl May whispered to himself and sang,

'With vassals and serfs by my si-i-de,
  And of all the assembly gathered there
  You were the joy and the pri-i-de.'

And well might he sing, and thus, as some months later he stepped from the back of a limousine and his sneakered foot touched conquered ground, while the Thames ran by as busy and significant as the ancient Euphrates.

Bethany Turner stepped out from the other side of the limousine and a different tune ran through her head. 'Shoo fly,' she whispered and hummed, 'shoo fly don't bother me, for I belong to somebody.' And she thought, of course, if she belonged to somebody, that somebody must be Carl May, her rich grey man, but she was wrong. Bethany loved, like a million million other women, someone who existed only in her head, who would never, in all her life, materialize. She loved a phantom, in whose image Carl May stood.

'What are you singing?' she asked Carl.
'Tunes from the dog-house,' he said. 'Tunes from the dog-house, that's all.'

It was a joke. For Carl's mother had kept him much of the time, when he was little and hungry and stole, chained up in the dog's kennel in the yard, to teach him a lesson. His father was a dead dog: his mother was a bitch. That much he learned. 'Marble Halls' would drift over the neighbouring fence, from next door's wind-up gramophone, and sustain his assaulted spirit. The child Carl shivered, he wept, he slept, he dreamed, and later he made the dream come true, as a few, just a few children, can.

'And you?' he asked. 'What are you singing?' For Carl heard everything, however soft, especially soft.

'Tunes from a childhood,' she said. 'That's all.' As for her, she'd been brought up in a whorehouse. Thrust people down when young and most stay down. A few rise up, like Carl and Bethany, and then if they're lucky they find each other.

He took her arm in his and they walked off to inspect this especially poignant part of his empire, there beside the Thames, and were happy for at least this one hour: he had found someone he truly desired, whom he could mould to his will, and she had found someone she truly admired, who would do as she wanted; the past, they thought, was now well and truly over. None so dangerous as those who believe they are happy, and are not. They flail around them, laying waste.

How at home they felt, young Bethany, old Carl, in this wasteland of razed warehouses and mean streets. Her high crocodile heels caught in crevices where weeds and grasses still found temporary hold, just enough dusty soil to live. His spongy-soled sneakers made light work of cracked, uneven surfaces. Soon builders and container-gardeners would move in and a new People's Park spring up all around: fast-food concessions in ferny precincts; disco dancing in leafy glades; Goofy and Peanuts and Garfield fighting it out in flowery pastures. Miniature sheep would graze on new enriched turf for the delight and wonder of young and old; there would be fireworks by night, TV stars by day, entrance £5 per head and few extras, and all thanks to the ingenuity and enterprising thrust of Riverside Gardens plc, the funding of the DTI, the involvement of local government, and Riverside Developments Inc.

Carl May was on the board of both Riverside Gardens and Developments. Six months after its no-doubt-royal opening,

Riverside Gardens was destined to pack up its container plants, crate its miniature sheep, fill whole lorries with stacks of well-watered turf and move on to the next inner-city waterside site. Then Riverside Developments would move in, all planning permission and social grants agreed by the local housing authority, to erect high-price housing for those young professionals who wanted a river view and easy access to the City, and who were prepared to pay for it.

In this way everyone would benefit: not only the people who flocked to the part Disneyland, part Garden Centre of the People's Park – in particular a thousand thousand dispossessed fathers who needed somewhere to take their children on access weekends – but those who would obtain a minimum of six months' employment in its running: that is to say craftsfolk, fast-food concessionaires, builders, painters, waitresses, gate-keepers, security men, artists and artistes, cleaners, hedgers and ditchers, occupational therapists and so on. And after they were gone there would be permanent employment for the servicing agents of the young property-owning incomers – janitors, hair-dressers, manicurists, dress designers, drivers, dentists and so forth. Yes indeed, all would benefit, and not least the profit and status of Carl May himself: Carl May of Riverside Parks plc, Riverside Developments Inc., and many other interlinking business concerns beside, including the one of which he was Chairman – British Nuclear Agents, Britnuc for short.

Bethany was twenty-four. She wore high crocodile shoes, ginger stockings, suspendered beneath ginger woollen jodhpurs held by leather bands at calf and waist, a not very clean white cotton shirt, highwayman's style and well unbuttoned, chains of gold butterflies round neck, waist and ankle. Her red hair had been untidily pinned up with a Spanish amber comb: she wore emerald-green contact lenses in her eyes. The look of the wanton was intentional, and as fake as her orgasms: she could do student, or executive wife, or lady doctor just as well. The only school exam she'd ever taken was Drama and she'd got a credit for that. But she could think of easier and livelier ways of making

16

a living than being an actress, and recognized it as folly to waste her father's training in being what men wanted.

Carl stood 5 foot 10 inches in his shoes, or had done last time he was measured, thirty years ago, in the days when he still needed life insurance to set against mortgages. Suspecting that time might have shrunk him, thinning the discs in his spine, as time does, he now wore elevated shoes. He knew the value of height when dealing with other men: but also that height is in the mind of the observer, it is a matter of bearing rather than actuality. He saw no deceit in the elevated shoes: he would have reached at least 6 foot 3 inches had it not been for severe malnutrition in early childhood, or so he had been told: he knew he was in essence a tall man. He wore carefully casual clothes for this outing with Bethany: he had a natural tendency to be dapper, to wear carnations in buttonholes, which he was at pains to overcome. To dress too carefully was to display nervousness. He had the well-developed chin of those accustomed to telling others what to do. His hair remained thick, though white.

The gap in their ages, the gulf in their manners, their way of dressing, the sense of his wealth in proportion to that wiliness born of helplessness in her, the very place in which they walked – exploiter and exploited (but which was which?) – made their perambulation altogether disreputable. People looked after them puzzled and not altogether pleased, as if expecting something sudden and terrible to happen any minute – as if a bulldog and a kitten, not a man and a woman, were out walking together. But Carl and Bethany saw in their looks only admiration and envy.

Carl and Bethany returned to their limousine to drive over rough ground to a site of special interest, where a brass plaque was to be set into the ground: a place of pilgrimage for future generations.

'Perhaps,' said Carl, modestly.

'How can you doubt it!' said Bethany, as expected of her.

The mythology of Carl's past had become familiar to the public, and even to himself: his childhood had indeed, by constant reference, been all but sucked dry of pain, drained of poison. Yet this pain, this poison, he knew well enough was the source of his energy, his power.

'Let there be buildings!' Carl May had only to cry, pointing to an arid landscape, and lo, so there would be. In the beginning, it is true, unlovely stubby concrete profitable blocks arose, but then, confidence breeding confidence, came the glassed towers and steel pinnacles of the finest architectural imagination. And all at Carl May's command – he, who until he was ten had lived in a shed down here by the river, chained with the dogs.

'Let there be beauty!' Carl May had only to murmur, he whose stepfather had battered and abused him, and lesser men would scurry forward with trees and flowers – albeit grown in container pots with soil substitute, well sterilized against all insect pests – and yes, there would be beauty, of a sort.

'Let there be light!' Carl May ordained, and nuclear power stations sprung up at his command and pumped their power into the National Grid. He, who was rescued by a teacher at the age of ten, half-dead, passed into council care, thence to foster parents and public school, Cambridge, business school and the Institute of Directors. He, who had everything except what he wanted – that is to say that which was not to be bought with money, that cluster of blessings which trip off the tongue as faith, hope and charity.

'See,' said the world, 'anyone can do it. It is perfectly possible to rise above circumstances, however dire those circumstances may have been. An unhappy past can be no excuse for the actions of murderers, sadists, child abusers, wife batterers, criminals of any kind. Carl May did it – so can you!'

It was to revive the pain and thus maintain the level of his achievement that Carl May took green-eyed Bethany down to the banks of the Thames. So, on this very pilgrimage, he had on occasion taken his blue-eyed wife Joanna. But that had been in the days when the mean and horrid streets still stood, before Carl May had conceived the idea of Riverside Parks plc, and Riverside Developments, and the main area of his fame and accomplishment (apart from his notable capacity to overcome

18

the rigours of the past) was seen to be in the new world of nuclear power, the harnessing of the atom for mankind's advancement, that peace, happiness and prosperity might reign henceforth, and so forth.

'Without my wife,' Carl May had said for all the world to hear on radio and TV, 'I am nothing.' He was brave enough to bare his soul in public, or at any rate such part of it as he wished the public to know. 'The love of a good woman', he had joked, 'behind any great man!' only half-joking, and popular psychologists at once put pen to paper. 'You see,' they said, 'the wife can do for a man what the mother did not. No one should give up hope: no personality is irredeemably lost, destroyed. The narrow eyes of the tormented, anxious child, the thin mouth of the frightened child – they need not be permanent. With time, and love, those eyes will open wide, the mouth fill out. Fear not.' Carl May believed it too.

5

A couple of days before Chernobyl went up, making a large world into a small one, by reason of our common fear of radiation – the invisible enemy, the silent murderer, that which, like age, creeps in the dark – in this case consisting of a myriad, all-but-immortal particles, too small for the eye to see, of one man-made radioactive isotope or another (selenium, caesium, strontium – you name it, we invented it) flying through the air and causing death and decay wherever it fell, at any rate in the popular imagination – I, Joanna May, read of another strange event.

A girl in Holloway, doing three years for cheque offences, plucked out her eye. The technical term for this is 'orbisecto de se', and very nasty it is, for those who have to clear up afterwards and put flesh and head back together. The human eye, if you regard it without emotion, is a glob of light-sensitive jelly attached by strings of nerves and muscles to the convoluted tissue mass of the brain, in itself a fine ferment of electrical discharges. But it works, it works. The 'you', the 'me', the 'I' – behold, it sees! The soul in the dark prison that is the flesh looks out through the senses at the world: the senses are the windows to that dark prison. And what the soul longs to see is beauty; smiles, grace, balance – both physical and spiritual – love in the maternal eye. It longs to see evening light over summer landscapes: crimson roses in green grass: birds flying, fish leaping, happy children playing – all that stuff. Yes, all that stuff.

What the contemporary eye gets to see on a good day is Mickey Mouse: it can just about put up with that, some joke is intended in the ugliness. The white lacy Terylene of a wedding dress makes up for a lot. A nice strong erect penis, viewed, can reconcile a lustful girl to some grimy back alley. But three years in Holloway! What is the eye, the I, to make of that!

Three years in Holloway, three years of grey concrete, the stuff of anti-life, the stuff that keeps radioactivity in (at least temporarily) or out: three years of looking at old Tampaxes in corners and cigarette stubs and grime and grey tins holding the brown slime of institution stew, and any sane person would be tempted to pluck their eye out, let alone the mad, who more than anyone proceed by punning. The word in action. The deranged pursue their sanity down the only alley known to them: giving language more meaning, more significance, than it was ever meant to have.

If thine eye offend thee, pluck it out. And quite right too. Broadmoor's a handsome place, set grandly in the wild hills: a great sweep of dramatic sky; old bricks not new concrete. One eye in rural Broadmoor's better than two in suburban Holloway, any day. She plucked her eye out and got transferred to Broadmoor. That's where one-eyed girls go.

I wanted to write to Carl to say, 'Carl, Carl, did you read about the girl in Broadmoor who plucked out her eye?' but how could I? I had betrayed Carl, spoiled the achievement which was his life, made of him a murderer (how could one doubt Carl's hand in Isaac's death: as well believe that Kennedy's assassin — and his assassin's assassin, and his assassin's assassin's assassin — all died of random acts) and Carl May had divorced my mind as well as my body — of course he had. And that was the hardest thing of all to bear.

Instead I rang for Trevor and asked him to fetch me the *Yellow Pages*. I turned to 'I' and there found Investigation Agencies, and ran my finger down the list, passing by the Acme and Advance and Artemis (they cluster their names in the A's, these places, and advisedly) all of whom I had used in the past and from whom I had sucked all possible juice of entertainment, and presently came to Maverick Enquiries, an agreeably innocent

21

name, I thought – and dialled their number. It is my experience that the cool appearance of any Investigative Report, the comings and goings, contacts and activities of the investigatee neatly and impersonally described, acts like antihistamine ointment on a wasp sting to soothe the obsessional and tumultuous mind, if only – like the ointment – for a time.

I did not report to Oliver what I had done. Oliver thought I should just forget Carl. Oliver thought such a thing was possible – of course he did. Oliver was a nice guy, and young with it. But I had been married to Carl for over thirty years, and Carl was intertwined in my mind and body like the strands of dry rot fungi in the damp bricks of an empty house.

Let Oliver say as often as he liked, 'Forget him, Joanna, as he's forgotten you,' the simple fact was that Oliver had not been alive as many years as Carl and I had been married. But I liked to hear him say it. The young find everything so simple. That is why their company is refreshing. The young, moreover, see it as their duty to be happy and do their best to be so. I was brought up to be happy to do my duty, and so tend to equate happiness with boredom.

I would say to Oliver (or words to this effect), 'If Carl May has forgotten me why hasn't he found himself a wife, or even a girlfriend; why does he stay celibate?' and Oliver would reply (or words to this effect), 'Because he's so busy making money.' Oliver was kind. He could have said, 'Because he's in his sixties; too old to get it together,' but he didn't, in case I was reminded of my own age, and suffered. Isaac was kind, in the same way as Oliver. He too tried to smooth the path that ran before my thoughts. Too kind, when it came to it, to live in the same world as Carl May. My fault.

If thine eye offend thee, pluck it out! I wait for the arrival of the soothing ointment, the person from Maverick Enquiries. I want to be told, as I have been told so often in the past, that Carl still lives as a celibate, in memory of me.

22

6

How had it come about that Joanna Parsons, that English rose, had married Carl May, this upstart from a kennel? Why, because she fell in love with him, of course, and he with her, and her father was too busy and her mother too complacent to interfere with the course of true love. Nor were Carl's natural parents in any position to object to the match, being dead, and his foster parents were only too happy at this sudden uxorious turn of events: proof that the trouble they had taken with the boy, and the love and money they had expended upon him, were to be rewarded as they had hoped. He had joined the ranks of the achieving middle classes.

Little Joanna – for this is the way fate often works; sealing in our memories what is yet to come – had, when she was a child, read about the strange case of Carl May in a daily newspaper. The image of the abused and abandoned boy stayed in her mind, waiting, as it were, to pounce. The one to whom she, who had so much, could give so much!

How was it possible, thought little Joanna at the age of ten, weeping (unusually for her) into her porridge and cream, served by a maid, the plate so prettily laid on the white linen cloth, how was it possible that a world that contained so much excellence, pleasure and refinement should be the same world in which a boy could be kept in a kennel, beaten and abused, all but starved to death, have to teach himself to read from scraps of newspaper; a boy whose mother would then kill herself and whose stepfather be battered to death in prison at the hands of a vengeful mob? What, all this, and porridge and cream and dab your mouth as well? What a strange and upsetting world it was turning out to be!

'That child should not be allowed to read the newspapers,' her father said, observing her tears. The Parsons lived in Harley Street, above the shop: that is to say his consulting rooms. It was Dr Parsons' joke. Joanna's father was a physician: his speciality ear, nose and throat; two windows from the soul's prison on to the outside world, one organ of communication. The doctor's function was to keep all three bright, clean and properly receptive. Dr Parsons smoked a good deal, and coughed quite often, and presently was to die of lung cancer, but never made the connection between cigarette smoke and his ill health.

'The newspapers should print only what is happy and good,' said her mother, 'not upset people the way they do.'

Dr Parsons had disappointed a family of generals and majors to go into medicine. He was a man of moderate height with regular features, fair hair and bright blue eyes – the latter a recessive gene. He came from the North East – he was of Scandinavian stock.

Mrs Parsons, daughter of a West Country solicitor, had pleased her family by marrying a man a notch or so above her in the social scale, three inches taller, four years her senior, and well able to support her. She was slightly built and reckoned beautiful, with high cheekbones, wide green eyes, and the red hair sometimes inherited from two black-haired parents. She was of mixed Norman and Celtic stock. The strands of the different races met in their child, Joanna: she was beautiful, strong, healthy and bright, as if to encourage just such a blending.

'Do stop that child snivelling,' said Dr Parsons. 'Take away that newspaper.' The maid did so.

Mrs Parsons dabbed Joanna's eyes tenderly while rebuking

her crossly. 'You have no business crying,' she said. 'Remember there are others far worse off than you!'

It is the custom of intelligent and competent men to marry women less intelligent and less competent than themselves. So mothers often have daughters brighter than they, and fathers have sons more stupid. It does not make for happiness. Nature looks after the race, not the individual.

Joanna stopped crying the better to puzzle it all out. But she did not forget Carl May. She saved him up, as it were, till later: stored him in her mind. One day she would make it all up to him. In the meantime she learned her letters and presently Latin and Greek, at an all-girls' school, and amazingly nobody stopped her, for the more a girl knows the more trouble she has finding a husband who knows more. But then prudence prevailed and she went on not to university but to a finishing school in Switzerland, where, in the interests of a future marriage, she was taught the mastery of flower arrangements, the organizing of dinner parties, the proper control of drunks (speak firmly but politely), servants (likewise), and the finer points of deportment. She 'came out' gracefully, being presented at Court, in the traditional way, when the ceremony was revived at the end of the war, and at her very first dance just so happened to meet Carl May, a pale, intense, not very tall but good-looking young man who worked at the Medical Research Council in Hampstead. He had not been on Active Service: his was a reserved occupation.

Carl May was famous already as the young man who'd started life in a kennel. Joanna Parsons' heart went out to him at once: she saw him as the solution to a puzzle which had worried her all her life. His body went out to her, in trust and confidence; and though his head regretted she was not of the titled, moneyed classes, he thought he could put up with that. He needed a wife to look after him and he needed one now. He did not need children, but he did not tell her that, not at once.

'I love him so much, Mummy,' said Joanna. 'I do so want to marry him. I want to make the past up to him. I want to make him happy.'

'If you love him you should marry him,' said Mummy. 'After all, I loved your father.' It was 1949, the nation was three years into socialism, everything was upside down. The young man had fought through heavy odds to end up well educated and well spoken: what were a few years in a kennel? They would make him appreciate her daughter the more. It was time the girl was out of the house: she made her mother feel faded, dusty and stupid. Mrs Parsons wanted Dr Parsons to herself again.

'I want to marry him, Daddy,' said Joanna, waiting for opposition. But none, to her disappointment, came.

'Why not?' was all her father said. He'd rather she'd married a doctor and perpetuated a race of physicians; he'd rather the young man had faced up to Hitler directly, but those few hard early years should at least help keep the young man's feet on the ground, and besides, Dr Parsons was busy. Men had brought back odd diseases from the African deserts and the jungles of the Far East; ears heard wrongly, noses smelt falsely and words came strangely from tortured throats. And it was time the girl was out of the house. The vivid presence of the daughter made him discontented with the mother.

Only Joanna's Aunt Anne was against the match: she said, 'the child who's beaten grows up to beat,' but she was years ahead of her time and regarded as an hysteric. What a hopeless doctrine it would be, if true! That we never recovered from our past! What price progress then? For what applied to individuals applied to nations, and societies too. So much the world was beginning to see.

Now Joanna was sixty, and disgraced: she had failed, in the end, to make the past up to her husband, failed to make him happy. And Carl was sixty-three. Age wears out the resolution of youth: or look at it another way – the past seeps through into the present, as the garish colour of underlying old wallpaper, left unstripped for one reason or another, but usually financial, will eventually show through to the pale expensive layer on top and spoil everything.

7

'She should be thoroughly punished for making you so unhappy,' said Bethany to Carl, when he ran through his life for her, the way new lovers do.

'My mother is dead,' he said, surprised.

'I didn't mean your mother,' she said. 'I meant your wife.'

'Oh that old woman, that Joanna May,' said Carl, 'who cares about her?'

Bethany had heard that kind of thing before, for all she was so young. On the night she met Carl, she turned over in bed and said, 'I'm twenty-four going on forty-two and you're sixty-three going on thirty-six, so who's counting?' And Carl stopped counting there and then, though of course the world did not.

That first night he said to her, 'You're the second woman I've slept with in all my life,' and she said, 'I don't believe you,' and he did not care if she believed or not: he just got out of bed to make some calls to Australia, and so she believed him.

'I was totally faithful to Joanna all my married life,' he said, when he had finished his calls and got back into bed. He had skinny white hairless shins but she did not care. 'That was my folly.'

'What happened?' asked Bethany, though she knew pretty well; these things do not go unnoticed, even in circles of power, where policemen seldom enter in.

'I found her with another man,' said Carl, easily, though this was the first time for several years he had found words for the event. Well, who had there been to speak to? And in so saying, he bound Bethany to himself, or so she thought. She was safe with him now, she told herself: he would not, could not, surely, pass her on to some subordinate.

'What did you do?' asked Bethany audaciously, and audacity was rewarded, as it so often is.

'I killed him,' said Carl, even more easily. 'That is to say, I had him killed. But it amounts to the same thing.'

Bethany wondered how the deed had been done, but did not like to ask. Screams in the soft suburban night had many a time disturbed her childish sleep; she had never liked to ask. Once she did and her mother slapped her. 'What you don't know can't hurt you,' Mother said, and Bethany had believed her.

'Why him not her?' Bethany enquired further, now, of Carl. 'Most men kill the woman and leave the man.' Twenty-four going on forty-two, no doubt about it, reared in a whorehouse! The things she knew for all she never asked.

'I left her alive,' said Carl dreamily, 'to suffer from the loss of me.'

'Most women left alone for that reason,' said Bethany, 'just find someone else.'

'Not when they're old,' said Carl. 'Don't you want me to tell you how I disposed of her lover?'

'No, I don't,' she said, so he didn't. Confidences are dangerous. Witnesses get killed. Those who know too much disappear. The world is not a safe place, even for the well intentioned; especially the well intentioned.

'Why did Joanna betray me?' asked Carl May, that first night, he who so seldom displayed ignorance or doubt, thus suddenly loquacious. 'I don't know much about women. What did my wife need that she didn't have? I still can't understand it. We'd been married nearly thirty years. She was never much interested in sex; what did she want with another man? She had more than enough to do – the house to look after and so forth; I was good to her: attentive when I had the time: generous – she could spend as much money as she liked on clothes, though she never would: ask Joanna to choose between Dior and Marks & Spencer and she'd choose Marks & Spencer. It was her background — middle of middle. Revenge of some kind? Insanity? She liked animals more than people: she said so: it hurt me. She had a little grey cat which died. That upset her. And then of course the dogs — it's true I got rid of the dogs. But she never found out about that. It can't have had anything to do with that. No, it was just in her female nature, buried deep, but there it was. The need to betray, to spoil, to turn what is good bad. The bitch goddess, at it again.'

'How do you mean, Carl? Got rid of the dogs?'

He was not in the habit of explaining himself, and she knew it. But still she asked, and he replied, as she knew he would. As he trusted her body, so he began to trust her mind.

'I was jealous,' said Carl May to Bethany. 'I didn't like the way she stroked the dogs. I didn't like the way they nuzzled her, as if they'd been there many a time before. Or how she'd talk to them instead of me. It upset me — a kind of spasm attacked my throat: such a lump in it I couldn't swallow. Once, looking at her with them, I almost fainted. A lot of people depend upon me. I have to keep myself steady for their sake. I had the animals stolen: I was going to sell them; then I realized I'd have to have them poisoned. You know how dogs will find their way back home. But enough of all that.'

'You did the right thing,' said Bethany, who felt quite safe, having no dogs to poison, no lover (so far) for Carl May to destroy.

Bethany knew well enough the value of the benefits she offered her new lover; how hard, once enjoyed, they were to do without: the sheer surprise, the sudden joyful restoration of self-esteem, as conferred by the sexual act when performed with the right (even though unlikely — especially the unlikely) person. Moreover, Bethany surprised even herself: she had never known the magic work so well before: not in the many sometimes profitable, sometimes distressing couplings of her adolescent days; not even when she moved away from home and the suburbs to the nightclubs of the fashionable world, not even then had she and whoever come even near it; no, not even with Hughie Scotland, Carl's predecessor, not for all his fame as a media stud. Those others had not seemed to notice any lack of anything. Those others had given her money, cars, racing tips, sexual satisfaction, all kinds of things – but what Carl May gave Bethany, in return for his pleasure, was confidence. And what she felt he felt too. Oh yes, she was safe enough. He wouldn't want to do without her. So Bethany believed. So Joanna had believed.

'You be careful,' said Patsy, Bethany's mother, when Bethany reported back to her that she was moving on from Hughie Scotland to Carl, and rather liked the new arrangement. 'Don't go falling in love. Love's all misery and muddle and never any profit.'

'Don't talk like that!' said Bill, Bethany's father, to his wife. 'You and I are in love, always have been, and look at the profit we've made! Look at the child we made! Our Bethany, child of love. No wonder she's sought after; and fate is on her side, it's obvious. Carl May! That really is the big time.'

Patsy and Bill, ex-flower-folk, kept a house of moderate ill fame in an outer-London suburb, halfway down a very long quiet street. They went together to local pubs: he brought home lonely men, she brought home lonely women. They brought them together in the upstairs bedrooms of the large suburban house, charging an agency fee. Bill mowed lawns for the neighbours; Patsy would meet their children out of school if they were ever in a fix: they were an obliging pair, they took care to be, no one ever complained. Where did altruism stop, self-interest begin? Hard to tell. Whoever can, of other people or themselves?

Patsy and Bill met in the fifties, at the cinema. *Gigi* was showing: Audrey Hepburn of the wide brown eyes as the girl reared in the brothel who found true love, Maurice Chevalier as her protector. 'Thank heaven for little girls,' he sang, with all the faux-innocence of that sickly decade. There at the cinema, to that tune, Patsy and Bill fell in love, and reaffirmed that love at a rerun in the sixties, at a half-empty local cinema, while they were trawling for custom amongst the dispossessed and empty-lifers at a Tuesday matinée, and there, in the back row, Bethany was conceived in a fit of wholesome life-trust. How else should they rear her but as Gigi was reared? So the beauty advice came from women's magazines, and the style was suburban not *fin-de-siècle* Parisian, but never mind, never mind! Bethany was created.

And Patsy and Bill, proud in their achievement, while valuing the joy of sex, all sex, and perhaps overvaluing Bethany their daughter, for a time all but priced her out of the market; many was the boring night she spent alone: lying empty, as a house may lie empty while its value increases. That was when she was fifteen. Noticing what was happening, they brought the price down.

All things are chance, thought Bethany, who bore no malice against her parents, no resentment for the manner of her upbringing, or thought she did not. I might have been born in Africa in time of drought, she thought, and had stick arms and legs, and a stomach which stuck out: I might have been born an Eskimo, and hardly seen my legs and arms at all, so cold would it be to undress: as it was I was born to Patsy and Bill, and if they had not been so foolish, so trusting, and so adored Audrey Hepburn, would I have been born at all? And now here I am with Carl, and happy and safe, so what's the point of complaining? But he still hasn't got his wife out of his system. Something must be done about that.

'Well,' said Bethany, 'it seems to me your wife lived an empty life and was a shallow woman and you're well rid of her. But perhaps her life was boring. Perhaps she was just bored. Some women will do anything not to be bored.'

'She could have gone to classes,' said Carl. 'She had no reason to be bored. She had me. Boredom is no excuse for infidelity.'

'She should have had babies,' said Bethany, 'with all that time to spare. Why didn't she?' Not that she wanted or anticipated children herself, belonging to a younger generation, one which did not define women as people who had babies.

'She did,' said Carl, cunningly, 'but she never knew it.'

'That's impossible,' said Bethany. 'How can you have a baby and not know it?'

'In the same way,' said Carl, 'as you can have an hysterical

32

pregnancy and be convinced you're growing a baby when you're not. That's what Joanna did to me when she was thirty. She got morning sickness: her belly swelled up. She looked terrible. I took her to this doctor friend of mine, Dr Holly; a very clever man. He just looked her over and sent her out of the room and said to me, "Your wife and Mary Queen of Scots! There's no baby there, only air and wind." "What's the cure?" I asked. "Love and kisses," he said, "or failing that, a mock abortion, a ceremony of death." Almost nothing he didn't know about women. So that's what we did. Told her she was to have a termination, anaesthetized her, and whee-e-ee, like a balloon going down, went Joanna's belly. When she woke up she was cured. My lovely wife, slim and fresh and all for me again!'

'But that's not having babies and not knowing it,' said Bethany, 'that's not having a non-baby.'

'Oh so clever she'll cut herself,' said Carl May, his old finger running sharply down the skin between Bethany's breasts, where she should have buttoned her blouse, lifting the white nylon rosebud in the centre of her bra and snapping it back so she jumped. 'Wait! Joanna knew well enough I didn't want children: I told her the day before our wedding: she accepted that when she married me. I took that phantom pregnancy of hers badly, an imagined one seemed to me worse than the real thing; let her conscious mind be loyal and loving, in her unconscious, in the depths of her being, Joanna May betrayed me, went against me.'

'You were to be all in all to each other! Just you, just her! I think that's sweet – my mother and father were like that, in the beginning. Then they had me, and felt differently.'

'How could Joanna and I have had children? Do you understand just what sort of inheritance I have? What do you think it's been like for me, knowing what kind of parents I had, what sort of bestial blood flows in my veins?'

'Your parents were mentally ill, Carl, that's all. They must have been.'

'That's all? Insanity? All?'

How white he suddenly was. She ran her finger over his lips. They were dry and trembling. He calmed. She had not known he could be upset. She felt privileged, and powerful. Carl May,

33

Chairman of Britnuc, power in the land, TV personality, calmed by Bethany's young finger.

'I had myself sterilized when I was eighteen,' he said. 'A vasectomy. I would be the end of the line: that particular experiment of nature's. I chopped down the family tree.'

'Joanna didn't mind?'

'Joanna didn't know,' he said. 'Why should she? What difference did it make? She understood my mind when we were married; we would have no children. There'd be just the two of us.'

'Tea for two,' said Bethany dreamily. 'Just me and you. Two for tea and baby makes three.'

'Baby makes five,' said Carl sharply, and nipped her finger suddenly with teeth made sharp and fine by the passage of sixty-three years. 'While she was opened up we took away a nice ripe egg; whisked it down to the lab: shook it up and irritated it in amniotic fluid till the nucleus split, and split again, and then there were four. Holly thought we could have got it to eight, but I said no. Growth begins so quickly: there wasn't time. A truly vigorous egg, that one. We kept the embryos in culture for four whole weeks, had four nice healthy waiting wombs at hand and on tap, for implantation. All four took like a dream: there they grew until they popped into the world, alive and kicking and well. Four nice assorted ladies, desperate for babies, got four very pretty little girls: little Joanna clones. Not cloning in the modern sense, but parthenogenesis plus implantation, and a good time had by all. We kept it quiet. So quiet one of the mothers didn't even know we'd done it. What passive creatures women are: they just lie there, trusting, and let the medical profession do what it wants.'

'That's two for tea and four babies make six, Carl, not five.'

Carl bit Bethany again. 'Wrong!' This time she yelped, and quite reminded him of his younger days. 'There wasn't anyone to tea. There ain't a father in the whole wide world,' crooned Carl May, 'that gave help to my poor old dutch. All on her lonesome ownsome. Her DNA and hers alone. She was thirty. She was growing little hairlines round her eyes: so I gave time itself a kick in the teeth. It seemed a pity to let it all go to waste, when you could save it so easily.'

34

'Like an old Magnox power station,' said Bethany; he looked at her sharply.

'Don't be so cutesy,' he said, not even bothering to bite, so she desisted.

'Well,' said Bethany, 'all I know is if it was me I'd have told her. I'd never have managed to keep it to myself. I can't keep the smallest secret, let alone cloning someone and not telling them!'

'It's sensible to keep things in reserve,' said Carl May. 'Information may not be wisdom, let no one tell you it is: but knowledge – ah, when it's secret knowledge is power.' And Carl May looked at Bethany hard, until she wondered which of her secrets he knew and wasn't saying.

'No,' said Carl May, 'she'll never get it out of me. Let her go to her grave not knowing. She chose loneliness: let her be forever lonely.'

'But now I know,' Bethany said, 'what about me?' and wished at once she hadn't opened her mouth.

'You'll keep it to yourself,' Carl May said, and she thought, yes, I will: on the whole I better had. I can see I better had.

'One day you might tell her,' she said. 'You never know what's going to happen next. One day you might, to punish her. To take away her singularity.'

'A long word for such a little girl,' he said, and pinched her with sharp-filed fingernails – she'd given him a manicure: he enjoyed that: he on the chair, she crouched on the floor, red hair falling – better, she could see, in future, to file his nails less sharp or use words that were less long, or both.

'What can happen next,' asked Carl May, 'that I don't know about: what can surprise a man like me? I win. I always win. I need to win, as other people need sex, or food, and that's all there is to it.'

Bethany shivered, and hoped Carl May hadn't noticed, but of course he had. So she looked and spoke as bright as could be. 'I wouldn't like to have a lot of little me's walking about,' she observed. 'One of me is quite enough,' and the jabbing nail

35

turned into a stroking hand, a pressing mouth, and she felt safe: yes, she felt safe enough. One of her, she told herself, was more than enough for him. Besides, she wasn't perfect, not like Joanna: on the contrary, she was flawed; she knew it: people had told her so often enough. Now she was glad, not sorry, Carl May had noticed. If the penalty of perfection was reproduction she could do without it. Her bone structure was not good: she was pretty rather than beautiful — she had her mother's chin: it would droop and double by the time she was thirty: she was all artifice: she inspired lust not love: she was cunning not wise: bright not clever: could memorize well but not categorize easily: was a good guest but an over-effusive hostess: affectionate but not constant — being able, at will, to switch that affection in the direction which most suited her, and often tempted to do so. These things Bethany knew about herself. She was in fact too vulnerable to the passage of time. She was the kind who went off early. Never mind, when she lost her capacity to charm she would start a business: an employment agency: a chain of them perhaps: Carl May would help her, pension her off: she would be powerful through money, that safe and snazzy stand-in for sexual pleasure. She liked to be safe. She didn't like to be bored. It was difficult to keep a balance between the two.

'What a pity you can't have babies,' she said, quite forgetting to whom she was speaking. 'I'd like to have your babies. Then I'd always have something of you to love!' Men liked to hear that kind of junk, but Carl merely shook his head impatiently, as if some gnat had bitten him, so she shut up and let him get on with it.

8

The day they went down to the river, Carl May returned to the subject of his ex-wife, and his secret knowledge. He and Bethany sat side by side in the back of the limousine. Perhaps he thought she was too confident: he liked to have her a little frightened. He knew how to frighten her. It's always pleasant to do what you're good at doing: hard to refrain from doing it. Anyway, Carl May had said, 'You could always give birth to one of my clones. I could use your womb to implant me.'

'What a lovely idea!' said Bethany, in her best and politest voice. 'They can't really do that, can they?'

'Oh yes they can,' said Carl May. 'I'll take you down to my friend Holly. There's an advance on freezing now: the rage is all for drying: keeps the nuclei intact. It used to be just frogs and below: now it's sows and upwards. Shall I take you down to Holly? Prickly Holly?' He pinched the tip of her little finger, and they watched it turn blue between the bloodless nails of his thumb and third finger.

'He must be rather old by now,' said Bethany, and wished she hadn't.

'No older than me,' said Carl May, but added kindly, 'Lost his nerve, lost his bottle, you're quite right,' and he let her finger go. She sucked it. He liked that.

'One of you,' said Bethany, 'is more than enough for me. I'd be exhausted. I want you, not your clone. What would be the point of a clone?'

He nipped her neck. She was covered with little bruises in tender places: mementoes of Carl, he called them. She loved them.

'It would come in handy,' he said. 'It could stand in for me here and there — at banquets, for example, when all anyone needs is my presence; when my opinion counts for nothing. It would save my digestion.'

'But what would you do while you stayed home?' asked Bethany, whose idea of pleasure it was to be out, not in.

'Learn not to need to win,' he said and, as if to make up for a lifetime of over-controlled Joanna May, flung himself upon Bethany, digging his teeth vampire-like into her neck, tearing her blouse, his hand approaching her crotch from the top, not the bottom, down between her clothing and her skin, forcing her belt to give and break, without any thought at all for the presence of Philip the chauffeur in the front seat. Philip was indeed embarrassed by their moans and groans, but Carl May paid well: it was a privilege to work for such an employer, who had led a lonely and prudent life far too long, and the girl was not reluctant, on the contrary, so he put up with the embarrassment easily enough. He had faced worse in the course of his job – the poisoning of Joanna's dogs for one thing, the backing his car into and over Joanna's lover Isaac for another, as required of him by Carl May. Who was he to object to anything? What kind of moral stance could he take? What outrage would now be justified? Once a servant, an employee, has decided that loyalty to the one who pays him supersedes all other moral obligations, and has acted upon that decision, to change the mind becomes impractical, not to say dangerous. Reason and self-interest must be called upon to counteract the pangs of sensibility.

Philip kept his eyes on the road and drove slowly beside razed warehouses, over broken tarmac, where the weeds kept bursting through.

'You know far more about me than you should,' said Carl to Bethany, after his final climactic gasp.

'It was all just a story anyway,' said Bethany prudently. 'All that about clones. Just to frighten me.'

'Of course,' he said. Then he added, 'But just think, if there were more of me, and more of you, how much pleasure we would bring into the world!' and he actually smiled, and she remembered that she loved him and was pleased to give him pleasure.

He slept a little. Bethany stared out of the window on to a broken landscape. Philip parked the car. His employer woke up with an old man's start: a shiver: where was he? The river air was in his nostrils: the air of his childhood: a flowing tide of soot and despair mixed: there in his mind for ever, lying low but always there. He got out of the car. Bethany followed. The sun went in and a cold wind blew across the river.

'I brought you down here,' said Carl to Bethany, 'so you could see for yourself how I began. Of course it's all gone now – but where we stand used to be the corner of Jubilee Road and Bosnia Street. This is where the brass plaque is to be.'

And Bethany said, 'If it was all so nasty, why do you want to come back? Or is it like a loose tooth? You want to jiggle it even though it hurts?'

And Carl knew he had been deceived in her: she was not after all what he hoped. He was disappointed in her, hurt; he had forgotten what it was to be disappointed, hurt. Bethany did not begin to understand the significance of his achievement. She belonged to the TV age: nothing surprised, nothing impressed: real life rolled off a scriptwriter's pen. To have started here, yet come to this! Magnificent, but she could not see it.

The chauffeur buttoned his coat and straightened his cap, feeling the alteration in his master's mood: though if you'd asked him he'd have said, 'Just something in the air, that's all: just something in the air that chilled me, reminded me of this and that. I wouldn't work for anyone else: not for twice the wages and half the hours. It's an honour.' He'd been in tanks in the war and killed men for less reason than he killed for Carl, which was from loyalty, obedience and self-interest mixed.

'But it's all such a long time ago,' said Bethany, compounding her error. She felt the cold wind in her hair and round her chin and cutting down against the white and tender skin of her still partly unbuttoned bosom; harsh against the grazed skin where he had sucked and bitten her neck. Had he told her where they were going she would have worn boots and brought a scarf. With almost every step over the uneven ground she caught the leather on her high heels; they would be badly snagged: she

39

would have to have them rewrapped. He was thoughtless.

'If you're not interested we can go home,' said Carl. She understood then, too late, too late, that the cold wind was somehow his doing, and said, 'Of course I'm interested,' and then, 'They say one's childhood is never over. Do you think that's true?' But it was no use: the cold wind whipped and zapped through her red hair, and that was the only answer she got.

'You are not sufficiently interested,' Carl May said, 'for me to waste any more of my day on you.'

They rode home in silence, to the big boring house at 20 Eton Square, Belgravia, where the May collection of Egyptian art and artefacts was housed in what used to be the stable block, open to the public on the first Wednesday of every month. Very few of the public in fact took the trouble to attend. The windows had been blocked up to save specimens from the dangers of direct natural light; the ceiling rose to a central peak: the single door was arched: the room, though vast, was for all the world like a kennel. It was a dismal place. But Carl liked it, which was all that mattered.

As the chauffeur pulled up outside 20 Eton Square, a small group of reporters rushed to meet the car. Microphones were pushed under Carl's nose and flashbulbs popped. News was coming through that the power station at Chernobyl had blown, and in the light of the fact that two of Britnuc's plants, like Chernobyl, were WCRs, water-cooled reactors, could he make a statement? Was the public in any danger?

'Making electricity is not like making a sponge cake,' he said kindly in his soft gravelly voice. 'It is dangerous and things go wrong. When I know exactly what has happened at Chernobyl, if anything, I will be in a position to make a statement. Not before.'

'But, Mr May, the public is worried.'

'The public is right to be worried,' he said, smiling, and closed the front door, swiftly, and upon Bethany's right foot. The picture of the snagged and torn leather upon the six-inch heel of her shoe was upon the front cover of a tabloid newspaper the next day. 'May Faces Snags,' it said, going on to speak of the unseen killer which now stalked Eastern Europe. Other newspapers relegated the item to the middle pages. It was one of those stories which was to grow and grow, as wind patterns in the upper atmosphere made nonsense of national boundaries.

Carl went straight to his study to make telephone calls, his face still set cold against Bethany.

Bethany was a practical young woman. She dumped her shoes in the bin, feeling that since they brought her no luck they might as well be discarded, changed into more restrained clothes, dabbed ointment on her neck and, in the cold light of the bathroom, brought her hair under better control. She did not like the bathroom. It was too large, too full of marble, too brightly lit, and the washbasins were antique and their porcelain, being finely crazed, never looked quite clean. She did not like the house; Joanna's house. She did not like the servants; Joanna's servants – who did not like her, with her tiny knickers left everywhere and her strewn junk jewellery and hairpins, and her waterproof make-up smeared on sheets and cushions: but that was her role; how Carl liked it; they would just have to get used to it. In fact Bethany came to the conclusion she did not like Joanna, whose ladylike presence in the house was still too clearly felt for comfort.

The woman had no natural taste, that was apparent. She had re-created her father's consulting rooms in her husband's house: dark, highly polished mahogany furniture, dusty pale-green velvet curtains, over-plump greeny chintzy sofas and blue-and-white encrusted Chinese jars of arguable value standing on every available ledge. Twice a week the housekeeper would arrange fresh flowers – unnaturally large blooms – in the bleak white fluted floor-standing Italian vases which stood boringly in each corner of the room.

Bethany assumed, and rightly, that the twice weekly arrival of the peculiar flowers was an expression of gratitude from whatever container-gardener firm had been granted the contract to supply the Thameside Garden Park – a gift, of course, not a

41

bribe. Bethany well understood the difference. Many a gift had she received in her life, before or after a favour. But she could not be bribed – that would be an indignity.

Bethany bent to smell the flowers, which seemed to occupy some point between gladioli and chrysanthemum and withdrew her face at once. They had been sprayed with a strong flower perfume somewhere between violet and rose. It was not her place to comment or improve. She thought longingly of her parents' suburban garden, filled with nothing more exotic than pansies and roses, and settled down to read *The Layman's Guide to Nuclear Power*. It was one thing to appear ignorant; quite another to be so.

9

Carl was on the phone to a certain Gerald Coustain. This is how their conversation went:

Gerald Coustain said, 'What you're telling me is that there is no indication of additional radioactivity from any outside source at either Britnuc A or B?'

Carl May said, 'That is correct. I would add that this is hardly surprising since our instrumentation is not designed to pick any up.'

There was a short silence from Gerald Coustain, who worked for the Department of Energy.

'You're being remarkably frank with me,' he said.

'Why not?' enquired Carl, who was still in what Joanna had learned to call 'a mood'. Bethany had failed him. It was not his time he feared to waste, so much as his emotion – and what were referred to in a booklet he had recently received through the post on the subject of AIDS as 'bodily fluids'. He was aggrieved. He had made himself vulnerable. It was dangerous. If, as he felt, the experiences of his childhood energized his present, a fire to be fanned and nurtured back to life, that fire was as like as not to go out altogether under the thwack of cold water delivered by Bethany. There was a lot at stake here. A long time ago! What had that to do with it?

'I have done everything the inspectorate required,' said Carl May. 'I have followed its instructions to the letter, no matter how absurd those instructions were. Nowhere could I find regulations appertaining to the upper limits of instrumentation.'

Again there was a pause.

'Nuclear power is a new industry,' said Coustain, his voice receding as if he held the receiver further and yet further away.

'It is essential that the spirit of the law rather than the letter be followed.'

'Come off it,' said Carl May. 'You don't want Britnuc A and B off line every time instrumentation shows a rise in local activity any more than I do. You fellows have your own information-gathering network. Don't come bleating to me every time the shit hits the fan.'

Coustain, thinking he should perhaps make a virtue out of necessity, asked Carl May if he would make some reassuring statement on TV the next day: along the lines he had sketched out: and so Carl May did, in the programme seen by his ex-wife, Joanna May.

10

'God's last laugh,' I said, 'before he flew off,' I, the original of
the clones of Joanna May. I said it, of course, more for the sake
of a neat phrase than anything else: my way of vaguely invoking
the name of God whilst yet dismissing him. God was there once,
I safely maintain, thus explaining away some intimation of
immortality, some general notion we all have of 'more to this
than meets the eye' whilst disposing of him, whoever he may
be, for all practical purposes.

'Joanna, define your terms!' – Miss Watson, 1942. A certain
Miss Watson taught me English language when I was a school-
girl. She was in her eighties. Young women were at the time
busy making explosives in factories to blow young men up: they
had no time to teach their juniors anything. The old were
brought out of retirement to be of some use, while the young
finished each other off. No wonder the war was so popular
with everyone. A long, violent, riotous, disgraceful party! Miss
Watson died of a stroke on VE day; and quite right too – the
party was over.

If I'm forced into a corner by the ghost of Miss Watson, who
returns to me often in dreams, I would define God as the source
of all identity: the one true, the only 'I' from which flow the
myriad, myriad 'you's'. We acknowledge him in every 'I' we so
presumptuously utter. Now what could be more all-pervasive
than that?

Carl once told me God flew off the day Fat Boy was exploded
in the Nevada Desert, when man entered the atomic age (though
of course man – and woman – had in fact entered it long before,

45

when Pierre and Marie Curie first started sieving and filtering their dusty mounds of pitchblende), leaving the field to the likes of my husband. But I prefer to think He flew off when the first flicker of television appeared upon the screen. He knew he was beaten. For Lucifer read John Logie Baird, inventor of TV, toppling the Ultimate Identity from his seat of power: spoiling the currency of 'I' forever. The 'you' that is the real 'I', the one perceived by others, the one understood by the child in that initial bright vision, now watches the 'you' that that you perceives. There is no end to it. Our little shard, our little divine shred of identity, so precariously held, is altogether lost as we join the oneness that is audience. My clones and I. After I found out about the clones I began to worry a lot about 'I'.

As for evil – which everyone knows is the absence of God – what could it do when God took off but take up residence in the source of its trouble. The minute parents, those stoical folk, look away, evil creeps out of the TV set and settles in the wallpaper. The children ask for sneakers now, not proper shoes. Why? Because sneakers have long laces, long enough to hang a person by. And every year the laces get longer and tougher, the better to do it; to hang, to dangle yourself or others. Why bother to preserve the 'I'? It's seen too much of sights not fit for human eyes, it is not fit to live. It no longer believes in life: all it gets to see is corruption, seared, torn and melting flesh. There is no 'I' left for any of us. The great 'I' has fled, say the eyes in the wallpaper: only the clones remain, staring.

If the I offend thee pluck it out. Idopectomy.

My children who are myself pun too. Bloody clones. That was Carl's doing.

On hearing the first news from Chernobyl, I sent Trevor the butler to the Post Office with a telegram to Carl May my ex-husband saying, 'Yah boo sucks, signed Milly Molly Mandy', but Trevor came back saying the Post Office now sent only greetings telegrams – Happy Birthday, Congratulations on your Wedding, and so forth – and I decided silence was the better

46

policy. One must go with the flow of events. If waves slap against your face, turn back to shore.

The next day Carl made a statement to the press saying (or words to this effect), 'It can't happen here. Our reactors are constructed on a different principle from theirs. Children may safely drink milk though sheep may no longer safely graze on the uplands.' His lies were soft and persuasive, as ever: and his face calm and handsome. It had the tranquillity of a death mask: as if someone had placed a waxed cloth over his corpse's face – after it had been composed by the undertaker, of course – and moulded it into shape and propped body and mask up before the cameras and used puppet strings to work the mouth and eyelids. Carl was dead, pretending to be living. That is what a diet of lies does for you – and now I am no longer with him what else will Carl choose to eat but lies? There is no nourishment in them, the spongy junk food of the mind. The soul dies from malnutrition.

I longed to tell him so – yah, boo, told you so – to ease the itch of spited, spiteful love, watch the pale dead face suffuse with the living pink of rage, but I didn't. Let him stay dead. It was what he chose when he threw me out: it is why he lived without a woman after I was gone.

I dedicated my life to Carl: I threw away the children I could have had, for his sake, to keep him happy. Isaac was nothing; a side-show, a weak man: he died and I scarcely noticed. Oliver is nothing either, when it comes to it: a pet which curls up alongside, by a warm fire, or on a forbidden bed, to be indulged. Better than nothing, that's all, poor Oliver. Of course Carl is dead, dying: so am I, without him. But Carl is at least able to blow up the world while he waits. I'm not.

11

The clones of Joanna May also blamed their nearest and dearest for the accident at Chernobyl, with rather less reason than did their original.

In their case, of course, near did not necessarily or permanently mean dear, and this was either an affliction ironed into their genes, or the common cross of humanity, as may be decided by events. Nor was the tendency to blame irrationally peculiar to these four women, of course: it afflicts all mankind. When the weather is fine on polling day, the sitting government is returned. If the weather is wet, it gets thrown out. And that's that.

Jane Jarvis listened to the news on the radio and slammed her attic windows shut to keep the radioactivity out. A pity, because it was such a fine spring day, but to keep out the bad you had to keep out the good. Then she returned to the brass bed where her lover lay. It was Saturday, and lunchtime. Presently they'd get out of bed and walk into Soho for something to eat. Her flat was in Central London: she had the whole attic floor of a big house in Harley Street. She could afford it. Such was the reward of beauty, intelligence, education, and the capacity for making decisions others feared to – saying, simply and firmly, 'this is good but not profitable' or, 'this is bad but commercial', or 'this is neither good nor profitable', or, just occasionally, 'this is both good and commercial' and having the results bear her out. Tom designed book jackets and lived in half a house in Fulham, and earned a quarter of what she did, for eight times as much work. He would take her out to lunch, so she would have to eat spaghetti, not oysters.

Jane Jarvis was 5 foot 7 inches tall; precise and orderly in mind and body. She measured 36 inches around her chest, 24 inches at the waist and 36 round her hips, as had her original at the same age. Her nose was straight and perfect; her eyes widely spaced: her cheekbones high, her top lip a little short, the bottom lip a little thin: her gaze was direct. To wash her hair she dunked it in a basin of soapy water, rinsed it and towelled it dry. It frizzed out round her head. She belonged to some new, insouciant age. She walked like someone who knew herself to be free. She lived at the top of No. 30 Harley Street. Her original had spent her childhood in No. 34.

'I want the windows open,' said Tom, when she got back into bed. 'I can't sleep with the windows shut.'

'I didn't realize you had come here to sleep,' she said.

'Besides which, why bother?' he asked. 'If there is radioactivity out there glass isn't going to stop it.'

'It will stop alpha rays,' she said.

'Smarty pants,' he said.

'You can't bear it if I know things you don't,' she said.

A row was approaching through the window: no glass could stop it: the hideous black cloud of the spirit: tumulus and cumulus fighting it out: lightning flashes of dire perception, thunderclaps of rage, hail storms of battering distress; every passion and woe of the past returned to plague the present, bent on turning love to hate. They knew it, Jane and Tom: both looked uneasily out of the window: they could see rooftops and sky: no sign yet of the storm they expected to see, but they knew it was coming, in spite of there, in the real world, a blue sky, a few white clouds. On the bed the grey cat Hattie sensed their unease and stopped purring. Tom put his hand on Jane's thigh, the better to forget what was going on out there, seen or unseen.

'I thought you wanted to sleep,' she said.

'This is crazy,' he said. 'Why don't I live here? Then we could use beds the way other people use them. We wouldn't have to be in bed in the middle of the day.'

'I like it like this,' she said.

'You don't love me,' he said. 'It's obvious.' He removed his hand. 'You don't know the meaning of the word love,' he said.

'You're over-educated. What do you think I am, some kind of stud?'

It really made no difference what they were arguing about. Her reluctance to marry, settle, wash socks, have children – which he saw as just a habit of thought, a pattern of belief, an ongoing fear of change, something more to do with the ascendancy her mind had somehow gained over her body than anything to do with her essential nature; his failure to match his sexual desires to hers, which she registered as a hostile act; his intention to punish and humiliate her for earning more than he did; his fear of giving voice to his feelings; his inability to offer reassurance and comfort; his failure to acknowledge her equal status; her lack of taste, as he saw it; his lack of understanding, as she did. One way or another accusations and insults began to crackle in the air, feelings no longer contained but given voice to. You did this and you said that. Wimp and harpy, bastard, bitch. Unfaithful! Gutter slut and macho pig and the simple, friendly, curing pleasures of desire fulfilled denied – and just as well, perhaps, lest sex itself become the weapon, and then indeed there'd be an end to everything, and neither in their heart wants that. But spite and rage preferred – preferred, that's the shocking thing, the self-revelation that hurts and wounds – chosen above love and kindness not just by the other but by the self. Not so much the other hurt, humiliated by the other, as the self by the self. The row is with the self, the other stands witness, accepting the bruises: it is some kind of horrid, magic, contrapuntal duet: variations on a theme; how can the unloveable, my self, be loved by you; your fault that it cannot. Projection. Simple! He accuses her of his own deficiencies: he hands them over. She does the same to him. Outrageous! How can I be expected to put up with this? And what is more, and have you forgotten; accept this evidence, accept it or I'll kill you, that you do not love unloveable me! Unforgivable!

The row is vaporous: it circles blackly, out this window, into that: it never stops; when you make up others begin: their turn next; always someone's. It feeds on itself, it feeds on you, the more you give in to it, the bigger it grows, the more powerfully it affects your neighbours, down here in the shameful gutter world, up there in the reeling attic sky, breeding every ill that flesh is heir to.

Keep your mouth shut, keep it shut, take a pill to knock you out. How gently, silently, this ire crept, the first cold wet breath through slammed shut windows. *You* shut the window: *I* want it open: Why? Because *you* want it shut. *I* shut it, knowing *you* didn't want it. Why don't *you* love *me*? Why, because *I'm* unloveable, but not as unloveable as *you*. And what is radiation compared to this virus already in the bloodstream?

Oh yes, a virus. The row comes like a virus. Unseen, unheard, unknown. It comes in a droplet, through a break in the skin, the brushing of flesh, a flavour in the air, a particle inhaled. Once in the blood it's there for ever, an infection; a lingering, debilitating disease, flaring up from time to time. Once you're sensitized, the first time you succumb, there it is, yes, for ever; a spiritual TB, before the development of antibiotics; sometimes it kills, sometimes it doesn't: it just doesn't go away; it merely hides to wait its triggering. Can't wait! AIDS of the spirit.

In the end Jane Jarvis scratched and clawed Tom Jeffrey and he left the house saying he'd rather die than return to face the virago, and they didn't make it up till Sunday, when they went out to supper and she ordered oysters and he let her pay. He was growing a beard. Lemon juice trickled amongst the black bristle. He had a square jaw and even teeth. He was a good-looking man, a sensitive man, a talented man. One day the world would recognize him. He would make a good father. He wanted to be a father.

Oh yes, indeed a virus, caught somewhere along the way by Jane Jarvis, at Oxford perhaps. He certainly thought that was where she'd picked it up.

It could not be in the genes, could not be in the nature, must be culturally induced, caught. Joanna May suffered a severe attack at the age of sixty, but had not been previously afflicted. Her relationship with Carl had ended with the murder of a third party, true, but that was Carl's doing and coolly done; no one had ever shouted, screamed or clawed. No, there was this to be said for Joanna and Carl — they never descended hand in hand, step by step, into that shocking desert landscape where the air is rent with whining and spiteful complaint, and the self stands isolated and terrified in all its snarling, scratching fury.

Jane Jarvis said to her Tom as he left, in the rain, 'With people like you in the world, how can it be anything but doomed. I hope you inhale beta particles and die.'

And this was the man she loved, or tried to love, or hoped to love, and knew if she didn't love, who else would there be?

Julie Rainer heard on the news that a radioactive cloud hovered over the country, and blamed the Russians, since her husband was away on business as he so often was, and there was no one else to blame. She closed the windows and poured away the milk. She stalked her lonely, perfect, tasteless house and filled in yet another form for yet another adoption agency: checking her lies against a note of previous lies in a booklet kept solely for this purpose. Her husband could not have children: he was infertile. She had spent hours, hours of intensive life with doctors' fingers and spatulas inside her, investigating, before they turned their attention to him: it was her fate, her destiny, she felt, to have these prying feelers there. She despised herself. She lacked the courage to be artificially inseminated, she lacked the courage to leave her husband, though she did not love him, whatever that meant. She felt she would gain courage in the end: but by then it would be too late to have babies.

Time was against Julie, as it is against all women, in such gynaecological matters. In the meantime, she loved her animals, who gave her work in the way that babies do: removing dog

52

hairs from a sofa, replacing chewed seat belts, nursing aged cats, cleaning up after kittens, discouraging algae in the fishbowl – these things gave her pleasure, a sense of achievement . . .

'You love those animals more than me,' said Alec, closing his leather briefcase, off again, mini-computer in hand.

'I expect I do,' was all she said. She only told lies on forms.

She called up the vet to ask him what to do with the animals in view of the radioactive cloud and he said he doubted they would come to much harm, no one seemed to know how much radiation was about, or indeed what radiation actually was, but it would also do no damage to keep them in, and even perhaps to bath the dogs.

'But supposing the water's radioactive?'

He thought she was the most beautiful woman he'd ever met, but over-anxious. He thought her husband neglected her. He had the sense that she waited for her life to take its proper direction, and that also, if she was not careful, she would wait for ever. She was lost: in the wrong place: with the wrong fate: making herself neutral.

'Shall I come over?' he asked.

'No,' she said sadly.

'It's a pity your husband's away at such a time,' he said. 'Chernobyl has made everyone nervous, probably more nervous than they need to be.'

'You can't see it but it's always there,' she said, 'like my husband. I'll just call the animals in, shall I?'

'Good idea,' he said, and went to deliver a calf which had two heads. These things happen, with or without radiation. The farmer was inclined to blame Chernobyl, all the same, and however irrationally.

Gently, Julie Rainer, aged thirty, 5 foot 7 inches, 36–24–36, wiped the paws of Hilda her grey cat with a damp cloth, but Hilda took offence and scratched her. Julie watched a line of blood ooze along her white inner arm and threw the poor creature – the one she loved – across the room.

'Bloody animal,' she shrieked, 'bloody animal! It's all Alec's fault.' Later of course she stroked and cosseted the cat, who fortunately had not seemed to take deep offence, and then she went out into the night and breathed deeply, to punish herself.

———•••———

Cliff came home on time and Gina did not realize he'd been drinking until too late.

'Isn't it terrible about this thing at Chernobyl?' she said, when he came in. She was 5 foot 4 inches, 38 around the chest, 28 around the waist and 40 around the hips. Well, she had been seven weeks premature and reared in a less fortunate environment than Joanna May, her original.

'Don't give me any of that fancy stuff,' he said. 'Where's dinner?'

'Not quite ready,' said Gina. 'I had to get the kids back home from the park. It was raining; supposing what they say is right: the rain's radioactive?'

'I want some straight talking round here,' he said. 'Dinner is either ready or is not ready, and if it is not this is what happens,' and he hit her.

Now, the kind of row that occurred between Gina and Clifford was of a rather different genus than the one that slowly developed between Jane and Tom. It was not a black cloud that little by little took over a clear sky: not a virus sent to blight the life of the potentially happy. No, this was the kind of domestic discontent that runs like gutter sludge through the houses of the depressed and desperate, be they smart new bungalow, palace or slum – and once your children get their feet wet there's no drying them out. Mothers' noses get broken, eyes blacked, kidneys damaged, unborn babies killed; the little witnesses have a hard time of it; thwarted in their desire, their passion, to love someone, anyone, who is worthy of their love, they grow up to lay about them likewise. It is never over. Parents must be worthy of their children's love, and that's all there is to it. And whoever grows up, properly, finally? Not *you*, not *me*, not *him*, not *her*.

'Where's my dinner?' he says. He might be four. 'Not ready,' she says. She might be six. Wham he goes: he's all of fourteen.

54

'How can you?' she wails; fifteen if she's a day; and to the neighbours, grown-up at last, 'I walked into a lamp-post,' denying truth, so what sort of grown-up is that? And not so different in essence perhaps, just more swift, more desperate, more dangerous than Jane and Tom. Where's my dinner means did you care for me in my absence, did you notice I was gone, Mum oh Mum, how can I trust you? Not ready means no actually I didn't, I don't care about you one bit; wham means I can't express this sorrow, this grief, this disappointment, in words, you self-righteous bitch, you cow: the wham arrives reinforced by a great communal strength, the sudden surge of the male's hatred of the female who will not be possessed, will not be owned, will not be all body but will have a soul, and who in the refusing suggests some unattainable, other ideal. And then her tears, her silly tears of resentment mean see I knew you were like this, you've proved it again; her loyalty acknowledges that if I am punished it must be my fault, things will get better, you my neighbour can't possibly understand the complexity, not his fault, mine, I have failed, I have failed – the whole thing's impossible . . .

If there's no one around for Gina, and no one around for Cliff, either will kick the cat. There! Told you after all that I was unloveable. See what you've done?

In the next room the children turn up the TV – they'd have done better to stay in the park, in a different kind of fallout. Presently Gina comes in to say, 'Sorry about the explosion. It's all over now.' Except her nose is bleeding, so it clearly isn't. Why does she tell such lies? Why doesn't she leave? She doesn't leave because how can she leave, where can she go, she hasn't got the courage: one day perhaps she will, she says, leave. But leave what? Who? Herself – that's what she fails to understand, late with his dinner because Chernobyl exploded. How does she leave herself behind?

He is the product of her imagination taken flesh: she married him to make him flesh, he is what she deserves. She stood there

55

and said, 'I will, I will!', knowing his nature, the strength of his backhand, the cheap wine reddy-brown upon his teeth.

Those who have rows are more alive than those who don't: make better friends, more interesting companions. They may wreak havoc but they understand their imperfections – witness how they project them upon others – they cry to heaven for justice. They believe in it.

———•◦•———

Alice had a row with her agent. He was her nearest and dearest. Other men came and went, but he was the voice on the phone, unsweaty, unsmelly, a man firm and strong upon a letterhead.

He rang her to say Kiev was cancelled. She'd been going to do a show there.

'I don't believe it,' she said. 'You're doing it on purpose.'

'Alice, be reasonable,' he said. 'How could I make a nuclear power station explode?'

'You're using it as an excuse. You didn't want me to do this show. You don't want me to represent my country abroad. You want me to do some cheap swimsuit for some cheap mag because there's more in it for you.'

Alice was 5 foot 8 inches tall, 33 inches around the chest, 22 round the waist and 32 around the hips. She'd spent a week longer in the womb than Jane or Julie, and eight weeks longer than Gina. She exercised and dieted. She was in love with herself: she would stand naked in front of a mirror and run her hands across her body: she would do anything for herself.

'There's never anything in it for me,' he said. 'Ten per cent! A tip. That's all it ever is, a tip.'

'Perhaps it's time I got a new agent,' she said.

'Perhaps it is,' he said.

There she went again. Prove *you* love *me*, before *I* prove *you* don't. Later *he* called to apologize. *She* knew *he* would. *He* needed *her* more than *she* needed *him*.

Sometimes Alice felt alone in the world. She wished she'd had a sister: all she had for company was her little grey cat, and that was often left for neighbours to feed and so was cantankerous. Nevertheless the penalties of continual companionship, that is to say marriage, seemed too onerous to contemplate. What did she need with a husband in the flesh when her agent on the phone cared so much about her – how she looked, how she felt, where she'd been, what she earned – and all in exchange for a tip. Sex she could take or leave – and often left, for the sake of her looks. Not just because of the necessity of early nights if her eyes were to stay bright and large, but because sex made her screw up her face and that encouraged wrinkles.

One day she might marry, one day. Not yet. One day she might find the courage to marry.

So thought and felt the clones of Joanna May, before they discovered each other and themselves.

12

After his conversation with Carl May, Gerald Coustain put down his cordless telephone and said to his wife Angela, 'The man's a monster.' They sat in the garden. She was setting examination papers in A-level European history: she had lean academic fingers. He was potting out delphiniums: he had plump and clumsy ones: he was a civil servant of the stout complacent kind. She did not reply: what was the point: she knew Carl May was a monster. The sun went behind clouds; the wind was suddenly cold: there was rain in it.

'I think perhaps we should go indoors,' he said.

'Why's that?' she asked, absently, lost somewhere in the Boer War. 'It will stop in a minute: it's only spitting.'

'There is a possibility the rain is radioactive,' he said.

'Don't be absurd,' she said. 'Things like that don't happen.'

But she gathered up her papers and they went inside. He left the delphiniums to take their chances.

'Perhaps we should change our clothes and shower?' he said.

'I would rather die than do anything so extreme,' she said.

'Death itself is extreme,' he said.

'If you envisage this alleged radiation as life-threatening,' she said, 'shouldn't you be measuring it to find out? Or something?'

'Our organization is a little sketchy,' he said, 'and I am not getting much cooperation where I had hoped to find it. I can't get through to the Department. The lines are jammed.'

'Perhaps you should go in to the office,' she suggested.

'On a Sunday? I spend Sundays with my family.'

'All the same,' she said.

'Besides which,' he said, 'it's safer indoors. Bricks and mortar offer some small protection. No one would expect it of me, to go in to the office through radioactive streets on a Sunday.'

He felt her disapproval and stood out against it. He must be allowed to make his own decision, surely.

'How is poor Joanna?' he asked, to change the subject. Angela had been Joanna's best friend, until the divorce. After that, of course, the relationship had become difficult.

'Joanna was never poor,' said Angela. 'Nothing poor about Joanna. Her house would make two of this, she has a park rather than a garden, her month's alimony is my year's housekeeping.'

'In the circumstances, Carl May was generous. I would not be so generous, if I caught you at it.'

She laughed. It was hardly likely that he would. She was plain as a pikestaff, warts and moles all over the place and hairy legs. People were amazed at the match. He'd been a good-looking man when young: he could have done better for himself. But he hadn't wanted to: he'd wanted her: and as for her, she didn't give two figs for her looks. Their children, surprisingly, were all handsome, in a tall, strong-jawed way, and being male, their facial hair was not a matter for concern.

'That way he can control her,' said Angela. 'If she accepts his generosity.'

'I suppose it is better to be controlled than ignored,' he said. 'Poor thing.'

'She has a young friend,' said Angela. 'The gardener: the man who pots out her delphiniums.'

'You're making it up.' Gerald Coustain did not want to know this.

'But I saw him when I went round the other day. She was looking wonderful. Not quite so perfect and clear-cut as she usually is – a little blurred around the edges. Swollen-mouthed. Sex, I suppose.'

'What were you doing round there, in any case? I'd rather you didn't call on her. Meet for lunch, of course, in town, if you insist. But not too close, Angela. No home visits: especially not if what you say is true. Carl May might see you as an accomplice. Be prudent.'

'If your promotion depends on my prudence, you've had it anyway,' said Angela. 'Hadn't you better be getting along to the office?'

'There are no trains to speak of, not on Sundays.'

'Then get a taxi.'

'Certainly not. It is not a question of my promotion, Angela, but of your safety. God knows what Carl May might do next. He had his wife's lover written off, blanked out, knocked off the perch, however you want to express it –'

'Murdered. But there were special circumstances. One can't condone it, of course.'

'It has hardly reached "condone", Angela. One doesn't even know about it! Just don't get involved, that's all. I hope she has the sense not to boast about her lover to you ladies, or this one won't last two minutes either.'

'You ladies!' she scorned him. 'You ladies! Where has your courage gone? Can't say boo to Carl May, can't get to the office in case the rain's radioactive –'

In the end he went, as she knew he would. Angela served as her husband's conscience. Women who play this role are often as plain as pikestaffs – indeed, the plainer the better: Angela had a grey skin, a double chin, short grey greasy hair and wore belted navy blue around a waist almost larger than her hips, and her husband was never rude to her, or tried to make her unhappy.

13

The next day Angela called Joanna.

'How are you, darling?' she asked.

'Do you really want to know?' asked Joanna.

'Yes,' said Angela, settling in to listen. Angela had undertaken to see Joanna through her divorce: so much one woman will often do for another, although with luck the service may never have to be reciprocated. But you never know, you never know! The burden of guilt, indignation, upset, and general sense of injustice must be handed round, communally shouldered: it is too much for one person, one 'I', to bear. The 'you' must take a hand. At first the phone calls come at any time of day or night: the woman wronged, the 'I', has no idea of time, place or pertinence: then the notion of the otherness of the recipient, the sharer of distress, the *you* reasserts itself: the calls are at least prefaced by 'is the milk boiling over? the toast burning? is Hollywood on the other line? have you a minute?' and it's clear the healing process is under way. Joanna was by now far down the road to recovery: whole conversations could be held without mention of Carl. But of course Chernobyl and his face on the television screen that morning had stirred up what Angela saw as a good deal of muddy sediment: nasty little insects crawled again in and out of slime: they had only been playing dead: they were back again, spreading disease and discomfort.

'When I think how Carl has behaved to me!' said Joanna, and it was clear to Angela she had had quite a relapse. 'When I think how I wasted my life, simply threw it away! Why did my parents allow it? Carl May was a completely unsuitable match: it was unforgivable of them. They just wanted me out of the house. I was born to have children, but no, Carl May wouldn't have that: the day before we were married he told me he didn't want

61

any. What could I do? Everything arranged: all the guests: the presents: I had to agree. You know what he's like. I was so young I thought it didn't matter. Infatuated! His unhappiness had to be loaded on to me; that was what it was. He denied life, made me deny it too. He turned me into some sort of snow queen and when I made just one small attempt to thaw myself out he used it as an excuse to throw me out of his life – he set it all up, I swear he did. He was just waiting for the opportunity to be rid of me.'

'Yes, but Joanna –' said Angela, cautiously.

'I'm sorry, am I boring you? You do agree, don't you? I am right?'

'Carl may look at it a little differently. Carl came into his art gallery one day and found you and that Egyptologist together.'

'For heaven's sake, Angela, I was over fifty.'

'What has that got to do with it?' Angela sounded really interested: she really wanted to know.

'Obviously I was desperate and Carl should have understood that.'

'But Joanna, I'm over fifty and I'm not desperate.'

'But you're happily married!' Joanna's normally quiet voice was suddenly quite loud.

'And now you're not married at all,' replied Angela.

Joanna was silent. She sniffed a little.

'I don't know what's the matter with me today. Why did Carl choose to come into the gallery at that particular time? He never went in, normally. Besides, I thought he was away: he usually was.'

'Perhaps he suspected something. Perhaps you seemed unusually happy.'

'Oh, I was. Isaac was so much the opposite of Carl. But he had to put paid to that, didn't he? And then that accident – if accident it was.'

'Of course it was, Joanna.' Though nobody believed that for one minute – Isaac, crossing the road outside the Eton Square house, in too much of a hurry, knocked down and killed by Philip the chauffeur, reversing into the garage. Oh yes!

'Carl was so hard and cold about it all: not an ounce of sympathy for me.'

'Could you expect it?'

'Yes I could! We'd been married for thirty years and it was always me looking after him, worrying about him, listening to tales of his dreadful childhood; didn't I deserve anything in return? We were supposed to love each other.'

'I think that's what Carl believed, Joanna. And then you went and had an affair with another man; not even someone more important, or younger, or richer than him, but some penniless librarian with straggly hair. What an insult! Of course he reacted. I know you think he over-reacted, but men are like that, especially men like Carl, who are used to having their own way.'

'Whose side are you on, Angela?'

'Yours, Joanna, you know I am. But Carl did have a point of view.'

'Well, I don't see it. I suppose you're busy.'

'I am a bit.'

'Your children are about to visit you, I suppose.'

'Yes.'

'And the grandchildren?'

'Yes.'

'You see, you have everything and I have nothing.'

'Joanna,' said Angela briskly, 'you have a house worth two million pounds –'

'It's falling down, and Carl won't pay a penny for repairs.'

'You have a butler –'

'He's gay. Carl will only let me have gay servants. I'm surprised he doesn't have them castrated as well, just to be on the safe side.'

'And a gardener who shares your bed. Perhaps Carl is right. You are simply not to be trusted.'

'How do you know about Oliver?' asked Joanna, after a short silence.

'It's obvious.'

'Don't tell Carl,' said Joanna, 'or he'll kill me.'

'Or the young man, judging from past form,' said Angela, quite bleakly, and quite seriously.

'I'd thought of that,' said Joanna.

'And you let him take the risk?'

'If I do,' said Joanna, 'so can he. It's worth it. I don't care any more. I don't mind being dead. What have I got to live for? Next year's crocuses?'

Angela said, 'All I can say is, Joanna, keep your young man out of the garden for the time being. His parts might begin to glow in the dark, and you wouldn't like that. Gerald seems to think we're getting quite a lot of radioactivity over here.'

'How lucky you are,' was all Joanna said, 'to have Gerald.'

14

Angela is a good friend. She is a Doctor of European History, but she pretends to be less than Gerald in all matters because thus she preserves the domestic and marital peace, and she reckons those are of all things the most important to preserve, above dignity, truth and honour, and who is to say she is not right? She is married and I am not, and I am sufficiently a child of my generation to believe a woman who has neither husband nor children is scarcely a woman at all.

I, who revealed the truth one day, and lost everything, including dignity and honour, should be the last to suggest that she is wrong. Isaac of course lost more in a similar revelation; that is to say his life. But he had often told me he'd die for me if he had to. Fate listened, that was all: happened to be passing by, as he spoke, with its ear-muffs off. Alas, by dying, Isaac did me no good. He stepped without looking into the path of a reversing car just outside the May Gallery. There were no witnesses, and it was known that Isaac had left the gallery early with a migraine, and a man who has a migraine does not look carefully where he is going, so who was to doubt the driver's word – he being chauffeur to Carl May, and with a clean driving licence, and doing nothing more sinister at the time than backing into his own garage, albeit across the public pavement? And Isaac King had no family to dig away at the matter, to fling up dirt and dust until some nasty scandal was revealed, some bleached bone of unfleshed-out truth discovered.

Isaac was one of those rare and valuable people who are, or appear to be, totally innocent in their life's work: who, by pursuing their own interests, do no apparent harm to anyone.

An academic, an antiquarian, an Egyptologist, his imagination fired by Rider Haggard's Cleopatra when he was a boy, his fervour fanned in various university departments; and then, discovering the civilization of Ancient Egypt to be a culture of the wholly benign, the unmalicious, thereafter lived by sifting the desert sands for scraps and shards yet undetected, nodding politicly at museum curators, with impossible care and patience deciphering the all but indecipherable, piecing together fragments, writing up, collating, publishing papers only a handful of people anywhere in the world would understand. He wanted to bring the past to life. A benign and beautiful past, like no other.

'Is there any money in it, this Egyptology of yours?' asked Carl, at the interview. He was looking for a curator first and a collection second. He had a gallery: he wanted to put something in it: he wanted to be known as a cultured man. An enviable opportunity for the right person. I was there at the interview. I was to be involved. I was to be cultured too. I rather fancied Meissen, but Egyptology turned up.

Isaac smiled at Carl's question. He had a kindly but melancholy air. His smile was somehow forgiving. I understood then for the first time that Carl needed to be forgiven: the understanding cracked wide my wifely love and admiration, and through the crack all kinds of emotions and sensations came rushing unannounced.

'Twelve chairs of Egyptology in all the world?' Isaac King enquired. 'Six hundred devotees at most, turning up to the occasional conference, to compare notions and theories? Of course there's no money in it.'

And Carl, I knew, was both impressed and horrified by such selfless dedication. And as for me, I thought this Isaac King was just wonderful. A good man. So kindly was this man, so generous, so trusting, that coming across the embalmed mummy of a newborn baby, and discovering no body inside, but only sawdust, he concluded not that the embalming priests had cheated the grieving parents but, being too enthusiastic with their fluids, had disintegrated the body by accident, and decided

66

to go ahead with the funeral without telling the parents for fear of upsetting them.

Carl May would never have reached such a conclusion. Nor would my father. Nor indeed did I. But I loved Isaac for believing the best, and not the worst. We were in each other's company from time to time, in that musty vaulted room, the May Gallery, and the pleasures of ideas exchanged became the pleasure of emotion shared, and eventually touch as well. We were as close as we could get.

Carl had me locked in my room so I couldn't go to Isaac's funeral. It would not perhaps have been proper: in giving evidence at the inquest it was I who told the world Isaac had complained of a migraine. He had complained of no such thing – merely that I would not leave Carl there and then, discovered in flagrante delicto as we were, and go off and live with him in his bedsitting room in Ealing, which smelled of gas fire and tooth powder, for all his goodness and generosity. But I was guilty and afraid. I had betrayed Carl and been discovered. Yet I still hoped for Carl's forgiveness. Indeed, I expected it. I had made my demonstration of discontent: now I wanted things to be as before. But how could they be?

And so I moaned and groaned about the unfairness of it all to Angela, while trying not to acknowledge that, of the two of us, Isaac had had by far the worst deal. And she, to her credit, kept pointing it out, waiting for the day when I would have ears to hear. How *good* she is. This practising of so prudent a doctrine, of course, that of female subservience, does have some drawbacks. It renders Angela catty in her conversation: occasionally, one feels, out of sheer desperation, giddy in her behaviour and desperate in her undertakings. The unplucked whiskers on her chin, the straggly hair and wrinkled stockings, suggest some kind of revenge upon the world in general and on her husband in particular. But Gerald, dear Gerald, the amiable fool, seems not to notice, or care: they enfold each other happily enough at night, she tells me, her bulges against his paunch; her feet, untreated bunions and all, tangling with his softer, whiter, smoother ones. Gerald is a civil servant, he drives a car, his shoes are softest leather – his feet are in good shape. I saw his feet once, when the couple kindly asked me, the sorry divorcée, out to the local lido one weekend, to share with them the pleasures of an unexpectedly warm summer day: on littered grass crowded with suburban folk and children eating hot-dogs. Gerald and Angela are not smart at all: Carl couldn't abide them: once I too looked down on them; now I am grateful for them.

(Now Angela knows I am not so alone, of course; that Oliver leaves his nettle-pulling and rose pruning to slip into my bed, I may not get asked to the lido again. Pity may give way to envy – or so I pride myself.)

Something is going to happen. I can feel it. It is so quiet and orderly here in the house, it is unnatural. It is the lull before the storm. Even Oliver feels it. He makes love silently, as if afraid of disturbing someone, something. I am in the habit of being quiet in any case: Carl required very little sexual response from me, and seldom got it. Well, that suited me. Sex between us was a kind of formal dance: a ritual performed in the presence of my beauty, his power: confirmation that the one could be owned by the other. There was little sweaty enjoyment here, little ecstasy of the flesh – but it had its compulsion; like any rewarding habit it had become necessary – as going to church on Sunday might be for a religious-minded person. Or so it had seemed to me. Perhaps I was wrong? Perhaps it was central to his very existence – in which case I had indeed provoked him. How could I, when it came to it, feel on Carl's behalf, any more than I could think for him? I should have allowed him, even after thirty years or so of marriage, some independence of emotion.

Oliver has dirt under his nails, both finger and toe: his broad working hands assist me in altogether new pleasures: I daresay I should be too old for these responses but I find I am not. Does he love me? I don't know. Why should he? I think he likes the thought of screwing the rich older woman who employs him: kicking off his muddy boots at the door and walking barefoot (he seldom wears socks, finding them constricting) along thick carpets on his way to my room. I don't think he laughs at me or reports on me to his friends.

I am fairly sure Oliver likes me. Carl never liked me. But then I didn't like him. I loved him. I admired him and was awed by him: Lord of the dark domains, as he was, and myself the Ice Queen, having dominion over many secret things.

A woman may go out to work, earn her independence, spurn suitors, decline marriage, and be in every way her own mistress. But she will never wake in the morning with this particular gratification – she will never open her eyes to tranquillity and luxury, as I so often did, with the agreeable thought, 'Good Lord! Little me! All this, and just because I look the way I do, am the person I was born.' Enough for this woman just to *be*; not like the other to be forever proving, convincing, striving, placating, buying the comforts and respect of the world. Let someone else, for this fortunate, idle woman, do all that: let he who loves her, maintain her.

Of course it may all come to an abrupt end: the husband's, the lover's, favour may suddenly and dramatically be withdrawn. All the same, the flavour of that confidence remains: it is not forgotten . . . See how I crook my finger and young Oliver comes to my bed. The Ice Queen may be deposed, but she still knows who she is, and so does her subject. She who rules with the divine right of the old-fashioned female, she-who-must-be-obeyed, whose bag must be fetched, lawn mowed, glass kept filled. Someone has to do it.

I like Oliver. I like him for his implausibility, his trust in the future. He means to be a rock singer. He is getting it together. He has been doing this since he left college ten years ago. He lives by odd jobs; he can dry-stone-wall, dig ditches, lop trees, wire houses, clear blocked drains; he can paper and plaster, tell a comfrey from a borage leaf – the kind of things snow queens are not so hot at. Oliver looks like a young Elvis Presley and like him might presently run to fat. When things don't turn out right – the drummer loses his drums (how can anyone *lose* drums; they are so plentiful and bulky: still it's done) so the one

gig of the year can't be set up – his girlfriend sends the engage-
ment ring (such a *little* diamond!) back. She lives in Scotland:
he only sees her at Christmas and Easter: of course she sends it
back! Oliver simply smokes a joint or two, and ceases to worry.
I join him. We pass the magic weed from hand to hand, enjoying
– as no doubt they will presently say in the ads – a special
languid intimacy. I find simple things move me. When Oliver
rolls a joint for us both, unwraps a boiled sweet for me, my
heart turns over. Such kindness! I am unused to it. Carl would
mix me a gin and tonic before our dinner guests arrived and
hand it to me, smiling with his lips, but barking in his heart, a
high-pitched non-stop frantic bark: the gesture did not really
register as love, or kindness. Poor Carl. Poor me.

I try to forgive Carl: try not to burden my friends with
these sudden spasms of anger, misery and resentment. It is my
experience that a quiet mind is gained only by forgiveness: when
you cease to see the other as enemy, as merely yourself in another
guise, see the 'you' as perceived by the other, forget the notion
of 'I' – *I* shiver, *I* suffer, *I* bleed; *I* hate, *my* head will burst with
my resentments; *you* whom *I* hate for not acknowledging this *I*
– then peace descends. Our lives are our own again.

Until the next storm bursts.

15

Those who fear a storm breaking have it in their hearts to whip one up. So Joanna did, forthwith. She too had seen the press photograph of her own front door (or so she regarded it) closing upon the high heel of young Bethany, but shut her conscious mind to its significance, putting aside the yellow press with conventional murmurings of 'rubbish' and taking up *The Times*, who contented themselves with a ten-year-old library shot of her ex-husband at the opening of the May Gallery, the bearded face of Isaac in the background, just discernible. These things combined – the conscious, the barely conscious, the unconscious – to send winds both hot and cold, feverish and chill, through her mind to brew up a veritable hurricane. Well might she fear the lull before the storm.

Joanna paced her marble floor and then went out to find Oliver pruning and digging out rhododendron bushes.

'I mean to sell this house,' she said. 'I hate it.' The King's House stood on the edge of the Thames, near Maidenhead. The river divided around it, to form an island.

'It's a very special house,' he said.

'Oh yes,' she said, 'I know. Some king kept it for his mistresses. Now it does for discarded wives.'

'George the Third,' he said, 'had it renovated for Priscilla Evans. Part of the kitchens dates back to the sixteenth century.'

'Oh, you would know,' she said.

'Yes I would,' he said, 'because I am interested in what goes on around me, not just what happens in my head.'

'Does that make you better than me?'

'No. Just different.'

71

Clip, clip went the secateurs, firmly and sharply. He took care not to bruise the wood he cut. She found his concern for the bush insulting.

'I think it's a very vulgar house,' she said, 'but you wouldn't understand that. You think because it is old that justifies everything.'

It was true that the house was an uneasy mixture of the cosy and the elegant: much balconied, pink-washed outside, a nook-and-cranny effect inside, suggestive of weighty lovers chirruping at one another, peeking round corners. Successive purchasers had added marble floors and gold taps, and green watered-silk ruffled curtains of such expense Joanna had been reluctant to take them down, though only ever truly at home with crimson velvet curtains, round shiny mahogany tables and sideboards, patterned carpets and Chinese vases.

Oliver put down the secateurs and carefully brushed each small wound with bitumen paint.

'All that trouble for a bush,' she said. 'I mean to put this house on the market, I'm not joking.'

'I don't think you'd be wise,' he said. 'It would be a lot of trouble for nothing. If you're not happy here where would you be happy?'

'Somewhere far far away,' she said, 'and don't tell me wherever I go I'd have to take myself with me or I'll scream.'

He laughed, and took up the spade and began to drive it into the stony ground beneath the largest of the bushes. His arms were bare; the muscles moved beneath brown skin.

'I'm sorry about this,' he said.

'About what?'

'I was talking to the bush,' he said. 'I'm digging it up. I'm apologizing.'

She fretted and tapped her foot.

'Why are you digging it up anyway?' she asked.

'Because it's old and keeping out the light from the others,' he said, 'and because purple rhododendrons very easily become a pest.'

'Well anyway,' she said, 'I'm going down to the estate agents now.'

'Look,' he said, 'this is a perfectly good house with a fine garden which had been allowed to go to rack and ruin and I'm just about getting it into shape again. I like it here very much.'

'Well, I'm bored and lonely here,' she said, 'and since I pay, what I say counts.'

He raised his eyebrows.

'You're just in a bad mood,' he said.

'Of course I am,' she said, scornfully. 'And I'll do what I want, when I want, with my own house, my own garden.'

'Joanna,' he said, 'the garden can't be yours. Gardens are like children, they belong to whoever takes care of them.'

'Then stay round here and weed it for some other employer,' she said. 'Because it won't be me.'

'You need me, Joanna,' he said, and put down his spade. 'You have a very jealous nature. You're even jealous of rhododendrons. Why don't you help me dig them up? You'd feel much better.'

She looked at her long idle nails, her well-kept hands: she looked at his grimy and hardworking ones, no longer gardening, and felt better . . .

'It isn't in my nature,' she said, 'and besides, the air is full of radiation. Angela says it isn't wise to be out.'

'Perhaps I'd better come in then,' he said, 'or perhaps you'd better come under the bushes.'

And he would have pulled her under them there and then, and she would not have objected, or minded sharp stones against her back, her front, or twigs in her hair, or dirtying her purple dress, only the postman chose to come up the path at that moment, with a packet from the Maverick Enquiry Agency, which she could not ignore.

She left Oliver digging in the drifting outfall from Chernobyl and went inside, to read the report.

Fifteen minutes later she came out and said, 'I'm going to see Carl right now.'

'Why?' he asked.

'Because it's all too much to be endured,' she said.

'Don't go,' he said, and had she been listening, had she really

73

cared about him, she would have heard that tone in his voice which is used by bit-part film actors who know that a sudden fatal blow is about to fall, in the next few frames, and try not to show it. But she wasn't listening; she didn't care; she was going to see Carl.

16

'Yet each man kills the thing he loves,' murmured Carl May, as he paced his elegant office in the tower block in Reading which was the hub of Britnuc's empire. The building had been designed to dominate the city skyscape, and so it had, but not for long. No sooner had the foundations settled, no sooner the first window cleaner toppled to his death – always the mark of a properly finished office building – than all around arose the thrusting towers of usurping empires – leaner, taller, glassier – but doomed to crumble and collapse, built on the hot and shifting sands of finance, not the rock of industry, the cold power of the atom. Carl May was neither shaken nor dismayed, though the arch of sky he loved was now the merest tent of blue, so high and near the false towers crowded. He knew they would not last.

'What is that you said, my dear?' enquired Bethany, looking up from her VDU, upon which she played computer games. He'd had the contraption carried up from a lower floor. In this calm and spacious room all was grey and pink and empty surfaces: uncluttered: all that was needed here was mind: no tools of trade, no paper, pens, or telephones: he was too grand for that. But Bethany must have her toys.

'I was quoting,' he said, 'from *The Ballad of Reading Gaol.*' It was Carl May's joke. His empire, his prison! Oscar Wilde, once imprisoned for imprudence in Reading Gaol – still there, that gaunt grey building, still used, not a quarter of a mile away from where Carl May now had his throne – had through that imprisonment received his immortality.

'Do you think,' asked Carl May of Bethany, 'anyone would have taken any notice of Oscar Wilde if he hadn't gone to prison?'

But how was Bethany to answer a thing like that? She shrugged, and went on playing. He sighed. Carl May was restless. In the outer offices phones rang and minions ran; press officers dealt with queries concerning outfall and infall, becquerels and watertables, cladding and coolants, leukaemia and bone cancer, prevailing winds and drifting particles. Head Office personnel took calls from Britnucs A and D where staff threatened action over the recent tightening of various safety regulations, and from B and C where there was some anxiety that the tightening had not been sufficiently extreme. PR withdrew distribution to better facilitate the instant re-editing of an entire series of linked film for internal, external and educational purposes: no one could say Britnuc was not on its toes since Chernobyl went up; and the External Services division within the day had liaised with Concrete Casings – of which Carl May was also a director – to tender to the Soviet Union so many tonnes of special-grade radiation-resistant (though so far untested in the field) concrete for immediate shipment to Kiev.

Carl, confident in the efficiency and dedication of his staff, reserved his energies for the highest level – that is to say ministerial dealings; but the Government was, on the whole, wisely quiet, until such time as ignorance, panic and bad judgement in the lower levels were either cured, or covered up.

One female journalist did get through to Carl May that day by impersonating the Prime Minister's voice, but that was the only entertainment in an otherwise boring morning for Carl May. Those who have perfected the art of delegation tend to suffer, in emergencies, from too much peace.

In Carl May's childhood kennel, there had been a lot to do. Not only had he soothed the savage heart of Harry the bull-terrier but trained him to fetch him scraps of newsprint from the streets around: Carl May himself, being chained by a collar, was in no position to do so. Those were the worst days. But they had not been boring.

'I never saw a man who looked
With such a wistful eye
Upon that little tent of blue
Which prisoners call the sky'

said Carl May to Bethany, but her hand was upon the control
stick, her eyes upon the screen, and she seemed not to hear. In
theory she worked upon a special personal project of his, an
Open Day for Britnuc two years hence, thus avoiding bad feeling
amongst his other secretarial staff; it was an arrangement which
he could safely cancel nearer the time. He liked to have her close.
He realized he had been lonely, and resented his ex-wife Joanna
for having by her behaviour rendered him thus, so sadly and for
so long. With what great effort had he, Carl May, brought
himself to trust a cruel world, and how she had destroyed that
trust, completing what his mother had begun.

He wondered, as he sometimes did, whether to trace the clones
of Joanna May, and see how they had turned out, and whether
one of them might not do instead of Joanna, but he could see
the folly of it. The capacity for infidelity, Carl May suspected,
ran in the genes; it could not be in the rearing – for surely Joanna
had had a calm, tranquil and orderly rearing; she had seemed
neither too fond of her father nor too antagonistic to her mother,
and yet she had succumbed – and all he would do was set himself
up again for the same shock and sorrow. Joanna at half her age
would still be Joanna.

Bethany, thought Carl May; now Bethany was a different
matter. She knew where her bread and butter lay. She had been
bought. She acknowledged the transaction. He had taken, as it
were, an option out on Bethany, body and soul. When it ran
out, he would either renew on his terms, if he so chose, or let it
lapse, and she would be free to go. He felt well disposed towards
her. She gave him pleasure. He told her things he never told
anyone. It would not last.

He did not want it to last. He felt humiliated as well as
pleased, lessened as much as augmented. She was less than him
in everything but youth.

'It is sweet to dance to violins,
When love and life are fair,
To dance to flutes, to dance to lutes,
Is delicate and rare:
But it is not sweet with nimble feet
To dance upon the air –'

said Carl May aloud.

Bethany hummed a little song as she worked upon her game: little trills and tweets rose round her, as if flocks of tiny birds flowed from her machine: her red hair fell enchantingly upon her face.

'Do you understand that?' asked Carl May.

'Understand what?' she asked. Carl May felt a stab of displeasure: it cut between his ribs like a knife.

'To dance upon the air is to hang,' he said. 'Love is a hanging offence.'

'Why's that?' she said, not caring.

'Because each man kills the thing he loves,' he said, 'which was where we began.'

'You didn't kill Joanna,' said Bethany, 'only her boyfriend, so what are you going on about?' On her screen, in search of paradise, she dodged monsters and beheaded and delimbed her enemies with a sword which flailed every time she pressed the space key.

Carl May thought if he had Bethany cloned, he could perhaps undo the effects of her upbringing. If he got Holly to remove one of Bethany's eggs, fertilized it *in vitro* with any old semen, removed the resultant nuclei and reinserted the nuclei of any one of Bethany's DNA-bearing cells (which the new dehydrating technique had made just about possible), and then had the egg implanted in a womb as stable and orderly as that of Joanna's mother – and such wombs could be found, now as then; their owners crying out for implantation – why then Carl May might create a perfect woman, one who looked, listened, understood and was faithful. If he reimplanted the egg in Bethany herself – but no, that would be hopeless; she was spoiled, sullied, somehow she would reinfect herself.

'Shoo fly,' murmured Bethany. 'Shoo fly, don't bother me,'

and ping, ping, wimble, doodle, cheep cheep, splat went the little fluttering doves and ravens, the electronic sounds of victory and defeat – he'd made her turn the volume right down but still the small inanities, the false excitements, trembled and hovered in the air, insistent. He decided the cloning of Bethany would be more trouble than it was worth: it would require more time and energy than he had available. She made him feel tired, and that was the truth of it. Old King David's maidservant may have warmed his bed but she sure as hell carried him off quicker. He would be too old by the time Bethany was reissued, as it were, to get the benefit of it.

Now, if he had himself cloned, as he'd threatened Bethany – then the two younger versions of themselves could indeed pair off. But what use would that be to Carl May? Another body would feel the pleasure: another mind register it. Odd how the notion kept reasserting itself – that what one clone knew, would be known by all: what one felt, the others would feel; that to make clones was to create automatons, men without souls – soldiers, servants, deprived of will, decision. How could it be so? Did the common misconception suggest that the soul, whatever that was, would be split, divided out fairly amongst the repetitions – as if nature and God were indeed in some kind of partnership? For every new exercise in human diversity – a quarter of a million of them every day – God would dole out only one soul? They were in short supply? Nonsense! He wanted to talk to Joanna about it. Joanna the faithless, the betrayer: Joanna who mocked him, whispered about him behind his back, trapped and tortured him. Joanna Eve.

'Shoo fly,' murmured Bethany. 'Shoo fly, don't bother me!'
'What are you singing?' he asked.
'Just something that goes through my head,' she said.
'What's that?' he asked.
'It has no words,' said Bethany, but she lied. The words were clear in her head. If you went on from 'Shoo fly, don't bother me, For I belong to somebody,' you got to:

For an old man he is old,
And an old man he is grey,

79

But a young man's heart is full of love,
Get away, old man, get away.

Bethany stopped singing. She felt sad, to be so young and yet so old, twenty-four going on forty-two.

17

The clones of Joanna May would have been faithful if they could, but fate was against them. Like their master copy, Jane, Julie, Gina and Alice, for good or bad, were of a nature which preferred to have the itch of desire soothed, settled and out of the way rather than seeing in its gratification a source of energy and renewal. Here comes sex, they said in their hearts, here comes trouble! But trouble came. There was no stopping it, for them or anyone.

Of the four, Jane Jarvis made the best and closest approach to monogamy. Her chosen parents, Madge and Jeremy, were academics – chosen by Dr Holly of the Bulstrode Clinic in conjunction with Carl May, of course, rather than herself, but when did any infant have the choice of its environment? No, the child is landed with what it gets, albeit sharing with its natural parents a characteristic or so – his brown eyes and her crooked little finger and a tendency to sniff, not to mention the bad temper of a maternal great-grandmother, the musical ability of a paternal great-uncle – which may or may not make the family placing easier when the baby erupts into it. But little Jane, long awaited, painfully implanted, was eagerly received into the world by parents who knew she was nothing to do with them, and didn't care, and never said: she was cherished, taught, instructed, cosseted, pressured and expected to pass exams, which she obligingly did. At sixteen she appointed – or so her manner suggested – an unkempt and unsuitable lad as her permanent boyfriend, much to his surprise and gratification and her parents' initial dismay. While other girls moaned, giggled, sighed, heaved, chopped, changed, got pregnant, gang-banged, gossiped and groped themselves out of any hope of further education, pretty little Jane Jarvis sat studying, her faithful and besotted Tom beside her, making coffee and replenishing pens and paper as required.

When she was seventeen, her quasi-father Jeremy the economist, the most steady and rational of monetarists, owl-eyed, unimpassioned, kindly and distant, startled his family and the campus by making one of his junior lecturers pregnant. He seemed sorrowful that the event had caused distress and concern; he announced the news at breakfast the day after Jane sat her English A-level and the day before her Sociology exam, thus greatly compounding his offence. 'Surely it could have waited,' wept Madge the Eng. Lit. structuralist. 'Are you trying to destroy her as well as me?' Jeremy seemed puzzled: he said he was going with Laura to the ante-natal clinic so he would be late home for tea. Laura had been a frequent visitor to the house and had coached Jane in Economics, since Jane somehow cut off when offered instruction by her father.

Jane got a B in English and A's in Economics and Sociology. The results arrived the day Laura gave birth to a boy. 'You see,' said Jane to Tom, 'adversity just makes me concentrate the more.' Oxford let her in: she'd done the three A-levels in one year.

Madge wept and said to her husband at breakfast, the day the letter came from Oxford, 'I don't want you, I don't need you, go to her if that's what you want.'
'Look here –' he said.
'Go, go!' she screamed, so he went. Perhaps that was when Jane caught the row virus: her quasi-mother, rushing out of the room, beside herself, brushed one bare ageing arm against Jane's young one.

'It was their timing that was so awful,' Jane lamented to Tom later. When she went up to Oxford, leaving her mother alone in the big house, with its many bookshelves and bicycles and good prints, she found she was pregnant. Madge offered to have the baby; she needed something, anything, and Jane almost consented, but in the end she couldn't, she didn't, she had her future to think about. She had a termination at twelve weeks: a boy. A couple of years later Jeremy returned home: so that was just as well. It had been a kind of convulsion in all their lives, that was all. Everything smoothed out again. Laura married someone her own age and went to Sweden with the child. Madge became Professor of American Studies. Jeremy just seemed somehow older, and more tired, as if he'd tried something terribly important, and had failed at the last hurdle.

At the degree ceremony – she got a First in Eng. Lit. – he kissed the back of her neck with dry tired lips and said, 'I'm proud of you. I wish you were mine,' and she did not understand that, or pursue it, as she would have had it been some puzzling line in *Beowulf* or *Sir Gawain*. Some things are safer thought about than others.

And she'd ditched Tom by then. She had to. He was off at Art College in London, making a mess of things, quarrelling with his tutor, refusing to train for a career in advertising, too proud for this, too good for that, scratched and sore about the abortion, no matter that he understood the necessity, approved in theory, knew her body was her own, and so forth, knew there was lots of time for both of them – it had just been *that* baby, at *that* time – but he would keep reminding her, would keep upsetting her, and she needed a boyfriend on the spot, to save trouble and tantrums all around. Tom had to go.

Men pursued her, waylaid her, entreated her favours; yet when and if she looked in a mirror she could see only an ordinary, expected face, nothing special. Madge had never noticed how she looked, only what went on in her head. No one at home had told her she was pretty: Jeremy had seemed to notice her exam results more than herself, though responsive enough, it had seemed, to Laura. It was all a bother; too much to think about. She took up with a young man, a certain Stephen, a mathematician, good-looking, undemanding, as quiet and steady as Tom was noisy and wayward.

'You faithless bitch,' yelled Tom down the phone. 'You're never *here*,' she moaned, 'and when you are you're horrid.' 'I have to get my degree,' he shrieked, 'how can I be there?' 'I don't see why you can't be here,' she murmured. 'What do artists need with degrees?' 'You're cold, manipulative, selfish,' he said. 'You want to own me, control me. You treat me halfway between a little boy and a stud.' 'Then you're well rid of me,' she said. And he said, 'It's education has done this to you. It's changed you. Everything's in your head: there's nothing left in your heart. You don't know how to be natural any more: last time I was with you, you actually poured my coffee into a dirty mug. You've even forgotten how to wash up.'

'Good,' she said, and put the phone down. She stayed with Stephen for six years but wouldn't marry him, as he had hoped and expected, because of the problem of her needing to be in London – she had a good first job as a reader for MGM – and him having to begin his life as a chartered accountant in Newcastle, which was the only place he could get a job, so, coolly, she did without him. Well, fate was against her. If he'd been offered a job in London she would have stayed with him.

Madge and Jeremy were disappointed. When it came to it, it seemed they wanted her to be settled and ordinary, not independent and special. So much of it had been all talk.

And then Tom came back into her life, as they say in the magazines and, although it hardly seemed what she wanted, it was familiar, and would do. He filled her bed and sat opposite her in restaurants and they shared the bill, but he always had the feeling, did Tom, that she was looking over his naked shoulder – him on top of her, no variations considered – to see who was there, who had come to the party more important, more interesting, than he. And she would croon and stroke her little grey cat, sadly, even directly after they'd made love, as if it was his fault, as if he were the gatekeeper to some other, more richly sensuous world than this, but would not let her in. When actually it was the other way round.

———◦◦———

Julie Rainer's chosen parents were not academics and did not believe in girls taking examinations: on the contrary: they had a feeling, vague though it was, that too much thinking made girls undomesticated and argumentative. If Julie was seen with a book, her mother Katie would say, 'Don't mope about reading: why don't you go for a nice walk?' or 'Look, there's some washing-up to do,' and Julie would obligingly put the book away. Her father, Harold, worked in Sheffield for a firm of stockbrokers: Kate did voluntary work around and about: they lived in a pleasant house with a large garden.

Harold and Katie had tried to have children for eight years, unsuccessfully, before they agreed on the new and risky method suggested by Dr Holly, and Katie had the little female foetus implanted: but being pregnant, swelling up, did not bring the ease she'd hoped for, the sense of fulfilment she'd been promised. The fact that the baby was so close did not, when it came to it, make it feel less of a little foreigner, on the contrary: and Harold would not be present at the birth, which was just beginning to be fashionable, and in the end she'd have preferred to have adopted a baby in the usual way, actually *seeing* what she was going to have to live with for years and years, making much the same kind of choice as she had when she married Harry. 'Like that, want it.' Not a bad way, when it came to it. She was happy enough with Harry: they'd wanted a baby badly, so badly, because they wanted it, couldn't have it.

Nothing wrong with little Julie, on the contrary: the brightest, prettiest, easiest little thing, Harry's pet, too much Harry's pet at first, perhaps that was the trouble, always sitting on his knee, him fondling perhaps overmuch, but how could one say a thing like that, except the baby wasn't Harry's flesh and blood, was it, and he knew it. Dr Holly might have been right when he suggested Katie didn't tell Harry about the implantation, simply went home and said, 'We're pregnant! A miracle!' but she hadn't taken Dr Holly's advice though, had she? Then the miracle did happen; when Julie was five (and playing Mary in the school Nativity play, of course) Katie did become pregnant, in the ordinary marital way, with a boy, a son, a firstborn no matter what Harry said, a wonderfully easy, natural birth, and Harry was there to hold her hand, and they called him Adam, and after that, really, though she was always perfectly kind to Julie, of course, that went without question, Adam was her real child, her only child, and when Julie, by then trained as a secretary and working in a local estate agent's office, came home one day and said, 'Mummy, I've met this wonderful man, Alec: he's my boss, actually: I want to marry him,' Katie said, 'Of course, darling, if you really and truly love him' and Julie said, 'I love him with all my heart and soul,' and who knew enough about her to disbelieve her, and Harry, who was having a secret affair with his own secretary, a girl Julie's age, a serious affair, true love, and wondering whether he had the courage to leave Kate, and if he did would Julie and Adam ever forgive him, said, 'Her life, her choice: pity about his wall-eye, but I suppose it makes the one that works the more acute, and the fellow's got a good business future, that's the main thing. When the chips are down it's income that counts.'

And Julie married Alec, dressed appropriately in virginal white. (Neither believed in sex-before-marriage:
Julie: '*What would Daddy think of me? He'd die.*'
Alec: '*I think marriage should be a sacrament: should really mean something.*')

The wedding took place in the village church, and it was written up in the *Daily Telegraph*, and their first house was on an executive estate. And after Alec had had his wall-eye fixed, thanks to new laser surgical techniques, there was no stopping him: they moved to bigger and grander estates, and he was away most of the time, developing holiday resorts, flying the world Club Class British Airways with his computer on his knee: and she never worried about other women: Alec really wasn't interested, she knew that and she didn't think she was or why would she have married him? She would have loved children but Alec couldn't have them: and her father had left her mother and gone off with his secretary which had thoroughly upset Julie, but she had the cats and the dogs and the fish, and loved them, especially her little grey cat; she could run her hand over its soft fur and watch the light catch the grey and turn it into a hundred different changing shades and now suddenly she found herself in love with the vet, or rather he was in love with her, and it hadn't been sex, really, just closeness – but who in the world was there to talk to about these things? Not Alec. For Alec the past was over. Like his wall-eye, better not remembered.

And how could you talk to someone who wasn't there, but flying about the skies all the time? How could you talk to your husband about your lover?

There was no talking to her mother. Her mother had gone downhill since her father left. She ranted and raved and said odd things, which hurt. Julie thought she drank too much. 'You're no flesh of mine,' she'd say to Julie, and in the same breath complain that Harry hadn't been there at Julie's birth, and Julie had bitten her on the way out: she'd been born with one tooth already cut. So how could she talk to a mother who wanted only to hurt and confuse her? And how could she not go to bed with the vet, because it was bed first and talking after, with him. She'd have been faithful if she could, but fate was against her. If she'd had friends, it might not have happened. She could have talked to them. But friends where she lived came in couples, talked in couples; you could go out to dinner and talk non-stop and say nothing: and disloyalty over morning coffee was not allowed: and besides, the others had children, and she did not. She was an outsider, alone and lonely. Of course she went to bed with the vet. But she didn't want to. She would rather have been happily married.

———◦○◦———

And Gina? Ah well, Gina. Gina lifted her skirt to show the boys her knickers when she was nine, and took off her knickers to show them more when she was ten, and at twelve was deflowered in the back seat of a cinema, and at thirteen was hitchhiking down the A1 for the fun of it, and at fourteen was declared beyond parental control, and by sixteen was back home again and quite reformed and at eighteen was pregnant and married to Cliff, a would-be pop singer, and garage mechanic, and by twenty-eight had three children by two different fathers, but she'd still have been monogamous if she could. She'd had sexual encounters with some thirty men by the time she was married, fate being against her, and had felt altogether happy and at ease for perhaps ninety minutes of her life till then: the minutes in which she exercised proper sexual power over men, became the magnet to which they were drawn which could never fail; the minutes, however brief, just before actual penetration. From then on the man's energies took over, she was neither here nor there, and it was no fun: sometimes, depending on circumstance, it was even horrific. The more of them, the less of her. She felt it.

Perhaps the seven-day-old Joanna-foetus that was to become Gina lacked some vital energy, or, if you look at it another way, perhaps some segment of the double helix of the DNA which so strongly and happily composed Joanna, Jane, Julie and Alice had become fused and blurred in Gina. These things do happen, chance intervenes, being no respecter of the wishes and intentions of geneticists, let alone microbiologists. Gina was implanted in the womb of an impetuous young woman, by name Annette, who'd come south from Scotland to start her life afresh, and had been swept off her feet by an earnest and intellectual bookseller named Douglas with exotic tastes and a wen on his almost bald head.

They were married within the week. She was a good cook and a fine bookkeeper and he needed both. She worked in the shop, typed the bills, learned the book trade, charmed the customers – and then she wanted a baby. Douglas didn't. Later, later, he said, standing over her every morning to make sure she took her contraceptive pill. He didn't trust her and was right not to. 'I'll do it another way,' thought Annette, and went to visit Dr Holly at the Bulstrode Clinic, whose fame had spread throughout London in the late fifties as the maker or taker away of babies, depending on which you wanted. She told Dr Holly what she hadn't told Douglas – that to date she'd had one stillborn baby, Down's Syndrome, and four abortions. And Dr Holly said, since her husband's sperm was unavailable, and her eggs not reliable, he could give her a baby of her own without either. And under local anaesthetic, there and then, he implanted little Gina.

Dr Holly wasn't sure how long he could keep the processes of cell division going outside the womb; he said time was running out for this particular foetus; he could feel it. Carl May said he saw no reason for or evidence of any such deterioration, but Carl May, Dr Holly said, thus offending his benefactor, had a layman's view of the material world – that is to say he thought there had to be a reason for things to go wrong. Things just happened, as any scientist could affirm. You knew by the pricking of your thumbs. Had Dr Holly not been in such a hurry, he might well have rejected Annette as a suitable birth parent: as it was, he trusted to luck. There were more than enough wombs to choose from; he had little excuse; they thronged the waiting room of the Bulstrode Clinic, brought there by rumour. There were women who wanted babies, and couldn't have them, or had babies and didn't want them, women trying to save babies, women trying to lose babies, and most of them weeping or on the verge of weeping. Dr Holly felt, and Carl felt with him, that an evolutionary process which caused so much grief could surely be improved upon by man: genetic engineering would hardly add to the sum of human misery, so great a sum that was, and might just possibly make matters a good deal better. No doubt in time the techniques of artificial reproduction would be further advanced and manipulation of DNA itself made possible so that improved and disease-resistant human beings could in the end be produced. In the meantime, Holly and May did what they could; May providing money and inspiration and Dr Holly surgical deftness and experience. It was just he was perhaps, this time, in rather too much of a hurry.

So there Annette was, pregnant with a diminutive Joanna, who seemed less and less likely to reach her potential as the pregnancy proceeded. Annette's husband, discovering her pregnant, threw her out of the house, claiming the baby was not his. She told him the truth, which made matters worse. (He'd tried to sue Dr Holly but lawyers would not take on his case: he was excitable and it sounded like sheer fantasy to them, a tale told by a guilty wife. In the end he gave up.) Annette, distressed, drank too much, smoked too much, went home to Scotland, had the baby six weeks early, failed to love it, left it with her parents, who, the more they feared their granddaughter would go the same way as their daughter, brought this fate upon her.

'Mum,' Annette would say, at the beginning, over the phone from as far away as possible, 'she can't inherit anything from me, because she isn't anything to do with me. Her genes are different. I know what you're going to say next. "We don't let her wear jeans. She always wears a dress." Christ, I could almost feel sorry for her.' Then Annette drifted away altogether. Grandfather had a stroke, grandmother's vision was impaired. Grandmother drank too much, mostly sherry. There were no books in the house. Gina learned to read from the back of the cornflake packet and the fronts of buses. She had a weak bladder and wet her knickers a lot which made her unpopular at school – a graffitied, run-down place – with both teacher and pupils. She was classified as disturbed, she was unhappy with herself, unhappy at home, beaten by teachers for answering back, frequently locked in her bedroom by her grandmother as a punishment for 'being dirty', frequently climbed out of the bedroom window, and on one occasion was helped by a passing alcoholic; as a result of which, being observed, she was taken to the police station as being out of control and put in a children's home from which Annette reluctantly rescued her.

Annette who by now kept a junk stall on the Portobello Road and lived with a Rastafarian drug dealer.

'You're not mine,' she'd keep telling Gina, 'but no one deserves my mum and dad,' and Gina would look down her straight disdainful nose and lower the lids of her bright blue eyes, in the sexy way she'd lately acquired, and wonder where she'd come from, if not out of Annette, and ate another chocolate bar to keep her somehow rooted, tied to the earth. The world outside kept changing, without apparent cause or reason, out of her control. She had a weight problem. If she didn't keep herself heavy she'd fly off and be lost, like a piece of scrap paper. She went round with boiled sweets in her pocket, and boys knew by just looking at her she was anyone's, which these days she wasn't: her stepdad Bilbo belted her if she was, though Annette jumped up and down and told him he was a savage.

Gina liked Bilbo: he seemed to care what happened to her, and actually stir himself to do something about it, however painful. They ate good food, hot and rich with chillies; they watched a lot of TV; the cat had kittens: Gina begged and pleaded to keep the fluffy grey one for herself, and was allowed. Life was almost good. She did OK in school, too: caught up, quickly: would have passed exams and even gone to college (she wanted to be a doctor: how her mother laughed) except she met Cliff, got pregnant, wouldn't have the abortion Annette suggested – 'But it's murder, Mum' – and married him, and there was young Cliff, son of a Portobello repairer of clocks, who wanted to be a pop singer, obliged to be a garage mechanic the better to support her and baby Ben. And Cliff drank too much, though he went into car sales and ended up selling second-hand old Rolls-Royces, which you can buy for a couple of hundred in the trade and sell for a couple of thousand to fools, so they lived OK, except Cliff began hitting her, and she knew somewhere she deserved it, and she could no longer look down her nose so well, if only because it had been broken a couple of times. He was always sorry afterwards, and she was sorry for him and bound to him, and loved him in a kind of way; but she was never quite sure Sue was his, though she hoped so – it had been an accident, a one-night stand when she was really miserable, between a black eye and an apology, right at the beginning – and Cliff certainly had no idea, he would *really* have killed her, and in a way she was killing herself, she knew it, but how did you stop, once you had begun? But she would have been faithful, if she could. One life, one man. But fate was against her.

And Alice? Alice was implanted in the womb of Honeybell Lee Morthampton, a mother of four boys so anxious to have a girl she would not take the chance of another boy.

'Let's see,' said Dr Holly, 'we've only had frustrated wombs to date, eager and waiting. If we can make this one stick in an elderly multigravida with a history of rejecting females, we've really got it right.'

'I don't see,' said Carl May, 'why the womb history should make any difference; if hormone levels are sound, how can it? It's like believing that a pedigree bitch, once it's had pups by a mongrel, never breeds true again.'

'But it doesn't,' said Dr Holly. 'I have one and I know. The fleeting flavour of the brat about her last litter, purebred labrador though they are. Pure in theory, not in practice. There's more goes on inside the womb than meets the eye. Flavours are caught. Call it propensity, synchronicity, call it God, what you like: at the last fractional moment balances are tipped, this way and that. Interesting.'

'You mean we ought to *pray* this one sticks,' said Carl May derisively.

'I do,' said Dr Holly, and though neither of them prayed, little Alice stuck, and grew up, pretty little sister to four big brothers, alternately bullying and protective, resentful and admiring, lecherous and rejecting, mother's little helper, sweeping, cooking, wiping, serving, flirting, sulking, weeping, giggling, absurdly tender-hearted or else cruel beyond belief, valued for the sheer femaleness of her being, brought up with an amiable father and four big brothers no real kin to her.

Alice entered a beauty contest when she was fifteen, was 'discovered', won a holiday in Florida, kept the company of long-legged beach girls with millionaire boyfriends, came back, went to charm school, discovered the value of disdain, the power of active nonpleasing, failing to placate; she looked at her perfect self in a mirror one day and decided not to have children, not to get married. Who could she ever find to love better than she? Who better to be faithful to, than herself? Men were useful as admirers: sex kept them quiet: love was for suckers: when she felt the first pangs of love, lust, she went home to Honeybell Lee, the dogs, the cats, the nieces and nephews, love, muddle and mess abounding, and was cured.

'She's not like the rest of us,' said Honeybell Lee, puzzled. Honeybell Lee believed Alice to be her natural child: so far as she was aware the Bulstrode Clinic had carried out a simple investigation under local anaesthetic to change the acid/alkaline balance of her internal secretions in favour of the survival of sperm carrying female chromosomes when next it arrived. And it had worked to the great pleasure and satisfaction of all concerned.

And Alice would have been truly faithful to herself, if only fate had so allowed, and not pushed men into her bed, photographers and clients and so forth. Her infidelity brought her no pleasure. She really preferred to sleep alone, being of a nature that saw sex as a drain on her personal resources, not something that enriched them.

Jane, Julie, Gina and Alice.

18

So it was that the four clones, Jane, Julie, Gina and Alice, produced by the irritation of a single egg, were successfully implanted in waiting wombs. Beyond confirming that growth was normal and the infants were successfully born, Holly and May made no attempt to follow the fortunes of the children, or to do the personality studies that would, both agreed, be interesting, if only to make some contribution to the nature/ nurture debate. But the complications of setting up such studies would be immense; their research would come under an ethical and legal scrutiny it could not for the time being afford; and it would, they told themselves, be difficult for the four little girls to live normal lives under scrutiny. Nor did they see any good reason to tell Joanna May herself what they had done. Joanna May, the calm, normal, healthy, beautiful and apparently well-balanced woman whom they had, out of love, respect and admiration so successfully reproduced, was still a woman, and therefore liable to extreme, hysterical and unhelpful reaction: she was a creature of the emotions, rather than reason. That was the female lot. And look at it this way: if the population of, say, Egypt increased by a million every nine months, why then, were four more Joannas dropped into the pool – rather than one each of a female Madge/ Jeremy, Harold/Katie, Douglas/Annette, Honeybell/Patrick (un- likely in any case to come into existence because of nature's own inefficiency) – to be in any way abhorred? Holly and May had done no harm to anyone, so far as they could see, or anything: though Holly sometimes, when reviewing the past, did wonder a little about Carl May's motives: could a man brought up in a kennel, barking in his heart, baying at the moon, really ever know himself? Did anyone?

The Bulstrode Clinic experiments in parthenogenesis had long since ceased, becoming irrelevant as the whole field of genetic engineering and microbiology opened up. Dr Holly had moved on to run an enterprising and well-funded Research and Development unit at Martins Pharmaceuticals, an international conglomerate of which Carl May presently became a director. Here his field was at first the decoding of DNA; at which time the visits and special requests of Carl May became less frequent, rather to Dr Holly's relief. But later Holly moved on to the development of dehydration techniques in relation to egg-cell nuclei; there was much excitement and talk of Nobel Prizes – and all of a sudden Carl May was back again, having met up with Isaac King, requiring that Holly drop everything and search the gut of an ancient Egyptian body, dehydrated rather than mummified, which he just so happened to have in his possession, for cells with sufficient intact and living DNA for nuclei transference to be possible. Holly hinted, rather than protested, that he had better things to do than bring the past to life, since the present was surely difficult enough to cope with. He tried to keep the matter light in the interest of his funding, and in the attempt made matters worse than he had thought possible.

'If our motives are impure,' said Dr Holly blithely, 'we will suffer for it: we will be caught like birds in a trap.' The Curse of the Pharaohs was in his mind: Tutankhamen's curse which, according to Isaac King, pursued leading Egyptologists all over the world – tumours and heart attacks killing at an unusually early age, cancers and road accidents striking others down – so that the quality, forget the number, of professors in the subject fell as the best and brightest of them were removed from the human race. Dr Holly half-believed it, half did not, could joke about it.

Carl May did not consider it a joking matter. Carl May dismissed the matter of the Curse of the Pharaohs as the merest, most vulgar of superstitions; how could any scientist even half-believe such junk? Handling a lot of dusty, ancient, possibly carcinogenic material could well result in early death. Road accidents? Well, Egyptologists were by their nature impractical and vague. The myth of the absent-minded professor had its roots in truth. They just didn't look where they were going.

They got killed. Dr Holly, rashly, disagreed. He was a professor himself, he reminded Carl May. He was not absent-minded, not in the least.

The Curse of the Pharaohs, Carl May then pointed out, was no more than a warning, albeit engraved in stringent stone and in a prominent position. It was the Ancient Egyptian equivalent of a burglar alarm: 'If anyone enters my tomb with unworthy intentions, be warned. I will catch him like a bird in a trap and stand witness against him by the throne of the Lord of Eternity.' The Ancient Egyptians, Isaac King had explained to Carl May, who now took the trouble – and he was a busy man – to explain it to Dr Holly, caught their birds in clapnets, the two wooden sides of a net coming smartly and suddenly together, and that for the bird was that: kept trapped until it was time to be killed and eaten, or killed and embalmed by some patron who would gain credit in the afterlife for so doing. Absurd!

'You never know,' laughed Dr Holly, 'just when the past will catch up with you! You should always be prepared. Embalm a bird or two!'

Carl May did not laugh. Carl May took irrational offence. 'Gobbledygook!' he cried, and Dr Holly found his department's grant cut presently by many millions. For once too piqued to apologize or oblige, Dr Holly allowed his department to limp on as best it could, left the pursuit of Nobel Prizes to others, and diversified into the safe, cheap and interesting study of brain-cell activity in identical twins. Carl May did not take this side-stepping sitting down: no, he fretted, threatened and fumed – but shortly afterwards came the unfortunate matter of Isaac King's death, and the divorce of his wife, and he was quiet. Something seemed to have knocked the spirit out of him, at least for a time.

19

I, Joanna May.

Isaac King taught me many important things. Carl May taught me many boring things, mostly about how to keep him happy.

Isaac taught me that there need never be an end to seeing. Isaac insisted that I could look at the stubbed-out cigarettes in an ashtray and see beyond it to the meaning behind – know that everything has significance, even if it comes, for a time, to this trash. Those who grew the leaf and waited and prayed for the rain to come: those who profited by its processing and selling: those who smoked it, and defied death: those who stubbed it out, envisaging life – all are part of it. Even in that detritus of ash and grime was something to be marvelled at, something to make you quite giddy with delight. Isaac smoked, of course, and had no intention of stopping, and as it turned out, he was justified, his death by misadventure preceding any major damage to lungs or circulatory system. Carl did not smoke. Carl meant to live for ever in perfect health in a world he hated.

Isaac King taught me that patterns are being woven around us every minute of the day: if we have eyes to see them, they are there to see. When the stray cat miaowing on the doorstep one morning turns out to be the illegitimate grandchild of the grey Persian owned by your father's favourite patient, long deceased, there is no need for surprise. All things are interrelated: the cat was lost and found just to make sure all the cogs were locking properly; or some loose overlap, perhaps, needed to be sealed. The Egyptians knew how cats, who have their own strong familial links, interweave with ours, and our friendships and ventures. Fate offers us hints: shrugs if we don't take notice. No skin off its nose. Isaac taught me to accept mystery. Carl May believed in cause and effect, action and consequence, and nothing much else, except the laws of probability. He thought it was so obvious it didn't need teaching, or no doubt he would have. Brides get taught.

I once tried to explain to Carl what I meant by 'fate' but he didn't listen: he went on reading the *Financial Times*, fidgeting slightly to demonstrate his irritation. That was after Isaac and I had started sorting out exhibits together, but before our further intimacy.

The word 'fate', of course, did not help me, being inadequate to describe the sense of a multifarious, infinitely complex, dreamy yet purposeful universe which I had in mind – being altogether too singular a word, too single-purposed, like a chisel driven hard into the delicacy of experience. A single brain cell, one amongst millions, millions, were it self-conscious, might I suppose have just such an inkling of what was going on around it. The 'Fates' had it better, being at least plural, something capable of consensus, though separately driven.

Miss Watson taught me, I remember, that the concept of One God, Jehovah, was a great step forward for mankind – an end to all those piddly little Gods with brazen feet it thereafter became a capital offence to worship. I had done my best to believe her, but as Isaac and I unpacked and recorded from straw and sand the little artefacts, the various little deities of Ancient Egypt, our eyes melting from time to time and hastily looking away, I began to see the concept of a single God as a narrowing of our perception, not an expansion: the beginning of the long slow end of civilization and not its dawn at all – this cowardly insistence of ours on leaders, fuehrers, the someone who knows exactly what's going on and what's best for everyone; the One above All who demands our loyalty, our obeisance. Undemocratic. The truth is many, not one. Carl May was my Jehovah: it did me no good. I preferred Isaac. Now there's Oliver.

More, more! More and more Gods, each to be worshipped in a different way before lightning strikes us to death.

Isaac King nudged and nurtured my body into a capacity for orgasm, that stretching of the body until it meets the soul, with its astonishing shudder of recognition, elation. Proof, proof, cries the body, proof of my purpose, sinking back into languor, all passion spent: I knew it was there if only I looked hard enough. I perceived it, stretched for it, touched it, just with my fingertips encountered the infinite for an instant! I told you so! We're all in this together – we share it, one day we'll know this joy for ever, out of body. Those of us who can – which does not include those faithfully married to Carl May – must pass the message on to those who can't. It's OK. I told Carl May that day in the gallery just what pleasure Isaac gave me, and he seemed not to understand what I was talking about. Well, he wouldn't want to, would he?

Isaac King taught me about the Tarot pack and how it was possible to contain the world in just seventy-eight cards – shuffle the pack, deal them, and observe the pattern of the times: the Ancient Egyptians were great diviners. That there was a Major Arcana of twenty-two cards, which represented the great guiding passions of mankind; intellectual, moral, material. That there were four suits, Wands, Pentacles, Swords and Cups, from which our ordinary Diamonds, Clubs, Spades and Hearts derive. How, broadly, Wands stand for the power of the intellect, Pentacles the strength of the material world, Swords the capacity for endurance, Cups for aesthetic and sensual perception. Or so Isaac interpreted the cards; the power to interpret hieroglyphics at the tips of his fingers. Isaac was so *clever*: I was so proud of him: I felt I caught intelligence from him: and also, I daresay, something of his impracticality. It is wonderful to be taught: it is almost worth the years of ignorance to have it so suddenly, wonderfully stop. But I wanted my fortune told: I wanted to know the future. His future, my future. The cards are not for telling fortunes, Isaac said. They're for focusing the mind on the patterns which the world around you makes. But I wouldn't have it.

99

That was before we'd been to bed. Sex was in the air: it was inevitable: it was the best, the most powerful of times.

'Tell my fortune,' I repeated.

'What do you want to know?' he asked.

Will we go to bed, I wanted to know. When, where, how, what will happen next? Will you be the fulfilment of my life, will you take the cup of my emptiness and fill it to the brim, and so forth. But I didn't tell Isaac any of that. I wasn't quite such a fool.

'I just want to know,' I said, 'what's going to happen next.'

Isaac acquiesced. Isaac shuffled the pack, picked out the four queens: Wands, Pentacles, Swords and Cups. 'Pick the one that most represents you,' he said, but none seemed quite right to me. I reached for the Empress instead: a card from the Major Arcana. She held the world in her hands: it was what I felt like at that moment. 'Work with that,' I said.

So Isaac took out the Empress, put back the Queens. I shuffled the cards. He laid them face down:

The Empress in the middle was at number one. Above me, two was what ruled me: beneath me, three was what underlay me. Four was what I was leaving. Five was what I was approaching. The significance of the positions of six, seven and eight I can't

100

remember – it scarcely seemed important at the time. Nine was the final outcome: that was what I waited for.

Isaac King turned over the cards.

The four Queens surrounded me. Wands, Pentacles, Swords and Cups: above, below, to left and right. I cannot remember what stood at six and seven; but at eight there was the Hierophant; at nine, Death, a skeleton riding on horseback.

Isaac looked at the Hierophant and laughed.
'There's Carl,' he said.
I, Joanna May, looked at Death and moaned.
'Death means nothing,' said Isaac. 'The card's reversed. It means rebirth, new life; not what you think at all.'
'That's your story,' I said.
'But those four Queens,' said Isaac King, 'that's really something. I don't understand it.'
'I do,' I said. 'I didn't shuffle the pack properly, that's all that means.'
He laughed and swept the cards together and wouldn't say any more. I begged him to tell me more. I touched him in the begging, and though he wouldn't tell the cards for me, he kissed me and that was the beginning, and I forgot about the Tarot.

Except I told Carl that Isaac was teaching me about the Tarot pack: I couldn't resist it. I told Carl about the hand the Fates had dealt me, I tried to suggest to my husband that perhaps there was more to life than here and now, birth and death, that 'because' was a more complex word than he dreamt of – but he wouldn't have it, of course he wouldn't.

'I thought he was some kind of academic,' said Carl May, 'and he turns out to be a charlatan. Is the fellow weak-minded? Is his brain as limp as his shirt collar? Will I get a proper PR return on the gallery? Who does this fellow think he is?'

It did not occur to Carl May to be sexually jealous. How could the servant be preferred to the master? I was affronted. Pique made me guiltless. The more he spoke, poor blinkered Carl May, the

101

more I lost my respect for him, my fear of him. I felt justified in infidelity: it was a wonderful feeling: my spirit soared like a bird, circling, dancing, dizzy with sunlight: I was allowed to be happy. I was born to be happy. I remember sitting on my hands to weigh myself down, as though the very discovery would somehow waft me away. We were sitting, as I remember, in some riverside restaurant. It was night. Lights flickered over running water, and made patterns on the deep red silk of the dress I was wearing. There were only the two of us. It must have been our wedding anniversary, or we'd have been in company – some politician, or magnate, accompanied by boring wife. I've no doubt but that I appeared equally boring. Who is she? Oh, Carl May's wife. What does she do? Nothing. She is Carl May's wife. What does she think? Nothing. She is Carl May's wife. What does she feel? Nothing. She is Carl May's wife. My mother died on the fourth anniversary of my wedding to Carl May. I felt nothing. Carl May had somehow made my feelings for my own mother illicit – as if my life began with my marriage, and that nothing that went before was of any significance: not even the root of my very being, my mother. I went to the funeral alone. Carl May was in China. He did send a telegram and flowers: a wreath, too enormous for the coffin. My poor mother. Everyone should be mourned: remembered: somehow sustained in their journey through the afterlife, until the need for it is gone. Isaac taught me that as well: but I had never until that moment connected it to my mother.

'Superstitious nonsense,' Carl was saying. 'And by God I'll prove it nonsense.'

'How will you do that, Carl?' I asked, politely. 'People have been trying to prove or disprove magic, prophecy, ESP, since the beginning of time, and haven't succeeded.'

'I'll prove it,' he said, 'if it kills me.' And he started the Divination Department. I was glad to think the conversation had at least had some effect upon him. And in that original hand of cards – the first time the cards are dealt for someone the reading is always clear, always significant – was indeed my future. It was just that Isaac was to die, not me. No wonder he swept the cards up and reshuffled as quick as he could.

And I remember now what the cards at six and seven were. Six was the Star, kneeling by her pool beneath a sliver of moon; seven was the Fool, reversed. Treachery, one would imagine: self-delusion. I talked too much. I betrayed Carl, by finding sexual fulfilment with Isaac; and Isaac, because I couldn't resist telling Carl.

I, Joanna May. No longer 'Eye'. Acting; not observing. Doing, not looking. Dangerous, murderous, and not even knowing it.

20

Joanna May, impassioned at last by virtue of the blue-foldered report from the Maverick Enquiry Agency, which told of Bethany's existence, went straight to the heart of Carl May's evil empire, his glassy prison. She meant to tell him a thing or two. She rose by means of a pink and white escalator from the fountains and greenery, marble and glass of the reception levels, and smoothly ascended through layer upon layer of noise and tumult, panic and excitement, bells and clatter, of messengers running, girl clerks checking and pot plants wilting unattended. Then, audacious, was whisked up unchecked in a cage of green glass studded with yellow lights, right into the still centre of the storm, the quiet nexus of energy, the Executive Floor. She walked straight past secretaries on her expensive sensible heels and right into Carl May's office suite where all was silent, sparse and aesthetically correct. The nerve of it! There she found her husband, her ex-husband, flesh of her flesh, heart of her heart, with that tragic ruined girl, that Bethany, that almost beauty, with her sad brightness and her ersatz emerald eyes, his long pale tampering fingers tangled in her hennaed hair. And some might think it served Joanna May right, but she did not.

No. Joanna May spoke the truth to Carl May, or the only truth she knew: that once long ago she'd handed her life to him for keeps, as she was expected by all and sundry to do, being nothing but a girl, in truth, love, and hope, and what had Carl May done? Why, he had not only rendered these things sour for her forever, but drained her being dry as if it were an orange; with powerful lips sucked up the juice and the flesh through a hole in the skin the size of a sixpence, and then thrown the poor flabby thing away. And now look, now look, now look, Joanna May wept, self-pity overcoming rage. Look at me!

An orange, Carl May laughed, an orange. I thought women got thrown away like old gloves, not old oranges, and Joanna May screamed and shouted and banged her fists against his chest, and he didn't even catch hold of them to stop them, so distasteful did he find her flesh, or pretended to. And Bethany thought at last, at last, boredom is ending here, at last something's happening, not this quiet, this still, this nothingness, from which all things emanate but yet is nothing. So bored, she thought, I've been so bored. Ex-wives are better than nothing.

You have destroyed me, Joanna May said to her husband, in essence, used up my youth, my best years and thrown me out.

Carl May said to Joanna, men do not destroy women, some women destroy themselves, that's all; if Joanna May is indeed destroyed, why then he's glad for her sake since that was clearly what she wanted. Women choose the man they want, said Carl May, the man their calculating eye first falls upon; then, lacking the capacity and the will to stick by that decision, must chew away at their own loyalty – self-devourers all, rapacious of grievance, noisy in complaint – gossiping to neighbours and friends over fences and tables, round fires and out shopping, the yackety yak of the female affronted: first he did this and then he did that, can you imagine, and can you believe it, after all that she does for him how much she loves him the bastard, the brute! And how after all that complaint how can a woman expect to find in her own heart constancy, loyalty, truth or affection? Split a plain and single path into a thousand tracks of conversational interest and how can you expect to find yourself ever back upon the right one? In other words, Joanna May, in the course of our marriage, you talked about me to your friends, committed disloyalty with your mind and after that with your body which was how it was bound to end up. Your fault not mine, said Carl May, your fault, your fault, your fault, not mine. What's more, I just behaved as any man would behave, said Carl May.

What, murder? enquired Joanna May and Carl May said you're mad, you're insolent, my chauffeur knocked him down, that's all. An absent-minded Egyptologist, how could he ever bring the dead to life, and you were dead enough yourself by then. Old. A weak man, a *nebbitch*, a nothing, a better-dead, dead already so far as anyone had ever seen. Trust you to pick a zombie, Joanna May. Your fault for not finding a better man: how could you find a better man, a zombie the best that you could do, your fault that now he's dead, as dead as you, and you're alone. Lost him and lost me, lost us both, silly old you.

Oh phooey, she said, it's all men's fault, everyone knows it's all men's fault. Ask anyone.

Just a woman, only a woman, he said next. You should have died twenty years ago, what use to the world are you? A woman without youth, without children, without interest, a woman without a husband; old women have husbands by the skin of their teeth and there is no skin left to your teeth, Joanna May, your yellow discoloured teeth.

My teeth are not so yellow, said Joanna May, they're perfectly pearly white as ever. You're talking about your own miserable molars. And Carl May gnashed them and said he was a man, he was immortal, his immortality lay here in this building, this achievement – by his name on a hundred powerful letterheads he would outrun his death; but what was a woman such as Joanna May, a woman without children, here and now and gone with a puff, blown away like a withered leaf, just for an instant a stretch of limb, a flash of thigh, and gone, a flower that never left a seed, the merest annual, passing thing, a nothing. Here today, gone tomorrow.

I am so something, said Joanna May. Ask my lover, he'll tell you what a thing I am, how far from nothing, here today and here tomorrow. I have my lover, my young lover, I have a man a thousand times better than you, who makes me happy and satisfied, which is what you never did. Never, never, never, never.

106

Carl May was silent.

Oh ouch – thought Bethany, better she hadn't said that, better she'd kept quiet.

Then the fat was in the fire, oh yes it was. How it spat, how it sizzled and spat.

Carl May's eyes seemed to turn a kind of yellow red, as false a colour as Bethany's own emerald eyes, but the pupil went to slits through which a blackness showed, as her own would never do, or so Bethany hoped.

Then Carl May said in a voice as cold and clear as ice made from bottled water, let your poor old flabby legs be parted by whom you choose, it will be for money not love – Not true, not true, Joanna May began to say, but of course it was, it was perfectly true – so why then, she said, it's true for you too you poor old man; and he said no it's not, you poor Joanna May, you female, the music stops for women long before it stops for men, and pitiful and degraded are the ones who dance on when the silence falls; your dance is over, Joanna May, you thoroughly useless lonely person, and mine is not, why don't you go away and die?
Oh flesh of my flesh, love of my soul, husband of my heart, she weeps, to speak to me like this. How can you!
Because I am Lord of the Dance, he says, and I am man and you are only woman, and I am something indeed and you are nothing at all, in spite of your young lover. If he exists, which I take leave to doubt.
I am so something, she wept, I am, I am, and he does exist and I love him, but already she felt herself vanishing, though she still beat her hands against his neatly suited breast and Bethany yawned to hide her nerves and looked around for a door to leave by, but there seemed to be none, so perfectly, architecturally flush were they with the wall. You have to have good eyesight to detect those very expensive doors and Bethany's contact lenses had slipped and chafed and her eyes were watering and she couldn't see a way out at all.

You are nothing, said Carl May, quite bright and glittery all of a sudden as if the sun had come out to shine on a world of icebergs, hot in pursuit but chilly with it, and what's more I proved you nothing thirty years ago and I've known it ever since, and I swore I'd never tell you, but now I will. I proved then you were nothing so particular after all, and that, to be frank, is when I lost interest in you. I proved it by making more of you, and the more I made of you the less of you there was, so it hardly mattered when you betrayed me, because how can what does not exist betray. One a penny, two a penny, hot cross buns; more buns came out of that oven than ever went in.

What do you mean, she asked, quite soft and quiet all of a sudden, and listening hard, of course she did, so he told her – I cloned you, Carl May said, I cloned you, added another four of you to the world, and he told her how he did it, and Bethany put her oar in and said Carl only did it because he loved you really, did it as a compliment, take no notice of what he says today, he's bitter and twisted and furious because you've got a boyfriend, that's all, at which Carl May gave Bethany a push and a shove and would have sent her right through the window and windmilling to her death thirty floors below but the windows didn't open (and just as well, or how the bodies would have piled below, from hatred and self-hatred) so he didn't bother, just forgot.

Joanna May, shocked into calmness, paced and thought and considered herself split into five and her gorge rose into her throat.

Carl May smiled and it seemed to Bethany that his teeth were fangs and growing as long as the wolf's ever were in 'Red Riding Hood'.

There are many of you and many of you gloated Carl May and that means there are none of you because you amounted to so little in the first place. Now see how you like that.

Joanna May thought a little. All the more of us to hate and despise you, she said, flickering into defiance, and make wax models of you and stick pins into you. See how you like that!

Superstitious junk, he shouted, and I'm proving it, I'm proving it. Do you know who I am? I am master of mortality.

Bethany sighed: the children were squabbling again, that was all, perhaps that was all, perhaps it was nothing, could be sighed away, would vanish away like a thirties film disintegrating, unseen in its vault – the mad male cloning scientist crumbling into the dust of fantasy, Frankenstein dissolved, the monster only a dream, a fright, and the world return to normal. But no. It was real. It was true. It was the present – not the future. And it was all Carl May's fault. It was his fault.

You're the devil, said Joanna May, you're the devil. Your mother was right to chain you up with the beasts, she knew the truth about you. I wish they'd gnawed you to death, eaten you up, why have you done this terrible thing to me, imprisoned me forever in a bad bad dream?

You did a terrible thing to me, he said, you made your bed and didn't lie on it, chose a man and wouldn't stick with him; you're a piece of drifting slime in a murky female pool. You're all alike, you women.

Carl May, said Joanna May, I'm sorry for you. You look out of the dark prison of your soul which is your body, and the only windows you have are your eyes, your ears, your nose, your touch, and what can you know but what those windows look upon and it isn't up to much, never has been: a little tent of sky outside a kennel. What a pity you slipped your leash, you should have stayed forever, baying at the moon. I see a different world, said Joanna May, I see one which is perfectible without your tampering.

I don't, said Carl May, and my view is the true one, however disagreeable. I see a world of accident and not design, never perfectible left to itself. Besides, I want to amuse myself. I can make a thousand thousand of you if I choose, fragment all living things and re-create them. I can splice a gene or two, can make you walk with a monkey's head or run on a bitch's legs or see through the eyes of a newt: I can entertain myself by making you whatever I feel like, and as I feel like so shall I do. Whatever I choose from now on for ever.

I don't believe you, said Joanna May.

Believe what you like, said Carl May. Chernobyl has exploded and now all things impossible are possible, from now on in.

And then Joanna May just laughed and said do what you like but you can't catch me, you'll never catch me, I am myself. Nail me and alter me, fix me and distort me, I'll still have windows on the world to make of it what I decide. I'll be myself. Multiply me and multiply my soul: divide me, split me; you just make more of me, not less. I will look out from more and different windows, that's all you will have done, and I will watch the world go by in all its multifarious forms, and there will be no end to my seeing. I will lift up my heart to the hills, that's all, to glorify a maker who is not you. I should carry on if I were you, cloning and meddling, you might end up doing more good than harm, in spite of yourself, if only by mistake.

Carl May snarled and his eyes grew redder still for this was the heart of the evil empire and he was its lord, or so it seemed to Bethany, and he dug his yellow fangs into Joanna's neck just above her genteel string of pearls and he scraped up a piece of her skin with those disgusting teeth and went to the little designer fridge where he kept his whisky (for guests) and his Perrier (for him) and he took out a little box and with a spatula scraped the flesh, the living tissue, of Joanna May off the teeth and shook it into the box with a short sharp shake and put it back in the fridge and said now I'll grow you into what I want, he said, I can and will, see how you like that, I'll make you live in pain and shame for ever more, I have brought hell to earth.

Joanna May just laughed and said Carl May you've really flipped, wait till I tell Oliver about this, Oliver loves my soul not my body he loves my mind, my hope, my courage, me: he loves about me what you loved, Carl May, and still do, you silly spiteful thing, judging from how you behave. I was made in heaven not hell, as you were. You're not king of the Dark Domains, that's all in your mind, you're just head of Britnuc and in a state because of Chernobyl and the guilt and responsibility you feel and the whole world nagging on.

Carl May said if you'd loved me properly, Joanna May, if you had kept your word, I would make roses without thorns, I would make dogs who didn't want to bite, I would make all men kind and good and wonderful, and women too, I would create a sinless race, I would perfect nature's universe, because nature is blind, and obsessive, and absurd – consider the ostrich – and has no judgement, only insists on our survival, somehow, any old how: nature is only chance, not good or bad. All I want is the any old how properly under control, directed, working better: I, man, want to teach nature a thing or two, in particular the difference between good and bad; for who else is there to do it? But how can I, because woman makes man bad, I know it, I feel it. Joanna May, you nearly saved me once, you nearly made me good, and then you failed me, that is why I can't forgive you. You have made me bad, Joanna May: if I'm the devil that's your fault: if I create monsters, you've no one to blame but yourself.

Oh phooey, she said. So I'm Eve to your Adam, am I, that old thing. Take your own apple, bite its flesh, give me a break. All I wanted was a little conversation, for once: all I was doing was discussing the apple: if you chose to see that as temptation, God help you.

And Bethany saw them both standing in the Garden of Eden, Carl and Joanna May, or thought that was what she saw – Carl May long-limbed, tall, ruddy and eager, as he ought to have been, if everything had gone right, and Joanna May young again and looking down her perfect nose, as ever, just a sniff of disdain about her and in the sniff of that disdain the root of much trouble to come, perhaps even all of it, and between them they stared at the apple, red one side, green the other. Carl May bit first, choosing the red half, the better half, the riper half, and that made Joanna really spiteful. But Bethany had taken pills that morning, to get her through the day, as people will these days, and the pills were tiny and the pillbox in a muddle and as her lenses had scraped her eyes were blurred and she could easily mistake the yellow and the red, so who knows what she saw.

111

Thank you, Carl, for the gift you have given me, said Joanna May, cheerfully, and now I'm off to find my sisters, and I bet I find them different every one, different as sin and yet the same.

And with no apparent trouble at all she found a door in the perfect wall and was out of it and gone but on her way down in the lift she wept, and she nearly stumbled getting off the escalator, she trembled so. What woman of sixty would want to meet herself at thirty: rerun of some dreary old film, in which she gave a bad performance, like as not, and split-screen technique at that.

21

Bethany said to Carl May, 'That was a perfectly horrid thing to do, scraping her neck like that. You're nothing but a Dracula.'

And he said, still in a bad mood, 'Be careful or I'll do it to you too. You might be helped by a little sorting and a proper upbringing, so I should shut up if I were you, or you'll have a very sore neck indeed.'

So she did shut up, for a time. But unlike Joanna she could see the advantage of being more than one: the thought did not horrify her at all, not one bit. The more of her the better. She would sit back while the other clones did the shopping, yes she would; after all she could rely on them bringing back what she wanted, choosing what she would choose – until, thinking about it, she realized that was like believing you were Marie Antoinette in another incarnation, and not one of her maids, which was more likely statistically (one of Carl May's favourite words) there being so many more ordinary people than queens in the world. One of the other clones might seize command, and Bethany would be doing the shopping while the Queen clone was the one just sitting – and Bethany wouldn't know what was going on in the Queen's head, really, except she'd know it was pretty much what was going on in her own, which might or might not be a help. But somehow Bethany felt she would indeed have the benefit of extra strawberries and cream upon the tongue, not to mention all the lovemaking multiplied, because she'd know what the others would be tasting, feeling, doing, not just having to guess.

And, then again, though Bethany loved her parents, she could see they had not brought her up in a safe or sensible kind of way. Reared in another fashion, encouraged in different directions, Bethany might be a fashion designer, or fly an aircraft, not be just a girl who lived by her looks. Or would she? How could one tell? Except by trying.

Bethany said to Carl May later that evening, when he had calmed down and lost his satanic overtones, and she and he were in the bath – it was too small for their cavortings (she knocked her elbow quite painfully) and white, which she thought boring and old-fashioned – 'What happened to Joanna's clones? Didn't you want to find out?' and he said, 'Good heavens, you didn't really believe that tale did you? I was annoyed with Joanna, that's all.'

This time Bethany didn't believe him. Bethany said, 'You did so do it. You just frightened yourself with what you'd done. You realized, and stopped, the way people do. You set things marching you couldn't control, so you just shut your eyes, and left it to the other people to clear up the mess! Like the waste from your power plants. What's going to happen to that?'

Twenty-four going on forty-two. He got out of the bath. Either she annoyed him with her perspicacity, or irritated him with her stupidity. She confused him. He would be filled with tenderness and gratitude towards her, when she had rendered him some peculiar sexual favour – though in theory that was when he should most despise her – and yet wish to push her out of the window if she failed to read his mind properly, or was insensitive to his feelings. Carl May did not like being confused.

'Oh,' said Bethany, 'now what have I said? Why did you get out of the bath?'

'Because I banged my knee,' he said, wrapping himself in a towel, which smelt of Bethany, sweet and warm and agreeably cheap, 'and bed is more comfortable. Let's go to bed.'

In bed she said, 'If you were making it up about the clones – and you told me about them yourself once before; did you forget? – why did you take that piece from her neck?'

And he said, 'To frighten her off. Who wants ex-wives dropping in at any time of day or night, making scenes?'

'Well,' said Bethany, 'if you ask me, it was a bit drastic. Most

114

men don't behave like that when they find their ex-wife has a lover. And after all, it's only natural that she should. You have me, after all. And there can't be one law for men and another for women.'

'Oh yes, there can,' said he.

'Well, don't have him run over too,' said Bethany, 'or there'll be more talk. Punish him some other way. Have a thousand of him made, each one with a high sex drive but impotent. That should pay him out.'

'I'll pay him out the simple old-fashioned way,' he said, and looked at his watch and laughed aloud.

'Why are you looking at your watch?' she asked.

'Because it's the most expensive watch in the world,' he said.

He wondered how Dr Holly was doing; how long he would hold out, when he would give in and return to the fold. Men within a whisper of a Nobel Prize do not easily turn their backs on glory, renown and the plaudits of their peers. If Holly didn't, there were younger, smarter, more ambitious men in Holly's own department upon whom Carl May had his eye, more than ready to do a favour or two. But Holly was the best, the most creative, the most imaginative: the younger generation of scientists were more concerned with their careers than the marvels of the universe. You had to pay them to get them to think. He would confront Holly with hard evidence on the absent-mindedness of professors of Egyptology: how they did indeed step out in front of cars: how they died young for reasons which were nothing to do with the Curse of the Pharaohs. Dr Holly would admit Carl May was right, would agree to put at least a section of his department to searching the gut cells of the ancients for living DNA, and get his grant back, and off they'd go again, Holly and May, May and Holly!

Unless of course Joanna was herself the Curse of the Pharaohs. The thought made Carl May laugh aloud.

'Why are you laughing?' Bethany asked.

'Because you're such an idiot,' said Carl May, 'and that's the way I like it. I want you bright, I don't want you clever.'

'I may be cleverer than you suppose,' said Bethany.

115

'What great big teeth you have, Grandmama,' he said, which was silly, she thought, because she had very little white even teeth of which she was very proud, having spent many years wearing a brace, about which her parents had been very particular, allowing her to take it off only when being kind to their lame ducks, their lonely sea-captains, their newly widowed majors. 'One day you'll be pleased,' her father would say, when she moaned and groaned about the brace, and so she was.

Carl May looked at his watch again, and this time she didn't ask him why. He had the bright eyes and flushed cheeks of a delinquent child; he was up to something; she knew it, and she thought it might be better, safer, not to know exactly what it was, and she was right.

The next day Carl May took part in a TV programme about the Chernobyl disaster and the question of the threat or otherwise of radiation, which seemed to so absorb the nation. He took an aggressive and positive line, as suited both his whim, his business interests and the future of the nuclear industry; all of these being pretty much the same.

He said he doubted very much the story of 2000 dead and large areas laid waste and desolate, never to grow a blade of grass again. He deplored the scare stories in the media that death was raining down from skies all over the world. He drank a glass of milk front of camera, and said there was more to fear from cholesterol than radioactivity. He said he thought the death toll would be more like thirty-five – very modest for a major industrial accident (though of course tragic for those concerned: families, etc.) and naturally there would be a statistically calculable increase in cancers in those countries subject to fallout but certainly no more than would be produced by atmospheric pollution consequent upon the continued burning off of fossil fuels. These things had to be balanced.

Look, Carl May said, this argument that we should all live as long as we possibly can is barmy: who wants to live an extra five years in a walking frame anyway? Better an earlier death, be it cancer or heart attack, than a later one. It was an old-fashioned

116

sentiment which favoured length of life over way of life, quantity over quality. You found it the other end of the spectrum, when it came to how societies regarded birth: the old school, emotional, religious, said no contraception, no abortions, let the disabled live: the more life the better, regardless of quality of life. A younger, more reasonable, generation said no, let's have quality not quantity. Freely available birth control, worldwide family planning, sterilizations, vasectomies on demand, terminations all but compulsory for those diagnosed before birth as handicapped, every child a wanted child – and so forth, Carl May said, while Friends of the Earth, a Bishop and the Minister of Energy tried to get a word in edgeways.

Friends of the Earth managed 'What about childhood cancer? Leukaemia?' and Carl May replied briskly if this nation really cares about the lives of its children it will stop driving about in cars – how many get killed a year on the roads! – and increase family allowances: if it cares about cancers in the old it will ban cigarette smoking and free hospitals for the potentially healthy and those who have not brought their troubles on themselves.

Now look, said Carl May, people will work themselves up into a state about anything, especially if it's new. They thought the building of railway lines would destroy the nation, they thought TV would destroy its culture, they thought vaccination killed. ('They were right, they were right,' muttered the Bishop.) Nothing much to fear from radiation, compared to other dangers, compared to crossing the road, compared to smoking. A burst of intense radiation could kill you, sure. So could an overdose of aspirin. Nuclear power stations were, if you asked him, even more crippled by safety regulations than they were by the unions, and that was saying something. The unthinking and uninformed always fear an unseen enemy. From reds under the bed to radiation in the head, the public gets the wrong end of the stick, is ignorant and hysterical and impossible.

He stopped. Everyone in the studio was startled; even the camera crews were listening.

117

Next day Gerald Coustain called from the Department and said he thought Carl May had gone a little far in insulting the public so; it might not be a wise move considering the state of near-panic it appeared to be in. Let him at least appear to take the Chernobyl fallout seriously.

'OK, OK,' said Carl May. 'I'll bleat away in public if that's what you want.'

'We've now pulled together some very fine and modern instrumentation,' said Gerald, 'so we won't be calling on Britnuc any more. I have to tell you that in some parts of Cumbria, it now seems, the needles had been going once round the dials and back again, and our technicians simply hadn't noticed: they weren't expecting it. Human error's the real problem.'

'It certainly is,' said Carl May.

'Still, we've got the problem solved now, I think. We may have to take lamb off the market, though.'

'That'll just panic people more,' said Carl May. 'If Cumbrian lamb is twice as radioactive as Sussex lamb, why don't you ask people just to eat one Cumbrian lamb chop instead of their usual two? Or if they're *really* hungry, buy Sussex.'

'Because people's minds don't work like that,' said Gerald.

'I know,' said Carl May. 'That's the trouble with them.'

22

The world turned upside down. I went to Carl's office to have it out with him, but he had it out with me, and took some living cells from my neck, what's more: the kind of good fresh bloodless tissue that's rich in DNA: he could grow all kinds of me from that – he's right. Ugly, headless, always miserable, always in pain: five-legged, three-headed, double-spined: every leg with perpetual cramp, all heads schizophrenic, and spina bifida twice over. If he wanted, if he could persuade them to do it, that is – and he is a Director of Martins Pharmaceuticals, isn't he, and benefactor of this and that: an interesting experiment, he'd say, a favour. You do this for me and I'll do that for you. Would they? Snip and snap, create a monster? Not if Carl May put it like that, probably not, but if he said, humbly, in the cause of knowledge, just let's see if we *can*, just let's see. Only the once, then never again. (For once is ethical, twice is not.) Then you never know. They might. But what should *I* care; what is it to do with me? 'I' wouldn't suffer. The 'you's' might. Poor distorted things.

I saw my husband run his hands through her hennaed hair, that's what I remember, that's what makes the 'I' suffer, become well and truly me, with a shock which got to my solar plexus. I know he despises her. I could tell. Yet still he ran his fingers through her hair. Patronizing little bitch, little whore: in my home, bathing in my bath, her hairs blocking my plughole. I know. It was all in the blue-foldered report of the Maverick Enquiry Agency: there it stuck, a hennaed hair, long and silky, catching soap scum. Disgusting. Bethany! To be supplanted by a slut called Bethany: me, Joanna May. It would be easier if she was called Doris, or Betty, a name so ordinary it was deprived of resonance: became what I wanted it to be.

119

The world turned upside down: inside out, round and about; fire burn and cauldron bubble: bubbling vats of human cells, recombinant DNA surging and swelling, pulsing and heaving, multiplying by the million, the more the merrier: all the better, the more efficiently for biologists and their computers to work upon the structure of the living cell, the blueprints of our lives, decoding the DNA which is our inheritance. A snip here, a section there, excise this, insert that, slice and shuffle, find a marker, see what happens, what it grows: record it, collate it, work back and try again. Link up by computer to labs all over the world. Bang, goes Mr Nobel's gun, and off they go, false starts and fouling, panting and straining, proud hearts bursting, to understand and so control, to know what marks what and which – and better it. This DNA, this double helix, this bare substance of our chromosomal being, source of our sameness, root of our difference – this section gives us eyes, that segment of this section blue eyes, take it away and presto, no eyes – laid bare the better to cure us and heal us, change us and help us, deliver us from AIDS and give us two heads. And all of it glugging and growing in a culture of E.Coli – the bacteria of the human colon, tough, fecund, welcoming, just waiting around all that time to do its stuff at our behest – toss it, turn it, warm it, start it; nothing stops it. Well why not? Let the brave new world be based upon E.Coli – the stuff that gives us healthy shit. If our purpose on this earth is to salvage goodness from a material universe gone somehow wrong (which was what Oliver maintained) how more appropriately should it be done than by starting with shit and building up: creating not out of nothing, where's the glory in that, but forging miracles from debris, detritus. Now there's an accomplishment!

The vats are filled with pale, thin, milky translucent fluid, life itself, remarkably reflective of colour; slip, slop, plop. If the lab ceiling's green, then the culture shines green. Change the colour at will. Violet most impresses the visitors, but who wants a violet ceiling?

If you've got a good cow, don't breed from it, just repeat it: two by two, out of the ark. Take out the nucleus, cow-and-bull, mix in a newly fertilized cell, reintroduce an all-cow nucleus and what do you get, with any luck? Little twin clones, cow plus repetitions! I, Joanna May, beautiful and intelligent in my prime, now past it, am a woman plus repetitions, taken at my prime. Carl's fault, Carl's doing.

I am horrified, I am terrified, I don't know what to do with myself at all, whatever myself means now. I don't want to meet myself, I'm sure. I would look at myself with critical eyes, confound myself. I would see what I don't want to see, myself when young. I would see not immortality, but the inevitability of age and death. As I am, so they will become. Why bother? Why bother with them, why bother with me? What's the point? I can't bear it. I have to bear it. I can't even kill myself – they will go on. Now night will never fall.

I have never felt so old: I am all but paralysed. The back of my neck hurts where the vampire bit it. My heart aches where he struck at it.

I should have stayed home, as Oliver suggested.

23

Gerald Coustain said to his wife Angela, 'I don't know what's got into that fellow Carl May.'

Angela said, 'Is he any worse than he usually is?' They were eating fish and chips in a Chinese chippie with an eat-here section. With the meal, which included slices of white bread and butter, they drank sweet tea. This was their favourite food. They resented spending good money on food they liked less at expensive restaurants.

'Yes he is,' said Gerald. 'He's saying what he thinks on television. He's usually much too discreet for that. There'll be a public outcry. People can hear the sound of jackboots marching, the minute he opens his mouth.'

'I expect it's his new girlfriend,' said Angela. 'People who're foolish in one direction become foolish in them all.'

'What makes you think he has one?'

'Joanna rang me up in a state. Something had set her off.'

'That's not very reasonable of her,' he said, 'if what you say is true, that she's having it off with the gardener. What's sauce for the goose is sauce for the gander.'

'Yes,' said Angela, 'but neither likes the other having any.'

'Is he a good gardener?' asked Gerald, when he had absorbed this.

'She didn't say. I expect so. She's very fussy about that kind of thing. Always having her curtains cleaned and her wallpaper changed, and her kitchen units brought up to date.'

'I'm a good gardener,' said Gerald.

'I know you are, my dear,' she said. They each took a chip from the other's plate, in a gesture of continuing love and trust.

'Now she has a lover,' said Gerald, hopefully, 'we won't have to ask her to the lido again, will we? We won't have to be sorry for her.'

'I rather liked her coming to the lido with us. I think she enjoyed it. She looks very good in a cossie, I must say. Didn't you think so?'

'I didn't notice. She looked down her nose at me,' said Gerald. 'I had to stay wrapped in my towel. I didn't want her to see my paunch. There was nothing I could do about my varicose leg. She stared at that. No wonder Carl May got rid of her.'

'It would be a better idea,' said Angela, 'if you got rid of your paunch and your varicose veins. Eating here won't help. If only something healthier was our favourite food. Do you think the fish is radioactive?'

'Pretty well everything is,' said Gerald, sadly, 'if we're to go by our new monitoring equipment. But I'm not sure if it's been calibrated correctly. We'll just have to hope for the best. You don't mean to go round and see Joanna, I hope? You know my feelings about getting too close. All of us at the lido is obviously a good deed: you and her together smacks of a conspiracy.'

'She's my friend,' said Angela. 'I really do like her. She keeps saying things I don't expect!'

'If being her friend makes him your enemy, it isn't safe. I've told you that. I always take care to be very polite to him.'

'I think,' said Angela, 'they ought to get back together again. I think they still love each other in their hearts.'

He was pleased she thought so; a professor of Modern History both so wrong-headed and so romantic at heart; his wife, sharer of his chips.

24

Joanna May did not get back for many hours to her house on the banks of the Thames, where once a monarch had kept his vulgar mistress, and when she did she found Oliver dead. She'd wasted time talking to Angela, and then walking around Richmond Park to calm down. She found Oliver hanging by a rope around his ankles from a beam in the barn which was now a garage, swinging gently first this way, then that, his arms fastened gently across his chest as if he were an Egyptian mummy. His face was calm and not distressed, his eyes were open and everything he saw, if only the dead could see, was upside down. His bare young feet were smooth on top and rough-skinned underneath, but that was no surprise to Joanna May: she'd felt them often enough, and the nails were tough and horny and had earth beneath them as usual – the boots he liked the most to wear were not watertight. They stood neatly together in a corner of the garage, placed as if on guard. Who in the world would want them now, poor battered useless things? This way, that way, he swung. She sat down to adapt to a world deprived of this especial goodness, to recover from the shock. She grieved for his mother, and his friends, and the girl in Scotland he would never marry and the seedlings in the greenhouse which no one now would get round to planting out. She grieved for herself, of course she did. Who now would fill her bed? She was old. She was old: surely the old could be spared the shock of losing a lover, of understanding that the body that inspires you, fills you, is frail, mortal, corruptible, as liable to stop on the instant as anything else. This way that way. Through the grief and shock ran a thread of relief: it was over, finished: sharply, quickly: now he would never decide it wouldn't work: wouldn't one day see her wrinkling skin in a clear light, or some aspect

124

of her nature she could no longer hide and decide she wasn't the one for him, and be off (in the fallow season, of course) to some other garden in need, some other divorced lady with excellent alimony and a waiting bed. The back of her neck hurt when she moved it. The graze smarted.

Her fault, of course, her fault: she wailed aloud, and a bird fluttered down from the eaves and out the open door. (She thought it carried Oliver's soul with it, and now she was truly alone and he was truly gone.) His eyes had shut now, the lower eyelids drooping, as the flesh gave up its residual resilience. She was glad of that: he had seen more than enough upside down.

On the floor, beneath the hanging body, brushed by Oliver's hair, lay a single card from the Tarot pack. It was the Hanged Man, from the Minor Arcana, that benign and peaceful fellow suspended by his feet. Above, below, to right and left were four more cards, the Queens of Wands, Pentacles, Swords and Cups.

She should never, as a wife, have tried to discuss the nature of reality with Carl: her fault. She should never have told him about the Fates, about there being more gods than one God, about the Tarot pack: fidget as he might over the *Financial Times*, he heard, he heard: he did not forgive and he did not forget. As an ex-wife she should have faded away, ceased to exist: not quite murdered, not quite unmurdered. Her fault. She should never have told Carl May about Oliver, boasting, denying the inevitability of her desolation, her non-existence; her fault: she should never have answered back: her fault. She should never have gone in the first place, but listened to Oliver. She should have come straight home to warn him: her fault: she should never have allowed him into her bed: her fault. She had, she had, and now Oliver was dead. Her fault. A little niggle of anger arose, swelled; she screamed and screamed. Not her fault, not her fault at all. Carl May's fault. Carl May the murderer.

She went into the kitchen and found Trevor the butler, with his soft hands and soft round face, sitting at the scrubbed-elm table shaking and weeping; and the expensive wall-to-ceiling

kitchen units, which he so loved and Oliver found claustropho-
bic, rising like the walls of a mausoleum around him, and a
dozen hanging copper pans caught the reflection of his shock
and grief and threw it back and forth across the room, one to
another. Well, it was his world: it was fitting.

'What happened?' asked Joanna, and Trevor told her.

25

Why was Joanna so late home? Should not her instinct have been, having betrayed Oliver, to go straight back home and warn him? Of course, but her neck hurt, she was confused and upset; she was not convinced, even if she tried to persuade him of it, that Oliver would appreciate the danger he was in. He would say she was imagining it, and go on shaking off dahlia tubers, or whatever he was doing. It was difficult to convey the extraordinary and drastic nature of Carl's world to a young man whose concerns were so very horticultural, with a dash of rock guitar thrown in. He would be positive about the matter of the clones, which she was not sure she wanted him to be. He would say, 'Well, you always wanted a family: now you have them. Sisters and daughters both,' and if she complained that it was altogether too sudden, and done against her will besides, and Carl May's behaviour outrageous, he would have told her not to be so negative, or the peas wouldn't swell in the pods or the bees wouldn't fertilize the pears – some threat, at any rate, to hold over her head – and remind her that the reason she was no longer married to Carl May was because he was outrageous, so why act so surprised?

In the end she called Angela from a phone box and confided in her, and Angela was gratifyingly startled.
'You mean you didn't even know, Joanna?'
'No.'
'Cloned, and not known it?'
'That's right.'
'Well, I wouldn't like that.'
'Neither do I, Angela. That's why I'm calling.'
'Poor Joanna.'

'Because you know how all this time I've been complaining about having nothing – no children, no career, no family, no husband, nothing I've earned or worked for myself: a whole life wasted –'

'Yes, I do, Joanna –'

'Well, there was a kind of pride in that, Angela. It was my singularity. He has taken away my singularity. He has shovelled all these bits and pieces at me, and I hate it.'

'It would make me feel better, I think.'

'It made me feel like just nothing, Angela; and this makes me feel perfectly dreadful, I can tell you. All I can do is just wander about. I'm calling from a phone box, I'm not even home.'

'Why did he save it till now, do you think?'

'Because he was angry, I suppose.'

'I expect he was. Men don't much like their ex-wives bursting into their offices. Good old Carl, always has to be in the forefront of everything, even test-tube babies. Tinker tinker with the universe.'

'I don't know how you can say that: "Good old Carl."'

'I was being ironic, Joanna.'

'Oh. I see.'

'Joanna, would you say Carl was mad? Answer frankly.'

'No,' said Joanna, 'I'm afraid he isn't. I think he just likes to have his own way, and get his own back. He's childish.'

'I see,' said Angela. 'Can I tell Gerald about the clones?'

'If you feel you have to,' said Joanna, a little tearfully.

'Are you going to try and find these creatures?'

'I don't think so. I don't suppose they know. It might be an even worse shock for them than it has been for me.'

'I can see that. A kind of extra mother, dreadfully like one-self. Seeing what one would grow into. Thirty years ago, you say.'

'Yes.'

'What it amounts to is you've got four identical twins half your age walking round unclaimed.'

'I suppose so, yes.'

'Well, don't tell your Oliver or he might go after them.'

'You mean to kill them? Because they upset me? Like slugs, snails and greenfly?'

128

'No I don't mean that, Joanna. I mean he might fancy them.'

'Why should he?'

'Because they're half your age. You, but more so, Joanna.'

And Angela thought, but was too kind to say, even though she was jealous – how could she not be jealous with Joanna still beautiful, still pulling them in, at sixty – 'You'd be the first taste of a drug on his tongue, Joanna, and they the real stuff, the full flavour.' Instead, she said, 'I hope you didn't tell Carl about your gardener lover. I hope that wasn't why he was so angry?'

'Well yes, I did.'

'Oh dear,' said Angela. 'Wasn't that rather stupid?'

'Yes,' said Joanna.

'I hope your clones are more prudent than you,' said Angela, 'or their nearest and dearest will be having a terrible time. I think you should go straight back home and warn this gardener of yours. Gerald takes Carl quite seriously, you know.'

'I should hope so,' said Joanna.

Joanna went and walked about Richmond Park, in totally impractical shoes. When she was thirty she had imagined all her troubles would be over by forty, there would be nothing left to go wrong: at forty she had imagined the same about fifty, and at fifty she had given up: she still found herself walking about distracted and alone, carefully refraining from crying, just as she had when she was a child.

She remembered coming home from the Bulstrode Clinic and that time she had really wept, from physical weakness more than anything else, or so she had supposed. She remembered that the doctor's name had been Dr Holly. Holly and May, she'd thought at the time, berries and flowers. Red berries, white flowers, and nothing coming out of either.

Well, she'd been wrong about that. Too much had come out of it. She would go back to Oliver and tell him everything, everything, no matter what Angela said; they would go off for six months to some secret destination. New Zealand, perhaps. The soil was good, she believed, and the gardens were wonderful.

129

If he loved her, he would believe her; they would go. Or she would apologize to Carl; tell him she'd been making it all up. Something. Her head ached, her neck hurt: she had to sleep.

26

Angela went straight up to Gerald's office after she'd talked to Joanna; she took the car to the station, the train up to London, a taxi to the Department, and Gerald came straight out of a meeting to see her. She hadn't been to his office for eight years, he reminded her, not since the time their eldest son had made a passing girlfriend pregnant and she'd been upset.

It was Joanna May, she told him. Joanna had phoned her from a callbox on Reading station to tell her the most extraordinary story. Gerald said perhaps he'd better get back to his meeting, since it wasn't family, and the less he knew about the Mays the better and the same went for Angela, and the news from Chernobyl was not good, it was still belching peculiar things into the atmosphere, and there was more trouble with the monitoring equipment. He might have to go back to Britnuc for help. But he didn't return to the meeting, of course. They went to the canteen instead, for tea. Not liking the look of the pastries, he had the steak and kidney pie: she took the braised beef and mushrooms. Both had roast potatoes, boiled potatoes and buttered parsnips as well. It would keep them going until supper-time.

'It probably isn't the equipment's fault; it's just the technicians don't know how to use it,' said Angela, which hadn't occurred to Gerald. He admitted they were barely trained. The truth was, the nation was totally unprepared for such an emergency. If emergency it was – radiation was still pretty much an unknown quantity. The danger was not critical or immediate – damage would show up in the morbidity statistics of the future when a different government altogether would be in power.

'I hope you were careful,' said Gerald. 'I wouldn't put it past Carl May to have our phone tapped.'

'Neither would I,' said Angela. 'Is cloning someone without their knowledge illegal?'

'I have no idea,' said Gerald. 'I hope so.'

'The other thing that bothers me,' said Angela, 'is will Carl try and get rid of the gardener?'

'You mean fire him?'

'I mean kill him, like he did the professor. What Joanna calls "that thing with Isaac".'

'I shouldn't think so,' said Gerald. 'There was more to that than met the eye. I nipped over to the Home Office and had a look at the files.'

'Why did you do that?'

'Always useful to have a hold over a fellow like Carl May,' said Gerald, and there was a gleam in his eye she seldom saw but liked to see. Not for nothing had he risen through the ranks of public service; she used to know the reason well: these days, as his face grew softer and pudgier, she tended to forget. All round them people drank herbal tisanes and ate muesli bars. No one took tea seriously any more. She cleared their plates, and went to fetch spotted dick. Custard was off.

'I hope you like foam cream,' she said when she came back. 'There's no custard and it's kind of stiff without any lubrication at all. What did the files say?'

'Just that prosecution was against the public interest,' said Gerald. 'That fellow King had a pretty dicey record, anyway. He was collecting brain tissue from Egyptian mummies and taking it to some lab somewhere and trying to grow an ancient Egyptian. Garden Enterprises was funding the lab.'

'What a peculiar thing to want to do,' said Angela, 'considering how the population of Egypt grows of its own accord. By a million every nine months, I believe.'

'I don't know about peculiar,' said Gerald. 'It might have been rather interesting, if it had worked. Anyway the Home Office didn't seem too upset the professor was out of the way. So I don't reckon he was got rid of just because Carl was jealous. Something else was going on.'

'Poor Joanna,' said Angela, 'she won't like that at all. But at least it means the gardener is safe. Well, safe-ish.'

'So long as he keeps out of the rain,' said Gerald. 'That seems to be the main danger, these days. Personally, I hope he stays out in it, and his balls fall off. Are you sure there's no custard?'

'One wonders a little,' said Angela, 'about the wisdom of having a man such as Carl May in charge of quite so many nuclear power stations.'

'They're very old ones,' said Gerald.

'I should have thought that made matters worse.'

'Not really,' said Gerald. 'They're like old cars. You can patch them and repair them and keep them on the road; and they give you due warning when something bad is going to happen. They knock and clank a bit: in time for you to do something about it. It's the new ones that are the problem: all built-in, fail-safe factors, and non-labour-intensive, because human error is always the non-calculable hiccough, ergonomically speaking: nothing at all to go wrong in the new ones, but if it does, pow!'

'All the same,' said Angela.

'We'd never have him in charge of the new ones,' said Gerald, reassuringly. 'Don't you worry. As it is, he's a popular fellow and a public hero and good for the image of the nuclear power industry.'

'But he's a murderer,' said Angela.

'Hush,' said Gerald, 'that's a very strong way of putting it. All these fellows tend to dispose of their enemies one way or another: if governments can do it, they think, why can't they, quite ignoring the electoral mandate. One can't condone it but it does happen. At least Carl May confines his activities to the personal sphere.'

'Think about it, Gerald,' said Angela.

'He isn't mad,' said Gerald. 'One draws the line at people who're mad, in charge of anything.'

'I'm not so sure about that,' said Angela. 'I'm not so sure about him being sane.'

'We'll see what transpires,' said Gerald. 'We'll keep a careful eye on things. Are you really sure there's no proper custard?'

'Quite sure,' said Angela, brushing away a flake of suet pudding which stuck to her hairy chin.

'Pity,' said Gerald. 'This cream is rather much.'

133

27

Had Joanna bitten back her anger, jealousy and resentment, and not visited Carl, her life would have gone calmly on: as it was, she was saved. Without the assault of these passionate saving graces she would have aged slowly and gracefully, developed a touch of arthritis here, a backache there: Oliver would have drifted off – men with guitars seldom stay, as she knew in her heart; a few languorous, heart-strumming chords, and they're off – and her fate would have indeed been that of the elderly woman who has never been employed, has no husband, no children, no former colleagues or particular interests, a handful of friends still around, with any luck (though their particular loyalties stretched by distance, exhaustion, their own problems) but who is fortunate enough to have a lot of money.

She would have given up the King's House in time. It would have come to seem, as her body shrunk, too big, too echoey, too frightening, too empty. Most women end their lives in bedsitting rooms, one way or another; possessions exhaust; they get discarded. Even pets become too much of a responsibility. The walls close in as the years pass: rooms get smaller. Joanna might have joined, for a time, those groups of women who go from good hotel to good hotel, up and down the coasts in winter – in to the cathedral cities in summer – filling up the vacant rooms of hoteliers, who smile to see their income coming through the door, but whose hearts sink at the very sight of them, boredom and grievance incarnate. And how can these old ladies, these outlivers of men, not be boring, being so bored themselves? And how can they not complain, whose very life is a reproach to the young and vigorous? Joanna May's mind would have narrowed with her life: she would have stopped contemplating the nature of existence, stopped worrying about the constituents of identity, thought only of whether Tuesday's lamb chop and mint sauce was any more or less digestible than Wednesday's escalope and mushrooms. These terrible things she knew in her head: they lurked on the edge of her consciousness. And with that instinct for the preservation not just of life but of aliveness, not just the body but the soul, Joanna acted; driven by indignation, whipped-up emotion, frothed up to twice its proper size like a dollop of cream in a fast-food restaurant, she was moved to confront Carl in his lair, knowing perfectly well that he'd snarl and scratch, that his snarls and scratches were dangerous, and she was glad of it.

Why else had she married Carl May, in the first place, but to be saved from boredom? The boredom, the depression, of childhood, of home? Why had she brought about the divorce, but because boredom hadn't been routed, no: it had been creeping behind her for thirty years, waiting to pounce, and it had almost caught up with her again, peering out from behind soup tureens at official dinners, perching on the white ties of elderly gents at functions, waving; nothing to talk to Carl about any more: or anything he was prepared to listen to, his life so divorced from hers, yet she so used to him, he to her, they could hardly tell each other apart.

Something had to *happen*.

Isaac happened. Isaac talked, talked, everything interested him; more, he listened. Illicit excitement sent boredom running, far far away, over distant hills: but excitement, danger, was like a drug, you got used to it, you needed more. At first, sex in his bedsitting room was enough, more than enough, mad enough, with the strange smells of toothpowder, and undone laundry, and disorder, books and papers everywhere, bits of old pottery, half a mummy's head; dead flowers in a vase, from 4000 BC for all she knew, the old sometimes looked so new, the colours so bright, the shapes so distinct. And Isaac's voice wonderfully on and on, including her in his universe, and the universe seemed to have a history, a purpose, a meaning, which started in the past, collecting as it went, arriving at *now*. Carl's universe started

135

in the future and came back to today — it collected nothing. Well, that was understandable. Carl May's experience of the past was not pleasant, so he looked to the future, of course he did. But then Isaac's bedsitting room was not enough: she got used to it: it seemed too ordinary for something as extraordinary as Isaac and Joanna May, wife of Carl: boredom crept back, nearer, began to wave, sitting on mummy cases, on the edge of the chipped bath, sooty from an ancient gas-fired geyser, which puffed out black dust if you wanted hot water to wash. In the end the gallery was the only place he wouldn't come, this ghost of her own past, outdone at its own game by the half-haunted gloom, the watching eyes of history, which seemed to approve — or Isaac said they did; sex was just fine with the Ancient Egyptians, according to him — and of course in the gallery it was perfectly possible for Carl to come in at any time. They must have been mad. She must have been. But again, she was angry. A woman without children, now wanting children, too late to have children. Carl's fault. She loved Isaac, let Carl know it. He deserved it. Something had to happen. And one day it did: Carl pushed the door open.

And that stopped Carl being bored, for a time. He'd got too cosy anyway: he was the media's darling, the Government's blue-eyed boy. Garden Enterprises was under way. Britnuc was belching clean air into a threatened atmosphere — with only the occasional release of unscheduled radioactivity, which was in any case the least of many polluting evils. Something had to *happen*.

Carl May, before his wife's infidelity, was beginning to get pains in his chest. His was the kind of boredom which destroys life, like a slowly creeping fungus on a pear tree, causing leaves to wither and fruit to fall, unripened. Let him lose his wife, then, thought Joanna: that'll cure him: a swift blast of fungicide in the form of jealousy, outrage, anger. She'd been right. Carl shook himself and thrived. Only in the shaking he'd shaken her off too. She hadn't done it for his sake, had she, but for her own.

28

If thine eye offend thee, pluck it out! Now there's a desperate doctrine, a right dollop of lateral thinking, a fine biblical recipe for preserving thy view of thyself as a fine and upright person. Kill the bearer of the bad news, would you; much good may it do you. The enemy still advances over the hill. If thine eye lusts, sever the optical nerves; chop off your hand if it strays where it shouldn't: destroy your ears to keep out the seducing voice: eyeless, earless, legless, armless, roll around in the mire: you will still be in the valley of desire. Just unable to function. After the inquest, after I, Joanna May, had perjured myself and betrayed the memory and love of Isaac King, the better to protect the interests of my husband Carl, I walked back to Eton Square, to the big pillared house which was Carl's and my home. I walked up the steps, put my key in the lock, and found it would not turn. The key was the right key – it was the lock that had changed. I banged the knocker and rattled the handle but no one came. Yet I'd seen Anna's pudgy face at the window, just a glimpse of it, or thought I had.

I believed that by perjuring myself I would win Carl's forgiveness, that it would be over: it could be forgotten. That Isaac's death was sufficient punishment for me. I stamped and shouted and banged upon the step, and I expect I screamed and cried, I can't remember. The solid door stood between me and my marriage, my home, my friends, my clothes, my possessions, my past, my future, my life. Those strong upright houses of Pimlico are built to keep the poor out; to keep the rich secure, the noise of riot at a distance. Carl had cast me out of his life; I had become a supplicant: I belonged the wrong side of the door. I knew it was no accident. It bore the hallmark of Carl's vengeance. The sudden shock of horrid surprise which he knew so well how to deliver, the lightning stroke out of an apparently clear sky. First he lured you into complacency; then, clap, snap, he got you.

I went to the phone box on the corner and rang my own number but no one answered. I wondered what Anna was thinking as it rang and rang, and she knew it was me: poor Anna, straight from the Philippines, witnessing this cruelty, obliged to be part of it. Carl paid her wages. Would she be horrified, or would she just think this is what happens, always happens, always will happen, to women when they cease to please or, worse, step out of line. A plain girl herself, stocky and puffy-eyed, bad-complexioned, hesitant in English, used and abused, fleeing one set of harshnesses to run into another, still thinking herself lucky, allowed to pick up the crumbs of Carl's and my life. Poor Anna. She'd know whose side she was on: whichever hand had the power, held the food, would be the one she licked. I went back and stood on the step: it began to rain a little: I didn't know what to do: to go to friends would be to start a scandal: I was still Carl's wife.

And then the garage door whirred and opened, and the big Volvo backed out, black and shiny and somehow ordinary, with the dent still in the wing which had been the death of Isaac, and in the back was Poudry the solicitor, and in the front was Philip the murderer. And Poudry held the door open for me, and I got inside, because I didn't know what else to do. And while we drove to a small and rather grimy hotel in Paddington – where someone or other who needed their wages no doubt, and knew which side their bread was buttered, and that it wasn't my side, had unkindly booked me a room – Poudry told me Carl was divorcing me, that I would be bought a house and given an income, that I was not to set foot in Eton Square again, that I was to think myself lucky.

That my clothes had been destroyed, my papers and my books and my family photographs shredded, and my parents' marriage certificate and my father's death certificate too; and no sign of me was to be left in the house, all trace of me was to be destroyed. I was free to begin life again as he would be, without evidence of the past, and I should think myself lucky.

'Do you think I'm lucky?' I asked Mr Poudry.

'Yes, I do,' he said, after thinking about it for a little. We were, I think, both very conscious of the dent in the Volvo's back wing, and of Philip the chauffeur in the front. Mr Poudry hummed a little in a nonchalant way that reminded me of Pooh, in *The House at Pooh Corner*, singing a little song the better to sound at ease: 'How nice to be a cloud, floating in the blue. It makes me very proud, to be a little cloud.'

As it happened my husband was generous. Not that 'as it happened' is a phrase that was much bandied about in Carl May's life. It suited him, for reasons of his own not immediately plain to others, to be generous, or appear to be.

I moved out of the Suffolk Ease hotel only when the decorators finished in the King's House. I could have left at any time, but the hotel was a desperate place and suited me. I had a room to myself: others, immigrants, lived twenty-five to a room, in a stench of urine and cooking, refugees from one horror or another – flood, famine, persecution, torture, war. Carl, booking me in here, meant to tell me something. So I sat it out, recovering from my own desolation, my own sudden loss of home. I had no one. The other lodgers had each other. Night after night I sat alone in a room, sitting on a bed – damp stains on the wall, the murmur of human grief around, crying children – staring at television: a woman of more than fifty, whom even money couldn't save. And I wanted to see Carl, and he wouldn't: I wanted to talk to Carl, and he wouldn't. How could he do it? How could he wrench us apart? If it hurt me, surely it hurt him? I mourned Isaac but I mourned for my marriage more.

And all Mr Poudry would say, when I visited him in his office, was, 'You are very lucky, Mrs May,' and one day he added, 'It might be a good idea to move out of the Suffolk Ease: you'll forgive me for saying so, but there is beginning to be about you the pong of the underprivileged.' And I looked at him closely for the first time and saw he was not more than thirty: it was the weight of authority had aged him in my eyes. I wouldn't go. The hotel was where Carl wanted me to be. I was obedient. Only when I moved into the King's House did I begin to find my will again, or some of it. I washed, I dressed, I looked after myself: I became accustomed to life without Carl. Sometimes I even enjoyed it. I began to like the vision of myself, the drama of a woman lonely and alone, living in isolation, rejecting the world which rejected her.

Then I employed Oliver as a gardener: and one day he took out his guitar and sang some folk song to me, some wispy song of lust and longing, and asked me if I'd like to play the guitar, and I said yes, and he put the guitar in my arms, and stood behind me and put his arms round my arms, and that was that. I no longer thought about Carl. I was cured. I assumed he was cured too. I thought I was safe from Carl.

I thought all would be well if I did not love Oliver: I could not let myself love him. I knew quite well what would happen if I did. That if I cared when it ended − and it must, it must, I knew in my heart it must though my head pretended otherwise − the pain this time would kill me. A lump in my breast, a swollen lymph gland under the arm and that would be that. And who would there be to come to my funeral? Gerald (reluctantly) and Angela (weeping: if only for the loss of a good gossip) and Mr Poudry and the accountant, and a nurse from the hospital if I'd remembered to smile while dying; and Carl would not come, or if he did, it would be so the press didn't pick up the fact that he had not. The funeral was not worth the dying for: let Oliver be a nightly visitor to my bed, let him return me, little by little, to the fullness of the world, but that must be all. It should not be difficult. I had loved Carl May: having loved Carl May, I could not easily fall in love with, become emotionally dependent upon, sexually infatuated with, addicted to, a gardener who played rock guitar.

Oliver died and I found it was true. I had not loved him. You only know what you've got once it's gone, and it wasn't much. Trevor the butler gave an account of Oliver's death, his murder − and how could it be anything but murder: a man doesn't easily hang himself by his feet − and I heard the account with equanimity. I winced, for it was a horrid thought that a life which could bring me to life, purply-red, strong and pulsing, had changed suddenly and permanently into limp white rotting

140

tissue. I wept a little, because Oliver had been cut down in the spring of his life, and of the year, with the whole blossoming, blooming, fruiting season yet to go. I was saddened because now my evenings would have to be spent alone, the forbidden pleasure, the companionable calming marijuana joints no more. I was shocked, pale and shaking – a physical reaction, I imagined – but the roots of my being were untouched, steady, compacted in dry earth. I surprised even myself.

If thy love offend thee, pluck it out.

29

The gardens of the King's House ran down to the river Thames, gently sloping, occasionally terraced. The river split to form an island, shared by a little group of houses, of which Joanna's was the biggest and best. The jetty, however, was seldom used. Oliver did not like the water, and Joanna mistrusted it. The garden was old; first established in the eighteenth century, used originally as an overflow for Kew Gardens, neglected and cosseted by turns. 'What a pity you don't like gardening,' Oliver would say to Joanna. 'Looking after a garden is like looking after children. Feed plants and they grow, neglect them and they suffer. It's all rewards and punishments – with more than a dash of chance thrown in, in the form of weather. I'm sure you'd be good at it.'

But what Joanna liked was to sit out on a sunny morning, and breakfast at leisure, dressed in white as often as not, watching Oliver work: the garden and herself presently drifting into one: she the prize lily, a little past peak flowering perhaps, but still what the garden was all about: the culture and cultivation of beauty.

She liked to sit in the spring and summer and watch the pleasure boats go by, music approaching, passing, fading – while those who had the gift of life, the understanding of enjoyment, the privilege of friendship, went sailing by. Or so it seemed. Joanna did not doubt that on closer acquaintance the crews and guests aboard the yachts, steamers and launches were as vulgar and foolish as anyone else, as prone to anxiety, misery and jealousies as she: that the music masked a thousand discontents, and that the champagne moved to mock exhilaration, not necessarily the real thing: nevertheless the illusion was pleasant, there was no need to get too near. She did not grudge these river people the possibility of happiness, at least, and certainly admired their ambition to achieve it. 'Such a lovely day! Let's go on the river . . .' Still, she had managed the lido, with Gerald and Angela: that was water and outing enough.

On the afternoon of that day, the day Joanna, her own resentments finally focused, had gone to Reading to have it out with Carl, Oliver, having finished with the rhododendrons, was weeding out the herbaceous borders. He worked with a hoe, standing to unsettle the shallow roots of the clover which crept up from the river bank in spite of all efforts to prevent it; or, occasionally, kneeling, with fork and trowel, to dig out plantains, patiently easing out the long, stubborn root, loosening soil and levering back and forth until they gave up, apologizing as he did so for thus putting paid to their best endeavours. His habit of talking to plants of all sorts, including weeds, and especially weeds he meant to destroy, quite irritated Joanna.

'If you're going to kill them, kill them,' she'd say. Oliver would droop his lids over his soft brown eyes to mask his displeasure, giving him what she called his 'I meant to please but now look' spaniel look; his hippy look, of reverence to all things, gentle, kind and understanding; his Age of Aquarius look. Then she'd say, 'I don't know why you don't just use weedkiller, like anyone else,' just to incense him, to watch the pallor of determined sweetness give way to the pink of indignation, and then she'd laugh and he'd know she was teasing.

But these pleasures were over now. An expensive-looking pleasure launch of the kind Oliver least liked, being moulded in some kind of new fashion to give it rounded, bulbous lines, and in a colour Oliver knew to be called Whisper Pink, trimmed with Whisper Cream, its CD playing Elgar's 'Pomp and Circumstance', cut its engine, its music, on the stretch of river which ran by the King's House, slid slowly into the jetty and tied up. There were five young men on board, strangely dressed.

Oliver straightened up, and watched the five young men disembark and come towards him, up the garden path where the tiger tulips bloomed on either side. They smiled, but he knew they were not friendly: something about the tense way they held their necks; he knew at once that retreat would be more

143

dangerous than standing ground, that to placate would be safer than to challenge. They were, he thought, in their mid-twenties. They talked and joked amongst themselves, halfway between yobbo and yuppy: yobbo down below, layers of ragged and chain-strewn trouser; up above, collar, tie and suit jacket. Their heads were apparently shaven, and they wore bowler hats.

'Nice place you've got here,' the leader said. His name was Jacko. He was blond and beautiful. 'You the gardener?'

'Yes,' said Oliver, 'that's my trade.'

'Got quite a bit of age to it,' said the second in command. His name was Petie. He was dark and sulky. 'This garden has.'

'That is certainly so,' said Oliver. 'It was old when George Three bought it and renovated it for his mistress.'

'Did he now?' said Elwood, who was black and beautiful. 'Those old geezers weren't half naughty boys.'

And Haggie and Dougie, who were pale, thin and spotty, and didn't fill their trousers or their suit jackets nearly as well as the other three, kicked a tulip or two out of the ground.

'Pity to do that,' said Oliver, mildly. 'That's quite a rare flower. A black tulip. Not my favourite, as flowers go, a black flower being unnatural, if you ask me, but some people like them.'

In answer, Dougie and Haggie tore up handfuls of daffodils, and Oliver didn't mind that so much. They were more or less over and he'd been going to move them, in any case, to some less-overlooked patch of ground where they could deteriorate in peace and wait for their replanting in the autumn. But he pretended dismay, since that was what they wanted.

'Can I help you fellows?' he asked, wondering where Trevor was. Trevor would sometimes come out in the mornings with a cup of coffee, and sit on a stone wall in the sunshine and talk about the minutiae of his life with his lover – he was having an up-and-down relationship with a masseur at a nearby health farm – and Oliver would listen patiently and respond constructively. If Trevor looked out of the window and saw the young men he might, with any luck, call the police.

'Is the missus out?' asked Jacko.

'The missus is out,' said Oliver, 'but the master's in,' half a truth being in his book better than no truth at all, albeit in the

144

circumstances any lie might have been justifiable. Those capable of knocking off the heads of black tulips, in passing, were in Oliver's eyes quite capable of knocking off human heads.

'That's a lie and a half,' said Jacko. 'The mistress is out as we very well know – and what a naughty boy you are, Oliver, young enough to be the lady's son – and the master ain't here neither.'

'If you know,' said Oliver, brightly, 'then why ask me?' and was quite pleased with his own courage. He'd said the same thing, at the age of four – according to his proud mother – to his teacher when asked what three and two made. 'If you know, why ask me?'

Jacko took out his fob watch and looked at it, and took off his hat to reveal a topknot of golden curls, and nodded to Elwood, who opened his briefcase and took out a length of bamboo pipe. Petie took out a dart from the yellow child's lunch box he carried, and Petie carefully handed the dart to Elwood who put it in the hollow tube and blew the other end, hard and sharp, and it landed in the back of Oliver's hand, the one that was carrying the trowel.

'Ouch!' he said, and dropped it, and Jacko, Petie, Elwood, Dougie and Haggie counted to five in unison and Oliver felt numbness running up his arm and down to his heart. He noticed the sudden quietness of his whole body, as it stopped beating. He thought, this is what it must be like for a fuchsia killed by frost; when water turns to ice, and that was all he thought.

Trevor was coming out to meet the lads. He had seen the gleam of yellow hair when Jacko took off his hat, and the flash of handsome male profiles, and wanted to know what was going on. He feared no evil on his own home ground.

But they were bending over Oliver, whoever they were, and turned their smiling faces towards him, and one said, 'It can only be Trevor, the man's man,' and he detected in their smiles something which made him shiver. 'Better get in the house, Trevor, before it's you as well,' so he did. He walked smartly back into the house and locked the back door and slammed shut the stainless steel mesh shutters on the windows from the security

145

console. He watched through the mesh but they did not come after him, and he was affronted, as well as relieved. It seemed he was no business of theirs. Instead, they picked up Oliver and carried him shoulder high into the garage, which had once been a barn. Trevor thought they were singing something.

He did not call the police. He had enough trouble with the police. They followed him when he went out shopping, just waiting for him to go where they assumed he was going, to the public convenience that is, the better to pounce and get him for some disgusting act or other, which he would never perform, but they quite happily invent.

After five minutes Haggie reappeared and looked over the garden in a puzzled kind of way. He called to his friends, 'What's a shitty rose look like anyway?' and Petie came out and wrenched a branch off a rose bush, and went back into the garage, Haggie following.

After ten minutes or so all five men appeared again, without Oliver; marched down to the launch moored at the jetty, boarded it, and left in the direction of Reading. Trevor went out to the garage and found Oliver hanging as Joanna was later to find him. The back of his hand had been scratched by, presumably, thorns from the rose branch. A few petals lay on the floor. Oliver's boots had been pulled off and tossed aside. Out of custom, Trevor put them neatly together. On the floor, beneath the hanging body, brushed by Oliver's hair, lay a single card from the Tarot pack. Trevor recognized it as the Hanged Man. Trevor had had his fortune told often enough to know that the card was supposed to signify innocence and the overcoming of difficulties by sheer good luck, but he had always taken leave to doubt it; the Tarot pack in his opinion was more sinister than its diviners would often allow. In this case he could see the card signified what he had always suspected: death by hanging because you didn't look out. And above, below, and to the left and right of the signifier, the Hanged Man in person, were the four Queens. Oh, kinky, thought Trevor: what is going on?

He said goodbye to Oliver in the same spirit as Oliver would say goodbye to doomed weeds and went to sit in the kitchen. He opened the shutters. There seemed no point in keeping them closed. He would wait until Joanna came home and let her decide whether or not to call the police. If she did, he could explain the delay as the general inefficiency and stupidity of the man they insulted him by supposing him to be. He tried to call his friend Jamie but the line was dead. That did not surprise him.

He assumed Joanna would understand the significance of the four cards, and he was right.

'On either side the river lie,' quoted Carl May, from Tennyson,

   'Long fields of clover and of rye –'

'Barley,' said Bethany, and Carl May chose to ignore her. Once.

   'That clothe the wold
   And meet the sky
   And through the fields
   The road runs by
   To many-towered Camelot.'

   'That's where my ex-wife lives,' said Carl May, 'in Camelot.'
'I thought she lived at the King's House, Maidenhead,' said
Bethany. They lay in bed together. The sheets were white. There
were blankets, not a quilt. How quaint, had thought Bethany
once, how like him, how pure, but now she thought, how
old-fashioned, how uncomfortable, how like death. He ignored
her. Twice.

   'And up and down
   The people go
   Gazing where the lilies blow
   Round an island there below
   The island of Shalott –'

   'Shallots, onions,' said Bethany.
Thrice.

   'Four grey walls
   And four grey towers
   Overlook a space of flowers,
   And the silent isle embowers
   The Lady of Shalott.'

'Yes, I know,' said Bethany, '"She left the web, she left the loom, she made three paces through the room" — we did it for diction — "the mirror cracked from side to side, the curse is come upon me, cried the Lady of Shalott." Then she mooned about for a bit and topped herself from sheer boredom. Which reminds me that the curse has not come upon me. What are we to do, Carl?'

Carl was silent.

'I know you said you had a vasectomy, Carl, but it can't have worked because I'm pregnant and I've been with no one but you, Carl.'

Still Carl was silent.

'There, I've said it,' she said. 'I'd been getting really nervous.'

Carl sat up in bed, looked down at her bare breasts, her smooth narrow arms, her blue eyes — she took out her contact lenses at night — and rested his hand upon her throat. Then he moved it down over her body, on the whole quite gently, though tweaking her nipples rather sharply, to which she was not averse.

'You be careful,' said Carl, 'or you'll end up like Squirrel Nutkin,' but she didn't understand the reference. Nor did she have time to puzzle it out, as the whole of Carl May advanced upon her.

'You were only joking about being pregnant, I suppose,' he said, presently, disentangling his legs from hers reluctantly, but he felt the first twinge of cramp, to which he was prone.

'Of course,' said Bethany. 'Twice in one night. Wow! What a man!' She was tired. She used the language of porno films. She did not have the energy for finesse. He did not seem to notice. There was no real reason for her to be tired. She thought it might well be the effect of boredom.

'I had a man killed today,' said Carl, pleased with himself. 'Perhaps that's it.'

Bethany blinked, but was careful not to let her body tauten against Carl's. She no longer felt tired. Then she thought, well, one pregnancy joke deserves a murder joke. A death for a life. Silly old you.

'He didn't suffer,' said Carl.

149

'If you're going to kill a man,' said Bethany, 'why bother if he suffers or not?'

'One does bother,' he said. 'For some reason. I don't wish to inflict pain, or terror. Some lives simply need to stop. Have you ever had a termination, my dear?'

'Once.'

'Well, there you are. You understand.'

Bethany put on her contact lenses and turned her eyes green, and fluffed out her red hair, and pranced about the room. It could do no harm.

'Who was Squirrel Nutkin?' she asked.

'Squirrel Nutkin danced about in front of a wise old owl,' he said from the bed, 'taunting him and teasing him, asking riddles and telling jokes.'

'What sort of riddles?'

'Riddle me, riddle me, riddle me, ree,
  How many strawberries swim in the sea?
  I answered him as I thought good,
  As many red herrings as grow in the wood,'

said Carl May, 'for example.'

'What happened?'

'Nothing happened.'

'Then what was the point?'

'Nothing happened and nothing happened.'

'Then what?'

'Something happened. The old owl pounced and ate Squirrel Nutkin up and there was peace in the wood again.'

'Oh,' said Bethany, and put on her clothes rather quickly. Sometimes he did give her the creeps. But presently her spirits were restored, for she was indeed young and she found herself singing her favourite song:

'For a young man he is young
  And an old man he is grey,
  And a young man's back is good and strong,
  Get away, old man, get away.'

'I haven't finished yet,' said Carl May. 'Indeed I have only just started,' so she had to get back into bed again, but that was not really what he was talking about.

31

Thus thought Joanna May, missing Isaac King badly (for he *knew* what the cards meant, and she could only guess): now, if the four Queens of the Tarot pack, or, as some would have it, the long-lost Egyptian Book of Toth, are seen together, they denote nothing worse than arguments. If reversed, however, the argument might become excessive; fatal, even. In conjunction with the Hanged Man, a card from the Major Arcana, which when reversed denotes selfishness and sacrifice, rootlessness and riot, things don't look too good. If you laid all at the head of an actual hanging man, murdered, they might begin to look very bad indeed. And, as the Queens of Wands, Pentacles, Swords and Cups could be seen to represent all the women in the world – excepting only the few from the Major Arcana, the High Priestess and the Empress (positions Joanna May and Angela might contend for) or the female half of the Lovers (which might well suit Bethany), these great cards having in their own peculiar way dominion over all the humble folk of the four suits – why then, things might be looking quite appalling for all the women in the world.

Prudently, Joanna spoke none of this aloud. She merely said to Trevor, 'Gobbledygook. The police will not be interested in what they say is gobbledygook: they will not understand the insult and the threat involved: go and fetch those cards and put them in the kitchen drawer, and don't even mention them.'

Joanna May called the police. Of course she did. What else could she do? The duty sergeant she spoke to said they would send a police car the moment one was available. He was soothing and competent. He said if she was certain her gardener was dead, leave him where he was and touch nothing. It sounded, from her description, like some kind of inadvertent death by way of sexual perversion, and was at least less messy than a crucifixion. They'd had quite a lot of those lately: a lot of nuts in the homosexual community: they were sending an ambulance, but that might take even longer than the police car. Emergency services were stretched.

'I don't think he was gay,' said Joanna May.

'Gay, bi, hetero,' said the duty officer, 'makes no difference to us. We are not prejudiced. Where did you say? The King's House? The big place on the island? Wait, that's come up on the computer recently . . . yes, here we are . . . knew I'd seen it. Trevor Hopkins, occupation butler: indecent behaviour. And this one was the gardener, you say?'

'The charge against Mr Hopkins was not proven,' said Joanna May. 'In fact the charge was dropped. What's it doing on your computer?'

'You're quite right,' said the duty officer amiably. 'It shouldn't be there. No doubt it's on its way to wiping.'

It was an hour before they arrived, and an hour and a half before the ambulance came to take the body to a morgue. The police doctor said there'd be an autopsy but it looked to him as if the young man had had a heart attack while engaging in some kind of kinky sexual activity – there was no evidence of foul play. No end to the things that people got up to: a pity: from the look of his garden he was good at his job. The world was short of gardeners.

'And of police officers, too,' said the plainclothes man, hurrying him on. They had another suspicious death waiting. Four men had arrived. They questioned Trevor, but kindly, to his surprise. He told them nothing about the boat, about the bully boys: just that he'd gone out to the barn to take Oliver his coffee: had found him swinging, dead and upside down, and gone inside and just sat, till Joanna came home. If they thought there was more to it, they didn't say. It would only take everyone into the complex and miserable area of sexual deviance, and Mrs May's butler had, from the look of him, suffered enough.

'What we don't want', said the police officer, by way of

explanation, 'is copycatting. If it gets into the papers, before we know it everyone's hanging from their ankles trying to get heart attacks. We have enough to do –' and they left. The body had already gone, by ambulance.

Joanna May called Angela and told her all about it. Angela offered to come over but Joanna said she was OK. Only quite some time later did she begin to weep.

32

God flew off in three stages, if you ask me, Joanna May, the childless and the cloned, and none of them anything, I have now decided, to do with nuclear bombs or Logie Baird.

God the Father flew off on the day mankind first interfered with his plans for the procreation of the species: that was the day the first woman made a connection between semen and pregnancy and took pains to stop the passage by shoving some pounded, mud-steeped, leaf up inside her. He flew off in a pet. 'But this is *contraception*,' he cried, 'this is not what I meant. How can I work out my plan for your perfection and ultimate union with me if you start doing this kind of thing?'

God the Son flew off the day the first pregnant woman made the next connection and shoved a sharpened stick up inside her to put an end to morning sickness and whatever else was happening inside. 'But this is *abortion*,' he cried, 'it's revolting, and no place for a pro-lifer like me to be.'

And God the Holy Ghost flew off the day Dr Holly of the Bulstrode Clinic, back in the fifties, took one of my ripe eggs out and warmed it, and jiggled it, and irritated it in an amniotic brew until the nucleus split, and split again, and split again, and then started growing, each with matching chromosomes, with identical DNA, that is to say faults and propensities, physical and social, all included, blueprint for four more individuals, and only one soul between them.

Call me egocentric if you like, but that's when the Holy Ghost flew off, muttering, 'Christ, where is this going to end?' for it's been trouble ever since, hasn't it, all downhill; war, and riots, and crime, and drugs, and decadence, and dereliction, and delinquency, because there's no God. Well, there's no bringing him back; it's up to man to step in and take over. (I say 'man' advisedly; I don't think women will have the heart, the courage.) He gave us minds, didn't he, and the aspiration to do things right, as well as the tendency to do them wrong.

Carl may be wicked, but Carl's right. Takes a wicked man to be prepared to think like Carl, that's the trouble. I know how Carl May thinks: though not always what he thinks. I know what he was doing; I know why his teeth did not draw blood. Carl is not interested in my blood: blood cells do not contain DNA. A good place for obtaining DNA, from the tissue at the back of the neck. What Carl does with it depends upon what he feels like. So many things are possible. He could take a fertilized egg from, say, Bethany, give it the blueprint for my growth, put it back inside her, and she'd give birth to a little me. Would she like that? Perhaps she would. Perhaps mothering a man's first wife might make you feel altogether better about her. All these relationships are about incorporation, if you ask me, everyone in one big bed together – me, Carl, Oliver, Bethany, Isaac – all rolling around, warm and safe and companionable: we only get upset when we're left out in the cold. If I had a cell from Isaac I would ask Bethany to re-create him, in penance for taking Carl from me. And death would not divide us any more. If he were dug up from his grave, there'd still be enough residual DNA there, even now, to do it. But I won't do that: it seems forbidden, as forbidden as abortion ever was. I don't think Carl will do it: to impersonate God is a terrifying thing. Even for Carl, who as a child bayed at the moon. Microbiologists get so far, then lay down their tools, put aside their electron microscopes: take up gardening instead: they frighten even themselves. These days scientists talk a great deal more about God than does the rest of the world: they acknowledge magic – though they call it 'propensity', or 'something intervenes'. 'Something intervenes,' they say – as they break matter down to its smallest definable particles, the merest flicker in and out of existence of the most fragmented electric charge – 'or else our observation alters it.'

What is that but obeisance to the shadow of the God who ran off, the God they drove off, when bold and young and frightened of nothing!

What Carl could do, what Carl might well do, for Carl controls the scientists, since Carl has the money, is mix up some of my chromosomes with those of some other creature and set it growing, and know more or less what would get born, forget a fingernail or two. He could snip out the section that decrees I will have long and elegant legs, and snip in a section from someone else's DNA, someone with short piano legs, the kind without ankles. He could give me a dog's back legs. If he wanted, he could do horrible things. He could do good things: sometimes he wants to do good things. Just as man can use nuclear weapons to make war or keep peace, to destroy or build, Carl could make me live with arthritis for ever or keep me disease free, never to catch cold again. He could interfere with my mind: make me nicer, more gregarious, kinder, happier, more socially conscious: he couldn't control the environment I grew up in, not in the short term, but if everyone was kinder, happier, loved their children better, didn't shut them in kennels – why then presently the environment of the growing child would indeed change, improve, step by step, little by little. Look at it this way, Carl would say, every time a woman uses contraception or has an abortion, she interferes with natural selection. Not this baby, the next baby, says the mother, bold as brass, standing in nature's way. Let's go for a better father, or a better environment: let's hang on a bit. That's what it's about: that's what's important. Not the first baby that comes along but the best baby, the one that'll have a decent chance in life. And let's do better by the ones we have, stop at two, not six. Quality, not quantity. Choice, not randomness, and there being no God, why not? That's what Carl thinks.

In the meantime, being unreconstructed himself, and cured of the notion that death is final – for it isn't, not if he can keep the genetic line running – Carl May has killed Oliver, and now he means to kill the clones. He has told me so, by way of the cards. He thinks this will hurt me. He offered me a family: now he

157

snatches it away again. But I'm not at all sure that I recognize their right to life, these thefts from me, these depletings of my 'I', these early symptoms of the way the world is going. I might myself be rather in favour of termination. I must think about it.

Time to consult the Maverick Agency once again. I like the Maverick Agency. They make me feel the world is real, that the boats on the river, the cars on the road, are truly there. That a debt could affect you, a bullet kill you. Everything in this house is so still and quiet. The weather is warm. The windows are open. The watered-silk curtains, palest green, stir just a little. In the garden the weeds are growing, that's all, with no Oliver to clear them. And the caesium falls, and the strontium, and God knows what, silent, minute, invisible, as Carl makes his deadening presence felt.

33

Jane, Julie, Gina, Alice.

In the lives of the clones of Joanna May something stirred, some instinct of self-preservation was awakened, and not in that fact itself (for what woman does not wake in the morning once or twice in her life saying 'this can't go on a moment longer') but in the timing of that fact, lay whatever strangeness there might be to find. As Joanna May, Empress of inner space, fought for once to control her life, so too did the four Queens – Wands, Pentacles, Swords and Cups (rulers of the provinces, as it were), fight to control theirs, not quite sure what had moved them to action, groping for understanding of their own behaviour, and not quite finding it, so looking for justification instead.

———◦◦◦———

Jane received three letters by the same post. One was from her employers to announce the appointment of the new head of the London office: and it was not Jane but a snip of a girl of twenty-three, without a degree to her name, who got it. Too old at thirty! If you hadn't made it by thirty in the film world, you'd had it. The next was from someone she'd never heard of, a woman called Anne, written on thin blue paper in what looked like a drunken scrawl, saying she, Jane, should take her claws out of Tom and let him get on with his life, or she, Anne, would come round and personally strangle her, and the third was from the ground rent landlords, asking her for her £8000 contribution towards repairing the roof, a matter she'd never heard of until that moment.

She rang HBO and offered her resignation, which was accepted with an alacrity she found humiliating. She rang Tom and asked him who Anne was, or rather screamed at him about her, and Tom said she was just a friend: he'd come round. She rang the landlords and said it was monstrous, and they agreed, but nevertheless, there it was. If she did not hand over £8000 forthwith they could, if it came to it, foreclose on her mortgage and resell to raise the necessary funds. She rang her father, Jeremy, who said he feared she hadn't read the small print of her tenancy, and she said, 'Why couldn't you read it for me? Why have you never helped me?' and he said, 'Jane, you were always so self-sufficient, even from a baby: it came more easily to admire you than help you,' and for some reason this made her weep and weep more than did any of the other sudden and unexpected blows from fate.

Tom came round and showed her photographs of Anne, who was blowsy and uneducated and had a daughter called Roma, aged eleven. Anne was his landlady. Yes, he spent nights with Anne sometimes. Why not? Why had he never told her? It didn't seem anything to do with her, that was why: Jane only wanted half of him, so she could have half. She couldn't own him: they didn't have a child. Jane knew he wanted a child. Little Roma needed him. She didn't have a father of her own.

'You're not fair, you're not fair,' wept Jane. Once men, according to Madge, said if you don't sleep with me I'll find someone who will. Now the threat had changed, gotten worse: now it was if you don't have my baby other women will be only too glad.

Anne didn't have a degree: she worked down the council baths: she had a council house: she acted as his model: yes, he was painting nudes. No, he didn't want Jane as a model, she was too twitchy. She couldn't relax. He thought he would have an exhibition soon. He was sorry about her job, her roof, her father. But her job made her hard and smart and cynical; it was a good thing she'd lost it: if she sold her car she could pay for the roof: and she'd always been hopelessly in love with her father and how could he, Tom, compete: and yes of course he loved her, what was all this talk about love all of a sudden; if

160

he moved in with her and she settled down and they had a baby he would finish with Anne though of course he'd have to go on seeing Roma, she was only a child.

'You go back to Anne,' said Jane. 'That's the end, I don't need you, I don't want you, I don't want to see you ever again.'

So he went, and she wondered why it all felt so familiar. She began talking to friends and colleagues about possible openings not just in films, but in journalism, put her solicitors on to the matter of the roof, went round to the doctor and demanded a sterilization, which was refused. She did not argue, however.

For it seemed to her, as she advanced reasons, both laudable and derisory, in favour of her sterilization – her career, her freedom, her revulsion, her dislike of baby mess and smells, her figure, her need of sleep – that there was another one she was only just now beginning to put her finger on. She didn't want a boy; but who would understand that? If she had a boy it would be homosexual. It would have to be. Because how could she, being female, give birth to something male? Her little twelve-week foetus, which they'd said was male, had looked a real mess to her, and she wasn't surprised. She could understand how her body could somehow spit out a daughter, a replica: but the female was less than the male: how could the lesser give birth to the greater? How could she tell Tom a thing like that? Better forget the whole thing: just not have babies: just be in some other more rational arena, where life was for living not passing on. Nevertheless, when refused, she was remotely, somewhere, somehow, pleased. She had a coil put in, instead.

So much for the Queen of Wands.

———◆◆◆———

As for the Queen of Pentacles, Julie, well, her husband Alec flew in, ate supper without tasting it, went to bed without noticing her new provocative nightgown, let alone her determined serious sweetness – she had parted for ever (or so she really and truly believed) with her lover, for the sake of the marriage – was too tired to make love, rose in the morning, grumbled at the state of his shirts – though they were perfect – and flew straight off to West Berlin.

'This can't go on,' she said, and made an appointment to see a solicitor. Yet Alec had flown in and out, just so, a hundred times before.

Julie, Queen of Pentacles.

———••———

Gina, Queen of Swords, woke up to a usual kind of day and limped to the doctor's, as she often did. But while she was sitting in his waiting room – and she had to wait for a full hour with coughing young women and spluttering old ones all around, trying to reassure Ben (who had stayed off school to help her) and pacify little Anthony, who sat grizzling on the floor dealing harshly with the few old toys brought in by passing benefactors – she said something strange, to no one in particular. 'This can't go on,' she said.

'What, Mum?' asked Ben. 'What did you say?'

Ben always listened out anxiously as if his life's duty was to be on guard, waiting for something he could do nothing about, except watch for its coming.

'Never you mind,' she said. 'But don't worry. Things will get better,' and she'd said that to him a hundred times before, and it hadn't got better. But this time when she limped into the surgery – her knee stiffened and swelled with every hour that passed – and the doctor said grimly, 'I suppose you fell downstairs again,' she actually said, 'No, I was pushed. Will you write it down, please. I'll need some kind of record.'

The doctor wrote it down, with alacrity. The clones of Joanna May always found protectors: though it must be said that this particular clone seldom looked her best.

Gina, Queen of Swords.

———••———

And as for Alice, Queen of Cups, that morning Alice woke from a terrible dream in which she had been split into five from the waist up and four of them were eating alive, with fanged teeth, the one which was her, and when only one of her eyes was left and half her mouth, Alice woke screaming. She told the essence

162

of her dream to the photographer who happened to be with her and he said well that's you struggling for survival with your four big brothers, and having understood it, or thought she understood it, she felt better. Except that the one-eyed image continued to bother her, and instead of going back to sleep, she thought about it. One eyed, cock-eyed; something was wrong. She, usually so restrained, too controlled even to smile if she could possibly help it, suddenly kicked the sleeping photographer (his name was Radish; an absurd name) with a smooth, round muscular foot and shrieked, 'I can't stand it a moment longer. Go back to your wife' – for of course Radish was married: her relationships usually were with married men, who could be relied upon to go away – so he did go back to her, poor man, startled, surprised and upset. That is to say, he walked the streets until ten the next morning, when he was due back home, believing Alice had thrown him out because he was married, and had the evening before explained how he couldn't leave his wife, she being pregnant and relying upon him, and so forth. He could see it was all for the best: but it hurt, it hurt.

Alice had to take four sleeping pills before she could get back to sleep and as a consequence failed, for the first time in her life, to turn up for a 7.00 a.m. call. The studio had to send a taxi for her, and she arrived without her make-up box, and was, in fact, so thoroughly unprofessional all round they decided not to use her again. She was clearly paranoic. She claimed she was being followed by a young man carrying a child's lunch box, that he was standing outside the studio even now, and if they looked out they'd see him – and they looked to placate her – but there was nothing unusual to be seen, just people standing about on street corners waiting for taxis, and workmen waiting for other workmen and so forth, but no one looking out for Alice. Who did she think she was? Really beautiful women are admired and loved but seldom liked. She could not afford to step out of line, and she had. Alice, Queen of Cups.

34

Carl May did not believe in divinatory magic, of course he did not. To tell the cards, the stars, the lines of the palm, tea-leaves and so forth was to divine what was in the fortune-teller's heart, and that was all. How could it be otherwise, the clues to interpretation being so numerous and to reach that interpretation so many contradictory clues having to be taken into account? Moreover, the wisdom behind that interpretation – that is to say the sum of the experience of long-dead seers and necromancers – had always been so sloppily recorded and translated from one language to another, one culture to another, as to add up in the end to sheer gobbledygook.

Gobbledygook, and he would prove it.

To this end Carl May had started Britnuc's Divination Department, housed on the eighth floor, a floor which had heating and ventilation problems. Divination was made up of cartomancers, astrologers, crystal gazers and so on, and the greater part of its work involved participation in research, funded jointly by Britnuc and the University of Edinburgh, into the comparative validity or otherwise of the various occult disciplines. So far, as Carl May had expected, the balance was tipping otherwise. To justify the existence of the department in the eyes of his fellow directors and the shareholders its reports and prophecies were registered along with those of other sections: forward planning now included propitiousness of time in relation to event in its computerized forecasts. All other things being equal, which seldom happened, recommendations from the eighth floor would be allowed to tip the balance on minor decisions this way or that. Carl May reckoned it would be no worse than tossing a coin, which on occasion he had been known to do – though sitting alone at the head of the great board table as he did who was to say whether he reported its fall correctly?

Carl May was interested and displeased to observe how quickly the staff came to take the existence of the department for granted: how it had become common practice for Garden Developments to plant according to phases of the moon in spite of the virtual impossibility of controlled testing – variables in the rearing of plants being almost as numerous as they were for humans; how at lunchtimes the lifts to the eighth floor would be busy with not only female clerical staff (which he would have expected) on their way to have their fortunes told, but with middle and senior management as well. He wondered if there were a marker gene for gullibility: he waited impatiently for Holly to repent and come back on line. He would not wait for ever.

Since the Chernobyl event Carl May had had Divination, in conjunction with the University, working on maps of the British Isles, predicting regional variations of wind patterns and subsequent fallout. Now came a phone call through to his office from Edinburgh. A former music-hall entertainer, Wee Willie Bradley, who had the apparent gift, or talent, or capacity – call it what you like – of shutting his eyes and projecting imagined pictures on to ordinary black and white film, was proving successful in producing accurate maps two days in advance.

'How successful?' demanded Carl May, who was putting on his shirt.

'One hundred per cent,' said Edinburgh, smugly.

'Impossible,' said Carl May, 'because no one's maps are accurate. As well say today's instrumentation readings are influenced by Wee Willie's maps two days ago.' Which stumped Edinburgh, for a time.

'What's your star sign?' Carl May asked Bethany, who, dreamy and languid, still lay on the palely carpeted office floor, since she found the designer chairs too uncomfortable to sit upon. Since bits of carpet came off on her yellow cashmere sweater she hadn't bothered to put that back on. It was an idle kind of day.

165

'I can't remember,' said Bethany, prudently, for all Carl May was in a good mood. 'I don't really believe in all that junk.'

He wondered whether there might be a gene for the propensity to tell lies, and whether it would be desirable or undesirable to shuffle it out. Would Bethany honest be less or more desirable? He tickled her chest with his bare toes. The red light on the telephone blinked.

'What a busy day,' said Bethany.

It was Gerald Coustain. He had come back to Carl May, reluctantly, to ask if Britnuc could possibly make available to the Government one or two technicians properly trained in radiation diagnostic techniques, in the urgent national interest. Carl May was pleased to put at his disposal Britnuc's entire Divination Department.

'I don't quite understand,' said Gerald. 'What use are astrologers and palm-readers in this particular situation?'

'Our research shows,' said Carl May merrily, 'that they're as good at anticipating fallout as our technicians and they certainly cost less.'

'That may be,' said Gerald cautiously, 'because your diagnostic equipment is out of date. You have the technicians, the Department has the equipment; couldn't we just get them together?'

'I'll think about it,' said Carl May cheerfully. 'How's the family?'

'Just fine, thank you.'

'I hear you've been seeing something of my ex-wife.'

'We all had a jaunt to the lido, one day,' said Gerald, after only a second's pause.

'Joanna must have really liked that,' said Carl May. 'I'm glad to hear she's taken up swimming. Women need to look after themselves as they get older. Poor old thing, did you hear about her gardener?'

'I think she called Angela, just to say. Quite a shock.'

'Good domestic staff is always hard to find,' said Carl May, 'even more difficult than trained technicians and accurate, up-to-the-minute equipment in this ever-changing field of ours. Perhaps the Department of Energy will see its way to some form

166

of co-funding when this Chernobyl lark has calmed down. That way we could ensure Britnuc was always in a position to help you lot out.'

'I'll put it to my Department,' said Gerald.

'And I'll put your requirements to mine,' said Carl May. 'You're quite sure you can't make use of my Divination Department?'

'No thank you,' said Gerald.

'Pity,' said Carl May. 'What a lot of old stick-in-the-muds you civil servants are!' He was in a talkative mood. 'Reminds me of someone I used to have working for me. What was his name? King? That's it. Curator of the gallery – you know my gallery? The May Gallery? Egyptologist fellow. Well, never mind, it's a long story – he was interested in the Tarot pack. Hieroglyphics, and so forth. Poor fellow, he got knocked down in a road accident, killed.'

'I seem to remember that,' said Gerald, cautiously.

'That's the problem for stick-in-the-muds,' said Carl May. 'So stuck they can't even look where they're going!'

'Well,' said Gerald, 'it's been an interesting conversation, Carl. I'll come back to you when I've spoken to my Department.'

As Gerald Coustain put the phone down he heard Carl May laughing, and the sound of agreeable female giggles. He wondered if it were mad laughter and decided probably not: just that Carl May had discovered the answer to executive stress. You murdered the people who angered you, tormented those you despised, teased those who depended upon you, and kept bimbos in the office. He was about to pick up the phone and discuss these suppositions with Angela, but thought better of it. If Carl May knew about the trip to the lido, someone's phone was probably tapped: possibly even his own. It could wait till he got home.

35

The Queen of Swords and the Queen of Pentacles.

———∞———

The Queen of Swords left the doctor's surgery with one child in a pushchair and the other walking just a little behind her, as was his practice, and had been for years. She walked away from home, not towards it, she wasn't sure why.

'Where are we going?' Ben asked.

'I don't know,' she said, 'but I don't want to go home.'

'Where else is there to go?' he asked, which was of course the point. But he moved up to keep pace with her, and actually took charge of the pushchair, since she was limping, and it was the first time he'd done that — as if admitting their common interest, mother and son, in what was going on in the family, and encouraging this new train of thought in her: namely that things could not go on as they were, but would, unless she did something. At least for once she was walking away from home, away from Cliff, and not back towards him. They kept walking in the wrong direction until it was lunchtime — although Ben should have gone straight to school, and she would have been more prudent to have just sat down and rested her leg, as the doctor had instructed. Then they went to McDonald's, which was a luxury, and bad for them, but she had lost faith in a future in which care taken meant benefit returned. Ben ordered at the counter while she, her whole leg now painful and throbbing, unstrapped Anthony and heaved him out of the pushchair and into the high chair provided by McDonald's. He enjoyed sitting in it, which was something. She should never have had him, of course.

'These children that we should never have had,' she said aloud, 'still have to eat.'

———◆◆◆———

The Queen of Pentacles heard. Julie was sitting at the table next to Gina's. She had gone to visit her solicitor: he had not given her good news: she had no children and the house was in her husband's name: she was young and able-bodied: if she divorced she would be expected to shift for herself. At the same time she did not, as her solicitor pointed out, have the capacity, let alone the training, to earn a decent living. His advice, offered to her unasked, was to stay home and make the best of things. And so she had driven not home but in the wrong direction, not sure why or where, alone and lonely, childless and more than ever conscious of it, but also let it be said without the exhausting responsibilities that went with the company, the pleasure of children. This Julie recognized, and now tried not to stare curiously at Gina; this messy, overweight, distracted, sloppy woman of too many responsibilities who had said aloud something so remarkable. 'I might have been like that,' she thought, 'if I'd had too many children too young,' and envied the other woman but at the same time pitied her, and felt, if not grateful for her own lot, at least a little more reconciled to it. Her heart was breaking, but she would not, would not, see the vet again. He was married, so was she. Supposing Alec found out? A woman could lose everything, so easily.

Gina saw Julie watching and thought who does that woman think she is, staring, and why is she so familiar: do I know her from somewhere? And what was a woman like that doing, sitting in a McDonald's, in a pale cashmere jumper, trying to get her pearly teeth into a Big Mac when everyone knew you didn't bite but somehow drew the layered substance into your mouth. Prettier than me, thought Gina; taller, thinner, younger, certainly richer: dressed so you hardly noticed, but you could tell expensively, and looking miserable but down her nose. If things had gone differently for me, thought Gina, if I'd been given a chance in life, if I hadn't had these bloody children, if someone, anyone, had had the heart to stop me, got me to

169

school, let alone college – but they hadn't, had they. No one had cared. She felt herself beginning to cry. She was stuck here in McDonald's, marooned. Now she'd stopped walking and taken her foot off the ground she didn't think she could put it back down again. It would hurt too much. Moreover, she had set things in motion at the doctor's she could not control, and wished she hadn't: there would be more violence ahead: how was she going to collect Sue at four o'clock: she could send Ben, she supposed, but Ben would resent it, Ben had never wanted Sue to be born any more than Sue had wanted Ben to exist; and worse, she, Gina, wouldn't be there to stand between the two children and their father when they got home: and they were as likely to be met by blows, insult and humiliation, as chips and a video: you could never be sure with Cliff. Sue could walk home on her own, and would if no one turned up, but she would sulk for days and that would feed back tension into the whole family and make matters worse. Ben always wanted things to get better: Sue somehow wanted them to get worse, so whatever awful thing it was would be over quicker. Only, one row was just like another. When Cliff was sorry, and making amends, he was the best person in the world, but these days his being sorry was turning into a memory: a hope. She had failed her marriage, herself, her children.

Gina caught sight of her face in a mirror, and the tears running down it, and thought she didn't look so bad after all, almost glamorous, and then realized she wasn't looking at a reflection of herself but at the woman opposite, who was also in tears.

'Well,' said Gina, startled into friendliness, 'I suppose all women look the same when they're crying.'

'I don't cry,' said Julie, 'I never cry,' stopping on the instant, though the same thought had crossed her own mind: that looking at Gina she was looking at a reflection of herself. What a terrible thought! She gave up battling with the Big Mac and sipped a little black coffee and dabbed her eyes with a lace handkerchief. ('A lace handkerchief!' thought Gina, astounded, blowing her own nose on a McDonald's serviette.)

When Ben came back with the two Big Macs, one Chicken McNuggets, three large fries and two milk shakes, Julie gave up altogether and joined Gina at her table. Julie said, 'You're so lucky to have children; we can't have any,' and began to cry again. Gina wished she wouldn't cry in front of the children, but Ben seemed impervious to this extra distress, just stared stoically into space over his hamburger. He was a handsome child; but he did, she acknowledged, look pale and nervous. How would he grow up? 'You could have mine,' said Gina, joking, but Julie said, quite seriously, 'It's not the same. And I have this great house with no one to fill it, and somehow it makes things worse to have so much of what you don't want. I am never going back into that house again. I'm not. I don't care what anyone says.' Even as she spoke she realized she was, in her own mind, peopling her world with concerned observers, who of course in reality didn't exist. Lonely so lonely!

'Aren't you lucky,' said Gina. 'I have a house with too much to fill it, and I reckon I've got to go back into mine, I've no option.'

Gina looked across at Julie and again had a sense of familiarity. Had they known each other as children? At school? She couldn't put her finger on it. Julie looked at Gina and thought this woman is like the sister I never had, and doesn't she just need cheering up, cleaning up, and taking over. I could do some good here, for once in my life.

Ben said, 'Mum, there's a man following us. He was behind us when we left the doctor's and there he is, sitting over there –' and he pointed to where a young man in a suit sat behind a copy of the *Sun*, hiding his face. He had chosen a coffee and an apple tart. There was a briefcase on the empty chair beside him.

Gina said, 'Well, I haven't lost all my charms, then,' and Ben, who didn't seem to take to Julie but kept looking at her curiously all the same, went into a real sulk at being made, as he felt, to look a fool. Sometimes, when in a mood, he was so like his father, Gina quite disliked him. One of the problems about bringing yourself to divorce point, deciding this was the man you hated and not the man you loved, as you had rashly thought at the beginning, was not just the practical one of how you went

171

and where you went, or the emotional one of how you lived on your own, coped on your own and put up with loneliness, but how, if you hated the man, you went on loving the children, who were after all half his. You saw the father looking out of the eyes of the son. The whole business of it taking two to make one, Gina had long ago decided, made being a mother and doing it right all but impossible. She found her daughter easier. She just told her what to do and she did it. But that irritated her, too. Where was the girl's spirit? And she would snuggle up to Cliff, too, as if she was taking Cliff's side, as if she'd just move in with him the moment Cliff had battered her mother to death, and that drove Gina mad. It was all horrible; everything all went right or it all went wrong.

Julie said to Gina, 'Why don't you come home with me until you sort things out?'

Gina said to Julie, 'What about your husband? What would he say? He wouldn't like it.'

Julie said, 'He's never there, and if he does turn up, so what? The house may be in his name legally but it's mine morally, and it needs filling up with people. I do what I want with my own house.'

'Well,' said Gina, 'in that case, yes, OK,' and that took Julie aback, but she was not the kind of person to go back on her word.

'What a day of surprises,' Julie said, as she helped Gina limp to the car. Ben pushed Anthony.

'Yes, isn't it,' said Gina. 'But my motto is, something always turns up at the last moment!'

This had not been Julie's experience but she supposed that if you were consistently afflicted by misfortune, as Gina appeared to be, you would develop, as antidote to it, the art of optimism. Julie had never had the opportunity of so doing. The misfortunes that afflicted Julie masqueraded as good fortune, and so were the more difficult to locate, comprehend and deal with. If your husband blacked your eye and threw you downstairs, you at least knew there was something wrong. If your husband was away most of the time, but paid large cheques into your bank account, how could you tell what was going on?

'There is another child,' said Gina. 'A girl. We have to collect her from school.'

'Oh Good Lord,' said Julie, startled. 'Well, never mind. The more the merrier.'

If that husband came home to a house suddenly full of women and sticky, sulky, noisy children, none of them his own, it might force things to some kind of issue.

As the two women left the restaurant, two young men got up from separate tables and followed them. They met at the door, engaged in a brief conversation, and strolled down the street together. They got into the car parked behind Julie's, and when Julie pulled out, so did they. All this Ben noticed but did not say. His mother had laughed at him, now she would have to take the consequences. It was the same kind of drastic, horrid, nourishing feeling his father often had about his mother, and Ben knew it, and though he didn't like it there wasn't much he could do about it. You could stop how you acted, but hardly how you felt. This new friend of his mother's, picked up at random in a McDonald's, seemed to have something of the same quality. He didn't like it. And where were they all going? It seemed that their lives were about to change, and no one had the courtesy to explain it to him, let alone consult him. But he could see that simply to be away from home for a time, without the fear of bangs, crashes and screams in the night, not having to put up his own defences against his mother's terror or hurt, not to have to watch anxiously for the turns and changes in his father's mood, not to have to listen out for his mother's putting of her foot in it, which he sometimes thought she did on purpose, not to feel so confused about Sue, whom he felt obliged to protect but didn't want to, would be a great relief.

'You OK, darling?' asked Gina.

'I'm fine,' he said. He'd missed another day at school, and no one seemed to bother about that, either.

'Do you often go to McDonald's?' Gina asked Julie.

'No,' said Julie. 'Hardly ever. Only when I'm upset; then I like it. It's as if you were more like other people than you thought, and you might as well accept it. We're all in the same boat together.'

'That's what I feel too,' said Gina, feeling quite uneasy, that there was more to all this than met the eye. She wished there wasn't. In better times, she would have got out of the car there and then. But like so much else, once you had children, it became a matter of necessity, not choice. Where you were was where you stayed.

The car that followed them was white, all white, from its white-painted hubcaps to its white-coated aerial; a vehicle fit for angels from some phantasmagorical heaven and on the front seats, grey-suited, prosperous and clean, two young men who might have been God's accountants. The boot of the car was slightly open: part of a bicycle stuck out of it. People stared at them and forgot them.

Petie said to Elwood, 'Well, fancy you.'

Elwood said to Petie, 'Fancy you. Wheels within wheels. Just as well, my calves are aching.'

Petie said, 'That wasn't a coincidence, was it, that was drugs. That was the McDonald's connection.'

Elwood said, 'It was, and was I glad to see it. I'd begun to think that was no lady but a wild goose set up by Carl May to get his money's worth out of us.'

Petie said Carl May knows what he's doing and Elwood said you mean Jacko says Carl May knows what he's doing and Petie said it's the kids I'm sorry for and Elwood said we were all kids once even Carl May, especially Carl May, and Petie tuned the radio to rock but Elwood wanted classical so they had an argument about that, and Elwood drove rather hard around a corner just as Petie was feeling the sharpness of a knife against his thumb, so they ended up outside Julie's house with rather a lot of blood on the white upholstery. 'Serve you right,' said Petie, child at heart.

36

The Queen of Wands and the Queen of Cups.

—·•·—

The Queen of Wands tossed and turned in her penthouse bed and the moon shone in. 'I want, I want,' she said aloud, but she wasn't sure what it was she wanted, except perhaps what she couldn't have, that is to say Tom. And him she could have, if she would, which she wouldn't. Some barrier stood in her way: some wall of glass. She could not allow herself to be happy.

The attic was now a penthouse. Thus the landlords advertised it, threatening to call in her mortgage if she didn't cough up for the roof: they had put it on the market just to frighten her: they didn't have a legal leg to stand on: she'd put her solicitors on to them. It would be all right in the end, it would, it would, if only the moon didn't seem to rock so in the sky, if only her limbs didn't twitch with longing, the feel of Tom's body beside her so lacking, if only her savings would last for ever, if only she had the energy and will to go out and find another, better, less blackmailing lover than Tom, but she didn't, she couldn't.

All you had to do, she supposed, if you wanted sex, was to get dressed and go out in the night street and walk about, and see what happened next, and something would. Only such an act was unthinkable. Why? What did other people do? Did they have possible partners lined up, waiting? The longer she lived in the world the less she knew about it. It baffled her.

Other people had the gift of peopling their lives with friends and colleagues; went to outings, parties, reunions, but she remained solitary, distant, voices sounded from the other side of the glass wall, muffled: people's smiles were distorted. She waited for some kind of matching private intimacy to happen, but it didn't. She'd known Tom for so long he'd gotten through the wall, but perhaps he was the wrong one: how could the only one be the right one? Was that the trouble? Perhaps she just couldn't believe her luck?

She would go home for the weekend: she would retreat and lick her wounds a little: she would try and feel close to her parents. Difficult to look her father in the face since his strange adventure with Laura: difficult to feel close to her mother since she'd been so wounded: no matter how unaffected Madge seemed to be, how bright her intelligent eyes still shone behind her pebble glasses, she now sapped the energy of Jane's youth: she no longer fed it, nourished it. Madge had been mortally wounded, and that was the truth of it and there was no strength left in her.

'I'm depressed, that's all,' thought Jane, no longer wanting anything, and remembered standing as a small child in the hall of the big, pleasant house, and seeing through the glass door of the study her father working at his desk: and the other side of the study window the dim stumpy form of her mother, working in the garden. She'd begun to cry, for a reason she didn't then understand, from the sense of not-belonging, sense of having herself received some mortal wound, and knowing, with the clear prescience of a child, that she would thereafter limp through life: there was no healing this. Yet nothing had happened – just the sight of an ungainly woman through glass, and the understanding that beauty of spirit and beauty of body were not the same, and that the knowledge itself could maim for life.

She was grown-up now: she had controlled her life: she had remained free of emotional and domestic commitments for just such an eventuality as had now happened – she was free to move to Los Angeles where the obvious career opportunities were: the English were popular: their special talents appreciated. And now she didn't want to go. Nor did she want to lie where she was, in an empty bed, staring at a moon tossed by clouds. Where did clouds come from? She scarcely knew what clouds were, let alone why they were. It was all intolerable. The thing to do, obviously, was to let 'I want' get the better of 'I don't want'. Desire must triumph over reluctance. But how?

The Queen of Wands felt like the kitchen maid. She gave up sleep, got out of bed and switched on the light, and a sensor peeped gently in a van parked outside, and Haggie, who had been sleeping therein, woke and yawned and took out his notebook.

Jane got on with her work, her diversionary activity. She went through files and cuttings. She was writing a series of articles for *Film International* on 'Images of women: the changing generations'. She could not get excited about it, but it was work, it would keep her name up there in front of those who mattered. In the morning she could try and contact Alice Morthampton, who had the reputation of being a smart-arsed bitch. A year back she'd turned down a film part – typecasting, playing the lead, a model. She'd turned it down on moral grounds, the screen view of the model's life being so far from reality, she said, it was intolerable, and the producers refusing to change the script. Well, you were as moral as you could afford to be, supposed Jane. Alice Morthampton must be pretty rich. Pretty rich. She could not understand why Alice Morthampton was considered so beautiful. A face was just a face. The features were regular, it was true. There were two kinds of women, Jane supposed, the ones who looked like herself, and this Alice, and the others, the majority, who looked like Madge. Jane took out a ruler and measured the proportion of eyes to nose, to ears, to jaw on a fashion shot of Alice, and then did the same for herself, in the mirror. As she thought, pretty much the same. It proved something, she wasn't sure what. She was suddenly very tired.

Morthampton – house of death. She hoped not. Jane went back to bed and fell promptly asleep, forgetting to turn off the light, so Haggie was up pretty much all night.

The Queen of Cups.

Alice lay in bed with eyepads over her eyes and considered the emptiness of her life, and wondered why nobody liked her and decided it was because she didn't like them. She could see the justice in it. She thought if she called her agent and instructed him to double her fees she would then halve her work and be just as rich. If she priced herself out of the market altogether, why then she would have forced an issue: she would have no option but to change her life. She might have to anyway. She had a feeling sour looks were going out of fashion and smiles were coming back and she wasn't going to start smiling for anyone; before you knew where you were they'd have you doing idiot shots, up telegraph wires and under water on your head.

The phone rang. It was some woman journalist without an appointment; freelance, too, not even an assignment. Alice thought perhaps she'd better try to be pleasant. When it came to it, self-destruction was a frightening thing.

'So long as there's none of that crappy feminist junk about sexism in fashion,' said Alice, 'you can come on round now. This minute, before I change my mind.'

Jane came, within five minutes. She only lived around the corner it seemed, in Harley Street. Alice lived in Wigmore Street. Alice opened the door. Jane and Alice stared at each other. Alice's eyebrows were plucked and her hairline had been taken back to give her a high medieval forehead. Jane's frizzy hair fell down to her eyebrows and beyond. Alice thought she might be looking at herself on a bad day, when she was feeling particularly short and squat. Jane thought, 'I could look like that if I wanted to. Which I don't.'

Jane went inside and sat on a sofa covered in the same Liberty fabric as covered her own sofa, only hers was green and this was brown. Still, it was a fairly common fabric. But there was the same Picasso print on the wall. She said as much.

'Someone gave it to me,' said Alice. 'I don't know anything

about art. But there's a damp stain on the wall so I put it up – the roof's leaking. What's it meant to be?'

'Children playing,' said Jane.

'What, those splashes and dots? Well, write down I know nothing about art, and hate children. That should be a start. Who's it for?'

'*Film International*,' said Jane.

'Add I hate films too,' said Alice. 'I know nothing about them and don't want to.'

'But you did once turn down a part. It was that I wanted to talk to you about.'

'That old thing,' said Alice. 'I'm not an actress, I'm a model. I couldn't remember the lines.'

'I thought you turned the part down for moral reasons.'

'That's what my agent said. I was fired.'

Jane's pen stayed poised.

'People aren't going to want to hear that,' she said.

'You talk like me too,' said Alice. 'Only I try not to. This is going to be a crappy interview. So let's forget it.'

A little grey cat jumped up on to Jane's lap. Jane squealed.

'Don't tell me,' said Alice, 'you have a little grey cat just like that one and *Candid Camera* is hiding somewhere in the room. I warn you, I'll sue.'

'Would it be watching you or watching me?' asked Jane.

'Me, of course,' said Alice.

'Bloody egocentric,' said Jane, but both looked for signs of *Candid Camera*. There was no sign of hoax or hoaxer. They looked at each other.

'You should do something about your hair,' said Alice. 'It's an insult.'

'I like it as it is,' said Jane. 'I don't believe in artifice.'

'Then you're a fool,' said Alice, and both fell silent.

Presently Alice asked Jane when her birthday was and Jane replied September first, and Alice said, well, I was born on September thirteenth, so that's something, but Jane said not enough. Twins could be born as much as three weeks apart, even identical twins.

'Who's talking about twins?' said Alice.

179

'I am,' said Jane. Then she said, 'But I'm sure if I'd been a twin, someone would have told me. Besides, it's not in my parents' nature to give children away. If my mother Madge had had twins she'd have reared them both, and made a good job of it, at least in her terms.'

Alice said, 'You might have been the one given away. You're the one who's egocentric. My mother never did anything she didn't want. She'd have given away anyone.'

Jane said, 'I'm certainly not adopted, if that's what you're suggesting.'

Though when she came to think about it, she could see that not to be Madge's natural daughter would relieve her of a great deal of guilt. The wonder had always been that so pretty a child as she had come from a pair so rigorously plain as Jeremy and Madge: friends, both hers and theirs, had remarked on it: she'd hated it: she saw herself as the source of her parents' discomfiture. If you had no friends, you didn't have to put up with the pain they caused: she'd learned that early.

'My mind's going so fast,' she complained, 'I think I'm going to be sick.'

She was, in Alice's mirror-lined bathroom, so full of creams, unguents, oils and lotions she could only marvel. She kept books in hers. When she came out she said, 'I can't possibly be your twin; we're completely different,' but Alice was standing in front of yet another mirror and had combed her hair down over her eyes and there was no doubting it.

'My experience is,' said Alice, 'it's not that people tell you lies, so much as they forget to tell you the truth. Personally, I trust no one. But then I was brought up with four brothers. All the same, I can see we're going to have to face up to this. Who's going to see whose parents first?'

In the street outside, Haggie found himself double parked next to a manhole in which none other than Dougie was working on

180

telephone wires, yanking them out and then plugging them in. Dougie wore bright-yellow Telecom overalls.

'Well, fancy that,' said Dougie. 'Looks like yours has gone to visit mine. What's the connection?'

'Drugs?' said Haggie. 'Do you reckon?'

'More than likely,' said Dougie. 'Or prostitution. Women living alone.'

'It's too bad,' said Haggie, 'what goes on these days.'

'The world would be a cleaner place without their likes,' said Dougie, as Haggie joined him in the snugness of the manhole. 'Spreading disease with needles and sex.'

'This isn't a snuff mission,' said Haggie. 'It's a sniff mission.'

'One drifts into another, in my experience,' said Dougie.

'Mine's a tough cookie: no doubt about it,' said Haggie. 'No husband, no boyfriend, no children. Send a scrap of foreskin, or more, through the post, but if it's a stranger's what does she care?'

'You could slash my girl's face,' said Dougie, 'and all she'd do is call round the photographers, and there'd be even more of them in and out of her bed. Oh yes, they're tough. You have to admire them.'

'You don't,' said Haggie. 'You just have to stop them before they spoil the world for everyone else,' and Dougie said, 'I'm sure that yellow lead matched up to that yellow socket a moment ago,' and Haggie said, 'What the hell, Dougie, what the hell. At least Carl May knows what he's doing.'

'I suppose,' said Haggie.

181

37

'This Holly fellow has got nothing to hide,' Mavis of Maverick told Joanna, seeming disappointed, 'or if he has, he knows how to act innocent. Easy-peasy to trace.' Young Mavis strode into the house with muddy boots, reminding Joanna of Oliver, bringing the world with her.

The Bulstrode Clinic, according to Mavis, who – or so it said in the Maverick prospectus – had a First Class Honours Degree in Classics from Cambridge, was one of the first fertility clinics in the country, part NHS funded, part private, properly registered, licensed and inspected: it did legitimate terminations, blew fallopian tubes and stuff (said Mavis, with distaste) and carried out a few properly authorized tests on artificial insemination and ex-utero fertilization (makes you puke, doesn't it, said Mavis. Why do women *want* babies?). They also did vasectomies (more like it, said Mavis). When it closed there were letters to the papers saying what were women to do now? (What they did, said Mavis, was to come out as lesbians and sod the men.)

Holly had moved on to the Genetics Research Department of Martins Pharmaceuticals, where he'd been ever since: some files he left, a few he took with him: a common enough practice, in research. He was married, had grown children, lived within a comfortable income, contributed to the odd learned paper: apart from dabbling about in women's insides, said Mavis, he seemed OK. He wasn't making an illegal fortune, so far as anyone could see. Of course your ex is a director of Martins, said Mavis, but then he's on the board of most things, isn't he, so it probably doesn't mean much.

Martins Pharmaceuticals, said Mavis, specialized in the manufacture of synthetic hormones and made a particularly popular brand of birth-control pill with good sales in Third World countries, and drugs for hormone-replacement therapy in the West for, said Mavis, spoilt old women who wouldn't give in. Martins had a good reputation, compared to other pharmaceutical companies, for responsibility and reliability – which wasn't difficult. They had been known to take drugs off the market as soon as dangerous side effects were notified, and not fight through the courts for years to keep them on: they had been known to pay damages voluntarily to people whom their products had blinded and maimed, and their gifts to the medical profession could not be said to amount to bribes. Martins maintained large biotechnology departments in their various divisions, and their latest claim to reputation was the development of a certain Factor 10, which almost amounted to altruism, inasmuch as it offered hope of treatment to sufferers from sickle cell anaemia and everyone knew genetic engineering would eventually breed the disease out of the human race so Factor 10 was not even a long-term money spinner. They've cost-accounted integrity, said Mavis, and found it pays.

'Why do you want to know all this?' Mavis asked Joanna May.

Joanna May told her.

'Bloody men,' said Mavis, 'so competitive, always muscling in on women's wombs. I hope you're not going to barge into the lives of these wretched young women and stir everything up.'

'I don't know,' said Joanna.

'Well, think about it,' said Mavis. 'Thirty years on! How would you like it if your ninety-year-old self came walking through the door?'

'I wouldn't mind,' said Joanna, but she wasn't sure.

'Unless you have another reason,' said Mavis, booted feet up on the sofa, 'you're not being straight with me. What else is your ex-husband up to?'

Joanna May told her.

'I don't know anything about Tarot cards,' said Mavis, 'or all that gobbledygook, but that's a nasty wound you have there on the back of your neck, and you should get it seen to. A man who can do that to a woman, forget what he can do to other men – which is really of no interest to me, murder-schmurder, call it what you like, it's a man's gotta do what a man's gotta do affair, and boring with it – but I don't think he should be let loose on your young versions. God knows what he'll do, vindictive bastard, since no doubt he thinks he owns them, typical male, taking claim for their creation.'

'He had a very hard childhood,' said Joanna May.

'Childhood-schmildhood,' said Mavis, 'reclaim your sisters! I speak both in the political and the family sense.' She sat on the sofa where Oliver had been accustomed to sit, and, like him, she smoked; and like him she coughed. Her skin was tough, her hair was frizzy, her T-shirt none too clean, but she brought with her energy, common sense and determination. The world was not too much for her: it was for action, not contemplation.

'Well,' said Joanna. 'Perhaps.'

'Perhaps is not enough,' said Mavis. 'You must go to Dr Holly straight away. You must insist that he opens his records to you, the ones he took with him.'

'Can't you see him for me?'

'No,' said Mavis, crossly. 'There isn't time. You do it. What are you frightened of? What did men do to you that has made your generation so timid? I accept that Carl May is a special case, he scares even me, but an old fruit like Dr Holly?'

'He wore such a white coat,' said Joanna, remembering. 'He was so kind, he was so clever; and I, I was doing something so very wrong, something I didn't want to do. I was getting rid of a baby; I was having my husband's abortion, not his child. I put the Bulstrode Clinic out of my mind and tried not to think about it again. What I did was so very wrong.'

'It wasn't,' said Mavis. 'You weren't pregnant. Two psychiatrists certified it as an hysterical pregnancy.'

Joanna May's hands moved to her small waist, her flat belly, no longer young; she felt her belly swell – she knew it could still. She understood her body's desire to do just that – its capacity to think wilfully, to deceive itself. She felt herself widen and grow, and then she felt herself shrink again, defeated. Tumescence and detumescence.

'Oh,' said Joanna May, cheated all her life.

'Your husband had a vasectomy early on,' said Mavis.
'I see,' said Joanna May.

Joanna May saw. Joanna May saw back into the pattern of her life, black and white, greys and duns. There are no colours in the inner landscape. She saw a dull web of non-response, picked out by miseries and misconceptions, disappointments and remorse, sparkling away with courage where no courage was needed, glittering with hope where no hope was; of trials overcome where no trials were; a false web, not her own, woven by Carl May: and she was the wretched fly and he the whimsical, scuttling spider.

'I'm pregnant,' she had said to Carl May. Where had they been? The States. Boston. She remembered a hotel suite, and a big white boxed-in bath, and taps out of which water gushed with terrifying power. She had been afraid to say it: fear where no fear should be. He did not want children. The day before the wedding he'd told her so – a walk in the park, a moon, a lake, romance, as the world knew it – he'd said, 'Just you and me, forever, no one else, no children, I don't want children, to be a child is to suffer . . .'

'Not my child, my child wouldn't suffer, I'd protect it.'

'Yes, your child too, anyone's child – to be helpless is to suffer: there's no escape. Let the human race end here, with us, its triumph, love complete and final, whole.' And in that understanding she had agreed – only you, Carl, you and me: our no-children and our perfect love thus linked: and the stars, the treacherous messengers of fate, looked down and smiled. Carl and Joanna May, hand in hand.

Yet there she was in New York, ten, eleven years later, with her breasts heavy and sore, like the breasts of her friend Nancy, and feeling sick, as her friend Helen had been, and all her being focused in on this one wonderful fact: a baby, a baby! Treachery to Carl, but he'd understand, he'd forgive; surely their meshing was not so tight now, not so complete, as to forbid a little budding-off to come between; his past must seem a little further off, the remembrance of it not so desperate. Surely! What was her love worth if it hadn't healed him, hadn't undone the past sufficiently to make the future possible? Carl May had been kind. But he had said no.

And now, see! The kindness a lie: the no unnecessary. No living baby there: a notional baby in the head, not a real one in the womb. She'd had a spaniel once, whose nipples grew, whose sides heaved – nothing there, said the vet: an hysterical pregnancy. Animals do it a lot, said the vet, if you stand between them and their purposes. The bitch, Carl May had said; I've half a mind to have the thing put down. He'd laughed. A joke. Kick it and that will cure it. Later the animal had simply disappeared: it and its labrador companion. Dog thieves, people said. Now she wondered. A lifetime believing Carl May was sane, seeing black where white was, white where black was; if you practised too long you could no longer tell. You just saw what was convenient, what sounded best, what kept you out of trouble. Perhaps he'd envied even her dogs.

'Just you and me,' Carl May had said. 'Just you and me.' So back from Boston to England, off to the Bulstrode, to meet charming Dr Holly. Really nice, when it came to it, understanding so much, interested in everything. After the termination she'd felt he owned her body. She would have run off with him if she could, if she'd known how to go about it. But she never knew how; she'd had no practice. It was a trick you learned: as a kitten learns to scratch earth to cover its mess. If there's no one to teach it, it never learns. Tales of Joanna May, the deceived, the self-deceiver.

No baby, no abortion. No pleasure in the sadness, no delight in the grief, no soaring knowledge of I can, I can, I have, I am real, a woman, a grown woman, here's proof of it at last – likewise no regret, no shame, no sense of courage failed, of having thrown a child away, because that child's life was not worth hers. Selective breeding, Carl May had said. Come now, Joanna, if you make a fuss, if you weep and wail, I'll think you don't love me wholly, totally, as you promised you would, for ever and ever, in the park, with the moon, the most perfect moment of my life. Was it yours? Oh yes, Carl, yes. A sacrifice on the altar of Joanna's love for Carl, Carl's love for Joanna.

186

All lies, all lies. What was a mountain was in fact a chasm: what looked a chasm had been a mountain. Falling when you thought you were climbing. What a fool she'd been. What fools women were: they didn't need mothers to teach them folly.

Lonely and alone these last few years; used to it: liking it. I alone, Joanna May, in the perfection of my childlessness, the tragedy of this single drama: content here in the centre of the web of my life, what's left of it, repairing it as Carl May tears it: only not my web, it now turns out, a borrowed web, too late now, to build my own.

These clones, these sisters, these daughters, what are they to me? I know nothing about them. Let them die. Carl was perfectly right: to live is to suffer. And not just the child, but the adult too. It never stops. The clones, like their original, are better dead. I don't have the courage to die, to kill myself, to put an end to the shame, the rage, the desire, the fear that is Joanna May. But let them die, those other versions. No action is required by me. Leave it to Carl May to act. That at least is familiar, true, comforting.

'It must be upsetting,' said Mavis. 'All this kind of lovey-dovey complication.'

'It is a little,' said Joanna May, politely, vaguely.

Joanna May saw herself at the centre of a web: what did it matter who built it? It was no one's responsibility but her own. She perceived that she was held suspended, harmless and impotent, by the equal forces of the passions which stretched the web, one at each corner. Shame, outrage, fear and desire, the four saving and refining passions of the universe, holding her suspended, centring in her in exactly equal proportions, cancelled themselves, nullified Joanna May. The shame which should purify, the outrage which should move to action, the fear which should quieten, the desire which should sanctify, brought to nothing.

187

'Are you all right?' asked Mavis.
'I'm just fine,' said Joanna May.

And the greatest of these is desire, and the second greatest outrage, through which we recognize evil and sweep it away because it has no business hanging around, spoiling things. Joanna May willed: it was like using a muscle forgotten for years: you searched, focused, used – it hurt, but it worked. Enough.

'I want my life back,' said Joanna May, petulant and passionate as a child of five. 'The murdering bastard! He took Isaac, he took Oliver, but he shan't have the clones. I want them. I need them. They're *mine*.'
'That's better,' said Mavis.

38

'Hey ho, the holly,' said Carl May, bouncing into Dr Holly's office, 'this life is so jolly.'

Perhaps he's been taking rejuvenating hormones, thought Dr Holly, or is it just those old things, amphetamines, or perhaps youth is indeed in some measure infectious and he's caught a rather hefty dose of it from the young woman who keeps him company, but this is the third time in a week he's been to see me, and I wish he wouldn't. I don't like it. What does he want?

'Hey ho, the holly,' corrected Dr Holly, 'this life is most jolly.' Carl May is a powerful and wealthy man, why doesn't he get his secretary to call me on the phone, why doesn't he send his chauffeur, what is going on that he needs to see me in person? Does he have nobody to talk to? Or does he just want to show off his young companion? That was most likely.

'He's always getting things wrong,' said the young companion, and then, rather quickly, 'don't you, darling?' and she moved over to plant a kiss just above Carl May's eyes where the white hairs grew sparsely in stretched skin.

She seemed nervous. Just a two-a-penny scrubber, thought Dr Holly; an old man's toy, equivalent of a young man's Porsche, and then thought, no, that's just defensive, if she were mine I'd take her everywhere too, for all the world to see – could you breed from the emerald eyes? She wouldn't age well: the bone structure of the face was blurred – she had a look about the mouth: how was it you could tell the whore from other women, just by looking? Psychosomatic damage affected growth, as surely as did hunger: the failure to reach emotional potential left its evidence in the face: the outcome of the psycho-genetic battle was there for all to read. Poor thing. Poor damaged thing. As for Carl May, it was pathetic: a humiliation. Dr Holly did

189

not like to see it. The girl was so clearly bought. He wondered if there would be any point in trying to find the marker for the propensity to use younger members of the opposite sex as symbols of status – it might not be too difficult; some variant in the reproductive organs might well prove to have just such a behavioural link – but decided there were far more urgent matters to attend to. Future generations might locate and shuffle the marker out, if it existed. If they had a mind to. Certainly his own department, after his disagreement with Carl May over the absent-mindedness or otherwise of university professors, could not even begin to take it on board.

'Did you hear what I was saying, Holly?'

Dr Holly hadn't. Bad mark, Holly.

'When do they make you retire, Holly? Got to make way for the young ones, isn't that so, Bethany?'

'Young men are boring,' said Bethany. Then quickly, 'Anyway, Carl, you're not old.' Whew!

'I'm ageing better than he is,' said Carl May. 'I've pickled my bones in radioactivity, that's what it is!' He poked Bethany's young flesh with a bony finger. 'Isn't that so, Squirrel Nutkin?'

'Martins don't enforce a retirement age in their R & D departments,' said Dr Holly, whose beard was white but whose eyes were bright, alert, even kind. 'Good men are hard to find. There's a surplus of competence in the young, but not much imagination.'

'Is that so?' said Carl May. 'No fixed retirement age! I must have a word about that with my friend Henry.' Henry White, chief executive, Martins International, subsidiary of Britnuc. And Dr Holly wondered exactly what kind of task Carl May had in store for him and how he would get out of it. Certainly Carl May was building up to something.

Dr Holly had read about Carl May's divorce in the newspapers and had appreciated the silence which followed it. The man, he had hoped, was permanently subdued. But then he had turned up again, Bethany on his arm, bouncing about like a newly-inflated balloon.

On the first visit Carl May, on his way to a board meeting,

had talked amiably about the possibility of injecting more funds into Martins R & D. He had then left two specimens for dry-storage, which Dr Holly could see no reason to refuse. Carl May did not volunteer information about the nature of the specimens. Dr Holly did not ask. Bethany had worn white boots, black stockings, a scarlet miniskirt and an old grey-white torn T-shirt.

On the second visit they'd talked about the quest for the new non-addictive painkiller the world was looking for, and how after the expense of Factor 10 Martins deserved to be the ones to find it. Bethany had worn a grey suit, a white blouse and pearls and would have looked like a businesswoman only her hair kept falling out of its combs. On that occasion Carl May had been called away abruptly, back to Britnuc. Chernobyl was causing an uproar, apologized Carl May; the world had gone mad; and the thought came into Dr Holly's head that Carl May believed he was the world and was trying to tell him something. Carl May certainly had delusions of omnipotence.

On this occasion Bethany wore a long flowered skirt and an ethnic blouse, which kept falling open at the front where a buttonhole was too large for its button, and Carl May said, 'Tell me more about what you're doing,' and Dr Holly, who thought Carl May knew very well, told him more. He was studying brain-cell function in addiction, said Dr Holly, using identical twins as subject and control, stimulating the pleasure centres of the inner brain, rather than the pain centres – which would hardly be ethical –

'Impractical, shall we say,' said Carl May, 'since I daresay you're dependent upon volunteers, and only masochists would turn up, and then you'd have a biased sample.'

'Quite so,' said Dr Holly, calmly. 'How well you put it. Fortunately, you get much the same kind of hormonal excretion from the brain cells whether they're excited by pain or pleasure.'

'Much the same!' scorned Carl May. 'Time was when you wouldn't be satisfied with "much the same". Time was when you could have got a Nobel Prize, if only you'd pressed ahead, not backed out, sold out, let me down.'

'Well,' said Dr Holly, 'chance would have been a fine thing.

It just so happened that Martins halved my funding one fine day for no reason that I could see.'

'Perhaps they halved it,' said Carl May, 'because you, being a professor, were such an absent-minded old fart and only half there most of the time.'

Bethany stirred uneasily. Language! Another button popped open.

'Perhaps they did,' said Dr Holly, 'perhaps I am,' and Carl May smiled. He always won, in the end.

'Time was,' said Carl May, 'when you'd have bubbled the vats and brewed the broth and grown a million million brain cells and not have had the bother of asking in living twins and parking electrodes into their brains, and perhaps the time will come again, sooner than you think.'

'Do you think so?' asked Dr Holly. 'At least stimulating the pleasure centres of consenting twins, triplets, quads if we're very lucky, is ethical.'

'Ethical smethical,' said Carl May. 'What do you think Martins are doing in the other labs, or don't you ask? Pushing ahead with what you began but didn't have the guts to see through. The transfer of nuclei, perfect and whole, dried not frozen, from the frog right up to the mammal – and by mammal I mean human, you bet I do.'

'So much is interesting,' said Dr Holly. 'There is more to science than genetic engineering. Perhaps, as you say, the field should be left to younger men.'

'Potter on, potter on,' sang Carl May sweetly, which meant he was taken aback, 'to the end of the road, and you'll never walk again,' and he pinched Bethany so that she squealed and leant forward and the next button came undone.

'Walk on, walk on,' corrected Dr Holly, 'to the end of the road, and you'll never walk alone.'

'How's the wife?' asked Carl May kindly. 'She must be getting on.'

'She's very well,' said Dr Holly.

'No arthritis, no spondylitis? A fluttering of Alzheimer's in the brain?'

'A little,' admitted Dr Holly.

'Pottering on to the end of the road,' said Carl May. 'I really must take young Bethany home. Look at her! I'll be back for your answer within the week. A plague on your living twins, I say. I need you back in the field. Money no object.'

Dr Holly nodded and smiled vaguely as if he hadn't quite understood, but Carl May seemed satisfied and left with a cheery 'Hey ho, the holly', and when he was gone, in spite of the relief that he was gone, Dr Holly's office seemed oddly dull and quiet, as if Carl May had sucked out all the energy through the door, like juice from a hole in the skin of an orange, leaving nothing but pith and fibre behind. He wondered what would happen next and he hadn't wondered that for quite a while.

39

Dr Isadore Holly looked up from his desk and said, as Joanna May came into his office, 'Why, Mrs May,' he said, 'you've hardly changed at all.'

'Don't begin by telling lies,' she said. 'You haven't seen me for thirty years. You can't possibly remember me.'

'I'm not telling lies,' he protested. 'It's not in my habit to tell lies. I remember you very well. Naturally, you look older; time has passed: I merely remarked that you hadn't changed, and you may think of that as a compliment, or otherwise. You were the most beautiful of all my patients; your husband claimed you were perfection itself, and I had to agree. The mixture of Scandinavian, Celtic and Norman stock we call typically English sometimes turns out very well indeed. And you have aged well. That too is in the genes; of course. Like mother, like daughter, we find.'

'And you could say the same of identical twins, I daresay. Like this one, that one. No credit in it.'

'Truly identical twins are rare in nature,' he said. 'When the single fertilized ovum splits, it seems the division of the chromosomes is not necessarily exact. It is possible to get identical twins with different-coloured eyes, did you know that? And eye colour is known to influence behaviour, and therefore personality. But I don't suppose you've come here for idle chitchat. One must not suppose that one's life's passion is even remotely interesting to other folk.'

'Your life's passion, Dr Holly,' said Joanna May, 'has had quite an effect on me. Tell me, if someone came to you and asked you to grow a human with frog's legs, would you do it?'

'It wouldn't be a very practical proposition, Mrs May,' said Dr Holly, his shrewd eyes crinkling with artificial mirth. 'We have to respect the laws of physics. Such a creature wouldn't jump – it would be top heavy. And it wouldn't look very nice.'

'I was not talking about practicalities, Dr Holly, nor aesthetics.'

'You mean the ethical considerations? Rest assured we would not. We are not in the business, Mrs May, of creating monstrosities, but of removing disease and, in the fullness of time, and with all possible ethical and legal safeguards, mental illness – a tricky area, mind you, because what is defined as mental illness differs, as we know, from society to society, culture to culture: what seems insane to one nation is mere dissent in another – but no doubt we'll come to terms with it. And eventually we will have to tackle the genetic basis of behavioural problems, and that too will be ethically and politically tricky. But nowhere does anyone wish to create monstrosities, Mrs May. Do I look like a mad scientist to you? No, of course not! Don't you go believing what you read in the gutter press.'

Dr Holly smiled benignly. Joanna May did not smile back.

'But you *could* do it.'

'Of course.'

'And no one would do it just for money, say.'

'Good lord, no.' Dr Holly looked quite shocked.

'People do all kinds of things for money,' remarked Joanna May, 'they make instruments of torture and poison gas, for example. Why not me with frog's legs, for money: or worse, just for fun, to see just how far I jumped, or couldn't jump? Fun is a great incentive. There's always a shortage of it.'

'Mrs May,' said Dr Holly, 'this is very interesting, but I'm a busy man. Can I help you in any way?'

'I just wanted to know what kind of person I was dealing with,' said Joanna May. 'What kind of person you'd turned into since, under cover of performing an illegal abortion thirty years ago, you stole what was rightfully mine, one of my eggs, you and my husband between you. A lot can happen in thirty years. I have come for the names and addresses of the women in whose wombs you implanted my babies.'

Dr Holly was silent for a second or so.

'I think "my babies" is an unfortunate misnomer, Mrs May. I don't think ownership comes into it. Does a woman's egg, once fertilized, belong to her, or to the next generation?'

195

'Mine wasn't fertilized,' said Joanna May, 'that was the point. It was jiggled into life. So, yes, I reckon it was mine.'

'I should point out,' said Dr Holly, 'that there was no question of illegality, since as I remember there was no actual pregnancy. But these are interesting points; for lawyers to decide, not us. And, as I say, I am no longer personally engaged in genetic engineering. It's a young man's field, these days.'

He felt discouraged and resolved that he would stay with the study of brain cells. They at least would not turn up years later to pester and reproach him.

'The files,' said Joanna May. Mavis waited in the car outside, to make sure she persisted. 'Or has my husband been to see you already? Is that it?'

'Your husband?' Dr Holly seemed surprised. 'I haven't seen him for a couple of years, since he had this idea about cloning a mummy.'

'Cloning a mummy? An Egyptian mummy?'

'The idea was, if we could get enough tissue with at least some segments of DNA intact, we could shuffle it together, insert what we had into a growing egg cell, and the resulting child would have the same genetic make-up as an ancient Egyptian. What a lot we'd learn! Of course, the child's privacy would have to be respected. Just because someone dates from the past doesn't mean they don't have present rights.'

'How far did you get?' asked Joanna May. If Dr Holly was playing for time, she had enough of that and more to spare. This was the advantage of being useless. He was a busy man, she was not a busy woman.

'Well,' said Dr Holly, 'not very far, as it happened. Dead's dead, so far as I'm concerned, and in nature this turns out to be pretty much the case, though your husband finds it difficult to accept. On the whole such scraps of DNA as we managed to retrieve weren't sufficient for our purposes. We had such a deal of patching and joining to do, whatever we grew might well have had the odd toenail missing. Of course these days we can dehydrate the cell before freezing; every year brings new developments, and indeed, more promising ancient bodies to light. We reckon, eventually, to find a few gut cells inadvertently dehydrated. There's one fungus which will do it – before death –

196

which would help a lot. Your husband doesn't give in easily, does he?'

'No,' said Joanna.

'Unhappy childhood; to the point of trauma. Your husband represents the victory of nurture over nature: he is a great encouragement to us all. A source of inspiration. Interesting to reproduce him, wouldn't it be, and rear him in more benign circumstances, see just how it turned out.'

'It must have been fun,' said Joanna May, 'to clone me and see how that turned out.'

'Our major concern at the time,' said Dr Holly benignly, 'was in the successful implanting of fertilized eggs in stranger wombs, and testing the efficacy of certain immuno-suppressive drugs, rather than in personality studies, or making any contribution to the nurture-nature debate.'

'The records, Dr Holly.'

'I must say here and now, Mrs May, I would be happier if the request for information came from the child, rather than the natural parent.'

'I am not a parent, I am a twin.'

'You could look at it like that,' said Dr Holly. 'These personal and ethical ramifications do keep emerging – one hardly thought about them at the time. But, as I say, in ordinary adoption cases, the natural mother and child are brought together by the relevant agency only at the request of the child. The mother gave up certain rights, knowingly and willingly, when she gave up the child to adoption.'

'I neither knowingly nor willingly consented to anything at all,' said Joanna May, 'wriggle as you want, and I want those records now or I'll blow the whole disgraceful thing wide open.' She felt the pressure of Mavis waiting, filling the car with cigarette smoke, thicker and thicker as the minutes passed. She felt the dependence of the Queens of Wands, Pentacles, Swords and Cups: her sisters, her children, her family. They needed her.

'There is nothing to blow open,' said Dr Holly. 'Nothing that was not approved by the district medical ethics council at the time.' But he allowed her access to his records just the same.

40

I, Joanna May; not so young as I was, not so strong as I was, but braver: finding courage. My bed is empty again, but I dream it is filled, with lovers real and unreal, lovers I remember and men I never knew I wanted. I wake to find Joanna May sleeps alone, to face a day now peopled with the ghosts of the past: they throng around me, reminding me, instructing me. This, they say, relates to that. How simple! Why did you never see it before? But still the nights are stronger than the days. When the days triumph, I will act.

How the feelings of childhood haunt us. We think we forget, but we don't. Those initial pains grow stronger with the years: instead of fading, as one might expect, they merely afflict the present more and more. One image now torments me. I remember standing on the wide polished staircase in the big house in Harley Street. A scarlet carpet runner ran down the centre of the stairs. The pattern was both boring and complicated. I must have been very small. The front door bell rang and the receptionist walked through the hall. She wore a white coat, and was not friendly to me, or anyone. She opened the door to the patient. On the step stood an old woman. She had on a black coat with a fur collar and brought with her an air of what I can now see was genteel despair mingled with anxiety: the sense of a life misspent, of opportunities missed, of knights in white armour who never came, of husbands, children who were never grateful. So many of the patients were defeated women. Women, I perceived at that moment, were by their very nature supplicants. The outside world knocked on our front door and yielded up its goodies, and its goodies were nothing but female desolation, decay and disappointment. My father's voice sounded from behind closed doors in one direction: my mother's from another. My mama played bridge, and I was not supposed to disturb her. I ate in the kitchen, with the receptionist: rationing was in force. There was a war on. Food was simple and boring: so was conversation. My mother and I were not evacuated from London: she said we must defy Mr Hitler but I thought it was because she did not want to miss her bridge. My father said the same about Hitler and I thought that was because he did not want to miss his patients. Even fear was a deceit. Sometimes bombs fell and the outside world trembled and crashed and the door knocker banged of its own volition, but the house didn't fall down, which was what I wanted to happen.

I remember standing on the stair as my father's patient was let into the house, and voices sounded, muffled by closed doors, and I knew I was cut off from the real world; that I was alone: that other people would never quite touch me, or me them: that I was only acting this child upon the stair: there was no real and undeceitful me: therefore the voices that came would always be muffled. The prescience was true: children fall into uncontrollable grief when they realize, small as they are, certain truths about the world, and about themselves. 'I just feel like crying,' the small child will explain. Don't believe it. The future is seen: the grief is real and profound.

Only Carl could I hear loud and clear; his voice came through to me not muted, but somehow at first hand. I didn't like what he said or did: that didn't matter, it wasn't the point. When I met him I thought he was rude and plain and rather short, but his edges were somehow defined; quivery, like a real person superimposed against a fake background in an old film. And that was that. I don't suppose it was love I felt; I think I just recognized an opportunity for being healed, for becoming real, breaking through the shrouding veils and mists, and that for me was all, at the time, I needed. I somehow knew what Carl knew, though I had come to the knowledge in a different way than he. Carl had suffered cruelty and hardship and I had not. Carl's early world had been small, black, wretched, terrified, until suddenly the clouds had parted and revealed a new bright world, full of privilege, animation, possibility: and with the last drop of strength he had leapt out of the one world into the other. And myself, female, given everything yet nothing, in my grey, muffled, lonely world, bred to serve, to be a supplicant, knew a different kind of cruelty, but the same kind of terror – the inevitability of illness, age, death: the impotence of love. When I lifted my eyes to Carl's I thought how peculiar, how bright and naked they are – and then realized that was how eyes ought to be. It was other people's which were out of order, clouded by wishful thinking and self-deception. There were just the two of us, in all the world, who knew what the truth was, and how terrible it is. 'You have my kind of eyes,' he said.

It took little to persuade me that I didn't want children. How had it happened to me that I knew what Carl knew? The thought frightened me. How could you protect your own children from that one dreadful moment on the stair, the prescience of defeat and death? You could feed your children, love them, nurture them, act the good mother, do all you could to be close to them, and still it might happen. On that one occasion when I thought I was pregnant I was afraid. When I had what at the time I thought was a termination I was relieved, as well as angry. Let me not deny it.

When Isaac said of the card 'Death' that it meant rebirth too, I took leave to doubt it. But then Isaac's eyes did not have the naked brightness of Carl's. I liked Isaac because he talked to me. Even good wives get bored. What are stay-at-home wives, executive wives, determinedly childless, supposed to do, even if, like me, they are wives of captains of industry not the mere foot soldiers? It is all performance in the real executive estate. She must be like the others, or he will know the reason why, and so will they. She must act, in the first few years, as if she waited for a child: she must hold the babies of other women, and sigh with longing, although the little wriggling thing appals and upsets her. Is this the sum of woman then – to be the instrument of reproduction, a walking womb; the pulsing, gurgling, bloody redness inside the whole point of her being? Never, but let her dissemble! Later she must act out the emptiness of not having children; lament her inability to conceive: it is expected of her:

though she glories in the leisure of her mornings, the flatness of her belly, her peace of mind in a world where the lot of women appears to be worry, grief, toil and anxiety, as their children, their hostages to fortune, sap their cheerfulness, will and energy. Only later, when it's too late to change her mind, when the cyclical messiness has stopped, does a kind of truthful desolation set in, as the world around her empties; and she understands that of her own volition she has become one of nature's dead ends: an experiment set aside, because it didn't work. Then she may well blame whoever's around (as I do Carl), whoever, however unreasonably, she holds responsible for her initial decision, the tying of the knot that severs her from the future. She curses fate, instead of herself. Her executive husband has not got quite where he wanted, what he wanted: whoever does? She has seen him through an affair or so: smiled bravely and grimly through this or the other dinner party, when his mistress picked at her avocado and crab salad; worried through his threatened heart attack, put up with the bad temper and depression of his mid-life crisis; and at last she says what about me, me? Where is this promised life, this happiness, this fulfilment? It must be somewhere!

Perhaps, she says, she could be of service to the community. But how? She has learned something about the world, for all the comfort and security of her life: enough to know there's nothing she could tell the poor and oppressed that they didn't know already. That what the poor want is not advice but money. She knows above all the value of money: how it keeps people quiet and good. Put a hundred thousand pounds in the hands of a child abuser and he'd stop abusing. She can't even give all she has to the needy, because she has nothing of her own to give. It is his. The outside world knocks upon her door: she goes to open it, softly on deep carpets, and outside in the storm, begging for shelter, stands a crone, a beggar woman, and it is her future self. She slams the door, she closes her ears: calls up her bridge partner. If it's not too late, if she's kept her looks – and why shouldn't she? – she 'takes' a lover. Well, one just happens to come along, even if she's married to Carl May. Forget takes. A woman gets taken.

I, Joanna May! See how easily it comes to me to turn from 'I' to 'she' – joining my lot with other women, universalizing an experience, as if the better to justify myself. As if I, a woman who never gave birth but has four daughters, an only child with four sisters, could ever be quite like anyone else. Perhaps what Dr Holly took away from me at the Bulstrode Clinic was not so much my identity, as my universality. He made me particular, different from other women: he turned me into someone of scientific interest. Worse, he stole my soul, the thing that threads me through and back to the human race, and never mind that in my heart I'd tied a knot in it, it wasn't too late at thirty to change my mind, give it a sharp tug, untie it, take my chances along with everyone else, not let the moment on the stair last a whole life, but send my children and my children's children on down through the centuries, mingling and mixing with the others, sharing and partaking, into the future. I think when they took that part of me, the singular me, away, and interfered, they stopped me in my tracks. It isn't reasonable to think so, but when Dr Holly says to me, 'You haven't changed,' I think he's right, and I think it's his fault I haven't changed. He has stolen thirty years of life from me. And now it's too late. For me, but not for them. I have my four more chances, and that's how I must see it.

How had it been for the Queens of Wands, Pentacles, Swords and Cups? If Dr Holly was not interested, I was. I would ask them. I wondered if they lived their lives, or acted them. I wondered if they had their equivalent for the moment on the stairs, and if they had overcome it, as I, their master copy, had not. I felt what it was to be Dr Holly, to want to *find out*: I felt the pleasure of it. I felt what it was to be Carl, and want to change the world: I felt the power of it. But most of all, I wanted to see what I would be, born into a newer, more understanding world: one which allowed women choice, freedom and success. Perhaps I had merely been born thirty years too early and that was the only trouble. The young Queens of Wands, Pentacles, Swords and Cups: myself the ageing Empress: not devastating, frightening, shocking any more – just how very *interesting* to see how it all turned out. What fun it would be – that rare commodity.

It was with pleasure, animation and excitement that I waited impatiently for Mavis to come to me with the names and whereabouts of my sisters, my daughters, my twins, myself.

41

Angela called Joanna May.

'Darling, how are you?' asked Angela. 'I wondered if you had any clues as to your ex-husband's current mental health.'

'One or two,' said Joanna. 'Why?'

'Well,' said Angela, 'Gerald is getting quite alarmed. I tell him there's no need. I tell him that for a man to wipe out his wife's lovers may not be legal, or nice, but it doesn't mean he's insane.'

'Angela, I know you're only joking but I think this telephone may be tapped.'

'Ah. Well, listeners hear no good of themselves. My husband says your husband wants him to employ the entire staff of the Divination Department over this fallout business.'

'Then perhaps he should, Angela. I'm very fond of Gerald.'

'But then everyone will think *my* husband is insane.'

'He will at least be around to refute the view, Angela.'

'I see. You mean, on the whole, it's best to do what Carl May wants.'

'For the moment,' said Joanna May, 'yes.'

'In that case,' said Angela, 'Gerald is right. Gerald says it's quite alarming that this man should be in charge of such large sections of the nation's wealth and property.'

'These large companies more or less run themselves,' said Joanna. 'The man at the very top is so often a figurehead. Part of Carl's trouble is that he gets bored.'

'Gerald thinks something should be done about it.'

'Listeners may hear no good about themselves,' said Joanna, 'but they sometimes hear very useful things. Shall we meet and talk you know where?'

'Where's that?'

'Where I saw and admired Gerald's nice soft feet,' said Joanna.

'Ah, so that's what you were looking at,' said Angela. 'He thought it was his varicose veins. You sound much better.'

'Oh yes,' said Joanna, 'I'm better. I'm sorry about going on so the other day.'

'That's OK,' said Angela, of the hairy chin and thick legs, and the waist as broad as her hips, salt of a world fresh sown with salt. 'That's OK.'

42

'I'll be waiting at the corner
  Of the bottom of the street,
  In case a certain little lady goes by.
  Oh me, oh my,
  In case a certain little lady goes by'

sang Carl May. 'I wish I'd learned the ukelele,' he said, 'but in
the circles in which I moved when a child it wasn't done!'

He and Bethany were in the May Gallery. The morning sun
shone in the east window and made the place almost cheerful.
Workmen – they wore glasses and were elderly – gently inched
in from outside a large earthenware vat dating from the sixteenth
dynasty, the great days of Egypt. The hieroglyphics were worn:
it seemed to the untrained eye a rough-hewn if workmanlike
artefact.

'Why's it so special?' asked Bethany. She wondered how many
questions she'd asked in the last few weeks, in order to make
Carl feel good by supplying her with answers. She wondered
how she was going to get out of this. She wondered if Hughie
Scotland could help. She was frightened of Carl May, who
seemed to get happier and jollier with every day that passed.
She didn't even correct him, saying, 'I'm leaning on a lamp post
on the corner of the street,' and just as well, as it happened.

'This jar contains the dust of ancient liver,' said Carl May.
'Liver cells are rich in DNA. The ancient Egyptians mummified
their dead to keep them in good shape for their journey to the
next world. Nothing died unless you wanted it to in that fair
land, under the wide Mesopotamian sky: everything went on
for ever: so there was nothing to fear. The God Osiris died only
as the sun set: he rose again. The priestess aroused the God and

gave birth to the King and all was well in the world of men. And because there was no fear of death, no terror, simply a passing on, agreeable or disagreeable as it might be, all men were good, and all women too, and kind. Sometimes a bit stupid, of course. But they didn't shut their children up in kennels, or beat them, or torture them, or rape them, to express their disapproval of life, because life simply *was*, infinitely variable, infinitely long-lasting, and there was happiness upon earth. And the secret of it all lies there in the dust of all those livers, which are so very rich in DNA.'

'How do you know it's people's livers? Couldn't it just be dust?'

'Imperial Caesar, dead and turned to clay,' said Carl May, 'could stop a hole to keep the dust away. Dear little Bethany, we know it's liver because the hieroglyphics say so. Embalmers sucked the brains of the dead out through the nostrils, and the entrails out through I've forgotten where, including the liver, and saved them all in case of need in great big separate labelled jars like this one. This is a liver jar.'

Bethany felt quite dizzy and blackness made clouds around her. She'd never fainted in all her life, not even when her father had suggested she made a one-armed man happier than he ever had been in his life before – a service the complete in body must always surely be happy to render the incomplete – and she'd seen her father's choice for her had a hook instead of a hand, and she was only fourteen, but she thought she might faint now.

'I knew this existed,' said Carl May. 'That moony fellow Isaac King tried to say it didn't, but I knew he was lying. They had it at Liverpool University all the time. The pool of livers! I think we must get old Holly over and show him what we've found. Would you like that?'

Bethany hadn't liked the way Dr Holly had looked at her. She didn't much like the way anyone looked at her. At first she had thought the looks were admiration and envy; but now everyone seemed to think she was somehow cheating. She didn't know what she was supposed to have done. Carl May was being good to her. She was being good to him. Yet somehow she seemed to have stepped out of line. At home, there had never been this particular feeling of *unrightness*. Things at home were sometimes sleazy and sordid; here they never were: servants cleaned the bath and changed sheets: cats never passed worms on the table: but luxury seemed to make things worse, not better. Nothing was real. Perhaps she was just homesick.

'I liked Dr Holly very much,' said Bethany. 'It would be good to see him.'

And Carl May wondered, now what is the matter with this fragrant girl, this Scotland hand-on, this product of the outer suburbs, this despoiler of my celibacy, this firm-fleshed luxury, this stirrer to pleasure, this brightness which flickers on and off like the sun behind a yew tree on a windy day, this little liar — what is the matter with her? I know what it is, she has a lover. She can't be bothered to turn the brightness on for me. She's thinking of him and anything will do for me.

'Is something the matter, Bethany?'

'It was the thought of all those livers mixed up, that's all; it made me feel quite faint.'

'I hope they're not too mixed up, Bethany, or we'll have a hard task in front of us. I hope they're still nicely layered so we can tell one individual from the next. Are you sure that's all that the matter is?'

'Well, Uncle Carl . . .'

'Don't call me uncle, Bethany.'

'Sorry. It's what I used to call my father's friends, back home. And talking about my dad, I had a phone call from him yesterday. He's not too well.'

Then he knew she was lying. She'd had no such phone call. Every morning at Britnuc Carl May was handed a private pink folder, in which were reported the substance of all phone calls made and received at Eton Square, the King's House, the Coustain residence, and many another household besides, not to mention industrial firms and government departments. Knowledge is power, as Carl May had been told at school: '*Scientas est potentas*'. Carl May the sceptical, Carl May the shrewd, looking up the original text, found '*scientas est potestas*' instead. Knowing is to be empowered. More like it. But, understanding

208

why the misprint was preferred, he told no one; just hugged the empowering truth to himself. Truth was power. Truth was so disagreeable you could, if you had the stomach for it, keep it pretty much to yourself. Joanna his wife was one of the very few who understood these things; in her bones, in her blood, for no good reason: in her genes: Joanna May, Carl May's ex-wife, to whom he had trusted his being; here in this very room: this place, no longer young, no longer his, no good to him; but empowering him, proving yet again the world was what he knew it was, the empire of despair, beneath the little tent of blue that men call sky.

'She must die, or she'll go on to ruin other men,' said Carl May aloud, or just about. The removal men from Carling Antique and Rarities Specialist Transport let slip the giant jar – they felt it had a life of its own, sometimes, but hoped they were wrong – only a couple of inches, but it made quite a bang on the cold marble floor. Carl May seemed not to notice. They breathed again. Carling Transport was a subsidiary of Garden Developments. They specialized also in the moving of rare trees and plants.

'I'm sorry, darling, I didn't quite catch that,' said Bethany.

'Just something from *Othello*, my dear.'

'Oh. We didn't do *Othello* in diction.'

'No,' said Carl May. 'I daresay it's not often done in girls' schools.'

'Can I go home to see my dad, since he's poorly?'

'*Beauty and the Beast*,' Carl May said. 'Of course you can, my dear. But be back by five thirty this evening. Such a pity you can't come with me to the lido. I rather thought of going there this afternoon.'

'The lido?'

'The Brent Cross Lido. A charming place, prettily landscaped; though I'm afraid the chlorine fumes don't do the shrubs and flowers much good. Joanna's favourite place, it seems.'

'You be careful, my darling,' said Bethany, 'don't be outdoors too long. They say the fallout's dreadful: worse than Windscale. And to be frank with you, I'm not a lido sort of person. Now the south of France . . .'

209

Oh yes, she had a lover. She laid her hand on his arm, a pretty hand, long-fingered, each finger slightly trembling, promising pleasure, but promiscuous.

'I'll be back this evening,' she said and, suddenly giddy and happy again, whirled round the musky gallery, yellow skirt flaring, white shirt gleaming, gold shoes glittering, murmuring fond farewells to the embalmed remains of Gods and kings, waving goodbye to the stolid wooden funereal peasants, even dropping a quick brave appalled kiss on the crown of the liver jar, and then back once again to Carl.

'I don't think you got the *Othello* quote quite right,' said Bethany. 'But a good try, Carl-O-Carl! We didn't do it at diction, but my dad did take me to the theatre a lot. He said there was no need not to be cultured, just because I was kind.'

'Four,' said Carl, but Bethany did not even notice. Bethany said, 'And I may be the Beauty but you are not the Beast. You are not even a fiend in human form, you are just a little boy in a right old state, you silly thing!' And he was about to say 'five' – he'd given her to five – but Bethany was gone, emerald eyes and all, in a flash of yellow white and gold, and in strolled Jacko, Petie, Elwood, Dougie and Haggie so he let her go. The lads claimed to be a pop group. Theirs, they maintained, was a new close-harmony rock sound. They called themselves Barbers of the Bath. Carl backed them with recording studios, equipment, venues, wheels, even though they took little advantage musically of what was offered. Some people will do anything for money, the better to maintain the illusion that they have some purpose in life; and this failing, this conceit, suited Carl very well.

43

Jane, Julie, Gina and Alice.

────•◦•────

Gina left Julie in charge of her three children and went to visit her mum.

'You have let yourself go,' said Annette, kindly. Her hair was tight permed and blonde and her black plastic belt broad and close around a dieted waist. Bilbo had gone, Annette said. She was now with Nigel, an ex-policeman, something of a racist, but only thirty-five. It was over a bit of trouble with Bilbo, in fact, that Nigel had had to resign the Force. Bilbo was in hospital, more of a cabbage, said Annette, than a man. He'd suffered brain damage. A tragedy. She and Nigel were going to move to the country and open a pub. Start afresh. Nigel had quite a few enemies, Annette said, not without pride. She'd be sorry to sell up their little flat: could Gina take the cat, she'd always liked cats, hadn't she? How were the kids? How many did Gina have? She'd forgotten. She smelt strongly of sherry; a warm sweet smell which reminded Gina of her childhood.

'It was never your flat,' said Gina, 'it was Bilbo's flat.'

'Well, Bilbo's a cabbage, and what good's a fortune to a cabbage, and that's what this place is worth, a fortune. We can buy two pubs and still have some over.'

'Can we talk about me, Mum?' asked Gina.

'Little Miss self, self, self,' said Annette. 'Some people never change.' She looked closely at Gina. 'I told you not to marry what's-his-name,' she said, 'but you wouldn't listen. You never used to have a bust like that!'

'His name is Cliff,' said Gina, 'and you were all for my

211

marrying him. In fact you talked me out of a termination just to get me married and this place to yourself.'

'It was always just right for two, never for three,' said Annette. She kept budgerigars now, and the living room, with its view over the market, was warm and musty with the smell of birds, and birdseed, and the air stirred with the soft brush of feathers. 'And you mustn't be bitter. I'm sure you don't regret that little baby now! Mothers never do.'

Annette offered Gina tea and biscuits and when Gina accepted a biscuit raised her eyebrows.

'Mum,' began Gina, and Annette said, 'I'm sure I'm not old enough to be your mum, Gina. If you ask me I look more like your younger sister than your mother. I certainly weigh a lot less.'

'Don't worry, Mum,' said Gina. 'I'll be gone before your Nigel gets home,' and after that Annette was a little kinder.

'Mum,' said Gina. 'I met a woman who's exactly like me in all sorts of ways and we went to a clinic to be tissue-typed and it turns out we're identical twins.'

'What a peculiar thing to want to do,' said Annette. 'I expect all kinds of people are twins and don't know it. They certainly don't go rushing off to clinics to find out. It's rather like squeezing your breasts to see if you've got lumps: better not start or you'll only find them. A hit and miss kind of thing, I imagine, tissue-typing, whatever it is when it's at home, but you know what these clinics are. They told a friend of mine she had cancer and they'd got the slides mixed. She got the radium treatment and the worry while the other one stayed home happy and died. They'll tell you anything that suits them, these doctors.'

'Mum,' said Gina, 'I'm going to sit here until you tell me.'

Annette's mouth clamped shut, to demonstrate that she did not respond well to threats, but opened again soon enough.

'Don't you try and blackmail me, young lady.'

'I'm not blaming you, Mum,' said Gina. 'I can see twins are a real handful and my dad had thrown you out and you were very young and you couldn't be expected to cope. But I want to know. I have a right to know: was I twins?'

'No such thing as rights,' said Annette, acutely. 'Just such a

212

thing as it would be nice if only, only it usually isn't. All I can say is the doctor never said anything about twins to me. Mind you, I was under anaesthetic at the time. Anything could have happened. Anything. A girlfriend of mine was raped under anaesthetic, but would anyone believe her? No.'

She had some more sherry. She drank it by the teacup full. As she filled and refilled Gina's cup – and she proffered little thin china cups with saucers, flowered and gold-rimmed – with tea, she filled and refilled her own with sherry.

Gina wondered what Nigel was after: cosiness, or daftness, or pneumatic sex, or budgerigars, or just the money for two pubs and some over, or to have what Bilbo had, poor Bilbo, or perhaps it was true love, who could tell?

'You aren't telling fibs, are you?' she asked presently, hoping against hope for maternal reassurance, comfort. 'You didn't adopt me, by any chance? I wasn't some other mother's cast off twin?' to which Annette replied, 'No such luck. Split me coming out, you did; God knows why I did any of it. I must have been mad. All that fuss and trouble and pain and you not even my own child, from what I could make out, though I never could make out much. They talked so fast, the pair of them, and one of them not even a doctor. It was the end of my marriage, not the beginning of it, contrary to all their fine promises. If they were wrong in that what else were they wrong in, that's what I want to know. A twin! They should have told me that. If it was a boy you might have grown up to marry him. You'd have had to be warned. To tell you the truth I was glad when you got pregnant – at least it showed you were normal. I always had a feeling you mightn't be. Like a mule, that's the one, isn't it, or do I mean a donkey, the one that's a cross between a horse and a something else? At any rate, it's sterile. That's what I thought you might be. Sterile. Unnatural. I thought you ought to have that poor little baby. It might be your only chance. And Cliff wasn't so bad. You have to forgive me, Gina. I did the best I could.'

Gina sighed, amazed that she had once taken this woman so seriously, longed to please her, hoped to impress her, and with

213

the worldly competence that enveloped her like some cloud of embracing, protective mist the minute she was out of the children's company, soon had the details of her birth, and an old appointment card for Annette to see Dr Holly at the Bulstrode Clinic.

'I know you think I haven't a heart, dear,' said Annette, 'and sometimes I think you're right, but I kept that card as a memento. Time and time again, when the occasion arose to throw it out, I refrained. I knew it would come in handy. I've always done right by you. Didn't I come and rescue you from Granny and Gramps that time? Say what you like, when you needed me I was there.'

'Yes, Mum,' said Gina, 'you certainly were!' and was off to the Bulstrode Clinic by the next available Underground train. She went to Acton Central and took a bus down Acton Lane and found the Bulstrode Clinic. But it was now a lending library. A white car stood outside, all white, startlingly white. She noticed it. There were a lot of them about, these days. They must, she thought, be very hard to keep clean. Only very particular people would own them.

The librarian was of the old school, motherly, dustily dressed; she stood at the noticeboards and pinned up leaflets on rate support, rent rebate, family allowances and Citizens Advice.

'What do you want?' she said. 'We're about to close.'

'I want to know where the Bulstrode Clinic is,' Gina said. 'Where it went, if anywhere. Where Dr Holly can be found.'

'I've told you once,' said Mrs Avril Love, sublibrarian, for so her badge proclaimed her.

'No you didn't,' said Gina. 'I only just came in.'

Mrs Love looked at Gina more closely.

'I'm so sorry,' she said. 'I thought you were someone else. My eyesight is going, and then what use am I going to be to anyone? Mind you, all you young things look alike to me.'

She shut the library door, switched off the library computer; she offered Gina a cup of tea. She wanted company. She was in no hurry to get home: the later she got home the more likely someone else was to make the tea. Gina was the third young woman in a week to ask about the Bulstrode, after years and years of nothing. What was going on? Something finally come home to roost, the way things did? Birth would out, like murder. Funny things had happened up the Bulstrode, she'd always said so. They'd been fiddling around with women's eggs all that time ago, doing God knows what, the field even less regulated then than it was today. More people walking round who came out of a test-tube than anyone realized, said Mrs Love. She served tea in wholesome mugs, with biscuits. In the end the past caught up with you, said Mrs Love. No use running. She'd had an abortion there herself: she often wondered what they did with the poor dead foetus – and if it was dead. How could a woman know? They knocked you unconscious and did what they wanted: you couldn't object; what you were doing was wrong, illegal. She was sorry to have to speak like this, it sounded unhinged, but she'd never recovered from the experience, for all it was thirty-five years ago. She'd never married: the Mrs was a courtesy title. If Miss was on the library badge, the young mocked her and the old patronized. Ms didn't ring true, not for her. She never had more children: that had been her only chance, she'd blown it. Odd though, that she'd come to work in the very building where it had happened. Sometimes she thought life was just a pattern of spoiled expectations which you weren't allowed to forget. Was Gina a Catholic?

'No,' said Gina. Mrs Love said she nearly was. She'd taken a diet pill. It made her talkative. She was sorry. How old was Gina? Thirty? No. Too young to be her child grown-up. Because Mrs Love always had this notion that at the Bulstrode they'd take your baby away and just implant it in someone else's womb, like moving a fish from one tank to another. She hadn't killed her baby – somewhere it lived. Did Gina think that was possible?

Gina said she really didn't know. She thought it was more complicated, more difficult than that. She had begun to feel very tired. First her mother, then this.

'And to think,' said Mrs Love, 'I lost my baby here – well, gave it away, what kind of mother is that, to give her child away, hand it over to death, and now you lot come along, three of you, and say you were born here, and there's nothing here but books, books. Doesn't it make you feel funny? It did the

215

other ones who were in here asking. They were twins if you ask me, though they said they weren't.'

'Yes, it does,' said Gina, 'it makes me feel really very funny,' and went home feeling hunted and haunted, and told Julie she thought there might be more than just the two of them, and that she wasn't going to see Dr Holly on her own – Julie would have to come with her.

'In the meantime,' said Gina to Julie, 'it looks as if my mother's the one who had us. Yours just bought you in.'

———∘∘———

But Julie was in the honeymoon stage with the children: there were fish fingers and wet towels everywhere and she didn't mind one bit. She'd bought a tropical fish tank and set it up and called the vet to ask his advice, and he'd said he'd come round to see if it was fit for fish and she'd said OK but only to see the fish and he'd said of course and both knew different. She told everyone Gina was her sister. Her sister and her children had come to stay. Now when the neighbours talked about the price of children's shoes, so could she. Cliff called round, of course he did, and Julie wouldn't let him see Gina; Julie was cold and reasonable and said a cooling-off time was required, that was all, and he agreed but both knew differently. Cliff was intimidated by the cleanliness, the orderliness, the ordinariness of the house, the net curtains, the glimpse of parquet and framed prints when the front door was opened: this was how people were supposed to live, he could only imagine. He'd never somehow achieved it himself, or rather Gina had failed to achieve it for him. Weeds grew round his and Gina's door. What could he say, what could he offer? Cliff did not want to be a bad husband, he said so: it distressed him to be one: he was just too young to be a father of three: the wrong person to be Gina's husband, or else she was the wrong person to be his wife. 'Quite so,' said Julie, crisply, closing the door. 'Come back on Wednesday week and we'll see how things are. Who's right for who, if anyone.' He'd banged once or twice upon the door to prove a point and then left, apparently satisfied. No one had asked him for money.

216

'The more of us the better,' said Julie. 'There could be a hundred of us and I'd be glad.' As Gina had got thinner, she'd got plumper. They could wear each other's clothes.

When Alec rang from the airport she said, 'Look, why bother to come home? It's a long way. You'd rather be in an hotel.'

He said, 'There isn't an overnight laundry service.' After a short pause he said, rather pathetically, 'I'm sorry, Julie. I hadn't realized things had got so bad. I don't know what this is all about.'

She said, 'I do. If there aren't any children, there isn't any point.'

He said, over the noise of the airport, 'If only you *did* something: had a job. It's like coming home to a stage set. You hardly seem to exist.'

She said, 'But you didn't want me to work, you wouldn't let me. You wanted me there when you came home: you wanted proper home-cooked meals, you said you had enough plastic hotel food, airline food.'

He said, 'Did I say that? I can't remember.'

She said, 'I can hardly hear you. Why don't you check in at the Sheraton or the Holiday Inn —'

'— the Hilton,' he said.

'— and call me from there.'

'OK,' he said and he hung up, but he didn't call back.

'There could be a thousand of us and it'd be OK,' said Julie. 'The thing is, I'm not my mother's daughter. I thought I had to be like her, but I don't. I'm free to be me. Now everything can change.'

'You've still got to share,' said Gina. 'You got rid of her but now you've got me. You can still see your limits, your outline. And instead of your mother, you now have to put up with mine.'

'But it doesn't defeat me,' said Julie. 'How can I explain it to you? I don't know your mother, and since she didn't bring me up she doesn't count as my mother, and she's nowhere near as boring as the one who did. Boring, boring, boring. I thought I had to be boring, and I don't.' She danced about the house, elated.

Sue was wetting the bed; Julie didn't like that at all: it was smelly. She wanted to make Sue wash the sheets, but Gina said no, that made things worse. The children were upset. They'd lost their father. They were grieving.

'It can't be true,' said Julie. How could they miss a man like that!

'They were born loving him,' said Gina. 'And it's not so long since they were born.'

'There's such a thing as contraception,' said Julie. Women without children are smarter, tougher and more decisive than women who have children. Women with children are torn in so many directions they become kind, nice and hopeless in their own interests in the effort to understand themselves, let alone their children. Gina tried to be like Julie, and Julie like Gina.

The two grey cats slept next to each other on one or other of the children's beds, and Julie thought they ought to be in the kitchen.

'No,' said Gina, 'they need all the comfort they can get. Everyone does.' She missed Cliff; of course she did. Perhaps he'd change. If she went back now it might be different.

'No, it won't,' said Julie. 'You're just addicted, that's all. You've got pain and pleasure mixed.'

Little Anthony turned up the thermostat on the fish tank and one of the angelfish died. Julie slapped: the vet wouldn't like it one bit.

'Don't do that,' said Gina.

'What those children need is discipline,' said Julie.

'Don't you use that word to me,' said Gina. 'It was Cliff's favourite word. When are we going to see Dr Holly? We can't keep putting it off. It's getting on our nerves.'

And Ben said, 'Look Mum, look Auntie Julie, there's a man working on the gas main outside and there isn't gas down this street, only electricity.'

Ben had just started at a new school. They were hopeless at football which meant he was the best and to be the best player

218

in a losing team is easier than being the worst player in a winning one.

Ben said, 'He has a notebook and he writes things in it.'

Julie said, 'By the pricking of my thumbs, Something evil this way comes. There's more going on than meets the eye. We'll go to Dr Holly tomorrow. Ben, you'll have to stay off school and look after the little ones.'

'Oh, sh—' Ben began to say, and then, out of deference to his twin Aunt Julie, whom he had begun to quite like – he admired her toughness – 'Oh botheration. I don't want to miss too much school. I want to be a doctor. Or perhaps a vet.' He would be quite happy here if it wasn't for Sue, who kept getting on his nerves, so he'd start hitting her. He didn't want to, but he was sure she wet the bed on purpose, just to put everyone to trouble.

44

Jane, Julie, Gina and Alice.

———— ∘•∘ ————

Jane went home and announced: 'I've lost my job and I've lost my boyfriend and it looks as if I'm going to lose my home. That's the good news. The bad news is I've found a twin. Which means, Madge, either I'm adopted or you had twins and gave one away. I need to know which.'

They were having Friday supper. Jeremy had met Jane off the train, and been late. She'd had to stand about waiting for him in the outfall from Chernobyl for a full twenty minutes. The waiting room had been too full of cigarette smokers to afford acceptable shelter. When her father did arrive, she scarcely recognized him. She was used to a tall, albeit gangling, man. This one seemed shrivelled and shrunk, old. She didn't like it at all. She liked it even less when he said, 'I'm sorry I'm late. We have little Tobias staying. Not so little, of course. He's thirteen.'

'Who in God's name is Tobias?'

'Laura's little boy,' said Jeremy. 'He's over from Toronto to stay with us. I'm sorry, he's in your old room. We didn't know you'd be visiting. You so seldom do.'

'What a Godawful name,' said Jane. 'Tobias!' She had learned the power of bad temper from Alice, and the value of non-smiling. She practised them assiduously.

'He always was called Tobias,' said her father serenely, 'but you weren't listening.'

'I was too busy trying to pass my exams,' said Jane. 'Well, it's a wise child knows its own father.'

But her father did not rise to the bait. She found Madge shuffling round the kitchen, wearing slippers. Madge had a bunion, Madge said. The glass in her pebble lenses was thicker than ever, but not so thick that Jane couldn't see love for Tobias shining out from behind them. How could she! Madge's eyes had always shone with emotions that shouldn't be there: good emotion, noble emotion, masochism triumphant. They streamed out from her in a bright trail of kindly confusion. Now Madge loved Tobias, her rival's child, because he was there, because he was her husband's, because she should. How could she be like this and still teach grown people? Didn't she understand the value of the negative emotions? Have I, Jane, ever understood them, come to that? Would she ever let me? It was my mother made me what I am, and what I am is what I'm not. So thought Jane, as she looked for forks clean enough to lay the table with.

It was the better to annoy and upset, no doubt, that Jane kept her announcement until Jeremy, Madge, Tobias and herself were sitting round the table eating shepherd's pie – a typical English dish, Jane explained to Tobias, who was a beastly clear-skinned, thick-skinned Canadian lad, very plain, with his father's short-sighted eyes (no doubt there, alas). By a typical English dish, Jane implied, though did not say, she meant improperly cooked, fatty, stringy, English mince, hopelessly old-fashioned, unhealthy, and awful: even Canada could do better: sometimes Jane felt Madge did it on purpose to persecute Jeremy. After the mince she went on to her parentage.

'Well,' said Madge, 'I'm glad you've raised the matter but I hardly think this is the time.'

'Why not?' asked Jane.

'We don't want to upset the child,' said Madge.

'Either he's my brother or he's not,' said Jane. 'And he doesn't look like it to me. My belief is I'm adopted. Do I look like either of you two? No I do not.'

'You're upset,' observed Jeremy. 'You'll get indigestion.'

'If I'm upset it's Madge's cooking,' said Jane. 'Tough old shepherds, these, Tobias Tough and greasy. A great mistake to cook them, if you ask me.' Her parents were shocked into silence.

Jane felt terrible and began to cry. There was a kind of noise in her ears, as of breaking glass.

'Dear, dear, dear,' said Madge, 'it's as if she was six again.'

'She was like this at fifteen,' said Jeremy.

'But worse at six,' said Madge. And Jane had always had a vision of herself as a placid, easy, perfectly well-behaved child!

Madge made Jane go to bed in the spare room with a hot water bottle and sat on the edge of the bed, spare leg flesh swelling over the tops of her slippers, wispy hair awry – shouldn't she have hormone treatment, thought Jane, but she wouldn't, would she: she'd say she didn't want to interfere with nature; what she herself would have said, as little as a week ago, come to think of it. Since she'd met Alice she'd become a great deal less pious, but also a great deal more critical and, she began to see, really rather nasty. Alice had lent her a photographer for a bed companion and she'd found him so boring she'd asked him to go and buy a bottle of wine and then locked the door and pretended to be out when he came charging up the stairs again. She enjoyed that far more than she would the night in bed with him.

Madge said, 'Well, dear, to tell you the truth you're not quite adopted: I most certainly gave birth to you: your father isn't Jeremy: you weren't quite a test-tube baby: it wasn't quite artificial insemination by donor . . .'

'Stop it, stop it,' shrieked Jane. 'This is disgusting.'

'I don't think it's nearly as disgusting as sex,' said Madge.

'You always told me sex was wonderful,' said Jane.

'A child should think that,' said Madge. 'Just because it never went right for me didn't mean it would be the same for you.'

Jane opened and shut her mouth like a goldfish in a bowl hoping for sustenance, reassurance, information, nourishment, anything.

'So I must tell you that although Jeremy isn't technically your father – I was told he was a Harley Street surgeon – he really is your father in essence. What was it Brecht said in *Mother Courage*? "The child belongs to the one who looks after it."'

'Brecht is a man,' said Jane.

'I don't see what that's got to do with it,' said Madge, a little peevishly, Jane thought, in the circumstances. Surely she, Jane, was central to this drama. All the emotions should be hers.

'You mean you've never had sex with my father?' said Jane.

'No,' said Madge, 'and he isn't your father. It's all a long time ago and I think the best thing to do is go and see the Dr Holly who helped us to achieve you. He made a very good impression. I imagine that what's happened is that you and this other young woman share the same father. They may have used the same semen more than once.'

'Taken semen from the same batch, you mean,' said Jane.

'Well of course,' said Madge.

Jane was sick in the washhandbasin: she could not even get into the bathroom; Tobias was having a bath. The rest of the weekend went well enough. She got used to her father looking so old and her mother looking so soppy. She thought perhaps Brecht was right. These were the ones who had looked after her: these were her parents. She felt quite pleased, however, not to have to repress those qualities in herself she had always disliked in her father – the apathy, the sitting about, the slow movements, the grunts as his mind worked, as if some infinitely complicated inner machinery ground incessantly on. She could take of him what she wanted, and simply leave the rest. And the same went for her mother. She need take only what she fancied. She had been so amply served with a helping, she could well afford to be fussy.

She even took down Tobias's address in Canada and promised to write to him. But she didn't ask after his mother. She wouldn't go that far.

45

Jane, Julie, Gina and Alice.

———◦•◦———

At 10.30 a.m. on the third Tuesday in May, Jane and Alice sat in Dr Holly's outer office, by appointment, and waited for Dr Holly to return from, or so his secretary said, an important meeting. They sat as far from one another as they could. Just because they were sisters or half-sisters, they did not see why they should like one another, let alone resemble one another: in fact, the more they thought about it, the less they felt they did either. For the occasion Jane wore a tweed skirt and jacket; Alice wore jeans and a pink sweatshirt. Jane's hair was now cut remarkably short; Alice's was pulled back from her yet higher forehead by a sweatband but cascaded down her back. They came in separate cars. When Dr Holly's secretary Sarah said, 'Identical twins?' and neither replied, she said, 'You both turn your heads at the same time at the same angle. It's quite funny really.'

She went back to her word processor and Jane tapped with her fingers on the side of the chair until she noticed Alice was doing the same, so she stopped.

'Have you come in for the study?' asked Sarah. 'Is that what you want to see him about? Because they're not starting till next month. He is very busy.'

Neither replied.

'Oh well,' said Sarah, 'no skin off my nose. It may not even get off the ground, I warn you. I get these letters from the Biomedical Ethics people. He leaves me to answer them. Never a dull moment.'

Alice and Jane stared into space; four pure-blue eyes staring at nothing, giving nothing away if they could help it. Jane had lost some weight since she had discovered her twin, confronted her mother, and gone, as Tom put it, finally barmy. He kept out of the way. Alice had put on a little, since she'd begun losing so much work, and slept alone.

'Most of the twins are babes in arms,' said Sarah, filling in the reproachful silence. 'Lots more twins being born these days. Mothers have their babies later, when twinning's more likely; and they're healthier, so they carry both babies to term. One used to just get lost, before the mothers even knew. We get triplets and quads quite often, and nothing to do with fertility drugs. So it's not as if you two are a rarity. They might not even take you on.'

The blue eyes turned slowly towards her.

'At least it's just brain cells, these days. He's stopped doing all that egg-cell stuff: he got frightened. I wouldn't do it, I wouldn't have my eggs taken away in the cause of science, no matter how much money they paid. I don't want to even *have* eggs, it makes me feel like a hen. I'd rather not know about them.'

She thought she'd better shut up and get on with the mail. She was being disloyal to her employer. She had hoped for a decent conversation but seldom got it. Perhaps there was something wrong with her. People didn't like her. She did say sharp things, she supposed. She couldn't help it. She wished she could: was there a pill which would make you likeable? If not, no doubt Martins was working on it. Would she take it if there was? Probably.

Two more of them came down the corridor: the eleven o'clock appointments, no doubt. Sarah could see them through the glass door. She worked out the number of eyes that were now going to stare at her in disbelief, dislike and reproach: eight. These two did seem jollier, however, than the two already in the room. Both wore pink sweaters and jeans. She was glad to see they were at least not quite the same height. Too much similarity gave her the creeps. Reared separately, no doubt, though they'd end up much the same in the end. The impact of the rearing

225

environment wore away with time. In old age genes triumphed. Mind you, all old people seemed pretty much the same to her: as did small babies. People started out true to the broad human type, and ended the same way. Variation peaked in the child-bearing years.

'Oh, quads,' said Sarah, when the next two came in. 'That is a bit more interesting. But why didn't you all come in together? I'll see if Dr Holly can be brought out of his meeting.'

'You do just that,' said Gina, mother of three, accustomed to telling others what to do for their own good. 'And fast. We have a right to some kind of explanation.'

Like so many who have dealings with a beneficent but controlling state, she had a clearer view of her rights than many another, and was quicker to voice them. The others seemed stunned into silence. Not just two, but four. So far.

46

Gerald called Hamish Tovey of NBI – News Broadcast International – and said, 'The public are getting hysterical. They won't go out in the rain: they won't have picnics; I went to the lido with my wife and there was almost no one there, just us and a couple of friends. The farmers are complaining; the horticulturists are complaining; the fashion trade's complaining; and the Electric Power Authority are having kittens because the future of nuclear power is in jeopardy. Not only that, the vets are complaining of litters having two heads; I'm even getting tales of budgerigars exploding.'

'Budgerigars can explode if you feed them the wrong grain,' said the NBI man. 'We've just done a feature on it, nothing to do with Chernobyl.'

'Tell that to the public,' said Gerald, bitterly.

'That's what we are doing,' the NBI man pointed out, 'as best we can. But the public can't tell a roentgen from a rad, and to tell you the truth neither can anyone at NBI. If you could put some of your experts at our disposal to help our graphics team out, I'd be grateful. We've a world opportunity here and it's going to waste. It's sickening.'

Gerald said he thought Britnuc had some spare experts in the divinatory area, tested and proven in the field, and Hamish Tovey seemed as interested and grateful as a TV newsman can get: that is to say, he said, 'There just might be an interesting wind-up item there, I suppose. A light closing laugh. I could look into it. Now what can I do for you?'

Gerald said his Department could see the value of some kind of prize-winning news feature, fronted by someone from the commercial rather than the governmental sector – inasmuch as official announcements had lost credibility in this particular area. A popular yet authoritative figure, if such a person existed.

'Carl May?' suggested Hamish Tovey.

'Brilliant idea!' said Gerald Coustain.

'Did you see him drink that glass of milk on TV?' said Hamish Tovey, suddenly animated, 'defying the roentgens! Brilliant PR! How's he been since?'

'Fit as a fiddle, top of the world,' said Gerald. 'Perhaps we could get him to do something just as dramatic.'

'Or even more so,' said Hamish.

'So long as it's safe,' said Gerald. 'We don't want to lose him!'

'So long as the roentgens and the rads are as harmless as you lot make out,' said Hamish Tovey. 'I have my crew to think about, not to mention the union.'

'Back in 1957,' said Gerald, 'when Windscale caught fire and the instrumentation failed − twice round the clock and back again and no one noticed − the duty engineer lifted the lid of the pile to see what was going on. He stared right into the burning heart of the dragon. He's still alive to tell the tale. Head of the Nuclear Safety Inspectorate, as it happens.'

'Is that so!' said Hamish Tovey. 'Now that would be really something by way of a visual fix. Radiation's something we're all going to have to learn to live with, I guess.'

'I guess so,' said Gerald Coustain.

'Do you think Carl May would do it?' asked Hamish, wistful and dependent all of a sudden, like a greedy child lusting after a cream cake it knows its mother's purse can't afford.

'You can only ask him,' said Gerald. 'I have his personal number here, as it happens. He's not averse to publicity, of the right kind. If you took his astrologers and tea-leafers off his hands, he'd certainly feel obliged. I think his board aren't too happy about them.'

'I'll have to ask the boss about that,' said Hamish Tovey.

'I didn't know you had one,' said Gerald.

'When it suits me,' said Hamish.

'Mind you, these old Magnox stations of Britnuc's aren't the same as Windscale, or Sellafield as we call it now,' said Gerald, 'but I suppose they could raise a fuel rod from the pile and Mr May could clasp it to his bosom. How would that do? Or he could jump into the cooling ponds with his young companion: something like that might not go amiss.'

'Oh yes, the young companion,' said Hamish Tovey. 'I filmed her jumping into a trout pond with someone or other, once. Quite a looker. Amazing eyes. Now that's really interesting. It would have to be a zoom lens of course, this time. I don't see my crew with an underwater camera in a cooling pond.'

'Depends if they're running scared or not,' said Gerald, and left him to it.

Gerald was using the public phone at the lido. He knew better than to call from the office. He made a further call or so to contacts in Britnuc too low down the ranks of command to be directly under Carl May's eye, but men of action and responsibility, like himself. Then he went back to his family and friends.

The lido was almost deserted, in spite of the warm weather. Angela, Joanna and a brusque young woman with boots, who seemed a security risk of one kind or another, sat in the tearoom, under shelter. He didn't like them sitting out in the open: he'd asked them not to and they'd obliged. Angela had ordered the full tea for everyone – sandwiches, scones, cream, jam, muffins, cake. He went to join them.

47

Dr Isadore Holly beamed his goodwill towards the four Queens but they weren't having any of it. Interesting.

'Life,' said Dr Holly piously, 'is the only wealth, and I gave you life.'

'You did not,' snapped Cups.

'You just fiddled around in a test tube,' scorned Wands.

'Who do you think you are?' sneered Pentacles.

'God?' jeered Swords.

They had rapidly acquired the habit, now they were together, of dividing up a sentence amongst them and handing it out, with fourfold emphasis. So long, that is, as their emotions coincided, which fortunately was not always the case. They produced, or so thought Dr Holly, a kind of wave motion of feeling and thought, a trough in one giving way to a surge in the next. Alice had the sharpest peaks, the lowest troughs; Jane and Gina flowed more moderately in between: Julie was the smoothest, the most languid. He thought she was the most successful, or was this merely a sexist reaction in himself, what the man liked in the woman, a kind of acquiescence? More research, more research! But how could research into personality ever avoid the bias, the conditioning, of the observer? Interesting.

So God must have thought when the first sea creature grew a fin sufficiently strong to be called a leg and put his weight upon it – how much it hurt but how interesting!

Dr Holly sat on a swivel chair, and moved it gently to and fro in time with his thoughts; his short legs did not quite reach the ground; he had to use the muscles of his buttocks to provide the impetus for movement. He wished the women would go away and leave him alone with his thoughts, but they wouldn't. They came to ask questions, and stayed to nag. How much easier theory was than practice: how much more convenient the idea than the reality. And where was May, Carl May, whose theory, whose idea these women were, this multiplication of perfection out of technical ingenuity? He had thought to breed passivity and had manufactured its opposite. May should be here to witness this turn up for the books.

How they tapped their feet, how they drummed their fingers, these four handsome creatures, the clones of Joanna May; each one amounting to more than the original, by virtue – by virtue of what? What was it that gave the illusion that there was somehow more room in them than in their original, some sort of inner space not altogether taken up by flesh and bone, nerve, muscle, brain, blood; which gave them an energy, a freedom, a distinctiveness which Joanna May had never had? The life force skipped about in their bodies, toeing no particular line, if only because that line had opened out, widened, become fuzzy. These women were less the sum of their genes than was Joanna May, that was what it was, by virtue of being born into a later decade – as if time itself was a factor in the making of a personality, and ought to be included along with diet and education, and social expectation as a complementary building block. Each year its special character, as with wine, and due to something more than weather: rather some complex, so far undefined, pattern at work. Interesting. Except that it smacked of that insult to the civilized and rational mind, astrology.

'We're waiting,' said Alice.
'We've come a long way,' said Jane.
'We won't be put off,' said Gina.
'We have a right to know,' said Julie.
'Who our parents are.'
'What our relationship is.'
'Why this has been kept secret.'
'And are there more of us?' asked Julie, and a little breath of air stirred the air of the perfectly air-conditioned, even-temperatured room, as the other three drew their breath in surprise and alarm. More? It was intolerable.

'There is one more of you,' said Dr Holly, consolingly. 'But only one.'

Five of us!

They would not sit down. They moved about the room, their energy focused upon him. He had the feeling their energy bisected him. He expected their gratitude, but they had none to offer. Well, this was the fate of the prophet, the searcher after knowledge, the reformer, the artist, the innovator: he should not be surprised.

The room was acoustic-tiled, palest green: the light came from gently humming fluorescent tubes, the carpet was neutral oatmeal, the furniture pale ersatz oak veneer, the files a dingy yellow, computers, VDUs and faxes creamy white. No money had been spared: equally, none wasted. The room was male, male; straight-lined, hard-edged: he saw now what was wrong with it. No pot plants, no family photographs, no cushions – not an ashtray, not a coffee cup – nothing to bear witness to human frailty, everything to further unimpassioned thought, that divine inspiration, that necessary trigger if Utopia was ever to be achieved. And how else but by logical means, since all other ways had been tried, and had failed? Poet priests, and painter kings, all failed; empires crumbling as art and nonsense prevails: aspiration and practicalities always so little in accord: no, this was the way forward, through the digital clicking of information, the intricate matching of fact with fact, through memory forever retained, patching together the parts of wisdom to get at the wider vision: as DNA is logged and booked and coded and patched. Working up from minutiae rather than in from the macrocosm, for that could never be grasped in its entirety, only guessed at intuitively, and how much time and money you would waste if you got it wrong. Obviously, you had to start with the little bits and make them up into the whole. No wonder computers wrote such bad poetry.

'We're waiting,' or rather 'w–we–we'r–we're wait, waiti, waitin, waiting.' Odd, that; the ripple effect when they all said

232

the same thing at much the same time, just fractions of a second apart. Did it follow the same sequence as the initial cell division? Well, he would never know. He longed to know. How uppity they were, how irritating, these grown children of his invention. 'Which of our mothers had quins, then,' they demanded, 'was it a fertility drug, and who was our father? You?'

'Good God no,' said Dr Holly, shocked. 'You seem to be labouring under considerable misapprehensions.'

And Dr Holly explained to them the detail of their birth. ('Not birth,' snapped Alice, 'say genesis.') Afterwards they were silent for a little. He was glad he had shaken them.

'It isn't nice to be so unusual,' said Julie presently. 'To be implanted, not conceived.'

'We were so conceived,' said Gina. 'We were conceived in Harley Street sixty years ago. We are orphans. Our parents are dead.'

'Well if they're not,' said Alice, 'they needn't think I'm visiting them.'

Jane said, 'We were postponed for thirty years. We should sue.'

'I gave you life,' repeated Dr Holly. 'You should be grateful.'

They were not. Why only four, they demanded. Why not a hundred?

'We couldn't get more than four, in those days,' he apologized. 'We weren't in the business of swapping nuclei, shuffling genes, just parthenogenesis, and ex-utero conception.'

Then they despised him for a failure in ambition. He felt bad about it. He wished them out of existence, but they failed to dematerialize.

The clones turned their mind to Joanna May. They needed someone more exotic than Dr Holly to blame. She should never have let it happen. What sort of person could she be? How could you be cloned and simply not notice? Jane wanted to know.

'Easily enough,' said Gina, sadly, who had more experience of hospitals and doctors than her sisters.

'I don't want to meet her,' said Alice. 'She's so old we'd have nothing in common.'

But Julie said, 'You might learn something from yourself grown old,' and they pondered that.

Dr Holly rashly said sixty was not old, it was positively young, and they turned the energy of their attention back to him. They jeered.

'You have made orphans of us,' they said. 'Snatched away the ground from beneath our feet. We are unnatural, and all you can do is talk about yourself.'

Gina began to snivel at the notion of being unnatural. Alice slapped Gina: Julie comforted Gina; Jane restrained Alice's hand. They swirled around a little, touching, hugging, patting, settled down again.

'And now,' said Alice to Dr Holly, 'I suppose you think you're God and we should worship you. Well, we don't. We are much more likely to sue you.'

'The general opinion is,' said Dr Holly, kicking his feet against the central pillar of his chair, as if he were a little boy, 'that God is dead.'

He felt himself grow tall: his legs extended to the floor and below; his head to the ceiling and beyond. He floated. He felt himself swell, he thought he would burst. It was a most unpleasant feeling. Still his mind worked, computer racing, information pitted against wisdom. Interesting! The Gods were dead, starved to death by lack of belief, and when the Gods died the Titans returned, and he was a Titan untrammelled. Dr Isadore Titan Holly, suffering from gigantism of the head: outside the laboratory windows were the chimneys, the puffers, the suckers, the spitters and nibblers of Martins Worldwide Pharmacopoeia, patents taken throughout the universe, through all eternity, nothing too small, nothing too short, just everything, everything buzzing and whirring and blinding, swifter, faster, cleaner, neater, smarter, richer, glossier exploding markets, expanding universe, stretching time, smash, crack, ecstasy, smack, the cocaine culture, a faster mile, bigger muscles, sweeter smiles, shorter skirts, up their own arse and out again, he was part of it, feet through mud and head through clouds – and splat, he'd fallen flat on his face. The breath was knocked out of him. He

234

was having a fit: a bad one: perhaps this was the one which would carry him off?

Not one of them helped him up, these, the women of his creation. Not one of them loosened his collar or made his tongue safe. They stared down at him, watching him froth and twitch, waiting for him to die, or not, as the case might be.

'He can't die now,' said Alice eventually, brutally. 'There's more we need to know.'

He felt better, as if having been given permission to survive. He tried to speak. He couldn't. But his limbs moved now of his own volition, not of his brain's convulsion. That was something. Perhaps he should crawl out to Sarah? But they closed in on him. He thought they might kick him, even to death. Supposing they felt as entitled to end him as he had been to begin them? What would happen to his research? Had he remembered to put away his own dehydrated DNA? Yes, of course he had. A loss to humanity, otherwise. A multiplicity of ingenuity was what he had, and others had not. So much to be done, so very much it had frightened him off: nothing to do with Carl May. He had wanted the grant cut: he had wasted time unforgivably. Brain transplants: memory transfer: personality shuffling: all waiting for his attention. He of all people needed to be cloned, properly. Effective genetic engineering; not a hopeless dream: just a great deal of money and international cooperation. Another fifty years would do it. It would not be personal immortality for him, even so. It couldn't be. Just look at these four to know; to know what? Not one soul to go round, but a soul apiece and more to spare, and man, woman, was more than the animals, and God was there, and to find out that was enough for a lifetime.

But had he told Sarah where his DNA was? Where he'd put himself? Would she remember? Oh fallible, fallible! So much industrial security in a scientific arena; records always so secret: things got lost. Death was something you never expected. Four straight noses bending down. Perfect noses. Beautiful eyes. It couldn't be bad to have achieved this. He was proud of them. At least he was down to proper size. Little size, almost child size. Four short upper lips, four rather thin lower lips. Better breed clones than rely on finding twins: why had he doubted it! He would do what Carl May wanted: it was what he wanted. He was decided. He would take all the money and get going again. If they let him live. They did.

'What did you say?' asked Alice.
'Interesting,' managed Dr Holly, and they fetched Sarah.
'He had some kind of fit,' said Jane.
'Epileptic,' said Sarah. 'He must have forgotten his tablets. He'll be OK now. I expect you exhausted him. He's not as young as he was.'

The clones left, still angry: they blamed the bearer of bad news for the news: and the bad news was they were not who they thought they were, and that is always difficult to accept, no matter how little you may like being who you thought you were. Dr Holly had given them life and they'd drained the life out of him to the point of death, exhausted him, to punish him for every unpleasantness received and recorded during that life. Children do it to parents every day of their lives, to pay them out for not providing a perfect world to live in. They felt their own unreasonableness and it made them irritable rather than guilty. They felt the inherent guilt of the female, but not powerfully; being four that guilt was quartered. The soul was multiplied, the guilt divided. That was a great advance.

The realization cheered them up. They thought they should celebrate. The clones went back to Julie's house as soon as they could because Ben couldn't be left alone with the little ones for too long. A mild obligation, when divided by four. Alice said, at first, she wouldn't come, she wasn't interested, but in fact she did, she was. The others understood quickly that though Alice needed persuading, she was not difficult to persuade.

Julie and Gina went in Julie's small automatic Volvo, Jane followed in her Citroen Deux Chevaux, Alice in her Porsche. They were glad not to have chosen the same car.

'Alec likes Volvos,' said Julie.
'Tom only believes in Citroens,' said Jane.
'Mine's just more expensive than my brothers' cars,' said

Alice, cheering up. 'At least they're not really my brothers. Thank God, it wasn't incest, that on top of everything.'

'I never had time to learn to drive,' said Gina.

48

Carl May sent for Jacko, Petie, Elwood, Dougie and Haggie.

'Tell me about the clones,' he said. It was Thursday evening.

Carl May looked at his watch as he spoke, unusually conscious of the tyranny of time. So much to do, and so few years to do it in! The skin on his right calf itched; his circulation was bad. Would Bethany return of her own free will, and by five thirty, as she had promised, or would she have to be fetched? The hands of the watch blurred: the most expensive watch in the world, sleek, unobtrusive, infallible, but still the hands blurred. It was bitter. The fault lay in his eyes. They had tears in them. He wanted Bethany to return to him of her own free will. If she had to be fetched, he would feel discouraged and end up removing her from his scale of reference: that is to say from the material and current world. She would not die, or only so far as friends and relatives were concerned, and up to a point herself – though what that death experience was, who was to say? No, she would merely be put off to some other time, as Joanna's gardener had been. A pity for the genes of that particular talent, greenfingers, to be lost to the human race. The experience of Garden Developments plc was this, that – forget science, nutrients, temperature, humidity, and so forth – plants simply grew better in the care of certain individuals than in others. Greenfingers. He thought perhaps Bethany had pink fingers. See what happened to his circulation when she went away. He had been happier, calmer, of course, when married to Joanna. White fingers. But white fingers betrayed, strayed. If Bethany did not return, if Bethany removed herself from Carl May and the world – for were not the world and Carl May the same thing? – then perhaps one of the younger versions of Joanna May would do: white fingers he himself had made tolerable by tingeing them with youthful pink: redipping the faded stuff in stronger dye.

But Jacko was delivering the report on the clones. He was dyslexic. He held folders but spoke from memory. They were in Carl's penthouse office suite at the top of Britnuc's tower. Carl May sat in his architectural chair, and tried to find it comfortable. He thought for the first time that it was a young man's chair: it was uncushioned: it demanded resilient young flesh for its proper occupancy. The Barbers of the Bath did not sit, however, no matter how resilient their flesh. Their layered trousers were too bulky, or the chairs too narrow, to make it possible. He stared at Jacko's trousers: a ragged hole in dusty black cotton gave way to ripped green wool tartan, which showed slit red satin beneath, and that was patched and pinned. Three of them smoked: ash fell unnoticed on their clothes and on the pale floor. He would be glad when he was finished with them. He would not use a rock group again: they were easy to buy, easy to bribe, so unnecessarily cynical were they about the ways of the world – citing 'everyone does it' as cause and justification of their actions when of course the truth was everyone did *not* do it – and they were certainly stylish, but he felt more at ease with professional villains, who could make a proper distinction between criminal and ordinary citizenship, and stood their toddlers in a corner if they swore.

Jacko recited the qualities and lifestyles of the clones, rather as a nervous waiter recites a memorized menu, babbling a little, eyes to heaven. Carl May was accustomed to nervous waiters.

Carl May looked at his watch. He still could not make sense of it. Haggie took out his Victorian pocket timepiece 'Five thirty-five, sir,' Haggie said, rounding to the nearest figure, as people always used to, in the old world. Carl May was surprised that the lad could tell the time from a handed watch. So many of the younger generation could not. In the four Magnox stations under Britnuc's control, all clocks had of necessity been converted to digital display, at considerable expense. A wave of despair made Carl May catch his breath. All to no avail, all efforts on behalf of the human race; how could science hold

239

back this tide of stupidity, flesh and blood rioting, breeding uncontrollably, surplus upon surplus, so excess a quantity that quality went out the window, more and more and more, this plague of unthinking, all-feeling humans, no better than a plague of locusts, chattering, devouring, destructive, monstrous. To no avail, this latest heaven-sent breakthrough of the geneticists: the happenstance in nature of a dehydrating fungus, so that henceforth the nuclei of mammals could be treated and transferred unharmed, the building blocks complete. And not just transferred, but multiplied a million times in the E.Coli vats, so the shuffling of DNA, the improvement of physique and personality, could now be done at will. Jacko, Dougie, Haggie, Elwood, Petie. What could you do to them? Require the skill, refine the spirit, make *good* not bad. Too late, too late! Too many now. The random creations of nature would overwhelm the desires and designs of thinking man. Five thirty-six.

Carl tried to listen to Jacko's report. For the hors d'oeuvre, Alice, light and astringent (but too much lemon). For the fish, Julie, tentative and delicate (but a little stale, a little flat, too long out of the water). For the entrée, Gina, full-blooded but overcooked. Jane, a delectable dessert except salt not sugar had been put in the topping.

Faithful, monogamous? The Barbers of the Bath allowed themselves sounds of derision, close-harmonied snorts. Promiscuous at best, lesbians at worst. Carl May said perhaps it was because they had never met the right man, and the four young men shuffled their great Doc Martens eighteen-hole boots and looked uneasy: they had not expected words for the defence spoken by the prosecutor. They had understood their task to be to report adversely.

'So what's the message, sir? What's the next step?' Jacko asked.

Gina and Jane, meat and dessert. Too rich and indigestible. He had an old man's gut, it had to be faced. Those two would have to go. Alice and Julie would replace Bethany, one or the other. Which would he choose? Hors d'oeuvre or fish? One too lemony, one a little stale. Why not both together? They'd consent. They'd do as he asked, as Joanna always had. They'd love him, as Joanna had. Of course they would: they were Joanna. When he multiplied her he had not so much tried to multiply perfection – that was a tale for Holly – he had done it to multiply her love for him, Joanna May's love for Carl May, multiply it fourfold: to make up for what he'd never had: Carl May, the bitch's son. But love was strong, when it came to it: you couldn't stand too much of it: Joanna had been more than enough. It took Bethany, a sorbet between courses, tasted, relished, to restore a jaded palate, a tired appetite. Alice and Julie it would be. Five thirty-seven.

He tried to speak. His voice shook: he stopped.

'Instructions, sir?' asked Jacko. They sang the word, in inefficient close harmony. Inst-instr-instruct-instruction-instructions. He wished they wouldn't. His leg began to itch badly. There was a whining and whuffling in the air: it was the snuffling harmony of a bitch and her litter of pups. He'd lived amongst the excrement and the noisy, messy warmth of the litter and got quite fond of it. The need to love, for a child, is stronger than the need to be loved. When he was hungry, he'd sucked from her. But that had been when he was very small: he'd been told that: he didn't know if it was true. Five thirty-eight.

'Oh yes, instructions,' said Carl May. His voice came back, and his will. He told them Jane and Gina would have to go. Julie and Alice would be fetched. Their ten eighteen-hole Doc Martens boots marched out, blurred by a flurry of dangling fabrics.

49

When Bethany went home to Putney she found her father weeping and alone.

'I knew there was something wrong,' she said. 'I knew I wasn't lying. What's the matter?' Patsy had gone, torn the flowers from her greying hair, been born again as a Christian, and given up her life of sin, said her Dad. Now Patsy was living in an hotel for born-againers, going from door to door, converting as she went.

'But, Daddy, it wasn't sin,' said Bethany. Empty coffee cups stood around, and biscuit crumbs, and sugar bowls with mice droppings in them, and piles of stained sheets on the floor. He needed her. Upstairs there was the sound of revelry. 'It was never sin. Sometimes I'd wish I'd been brought up differently, sometimes I thought that you didn't know what you were doing, the pair of you. Sometimes I was so scared – you and Mum never knew quite what was going on, you thought what they did was just ordinary sex, but sometimes it wasn't, you have no idea. I tried to be kind, I tried to be loving, I tried to bring happiness into other people's lives, especially the disabled, but, Dad, they sometimes sure as hell weren't bringing happiness into mine.'

'Don't you start,' said Dad. 'I've had a bellyful. We had good times, didn't we? Don't take that away from me along with everything else. Your mum will be round here before long, trying to make me believe in Jesus Christ, and I can't, I just can't. Remember how he cursed the fig tree?'

'Well, I can't either,' said Bethany, sadly. 'I can't believe. We went to the theatre too often. You made me read too many books.'

'I suppose you hold that against me too,' he said.

'Of course I don't,' said Bethany. 'Let me help you get this place cleaned up before Mum comes back. She'll just die if she sees it like this.'

'You will stay, won't you?' said Dad. 'This is where you belong, your proper home.'

'I don't know,' said Bethany. 'I really don't know.'

It was three o'clock.

'Who's upstairs?' Bethany asked.

'That's another thing,' said Dad. 'I think I'm getting old. People don't seem to go. Once I used to tell them, quite quietly, it was time to get dressed and go, and they went.'

'You always were a big man,' said Bethany.

'I don't register that way any more,' said Dad. 'It's got worse since your mother moved out. Now I tell them to go and they don't: or worse, they turn up and walk in and use the bedrooms without so much as a by your leave, any time of day and night, as if this was Liberty Hall, and don't even put money in the box. I don't know who's up there, Bethany. You've got to help. I need you here.'

'But, Dad,' said Bethany. 'Carl May needs me too. I'm only on leave of absence, as it were.' And she cooked him a meal. Only omelette and beansprout salad, because of course he didn't eat meat, but better than boiled eggs and toast, on which he lived. It was four o'clock.

'Beauty and the Beast,' Bethany's father remarked, watching her clear and wash up. 'I must say you're looking good. Why bother with a beast? I'm proud of you. We were right about sex, weren't we, your mother and me? We grew you proud and true.'

Bethany's father had a cavernous, grizzled face. His thick hair had turned greyish since last she saw him. He reminded her of Father Christmas, the kind she'd been taken to in stores when little and on whose knee she most hated to sit; agony shone out from behind the joviality. You had to not notice, for fear of hurting feelings. To hurt feelings was the real sin. It was four thirty.

243

'We'd better put locks on the doors,' she said. 'And the front door, and the back door, and get a dog.'

'I don't believe in locks,' her father said. 'Lock the door and get robbed. The only time I ever locked my car was once in an underground car park and when I got back someone had broken into it and I had to get a new door.'

She'd heard the tale a hundred times, and taken many a lesson from it. If you kept the door unlocked, as it were, you didn't get raped. Some personal doors, alas, were on permanent lock; she sighed. Her father, for all his experience, for all his principles, was an innocent. She'd had stitches twice, and neither she nor her mother had liked to tell him. She was glad her mother was born-again. She hoped she was happy.

'We can't have strangers coming and going,' Bethany said. 'Things have got to change.'

'I don't like it,' he said. 'The world goes round on love and trust. I've always believed that. Besides, we have nothing to steal.' He made a concession. It was his principle to make concessions, save face wherever possible. 'But a dog, now . . . your mother always wanted a poodle.'

'I'll get you an Alsatian pup,' she said, and ran down the market and did so once she'd cleared up the rest of the house. The bedrooms were disgusting. It was five thirty-five. She'd said she'd be back at Britnuc at five thirty. She could feel Carl thinking about her. She didn't want to feel it. He spooked her. 'For a young man he is young, And an old man he is grey,' she sang as she cleaned, as much to dull the puppy's lamentations as anything else: it had been torn too young from its mother. But where was the young man? Where were they all? They so seldom travelled First Class and she so seldom Standard Fare. They never met.

'Don't lose your trust, Bethany,' her father said, petting the puppy in a way which once would have made her jealous, but which no longer did now her father was old. 'My little girl. Don't ever forget how to love. Keep the flag of faith flying.'

She said she'd try. Somehow there seemed no place between the two of them, Carl May and her father, where she could properly dwell. It had to be one or the other, and she didn't like cleaning, so that settled it. It was five forty-six. She called Carl May, and said she'd be late back, but she would be back. She was on her way.

50

How desperately I, Joanna May, tried to be myself, not Carl May's wife. Even in exile, even divorced, I was married to him, linked to him. She married to him is so different from he married to her. She occupies a little space in his head; he surrounds her, encloses her, as a white leucocyte surrounds some invading cell: if he puts his penis in her it's just to test the breeding warmth: he's really there already. He can escape, she can't. She is squeezed in there, in his head, without room to manoeuvre. Even in Isaac's bed, his uncomfortable, lumpy-mattressed bed, his comfortable arms, I was Carl May's wife, his employer's wife, source of his funding: he was my illicit lover. Therein lay the excitement, the pleasure. I could understand Carl's rage, I could understand my guilt, but not his jealousy. How could he be jealous when what I was doing could hardly be acting, could only be reacting? When Carl divorced me and Oliver climbed into my smooth, firm, clean and luxurious bed, Oliver was my comfort, my consolation, because Carl May had eased me out of his life, as the head's squeezed out, eased out, of a pimple. If Carl May did it painlessly, it was for his own sake, not mine: he didn't want any nasty, unsightly inflammation left behind.

When I acknowledged my sisters, my twins, my clones, my children, when I stood out against Carl May, I found myself: pop! I was out. He thought he would diminish me: he couldn't: he made me. I acknowledged fear – what would they think of me? I recognized shame – I am old, so old. I faced my rage – how dare they exist. I felt desire, and a great swelling energy, a surging pleasure, the joy of being one of a million million, part of the life of the universe, in all its absurdity, its tremulous glory: I was part of a living landscape, and the function of that life was to worship and laud its maker, and the maker was not Carl May: he had not made me: wife I might be, but only part of me, for all of a sudden there was more of me left. The bugles had sounded, reinforcements came racing over the hill; Joanna May was now Alice, Julie, Gina, Jane as well. Absurd but wonderful!

Carl May could not go on. I let Angela know, who let Gerald know; a man may murder his wife's lovers, but cannot be mad in charge of four nuclear power stations. I was no longer just a wife; I was a human being: I could see clearly now.

If thine eye offend me take a good look at yourself. If thine I offend thee, change it.

It's not lies that kill the soul, it's the effort to believe the lies, especially your own. Carl's dead, white face on the TV screen alarmed me, and should have alarmed the world sooner than it did. The walking dead can't be in charge. There is no room for zombies.

That day at the lido Gerald had a word with someone, who had a word with someone, who had a worker in the field, of course he did.

Sometimes accidents, or events as they are called, do occur without prompting in relation to the fuel rods of the old Magnox stations. Are bound to. The spent fuel rods – fissile uranium wrapped in magnesium – are removed from the pile when they've worn out their usefulness, are no longer capable, poor tired things, of sustaining a reaction. They're taken out, in sequence, en bloc, as they went in – some thirty at a time. But sometimes rods which are not quite spent, may even have quite a vigour to them, get in with the others: they too get dumped in the cooling ponds – square concrete-sided pools, open to the air. Such events do happen – it hardly seems to matter much. No one's going to swim in the pools, are they! What does it matter, if the dials do go round a second time, a third time, a tenth time, and no one notices – or in this particular case, cares to notice, gets paid not to notice; who's to say what goes on, no skin off anyone's nose, unless, that is, the owner of the nose is vain enough, proud enough, sufficient of a scorpion to sting himself to death. When it would be the scorpion's fault, no one else's. The old-fashioned dial readouts should have been converted to digital display long ago, but if management is mean, mean, whose fault is that? Management baying at the moon — snapping, howling: how dare you shine so bright! It doesn't stop the moon.

Accidents will happen. No such thing as an accident.

I, Joanna May. Or perhaps now, just Joanna.

51

Joanna, at the age of sixty, chaired the first meeting of her life. Her clones appointed her chairperson. The meeting took place in Julie's house, where Mavis had led her. On arrival they found a Volvo, a Citroen and a Porsche in the drive. They could hear the sound of children playing, or squabbling, not to mention TV-set, radio and hi-fi all turned up loud.

'How very peculiar,' said Mavis, who wore for the occasion a long brown woollen coat of amazing plainness. 'My report says this one, Julie, lives very quietly, and has no children. Isolated, rather the way you are. An "executive wife" is what they call this particular brand of woman.'

'Perhaps she's had no choice,' said Joanna. 'Or perhaps she lacked the courage to have friends. Look how brave I have to be to have Angela!' Joanna wore a nice little black suit and high heels to give herself confidence, or perhaps to annoy Mavis.

'Perhaps they've found each other already,' said Mavis.

'Yes, perhaps that's it. All of a sudden, like you, she has a family. And noise and drunkenness breaks out!'

Mavis rang the bell, because Joanna hung back, and knocked, and tapped upon the window, and finally was heard. The door was flung open.

'Mother!' cried the clones, elated and irreverent, 'it must be Mother!', as Joanna May stood in the doorway, startled. They crowded round, inspecting, touching, laughing. Even Joanna, accustomed to sobriety, could see they'd been drinking. But she was relieved they had recognized her with so little difficulty: had no doubt at all but that she was theirs.

'Mother!' she said. 'Oh, I see. I'm to be mother, am I!' She looked them up and down: she hushed them and tutted them.

She felt like her own mother, disapproving; she felt a flicker of forgiveness for the poor dead woman. Mother! The girls would have to take the consequences, the general brisk comment and interference for their own good. Joanna May, mother, refused champagne, fearing alcoholism; she accepted tea. (Mavis took what remained of Alec's whisky from the mahogany-and-glass cabinet.) Wildly, the clones asked Joanna for her opinion of them: they insisted, insisted. They wanted a proper mother's report – at last, they would have what every daughter wants, a mother to wholly appreciate them.

'I see,' said Joanna May. 'You want my true opinion, do you? My maternal view? Then here it is.'

She, Joanna, didn't like one bit the way Alice had taken back her hairline; it was vulgar; she felt Julie's sweatshirt was too informal considering this was her house and she had guests, and what is more she didn't care for the patterned drink coasters, they were common; she thought Jane should comb her hair properly – and it was much too short – and Gina should lose some weight and stop smoking. She couldn't help saying these things. They were true: she was right about them: they must listen to her. It was for their own good. She had been around longer than them: she *knew*.

Joanna felt resentment rising in her daughters; they were oppressed: they wanted her to go away, and yet she'd hardly said a word to them, had she, nothing that wasn't necessary. Just she didn't like this and she didn't like that. Which was true. And for their own good. And look how they drank – alcoholics, every one! They drummed and tapped with their fingers: they were one split into four: they defended each other: to attack one was to attack all. Joanna May stopped as suddenly as she began. She had shocked herself as well as them.

'I'm sorry,' said Joanna May, 'but this is the penalty of daughterhood. I remember it well. The mother must make the daughter as much like her as possible, unthread, unknit, the father in her. In this case, as it happens, my father is your father: you *are* me, so there's no point in me doing it, but still I can't help it.'

'I do it to Sue,' said Gina. 'I can't help that either. I don't do

250

it to the boys: I let them be themselves, I could never work out why. I suppose that's what it is: you try and unravel the father out of the daughter. How else can she be properly female?'

'Worm and the sperm!' said Jane.

'Disgusting,' said Julie and Alice together.

'I will not be your mother,' said Joanna May. 'I hereby renounce the role. If this is motherhood, save me from it. I always wanted it, but this is all it is! Nag, nag, nag!'

'She can't be our sister,' said Alice scornfully. 'She's much too old.'

'She'll only get jealous,' said Jane, 'of the way we are.'

'She does age well,' said Gina. 'I suppose that's something to look forward to.'

'I don't want to look forward,' said Julie. 'I want to live now.'

They allowed Joanna May no authority: she had disclaimed mother, she must take the consequences: they would not even accept her status as originator. They looked her up and down, inspected her, now their equal, their equivalent, but somehow dusty with it. So that was what the passage of the years did – it made you dusty. They resolved never to wear black. It did not suit them. They were in a manic state. As for Joanna, she wanted their pity, all of a sudden, their acknowledgement of her wrongs, but they'd allow her none of that. An easy life, a quiet life! Married for thirty years! To Carl May, the famous Carl! They had all been wronged, more than she, each one claimed. Joanna of all of them had her proper place in the world; she'd been born at the right time. They were a generation out. No wonder they'd been lonely: their lives had been in a mess. They could see now that was the trouble – they'd been lonely. They used men to stop them being lonely. No wonder it all went wrong. Now they had each other, nothing need be the same. They were delirious, giddy. It was absurd, wonderful. Joanna thought they were far too young, far too noisy, far too energetic. She wanted to be alone. She said so. They wouldn't have it.

'We'll make her chairman,' said Julie. 'That's what we'll do. That should keep her happy.'

'Chairperson,' said Jane. So that was what Joanna May consented to be: someone who controlled an agenda but couldn't vote. Mavis watched, and said nothing, but every now and then looked out the window, uneasily.

Ben came into the room and said 'Mum', and Julie and Gina both looked up. 'Those men are back,' he said. 'There are five of them this time, and if you don't do something about it I'm going to take Anthony somewhere safe. And Sue too, I suppose.'

Jane said, 'You let him watch TV, Gina, you shouldn't,' but Joanna said, 'No, we have to be careful. You don't know Carl.'

'I'd rather like to meet this Carl,' said Julie. 'Can it be managed?'

'At last,' said Alice, 'a man worth loving.'

'What everyone wants,' said Jane.

'If you did, Joanna,' said Gina, 'so could we.'

'To be able to love!' said Julie. 'Truly love.'

'He's a demon, a monster,' protested Joanna. 'It wasn't love I felt. Something else! He doesn't deserve to live. He is wicked, he is mad. It took me a lifetime to see it.'

'All that happened,' said Alice, 'is that you grew old.'

'Lost energy,' said Gina.

'Got the worst out of him, not the best,' said Julie.

'Any of us could manage him better,' said Jane.

'How would you do that?' asked Joanna.

'By not taking him seriously!' said Jane, and they all crowed with delight, and poured more champagne, and Joanna turned to Mavis in alarm.

All Mavis said was, 'I didn't think about the back,' and tried the telephone but there was no dialling tone when she lifted up the receiver.

Ben said, 'It's OK, I've already called the police. All the times I wanted to call the police, Mum, and never dared, because it made it worse for you.'

Jane, Julie, Alice and Joanna were shocked. They turned and looked hard at Gina, and Gina said, 'I know, I know, I can't cope, I'm an awful mother, I don't want to be a mother, please help me.'

Mavis and Ben seemed to understand each other, to comprehend that the world was a desperate and dangerous place. Police sirens sounded. Joanna said, 'Why did they come so quickly?' and Mavis said, 'It depends what Ben said,' and Ben said, 'Well, I'd better get it over,' and went out, and Mavis followed.

Alice said to Gina, 'Why don't you go after him, he's your son?' and Gina said, helplessly, 'Well, he's a boy,' and Alice said, 'This can't go on; personally I hate children but after all he is my nephew. Something has to be done about this.'

'About Gina, you mean,' said Jane.

'I'd like to help,' said Julie.

Mavis came back and said Ben's wonderful; he told them this tale of child assault, sex assault, five men in the car, and they believed him, and they took the men away; now they're going to have to talk themselves out of that. Ben's got to go down to the station. Someone ought to go with him.

Gina didn't stir. It was Julie who said, 'I'll go,' so that decided that.

Joanna, Jane, Julie, Gina, Alice.

52

A memo reached Carl May from the Divination Department: his PA thought it advisable to let this one through. The department was becoming an expensive joke, rumours of its existence having reached the media. The memo took it upon itself to warn Mr May fairly and squarely that the auspices for the day of the projected PR event in Wales were bad indeed. The common pack had produced the Ace of Spades 40 per cent above probability: the Tarot pack the Tower 90 per cent likewise; the *I Ching*, the Chinese Book of Oracles, that normally sedate and encouraging book, had come up with No.23 (Splitting Apart) four times running with mention of Tears of Blood; the prophetic dreamer had wakened screaming, the encephalic discs popping off of their own accord; so far undiagnosed telekinetic forces in the office had shredded the Welsh map, and the teacups came up repeatedly with coffins on the rim.

Carl May laughed aloud. 'Gobbledygook,' he said, and to the gratification of his PA dictated a memo back to Divination: 'If you have foretold anything it is the death of your own department: the end of your payslips,' and told his PA the Welsh PR event was now on and he himself would graciously participate.

A couple of days later, Hughie Scotland ran his finger down the M's in his private address book, and once again got straight through to Carl May.

'I take that back about you being a dry old stick,' said Hughie Scotland. 'I understand you mean to jump into a cooling pond to prove radiation's safe. Young Bethany has certainly brought you back to life. I hope you're grateful.'

'Moderately,' said Carl May, who sounded buoyant, almost

happy. 'It's the TV producer's idea. I must make a fool of myself, it seems, to bring the country to its senses.'

'I jumped into a trout pond for the same reason,' said Hughie Scotland, 'to popularize freshwater fish. These days we men of power must make sacrifices.'

'I thought you were drunk,' said Carl May. 'Bethany told me you did it because you were drunk.'

'Bethany tells lies,' said Scotland. 'How is Bethany? You know my wife's in Nigeria? Is Bethany jumping in the cooling pond, too?'

'The TV man says yes,' said Carl May. 'We're in his hands. And Bethany is looking forward to it.'

'What is a cooling pond exactly?' asked Scotland. 'Is it safe?'

'I wouldn't be jumping into it if it weren't,' said Carl May. 'It's where they put the old spent fuel rods to cool off, lose any short-term radioactivity they might have picked up in the pile, before they're carted off to Sellafield. No harm in them at all. The water's filtered and purified, monitored daily, just to be on the safe side, to keep the local populace happy.'

'I'd rather Bethany didn't jump in it,' said Hughie Scotland, 'all the same. I find I'm very fond of Bethany. Does she ever talk about me?'

'No,' said Carl May, 'and she is indeed jumping into the cooling pond with me. It can hardly be worse than into a trout pool with you. Personally I find freshwater fish unnatural. Our streams and rivers are a great deal more polluted than our seas, even the North Sea, and that's saying something. Well, good to speak to you, Hughie. I take it your men will be there in force, cameras and all. If one's going to do something like this, one might as well make as big a splash as possible.'

A joke too. Hughie Scotland winced.

'As it happens,' added Carl May, 'Bethany and I are getting married.' And he put the phone down. That last would stir up Scotland and his media troops.

Carl May told his secretary to confirm detailed arrangements with the NBI. He did not think he would marry Bethany, when it came to it, not even to annoy and upset Joanna. What he did not want, what he did not like, what upset him, was Bethany

255

staying away of her own accord. But when she was there, he could do without her. He could never win in his own head, only in the outside world.

Bethany looked up briefly from her computer game.

'I have the highest score ever,' she said. 'There's this little figure you have to guide through rooms full of demons and ghosts. I'm really good at it. What was that about you marrying me?'

'Only for the press,' said Carl May. 'We want them all there, not just the science boys. Why, do you want to marry me?'

'Of course I do,' said Bethany, but she wasn't sure. It would take her too much out of circulation. You could never divorce Carl May, and if he divorced you you'd be lucky to be alive to collect your decree absolute. The Barbers of the Bath might sing you to death.

'It was Hughie Scotland on the line,' said Carl May, waiting to see how she'd respond.

'That's nothing to me,' said Bethany, and for once she didn't lie. She had a short emotional memory which, considering her life, was just as well.

53

The journey to Britnuc B, in the heart of the Welsh hill country, impressed and awed as many of the journalists and newsmen who travelled down, by car, by train, by helicopter, to cover the media event of the year (for that, according to Britnuc's PR, was what it was) as it troubled and depressed others. The wild beauty of the hills, their sheer scale, the overwhelming presence of nature unorganized and unconfirmed, the indifference of the shaggy cattle, the unkempt quiet roads, the general dwarfing and rendering risible of mankind, inspired as much deference to nature as resentment of it.

Britnuc B had been carefully landscaped so as to offend the aesthetic sensibilities of landscape lovers as little as possible. Some – on the whole those with country cottages – shuddered as they approached the power-station complex, and their radios crackled and faded beneath the marching pylons. Others were thankful that something sensible, profitable and organized had at last, thanks to Britnuc, enlivened the rural torpor of the area.

Green grass grew wherever possible inside the security fence: the massive containment unit was so placed that it was all but dwarfed by the flat rock face that reached up to the sky behind it. Birds wheeled unconcerned above it, delighting in updraughts and downdraughts, the low, interesting, steady thunder of the heavy steam-driven turbines. As Carl May loved to say, 'What is a nuclear power station but a gigantic kettle? All we do here is boil water!'

Only the security gates themselves, the high fences, the handing out of security badges, the requiring of passes, the writing down and checking of names, made matters appear the least unusual: that here was the focus of a nation's terror, the very fount of paranoia.

Britnuc's PR teams made coffee, poured drinks, handed out booklets. Chernobyl could not happen here, the Russian designs were *other*, all *other*, hopelessly old-fashioned, and even if it did, would be no worse than a coal-mine explosion – less horrible, in fact, less likely to be a lethal accident. Nuclear power plants were the opposite of labour intensive! Carl May himself wished to make this very point. And if this proved too technical for the mass-circulation papers, middle rather than front page stuff, why, Carl May was engaged to be married – yes, he was free to marry – yes, he was divorced: a matter of mutual consent many years back: there would be a press handout presently. In the meantime, international TV was present on this wonderful day: a cinema film was being made, not just TV – though we're glad so many TV stations are represented here today: we really do have to get this message across to the general public. Yes, the film was to be part-funded by Britnuc: of course, why not? Part of the PR job – and look here, mementoes for everyone, on this splendid occasion. Choose from a genuine leather-bound Filofax or this genuine Barbour – if the rain should just possibly fall no one must get wet – and of course there'd be a buffet lunch after the event. Telephones, telex and fax facilities all available in the press office – and out, everyone out into the beautiful fresh air of Wales! The show's beginning. Carl May, nuclear magnate, and Bethany his bride – well soon to be his bride: no, the date wasn't quite fixed, but the press would, of course, be informed the minute it was – would ceremoniously jump into the cooling pond to prove low-level waste was no threat to anyone, and the future of nuclear power, clean, efficient, safe, would be assured.

And all trooped out into the clean, bright, windy air: a good day! A long way to come but at least Britnuc knew how to organize things.

'Do I have to jump?' asked Bethany. She stood on the edge of the concrete bunker looking down at the clean bluish water below. She'd felt the water with her long, nervy, trembly fingers. Pink fingers, as Carl kept saying. Pink fingers. It made her uneasy. The water was just nicely warm. Bethany wore a yellow bikini, with polka dots; it was cut high up the thigh to make her long legs longer. Her red hair flowed out in the wind. Her bosom was only just encased in yellow, polka-dotted fabric.

'This is really something,' murmured Hamish Tovey. 'Get a look of that!'

'This'll travel round the world,' said someone from a newspaper not in the Scotland chain. 'This'll really hit headlines.'

The Scotland chain were concentrating on the copycatting angle. They were rerunning the Scotland/Bethany trout-farm pics, to go out side by side with this one, inviting the reader to decide whether Bethany was going up or down in the world.

'Focus on the girl,' said Hamish, as Carl May joined Bethany on the concrete ramp. He wore black swimming trunks and was in good trim condition for a man of his age. But he was shorter than she was. 'Forget him.'

Carl looked Bethany up and down: he was elated.

'She wore a teeny weeny ultra-teeny
   Yellow polka-dot bikini –'

he chanted.

'No, Carl,' said Bethany. 'I'm sure it's not ultra-teeny.'

He pushed her in.

'Oh Christ,' shouted Hamish. 'What are you playing at? We'll have to do that again!' Though most of the press had got it, he wasn't yet rolling.

'We'll do it without the girl,' said Carl May. 'She's irrelevant,' and so they had to, because Carl May said so. The mood of the day changed. The media became bored and sour: what a waste of time: all the way to the Welsh mountains to get one old man, who had to hold in his paunch, jumping into a pond, top executive or not. Carl was in and out of the water six times before NBI was satisfied. They did not make it easy for him. As for Bethany, she'd scrambled to the side at once and had a really good hot shower straight away, and washed and dried her hair, and then sat gently crying. Carl May had finally really upset her. She hadn't wanted to do it in the first place: she had only said she would for the sake of the nation, for their moral health, as Carl put it: to keep the flag of faith flying, as her father did: doing the kind thing which was the right thing. And now Carl

259

was angry, swimming around in the water, doing stupid things for a camera, not himself – where was his pride? Where was his integrity? She had more than he had when it came to it, and now she was frightened again: Carl had taken the name of marriage in vain and would be punished for it: yet he knew no better. She found she was sorry for Carl, which was almost worse than being bored and she hated the countryside: green hills closed in around her. She wanted to be back in the city.

A man came up to her and said he was Hughie Scotland's PA: Hughie had said if she wanted a lift home, he could give her one. Bethany was doubtful. Then she looked over to where Carl May still thrashed about in the water of the cooling pond, white head bobbing.

'Hughie says not to worry,' said the PA, who was young, broad-shouldered, good-looking and interested. 'Hughie says he'll look after you. If you know what I mean.'

'OK,' said Bethany. 'I seem to remember what he means.'

She sat next to the PA in the car on the way back to London, not in the back as he'd expected. She felt shivery and a little sick presently, but it soon passed. She took out her contact lenses.

'I like your eyes grey,' he said, his own eyes off the road.

'Do watch where you're going,' she said, 'or you'll kill us both,' but she was pleased. Presently she started humming to herself:

'I do, I do, I do,
  And I ain't going to tell you who.
  But I belong to somebody,
  Yes indeed I do!'

and felt positively brave and cheerful, and as if her life had begun anew, which indeed it had.

54

Carl May sat amongst the Pharaohs and wept. 'I am a stranger in my own land,' he thought. He shivered and felt sick. Painted eyes stared at him, oval, beautiful and calm: the carved and soulful eyes of strange beasts, but there was no one to talk to. His impatience had driven them away. His own easy irritation, his flashing anger, his unreasonable demands, had seared a burnt and blasted space around and no one came near him. Why should they? He wouldn't if he were them. He lived in a kennel, and barked. If he'd been his own mother, he'd have put himself there.

He was dying. He did not care. Only that none of it had been what he wanted, none of it what he meant. He hoped Bethany would be all right. Death, he could see, was too great a punishment for the habit of correcting someone out of turn. Nausea made him feel kind: as if you needed strength to be cruel and kindness was just the easiest, most natural thing. There was no more time to investigate the notion. The mind had to die, that was the dreadful thing: bodies were two a penny, but that all the buzzing speculation of the individual mind had to go – therein lay the tragedy. He should never have got involved with the Barbers of the Bath. That had been insanity. He wished to apologize to the clones of Joanna May. But he didn't have the strength. Too late.

After he'd got out of the pond, towelled and walked back to the VIP room, the meters – the ones put in to reassure the visitors – had started to chatter. The area had been cleared, more or less. Media men will risk anything for a story, even stay round chattering meters. What a fuss! They'd wanted to put him in the isolation room and start emergency treatments, but he knew already it was no good. It had been foretold. Let them suck out as much bone marrow as they wanted, he was finished. Philip drove him back to Eton Square. Good for Philip. He'd make the alarms chatter now, too. He wondered if it had been an accident. Probably not. Who had fixed it? Coustain? His own Divination Department? Joanna? He wouldn't blame her. He wished she was with him. In spite of everything, he wished she was there. He thought Isaac was in the room; he hoped he was: it would be somebody to talk to. But there was no one, nothing animate. No sound at all, unless he was deaf. He would have to take his own journey through death, so alone, without servants, without friends; stand at the Throne of the Most High, and make his explanation there, without support, without witnesses. What could he say? I wanted to know what would happen next? Was that enough? There had not been time: he had been clapped like a bird in full flight, soaring. Fate was unkind, but just.

It wasn't Isaac. It was Joanna. He saw her blue eyes. He shivered so much he could hardly speak. He said, 'No, don't come too near.'

She said, 'I never did, I never dared. I should have been more brave.'

He said, 'I know all that. I know. My fault.'

She just stared at him, but at least her eyes moved. They weren't dead. He had, after all, spared her, saved her. Now he had his reward.

'Joanna,' Carl May said, 'take me, remake me. For God's sake, remake me.'

'All right,' said Joanna May.

55

That was a year of strange events, some wonderful, some terrible: and there are stranger years ahead, no doubt. They don't frighten me; even death has lost its sting. The future shouldn't alarm us: how could it possibly be worse than what's gone before? Little by little, wisdom replaces ignorance, self-knowledge overcomes stupidity, awareness gets the upper hand of cruelty. It is the past which is so terrifying, with its capacity to spoil and destroy the present. That can't get better.

Little Carl runs round my feet. He's three years old, an energetic, noisy little boy, with thick pale hair and bright red cheeks, interested in everything, bored by nothing. He can read and write already, and even recite nursery rhymes, which he loves to do, never getting them quite right. If I correct him he has a temper tantrum: he is beside himself with upset and indignation – I have failed to recognize the difficulties he has overcome, the achievement; so great a task for one so small – and his small frame cannot contain such passion. His whole body turns as red as his cheeks, he flails and kicks and beats the ground, the door, me, anything; and then I, hurt in mind and body, have to carry him, as best I can, to his room and shut him in until we both calm down and can begin again. I could beat him black and blue, and am still sometimes tempted to, to punish him for what he did to me, for the unlived life he gave me, so many years of it, the guilt he made me feel, the loss he made me endure, for the deaths of Isaac and of Oliver. Except this innocent has done nothing: I know he could, that's all, and knowing what he could do also know what I could do, sufficiently provoked; and so I have to forgive him, both in retrospect and in advance.

Easier not to correct him, one way or another, to avoid the confrontation, to let the error go unchecked. 'Spoiling,' Gina calls it. Now she has given her children away, how quickly she has taken on Julie's former role, and become censorious. But I'm older, I know better, I no longer fight for fairness, truth and justice. I just say, 'That's wonderful, Carl, how clever you are!' We christened him Rex, Alice and I. King. Why not? But Julie was against it – a dog's name, she said – and it soon drifted back to being Carl, little Carl.

Alice, of all of them, Queen of Cups, was the one who volunteered to give birth to little Carl, on condition she didn't have to rear him. Dr Holly, back in the business, used his own tried and tested techniques of nuclei transfer to bring it about. Alice proved a good and dutiful birth mother: didn't smoke, didn't drink, watched her health and her moods – trained as she was in keeping her body well under control. She relinquished the baby to me at six weeks, without protest – glad of a decent night's sleep, I daresay, and happy enough to let the simple pleasures of narcissism prevail over the more complicated snakes-and-ladders game of motherhood; anxious to get back to work; and knowing I'd bring up the child pretty much as she would. How could I not?

Julie, Queen of Pentacles, is happy bringing up Ben, and little Anthony too; Alec, their adoptive father, comes and goes. He is resigned to the noise, the mess, the constant upheaval; consoled by the sense of present and future, so long as he can fly off from time to time, leave it all behind and tread the clean and flattering corridors of world class hotels until such time as his strength returns and his self-esteem is restored.

Jane, Queen of Wands, no longer toys with the idea of working in film: she has settled happily and quite profitably as a journalist – the work suits her better, being more about facts, less about fantasy. She felt obliged to take Sue in because three was too much for Julie, and Alice had done her bit by actually giving birth to little Carl, and Gina wasn't fit, and a child will take any clone, it seems, for a mother. The essential nature is the same, after all: only the frills are different. Sue then felt the lack of a resident father, so Jane, running comfortably on only a quarter guilt, finally consented to allow Tom to move in. Jane is always out and about so Tom does much of the childminding and cooking, grumbling the while, but the three of them, Jane, Tom, Sue, seem happy enough. Sue sees her birth mother from time to time, of course, but prefers the Jane rather than the Gina version, or at any rate, she'd rather have Tom for a father than Cliff.

Gina, Queen of Swords, now childless, is at medical school but back with Cliff. He still drinks, he still hits her, but not so much or so hard. Pain is indeed addictive, and perhaps the effort of curing it is hardly worth it, if there are no children about. If it's pleasurable, why not? We've had so many oughts and shoulds, all of us, we've all but given up being critical of one another. Good for her, say we.

We would have been perfect people if we could, but our genes were against us. We would have been faithful, kind and true, but fate was against us. We are one woman split five ways, a hundred ways, a million million ways.

It's autumn. I, Joanna May, am out in the garden, raking leaves. I keep things tidy, and growing, in memory of Oliver, and besides, I like to do it. Little Carl runs round my feet and all but trips me up, and falls headlong into a pile of leaves. 'Careful,' I say, 'I'm not as young as I was,' and I pick him up and set him straight, and he laughs cheerfully and rushes off to set to flight a flock of seagulls, rashly gathered on the lawn: and when the wicked deed is done, and the birds have risen crossly and unwillingly into the air, where they hang around to wheel and squawk their reproach, he stands stock still, amazed at what he's done. I do love him. Never stopped.

265

FAY WELDON

AFFLICTION

PROLOGUE

'Who was that knocking at your front door?' asked Annette, as Spicer got back into bed and entwined his legs through hers.

'Only a gypsy woman,' he said. 'Dirty and fat and old.'

This was in London ten years ago.

'What did she want?' asked Annette, who was clean, slim and young.

'She wanted to tell my fortune,' said Spicer. 'For a fee.'

'Did you let her?' asked Annette.

Spicer looked down at her from above. His eyes were brown and intense; his hair was thick and blonde.

'Of course I didn't,' Spicer said. 'Superstitious nonsense! I told her to go away at once.'

'She can't have liked that,' observed Annette.

'She didn't,' said Spicer, 'but I wanted to get back to you. She said as she went, "I'll go but the bad luck will stay." She had an angry heart in the first place. Nothing to do with me.'

His mouth descended upon Annette's, his hand parted her legs and she forgot all about the gypsy woman.

'I shall give you half the house for your birthday,' said Spicer, eight days later. 'I will give it to you out of my natural love and affection, as it says in legal documents. We will share this house as we share our lives. I will see my lawyer as soon as I can.'

'Spicer,' warned Annette, 'aren't you being precipitate? We've known each other for only seven weeks, and most of that has been spent in bed.'

Spicer laughed.

'I'm a precipitate person,' he said. 'An all-or-nothing guy.'

Annette was leaning against an oak tree and Spicer was leaning into her, holding her fast, at the end of the overgrown garden. A little distance away Spicer's son Jason by his first wife Aileen, and Annette's daughter Susan by her husband Paddy, played together quietly in the long grasses. Jason had been in the world for two years and Susan for three.

'You know as well as I do, Annette,' said Spicer, 'that we're going to be married and live happily ever after.'

He kissed her on the lips and then drew away from her, but only because he could hear the children approaching. Both felt the loss of touch as pain, and moaned. Up above, the green oak leaves shivered in witness.

'But, Annette,' said Annette's mother Judy on the phone, three months later, 'this all comes so soon after your break with Paddy. I'm glad for you, because you've had such a wretched time, but please tell me more about this Spicer.'

Annette lay on the bed and Spicer lay beside her.

'He's so beautiful,' said Annette, 'you've no idea. And he lives in a lovely big house.'

'Don't be silly, Annette,' said Judy. 'And don't say I'm being patronising and put the phone down. Where and how did you meet him?'

'I met him at a party,' said Annette, 'and we've hardly been apart since.'

'He must go to work,' observed Judy.

'It's his own work, his own business; So I go with him. Spicer is heir to Horrocks and Sons Wine Imports, established 1793, though there's very little left to inherit.'

'Wine's not a good business to be in, in a time of recession,' said Judy. 'But I expect he had a good education.'

'Better than mine,' said Annette. 'Do you want references for the man I love; is that it?'

'It might be a good idea,' said Judy, 'and from his first wife too, since you say he's been married before.'

'She made him unhappy,' said Annette. 'Okay? She's depressive, manipulative and greedy, and tried to turn his little boy against him.'

'So now you can look after her little boy and he can give you and little Susan a home,' observed Judy.

'Well, yes,' said Annette, after a pause. 'Isn't that wonderful! Not just that we've found true love but we each answer the other's problems. Please be happy for me, Mother.'

'I'll try,' said Judy. 'I expect I'll manage.'

Annette brought the call to an end and with one hand lifted the phone from the bed and half-dropped it onto the floor. The receiver fell off its hook and lay neglected and buzzing at Spicer and Annette while they made love. This was before the advent of the new technology which cuts out the buzz after thirty seconds and instructs the user to re-dial.

'Everything moves faster now,' said Annette, some six months after her phone-call to her mother. 'Do you think it's because there are more and more people in the world, and time has to be shared out amongst them?'

'I am not as fanciful as you,' said Spicer. 'I'm just a wine merchant.'

They sat on the living room floor watching television. The room had been redecorated; the carpet was thick and clean; all trace of the miserable Aileen removed. Jason and Susan sprawled beside them.

'Shall we have a baby between us?' Spicer asked. 'That's one for you, one for me, one for us. That makes a real family.'

'I must think about that,' said Annette.

'Make me a bacon sandwich while you think about it,' said Spicer. 'No better food in all the world than the bacon sandwiches you make for me. White, soft bread, thinly spread butter, crisp brown bacon.'

'Too much cholesterol, too much salt,' warned Annette, but she rose to do Spicer's bidding.

'I shall live for ever in perfect health,' said Spicer, 'because I love you.'

When Annette came back from the kitchen, she said, 'We must have a baby between us, Spicer; there has to be something to sop up this abundance.'

But it was another ten years before she conceived.

'Annette,' said Spicer to his wife ten years and five months later, 'I won't be able to come with you to the Clinic this evening.'

'But, Spicer darling,' said Annette, 'why not?'

'Because I have matters to attend to that are more important.'

'What could be more important than the baby?'

'*I* could,' said Spicer, and he left the rest of his breakfast and went to work straight away without even calling goodbye to Susan or Jason. Nor did Spicer kiss Annette goodbye, as was his custom. The habit of years had been broken: the gears of the relationship shifted and changed.

Annette set about her household duties and after an hour called Spicer at his office.

'Mr Horrocks,' said Spicer's secretary Wendy. 'I have your wife on the phone.'

Wendy was kind and efficient. She was in her thirties, plain and a hockey-player. She lived with her mother.

'Spicer,' said Annette. 'How could you speak to me like that? If you knew how it upset me, you wouldn't do it. You being bad-tempered isn't good for the baby.'

'Annette,' said Spicer, 'I am in a meeting,' and he put the receiver down his end so that the one in Annette's hand buzzed. Annette and Spicer were the first in their road to own a mobile phone: their neighbours possessed newer, lighter, cheaper models. There can be a penalty for being first; especially in technological matters. Annette called Spicer's office again.

'Wendy,' asked Annette, 'is Spicer really in a meeting or is he just saying that?'

5

'Mr Horrocks is just saying it,' said Wendy, 'but in fact he's very busy. The auditors are due.'

'Wendy,' said Annette, 'has Spicer been a little, well, on edge lately?'

'No,' said Wendy. 'He's been just fine. Happy as a sandboy, in fact, as usual. Very chatty. We're all so looking forward to the baby. If she's born on Christmas Day she'll be a little Capricorn.'

'I don't know about things like that,' said Annette.

'Nor do I,' said Wendy. 'It's Mr Horrocks who tells me she'll be a little Capricorn. A little goat.'

'Oh,' said Annette. 'Well, I'll try and get used to the idea.'

Wendy said, 'When he's got a moment I'll say you called, shall I?' And Annette said, 'No, don't worry. It can wait till this evening,' and put the phone down, but not before she heard, or thought she heard, Wendy say, 'Sometimes I'm really glad I'm not married.'

Annette called her friend Gilda; they went to the same antenatal class. Gilda was seven months pregnant to Annette's five and lived four doors along from Annette, at No 17 Bella Crescent. People likened Gilda to Ginger Rogers, and indeed Gilda had red hair and had once been a dancer. But then people likened Annette to Meryl Streep for no better reason than she had a fair skin and small, straight nose, and a vulnerable air. Gilda and Annette worked as freelance researchers for a TV production company. Gilda's current task was an investigation into the history of heraldic beasts, and Annette's into the myth of Europa, ravished by Jupiter in the form of a bull.

'Hello, Gilda,' said Annette.

'What's the matter?' asked Gilda. 'I can tell from your voice something's wrong. Is the baby all right?'

'The baby's just fine,' said Annette, 'but Spicer won't come to Father's Night at the Clinic and he seems angry with me and I don't know why.'

'He was all right when we saw you at dinner on Tuesday,' said Gilda. 'In fact he was being very attentive and kind. Perhaps he has troubles at work?'

'His secretary said something about having the auditors in, but

6

so far as I know everything's okay. Profits are down but aren't everyone's?'

'It depends how far down,' said Gilda, whose journalist husband Steve was short, thin and pop-eyed, but kind and intelligent. 'Spicer's very protective of you, Annette, especially now you're pregnant. Perhaps he's trying to save you from bad financial news but taking it out on you at the same time. Men do that kind of thing.'

'It doesn't feel like that,' said Annette. 'It feels worse.'

'Spicer doesn't have a new secretary? He's still got Wendy?'

'Yes,' said Annette. 'And I don't think it's anything like that. The sex is still fine between us. It's just that we used always to speak a lot when we made love: each offer the other a running commentary, but for the last few weeks he hasn't liked me to speak. In fact if I say anything at all he covers my mouth with his hand. This isn't being recorded by the answerphone, I hope?'

'No,' said Gilda.

'Because,' said Annette, 'I don't like talking about things as personal as this in the first place: it feels disloyal: supposing your Steve ran the answerphone tape and heard me talking about my sex life with Spicer.'

'I'm your best friend,' said Gilda. 'You're allowed to talk to me. Think of the things *I've* told you!'

'In fact,' said Annette, 'it's rather as if Spicer were plunging about in the dark, in the silence, and it was nothing at all to do with me. I can't explain it exactly. I don't mind, I quite like it, it's just different. It's mindless. So long as it doesn't go on like this too long.'

'Perhaps the baby is the problem,' said Gilda.

'But Spicer was the one who always wanted me to be pregnant,' said Annette. ' "One of yours," he said, "one of mine, one of ours." And I don't think time has changed that.'

'Perhaps Spicer wanted a boy? Men tend to.'

'I don't think so. I was the one who so wanted to be told whether it was a girl or boy: Spicer preferred to leave it as a surprise. But to me it always seems peculiar if the hospital know the gender and don't tell the parents, as if everyone were playing some kind of cute game.'

7

'It seems to me,' said Gilda, 'you're just paying the foetus more attention than you are Spicer, and he doesn't like it. I'll have to go, Annette. My other phone's going.'

Annette prepared a special supper for Spicer that evening and put scent behind her ears. Spicer liked Annette to wear scent. Of recent months, Annette realised, she had neglected so to do.

Spicer returned at seven-fifty-one instead of six o'clock, his customary time. Annette took care not to reproach Spicer or ask him where he had been. Nor did he offer any apologies for, let alone any information about, his lateness.

'I'm sorry I called you at the office, Spicer,' said Annette. 'I know you like to ring me but not me to ring you. I just sometimes get a little upset if you go off in a mood in the morning.'

'Um,' Spicer said. 'I see you have opened the 1985 Saint Estephe.'

'I made a rather special dinner,' she said. 'Beef olives. I know you like those. So I thought we'd treat ourselves and open our best wine.'

They were in the drawing room. Annette had found some candles and polished the candlesticks. Their light made the heavy grey curtains shimmer agreeably. She had arranged roses in the vases: red and white. The room seemed delightful.

'I thought pregnant women weren't supposed to drink alcohol,' said Spicer.

'Just a glass or so doesn't hurt,' she said.

'I thought you'd be at the Clinic,' he said. 'Weren't you supposed to go?'

'It was Father's Night,' she said, 'so if you couldn't be there, there wasn't much point in my going. Steve went with Gilda, though. So I had time to cook us something special. And since Susan and Jason have gone to the cinema, we can have some time to ourselves. Shall we eat now?'

'I don't know why you cooked beef,' he said. 'I don't eat red meat. It goes against the grain.'

'Since when?' she asked. 'And what grain?' but he didn't reply. He was not in a jokey mood.

*

'I'm afraid that without the meat,' Annette apologised, serving her husband's food, 'the mangetout and the new potatoes look a little bleak.'

'It takes very little food to keep me going,' Spicer said. 'Fruit and vegetables; pulses occasionally. In fact, Annette, if you would keep the fruit bowl full, I could help myself when my appetite dictated and then we could do without the formality of the family meals which nobody wants; let alone the dinners à deux. They must be as trying for you as they are for me.'

And Spicer smiled at Annette politely and rose and went to the living room and, instead of opening the newspaper as was his custom in the evening after dinner, opened a book entitled *The Search for the Father*, which had a whooshy pattern of oranges and reds upon the cover, and began to read intently.

Annette cleared the table. The baby kicked. Annette hurled a plate across the room. It broke. Annette went into the living room and snatched the book from Spicer's hand and flung it in the fire.

'For fuck's sake, Spicer,' Annette shrieked, 'what is the *matter*?'
Spicer regarded his wife calmly, only occasionally looking away from her into the fireplace to watch the book burn. He could have saved it had he wished, but he did not so wish.
'Look at you!' said Spicer. 'Take a look at yourself in the mirror, ask yourself what the matter is, and try to calm down. You are quite insane.'
'But what have I done?'
'It isn't your fault,' said Spicer. 'You can't help yourself, I realise that. But shall we go through today's performance? First you call me at my office and try to disturb my peace there; you cannot bear me to escape from you, even for an hour or two; you then call my secretary and try to turn her against me. You spend the morning talking to Gilda on the phone about our sex life – I had lunch with Stephen – it looks as if he's being made redundant, by the way. You're totally self-centred and without loyalty. I do not take kindly to you discussing our intimate life with your lesbian friend. I wonder what hold she has over you? When I

9

come home late you're not even interested enough to ask me where I've been. You're wearing scent so I know that in your calculating way you have sex with me planned for tonight. You do apologise for calling me at the office, which is something, but then you follow it up with a remark designed to make me feel bad, about how much I upset you. You open a bottle of 1985 Saint Estephe without consulting me – you are so competitive it extends even into the world of wine! – and worse, do so without the slightest concern for the health of our baby. You have so much ambivalence about poor little Gillian, I'll be surprised if you manage to bring her to term. You don't go to the Clinic – cutting off your nose to spite my face because making me responsible for your actions is another way of controlling me, and you can't resist a little extra dig, mentioning that Steve went with Gilda. Poor Steve: he seems to have no will of his own. You must have me all to yourself so you send the poor kids off to the cinema, regardless of what they want, let alone the fact that I might want to see them. You cook beef although you know perfectly well the only protein I can eat these days is white meat – chicken or a little fish – and you overcook the mangetout in a way that can only be deliberate. Then you break some plates, follow me in here where I am peacefully reading, snatch the book from my hand, and fling it in the fire. Is that enough about what the matter is? Now for God's sake don't start crying or you'll upset the children. They're upset enough already. Okay?'

'Gilda,' said Annette on the phone early next morning, 'I am so miserable.'

'What's the matter now?' asked Gilda. 'What's the time?'

'It's well past nine,' said Annette. 'I'm sorry. But I have to speak to someone.'

'The baby kept me awake kicking all night,' said Gilda. 'I've only just got to sleep.'

'Well, I didn't sleep at all,' said Annette. 'I was suffering from terror. That's the only way I can describe it.'

'Tell me more,' said Gilda. 'Here's Steve with my cup of tea. Thank you, Steve. You are so good to me. Okay, Annette, go on. Forgive me if I slurp.'

'It's a kind of black pit within the periphery of myself,' said Annette. 'It's as black and empty as outer space, and everything spins down into it and is lost.'

'A black hole,' said Gilda. 'I used to feel that when Jackson my first husband left me and I didn't know how to pay the rent. I think you're describing anxiety, not terror. What's making you anxious?'

'The thought of me without Spicer,' said Annette. 'He said such terrible things to me last night, and I love him and I'm having his baby. How could he? Then he just went and slept all night in the spare room. He said he was frightened to sleep next to me in case I did him some terrible damage. He said I was a madwoman, and eaten up with hatred of men.'

'What had you done?'

'I broke some plates,' said Annette, 'and threw the book he was reading into the fire.'

'Well,' said Gilda, 'you ought to expect some reaction. If you behave like a madwoman you get called a madwoman.'

'He drove me to it,' said Annette. 'He wouldn't eat the dinner I cooked. And he was late home and wouldn't say why. And I lay alone on the bed all night with a headache and a black hole in my chest, and I must have dozed off because when I woke Spicer had left the house and gone to work, and without a word, without a note.'

'You told me you didn't sleep at all,' said Gilda.

'Gilda, this is serious. There was a difference in tone. I can't explain it. I'm terrified.'

'It doesn't sound serious to me,' said Gilda. 'He'll ring later in the morning and apologise.'

At ten-thirty precisely the phone rang. Wendy put Spicer through.

'Annette,' said Spicer, 'I hope you're okay. I left you sleeping. You look lovely asleep: I didn't want to wake you. I hope I didn't upset you last night. I seem to get these moods these days.'

'You upset me quite a lot,' she said.

'But you're better now? It's all forgotten?'

'Yes,' she said.

'I love you very much,' he said. 'None of it's your fault. You can't help being what you are any more than I can.'

'Well, thank you,' said Annette.

'Pauline just called. She and Christopher want us to join them at the opera tonight. I said yes. That's okay, isn't it? It's *Figaro*.'

'That's wonderful,' said Annette. 'Mozart is always soothing.'

There was a slight pause –

'That's not a dig, is it?' asked Spicer.

'Of course it isn't,' replied Annette. 'How could it be?'

'It could suggest you needed soothing, which means you're not going to let bygones be bygones. Well, never mind either way. We'll meet up at the Coliseum at seven then: eat afterwards. Wear something lovely, especially for me.'

'Of course,' said Annette. 'Don't I always? Spicer, you know you have a really remarkable memory? Last night you went through every single thing I said, in order, finding fault. The other side of appalled I was impressed.'

'I don't have time to talk now, darling,' said Spicer. 'Though I'd love to. I have a meeting. But yes, I do have a good memory. That's Saturn's doing, sextile my moon but, alas, also quincunx your sun.'

'What are you talking about?'

'Never mind,' said Spicer. 'Not your world. Must go. Kiss you.'

'Kiss you,' said Annette.

'Gilda,' said Annette, 'you were quite right. Spicer phoned. The black hole feeling has gone. Last night was incidental, accidental. Put it like this: it was a little bit of emotional flotsam, washed up by the tides of togetherness. In ten years there'd be quite a lot to wash up.'

'How poetical,' said Gilda.

'Thank you. I'm so relieved,' said Annette. 'And we're going to the opera. I don't know what Spicer was upset about and I suppose I'll never know, and it doesn't matter.'

'I know what it may have been,' said Gilda, 'and all I can say is I'm sorry. I was about to phone you. I told Steve a bit about what you told me about Spicer and you in bed, and he talked to Spicer about it over lunch, he now tells me. I'm not speaking to

Steve, it doesn't matter how many cups of tea he brings me. It was a confidence.'

'I knew that,' said Annette. 'I didn't bring it up. Spicer did mention it. I expect Steve was only trying to help.'

'Steve likes everyone to be happy,' said Gilda. 'That's his trouble.'

'It's over now anyway,' said Annette. 'It did upset Spicer. But all kinds of things seem to upset him nowadays.'

'What do you mean by nowadays? How long has this nowadays been going on?' asked Gilda.

'Two, three weeks. I don't know,' said Annette. 'Two or three years, for all I know. How would I know? Spicer keeps complaining I'm unperceptive. But how can I perceive things he doesn't tell me?'

'Steve expects me to read his mind and tell him what he's feeling,' said Gilda.

'If I tell Spicer what he feels he goes berserk,' said Annette. 'He says he doesn't like to think of me inside his head so I try to keep out of it. I take nothing for granted. Gilda, have you heard of the word quincunx? Spicer used it this morning.'

'No.'

'Neither had I. I felt stupid. I looked it up. It's a term used in astrology to denote a 150 degree separation of the planets in orbit: a stressful aspect, particularly in a compatibility chart.'

'Nobody could be expected to know that,' said Gilda.

'It was a funny kind of word for him to use in a general conversation,' said Annette. 'And then there was sextile. That's a good aspect, but it applied only to him, not to him and me.'

'Don't get paranoid, Annette,' said Gilda. 'If you worry about every little thing you'll wear yourself out. Perhaps Spicer's just getting you a his-and-hers chart for your birthday.'

'Spicer would never do anything like that,' said Annette. 'He hates all that kind of gobbledegook. The religion of weak minds. Squelchy. So do I. And another thing –'

'Yes?'

'I wish Spicer hadn't called at ten-thirty precisely. It's as if he had it worked out, and was clock-watching. I'll let her stew till ten-thirty, then I'll call. He didn't phone when he first arrived,

13

he didn't wait till after lunch. Those are the times he usually calls. But this wasn't even any old time, it was on the dot.'

'Annette, that's insane,' said Gilda. 'Ten-thirty is as much any old time as any other. It just happened to be on the dot.'

'I suppose so,' said Annette. 'Now I'm feeling uneasy again. There's a sub-text I don't understand. Well, I expect whatever it is will emerge: push itself out like the alien in the film, bursting out of the ribcage.'

'What a horrid image,' said Gilda. 'It can't be good for the baby.'

Annette lay down on the marital bed and put Optrex pads on her eyes.

'Mum?'

'Hello, Susan.'

'Are you okay? I've brought you a cup of tea.'

'Thanks.'

'You haven't been crying?'

'Of course not. Being pregnant makes your eyes puffy.'

'Yuk. It's time you had new wallpaper in here. This lot's dingy.'

'It's how Spicer and I like it,' said Annette.

'Why? It's early eighties drear. Browny dinge.'

'Because Spicer and I put it up together the week we moved in,' said Annette. 'There was no money for decorators.'

'That's why the pattern's slipped,' said Susan. 'None of the little flowers match up. It's a mess, and always has been.'

'If it's a mess it's because you and Jason were crawling round our ankles,' said Annette, 'and tripping us up. Well, you were toddling: Jason was crawling. We like it the way it is. It's our keepsake: our memento of the beginning.'

'That's nice,' said Susan.

'And if we tried to take it down,' said Annette, 'the whole wall would come down with it. We'd have to re-plaster the room. That wallpaper was too heavy when it went up ten years ago and it's heavier still today.'

'That isn't scientifically possible,' said Susan.

'Yes it is,' said Annette. 'It has sopped up pleasure, uxorious bliss.'

'What does that mean?' asked Susan.

14

'Never mind,' said Annette.

'I'll look it up,' said Susan.

'Look away,' said Annette.

The phone rang. Annette stretched out her hand. It was Gilda.

'Annette? Did I disturb you?'

'No. Not really,' said Annette.

'I think I know what the matter is,' said Gilda.

'What?'

'Your novel,' said Gilda. 'He's jealous because you're publishing a novel.'

'Why should Spicer be jealous of a novel?' asked Annette. 'It isn't even a proper novel. It's a novella. I only wrote it for fun. The children were growing up, and work was drying up, and I had some time left over. And it isn't coming out for months and months. No, that can't be the matter.'

'Steve says it might be,' said Gilda. 'Steve says perhaps your novella is about Spicer.'

'Of course it isn't about Spicer,' said Annette. 'If it's about anyone it's about my parents, and not even them, really. No, that's a silly idea. It was Spicer who gave the manuscript to Ernie Gromback. It was Spicer who wanted it to see the light of day. I wanted to just put it in a drawer and forget it. Do you know Ernie Gromback the publisher?'

'Everyone knows Ernie Gromback,' said Gilda. 'He's given herpes to at least a dozen people I know.'

'That's beside the point,' said Annette. 'And I'm sure it isn't true.'

'Perhaps Spicer assumed Ernie Gromback would turn the manuscript down and put you off writing novels for ever.'

'Well Ernie Gromback didn't turn it down,' said Annette, 'and why on earth should Spicer want to put me off writing novels? It might bring in some money.'

'Because he's the kind of man who needs a woman's full attention,' said Gilda, 'money or not.'

'Sometimes I think you don't like Spicer very much,' said Annette.

'You asked my opinion and I gave it,' said Gilda. 'If you didn't want it, why ask?'

'Don't get huffy, please, Gilda,' said Annette. 'That's the last thing I need. If anyone should be huffy, it's me. You telling Steve about me and Spicer in bed, and still discussing it so far as I can see.'

'Steve and I hate to see you and Spicer having marital problems,' said Gilda. 'Of course we discuss it. We couldn't bear anything to happen to you. Spicer and Annette go together so well. The names fit. You are central to a whole lot of existences round here. I hope you realise that.'

'Spicer and I are not having marital difficulties, Gilda,' said Annette. 'We are perfectly happy together. I just don't like him being in a bad mood and me not knowing why. If I knew why, I could do something about it. That's all.'

'Okay, okay, okay,' said Gilda. 'Have a good time at the opera.'

'Scent!' remarked Spicer, in the foyer of the Coliseum. 'I'd rather have you natural,' and he nipped the skin of her neck with his teeth.

'You bit me!' said Annette.

'I am showing my affection,' said Spicer, 'in a familiarly uxorious way. I thought you'd like it.'

'It's just a little public,' said Annette. 'And surprising. And actually, Spicer, I wear scent for me not you.'

'Surprise,' said Spicer, 'is the stuff of life. Why hello Pauline, hello Christopher! Pauline, you look wonderful! How is architecture?'

'In the doldrums,' said Pauline and Christopher. 'How's the wine business, Spicer?'

'Just fine,' said Spicer.

'How's the pregnancy, Annette?' asked Pauline.

'Just fine,' said Annette. 'No sickness, and lots of energy.'

'That's because it's a wanted baby,' said Pauline. 'One day we'll have time and money to have one. Not yet. The future just isn't certain enough. Everyone we know is redundant or bankrupt. But Mozart will soothe us. Civilisations crumble, art goes on for ever.'

'Good lord,' said Annette. 'There's Ernie Gromback and Marion. What are they doing at an opera?'

'Searching for the culture,' said Spicer, 'they both crave and need. Do you know who they remind me of? Bob Hoskins and his cartoon lady in *Who Killed Roger Rabbit?*. He short, squat and vulgar, she the dream of his delight. Unreal.'

'Everyone's delight,' said Christopher. 'But that's a harsh view of Ernie Gromback. He may be from the people but he's a decent guy and they say he has a nose for a good novel. Others fail but he prospers.'

'And besides,' said Pauline, 'he's our guest.'

'Why hello Ernie, hello Marion!' cried Spicer. 'Great to see you both!'

'Ernie,' said Annette, 'and Marion. What a surprise! I didn't know you were opera goers. Last time I saw you, Ernie, you told me you were a Marxist.'

'Marx has let us all down,' said Ernie. 'Now there's nothing left but the New Age. Marion drifts into it, and I drift after her. There's money in it. Didn't Pauline tell you we were coming, Annette? I asked her to tell you.'

'I told Spicer,' said Pauline, 'and I assumed he'd tell Annette: he's usually reliable. What else could I do? Chris only got the box at the very last minute: I was expected to fill it out of the blue. I can't in person keep everyone fully informed. All I can do is delegate. I work too, you know. Why are you all blaming me?'

'Okay, okay, okay,' said everyone. 'Mozart will soothe us.'

'Gilda!'

'Good lord, Annette,' said Gilda, 'I thought you were at the opera. Are you okay?'

'I am at the opera,' said Annette. 'It's half-time or whatever they call it. Gilda, I think I might have left the iron on in the bedroom and the kids are both out. You couldn't possibly go round and make sure I haven't? The key's under the rose-pot.'

'You are impossible,' said Gilda.

'Why does everyone think that?' asked Annette. 'All of a sudden. Or is it just I haven't noticed till now?'

'I mean keeping the key under the rose-pot,' said Gilda. 'That's all. Everyone leaves irons on. Of course I'll go. What are you wearing?'

'My yellow silk dress, with a bronze silk sash thing which more or less hides me being pregnant, and my silver earrings. I look

17

okay. In fact I look rather good. Pauline came straight from the office in a grey suit and I felt overdressed but then Ernie's Marion turned up in red jodhpurs, a white lace blouse, a black riding cap and diamanté earrings so I felt under-dressed. That means I'm probably about right.'

'Is Spicer being okay?' asked Gilda.

'I don't know. I just don't know. He said he didn't like me wearing scent and I was stupid enough to say I wore it for me, not him. It wasn't even true: I was just surprised. But I think he must have taken offence: he sat as far from me as he could and we usually sit together: you know? If we can. We even hold hands. And then Ernie Gromback annoyed him by talking about books, and falling hardback sales, and paperback deals and so on, and then he started talking about *Lucifette Fallen* which made matters worse.'

'Started talking about what?' asked Gilda.

'*Lucifette Fallen*,' said Annette. 'That's the book I wrote, goddamn it. Hang on while I put in another coin . . . They think I've gone to the Powder Room. You can take forever in the Powder Room at the opera. It's because everyone goes in their best clothes. Ernie said he wanted to bring publication forward to be nearer the baby's birth, say mid-December.'

'Is that good or bad?' asked Gilda.

'I've no idea. I said it all sounded unhealthily commercial to me, because I thought that was what Spicer would want me to say, but Spicer said in for a penny, in for a pound – I ought to make as much capital out of the baby as possible and I could always go into labour in the middle of a chat show and so command maximum media attention.'

'Was he being sarcastic?' asked Gilda.

'I don't know,' said Annette. 'I just don't know. I can't read him any more. So I can't tell you if Spicer is being okay or not: I'm just not having a good time, which is why I'm talking to you. It's all too nervy. Look, I really do have to go to the Powder Room now. I must go. Please check the iron. I'm sure it's okay. I'd just feel better if you checked.'

'I know, I know, I know,' said Gilda. 'Of course I will, Annette.'

*

'Is there a new one-way system or is this taxi taking us the long way home?' asked Spicer.

'There's a new system,' said Annette.

'You haven't the faintest idea whether there's a new system or not,' said Spicer. 'You just want everything to be easy and pleasant. Well, never mind. Here, give me your hand. You're quite right: Mozart is very soothing. Did you see they were advertising a concert of Indian music? No, you wouldn't have noticed. I expect you prefer the familiar tonic scale: Eastern music would pass you by. But I'll try and get to it, if I can find the time and you're prepared to let me out of your sight for an hour or two.'

'Spicer,' said Annette, 'are you sure nothing's wrong?'

'It is really irritating,' said Spicer, 'to be asked all the time if something's wrong. I can't be laughing and chattering all the time, though I know you'd like me to be. Spicer, life and soul of the party. You don't notice much, do you? From one-way traffic systems, to Indian music, to changes in me.'

'What sort of changes?'

'Everyone changes,' said Spicer. 'And it is normal for spouses to notice, unless they are hopelessly self-centred. Then it may indeed come as both a surprise and a threat.'

Two tears ran down Annette's cheek.

'Oh dear,' said Spicer, 'oh dear, oh dear, oh dear. You do know how to put the pressure on. How many years have I had of this?'

'It must be something in my stars,' said Annette, 'which makes me so impossible.'

'Many a true word spoken in jest,' said Spicer.

'I don't feel in the least like jesting,' said Annette. 'And why this sudden interest in Indian music and astrology? It's hurtful. It keeps me out.'

'Good God,' said Spicer, 'is a man to have no privacy? No space in his own head for his own interests? His own tastes? Must everything be shared? Common denominated? A very quick way to end a relationship! I hardly think it's your ambition to do that, Annette. There's too much at stake. Look, we've had a splendid evening out at the opera, your fan Ernie's talked prattling nonsense to you non-stop, surely you don't have to be quite so doleful? Sitting in the back of a taxi weeping when you have everything in the world a woman could want? I know you're pregnant, but you mustn't take it out on others.'

'I'm sorry, Spicer,' said Annette.

'That's okay,' said Spicer. 'Shall we kiss and make up?'

'How was the second act?' asked Gilda. 'We haven't spoken for days. Where have you been?'

'I've just been rather busy,' said Annette. 'You know how it is. I'm trying to get this thing on the Europa myth done but I keep falling asleep. I really can't remember much about the opera, Gilda. I was too worried about what Spicer was thinking to take much notice of it.'

'That seems a waste of an expensive ticket,' said Gilda.

'I hate it when Spicer's angry with me,' said Annette. 'I can't focus on anything.'

'He does seem to be angry with you rather a lot,' said Gilda. 'These days.'

'He wasn't very nice in the taxi home,' said Annette. 'But we've been fine since then. Really. In fact he's been sweet, in a really good mood. I can almost say what I like without thinking first. Almost. Except –'

'Except what?'

'He warned me on Saturday that the moon was full so I had to be extra careful in the traffic.'

'What's the matter with that? All kinds of people say that kind of thing,' said Gilda.

'But not Spicer,' said Annette, 'not in normal times. I looked it up in my *Dictionary of Superstitions* and it said there was some justification in the belief that the full moon exacerbated insanity. The moon pulls the tides about, and since the human body is ninety-seven per cent water the full moon may well make minimal changes in water pressure on the brain.'

'Are you suggesting Spicer's mad, Annette?'

'Of course not. But who's telling him these things? I can see the moon being full could affect the way people drove. Okay. But how can Spicer believe that the planet Saturn, which is 800 million miles away, in relation to a moon which is racing round the earth, be what gives him a good memory? It's nuts –'

'You're not still worrying about that? You're obsessive,' said Gilda.

'I can't help it,' said Annette. 'I expect it's being pregnant does it.'

'Being pregnant makes me happy,' said Gilda. 'Not anxious. Did you actually look up how many miles Saturn is from the earth?'

'Yes.'

'God help you,' said Gilda.

'On the other hand,' said Annette, 'Spicer brought me strawberries from the market early on Sunday morning and came back to bed and we had them with cream for breakfast. And he put his hand on my belly and felt Gillian kicking.'

'That's nice,' said Gilda. 'It can't be too bad.'

'It's wonderful,' said Annette. 'Just wonderful to have him in a good mood again.'

'You won't miss Clinic on Tuesday,' said Gilda, 'just because you're happy?'

'Of course I won't,' said Annette. 'See you there if I don't speak to you before. I expect it's all nothing.'

'I thought whatever it was had passed,' said Annette sadly, to Gilda.

They were at the Tuesday night antenatal class; they lay next to each other on the floor and waited for the relaxation teacher to return from assisting a woman in the Ready-to-Pop class who had gone into premature labour.

'What's he done now?' asked Gilda.

'Don't talk of Spicer as "he" like that, Gilda,' said Annette. 'I don't want to be the kind of woman who complains to other women about her husband. I don't want to get into the what's-he-done-now mentality. It's so vulgar.'

'This is meant to be a relaxation class,' said Gilda. 'And listen to you! So uptight! Don't talk to me about Spicer if you don't want to. I didn't ask, you offered. In fact, come to think of it, I'd rather not discuss it either. We can just talk about babies, I suppose, and dishwashers or, better still, not talk about anything at all to each other, ever again.'

'Sorry, Gilda,' said Annette, and her hand stretched out to hold her friend's, as it lay gently upturned on the wooden floor. Gilda's thick red hair lay, from the angle of Annette's vision, like a kind of flounced skirt around her head. 'I didn't mean to snap. I expect I snap at Spicer. I expect that's the trouble. I'm really difficult and neurotic and I just don't know it. I suppose we all think we're perfect and everyone else is to blame: when really we're the source of the trouble.' She took her hand away from Gilda's. 'I shouldn't hold your hand, I suppose. Spicer thinks we're having a lesbian relationship.' Gilda snatched her hand away and lifted her head from the floor the better to turn and stare at Annette.

'I was joking,' explained Annette. 'So was he. Oh God, I keep putting my foot in it. Spicer's right. I'm impossible.'

'Perhaps you should have some kind of anti-stress treatment,' said Gilda, 'for your head as well as your body. I wish Dr Elsie Spanner would return. This floor is very draughty. And I wish they wouldn't call the other class the "Ready-to-Pop". I'm sure it's calling it that which keeps sending women into premature labour. Pop they think and pop they go.'

'You mean me see a therapist?' asked Annette. 'Spicer and I don't believe in therapy. It's one of the core beliefs of the marriage. Therapists make people self-preoccupied, selfish and destructive. Spicer's first marriage broke up because his wife Aileen went into therapy. He said he thought they had just an ordinary happy marriage, but she started seeing this man and the next thing Spicer knew Aileen told him she was unhappy and Spicer was the cause of it, and she left him.'

'Perhaps it was true,' said Gilda.

'But she left Jason too, because the therapist said she couldn't have a child and be fulfilled as well; the child being the fruit of an unhappy marriage. It didn't sound responsible to me.'

'You should be grateful to this therapist or you wouldn't be married to Spicer now.'

'That's true,' said Annette. 'You don't think he married me just because he needed someone to help with Jason?'

'For God's sake,' said Gilda, 'go and see a therapist! Don't ask me. Whatever answer I give I'll be in trouble.'

The class was abandoned since Dr Elsie Spanner felt her greater duty was to accompany the woman in parturition to the hospital and help her with her breathing rather than to conduct the class. In the dressing room Gilda said, 'Well, what has Spicer done now to upset you? Notice I don't say "he".'

Annette said, 'My mother came to lunch. It was Monday. She often visits on Mondays. Spicer looked in from the office to see her and have a cup of coffee. You know how they get on. It's a relief. She hated my first husband. It was because he was called Paddy. She didn't like that: she said it reminded her of an Irish navvy, and then I'd have to defend Irish navvies. You know how it is. But she and Spicer get on so well I sometimes get the feeling they gang up on me. Certainly they refer to me as "she" quite a lot. My mother was talking about what it had been like giving birth to me and how quick and easy it had all been. She'd had me in the ambulance; it had to park in a lay-by and the back doors were open; it was early autumn and the morning sun was shining right into her eyes: she often tells that story. And Spicer interrupted and said, "Did you say morning sun? I thought it was evening." My mother said, "I should know, Spicer; I was there!" and Spicer looked at the cup of coffee I was pouring and said to me very angrily, "You know I don't drink coffee any more" and just walked out on us both and went back to work. I made excuses for him to my mother; I told her Spicer was overworking and me being pregnant made him edgy – gave him brainstorms. Poor Spicer, I said, he has so much responsibility: myself, Susan, Jason, work, the house, a recession: and only Spicer to look after us all.'

'You mean the kind of excuse you make to yourself,' said Gilda, 'for the way Spicer behaves.'

'It's not an excuse,' said Annette. 'It's true. But my mother stayed upset and went home with her jaw set and her teeth grinding, which gives her headaches, and I felt dreadful. I always feel responsible for my mother's peace of mind. So I made Wendy put me through to Spicer at work and told him he had to call my mother to apologise, and he just shouted at me down the phone and said I should do the apologising; I was a liar, and psychotic. If I was born in the morning why had I told him evening. Only mad people made up lies to no purpose.'

'Well, why did you tell him wrong?' asked Gilda.

'I just thought evening sounded nicer, I suppose,' said Annette. 'I can't remember either way. It didn't seem important at the time. I think Spicer might be right and I'm going mad. I really want to see a therapist, but I don't know how to tell Spicer. I'm frightened he'd be angry; he hates people with soggy brains.'

'Your brain never used to be soggy,' said Gilda.

'I think it's pregnancy,' said Annette.

'It might be Spicer,' said Gilda. 'We must consider that possibility. Spicer confusing you, making you think that what's his fault is your fault. Steve says he does that. Would you like me to ask around about therapists?'

'Yes, please, Gilda,' said Annette. 'Secret therapy. Find me a man, please. I'm sure I could talk to a man easier than a woman.'

'Hello, Mum,' said Susan, when Annette got home from the Clinic. 'You're early. I didn't expect you for another hour.'

'Why are all the windows open?' asked Annette.

'I've been smoking,' replied Susan.

'What kind of smoking?'

'Just ordinary cigarettes,' said Susan.

'How many?'

'Just one. I still feel sick.'

'Good,' said Annette.

'Spicer says dope is healthier than tobacco,' said Susan. 'If I knew how to get hold of it I would, to see if it made you any happier.'

'When did he say that?'

'At six o'clock this evening,' said Annette.

'Where is Spicer?' asked Annette. 'In the study?'

'No,' said Susan. 'Spicer went out at six-fifteen.'

'Did he say where?' asked Annette.

'No,' replied Susan. 'He looked very smart. Not suit and tie smart; leather jacket and Armani sweater smart. He was wearing aftershave. You don't think he has a sweetheart?'

'No, I don't, Susan,' said Annette.

'I was really shocked when he said that about dope.'

'I'm glad to hear it,' said Annette. 'So am I shocked. Could you make me a cup of tea, Susan?'

'Spicer says tea's bad for you. Ordinary tea, that is.'

'I'll have some all the same,' said Annette.

'Okay. Why was the class cancelled?'

'Because everything's collapsing,' said Annette, 'and it's the end of the world.'

'I hate it when you say that kind of thing, Mum. I'll go and stay with my Dad if you're not careful.'

'Off you go, then.'

'No, thanks all the same,' said Susan. 'I like it here. We can eat in our rooms. At Paddy and Pat's we have to sit up at table and wear clothes that fit. How's your blood-pressure?'

'They forgot to take it, in the muddle,' said Annette. 'I expect Spicer's gone to see a client. To sell them some end-of-bin at a knock-down price. Did he say when he'd be back?'

'No,' said Susan.

Spicer returned at seven forty-seven.

'You're home early,' he said. 'I thought I'd be back before you.'

'The class was cancelled,' said Annette. 'That's two in a row I've missed.'

'Now don't start,' said Spicer. 'It is these constant nagging reproaches: the drip, drip, drip into the ear. No wonder I'm in the state I am.'

Annette apologised and went into the kitchen and made bacon sandwiches and low-calorie hot chocolate.

'You know I don't like bacon sandwiches,' said Spicer.

'No, I didn't know that,' said Annette. 'When we first met we ate bacon sandwiches all the time. Don't you remember?'

'I'm sorry, Annette,' said Spicer. 'I don't.'

'Well, we did. I had just left Paddy and Aileen had just left you. Proper cooking seemed a waste of time we could otherwise spend in bed.'

'Then times have certainly changed,' said Spicer. 'Annette, I don't think it does either of us much good to dwell on an unhappy and

25

messy past. It's the future which should concern us. And in the meantime, I don't eat bacon sandwiches. Bacon's seductive, but pork is probably one of the worst meats.'

'In what way, Spicer?'

'Pigs are intelligent enough to know what's going on,' said Spicer, 'so they suffer more. On the whole, suffering is always the fate of the intelligent. But one can't be party to it, just because it's the way of the world. What is this drink?'

'It's a kind of cocoa without the calories,' said Annette.

'As advertised on TV?'

'Yes,' said Annette. 'As it happens.'

'Pregnancy seems to have affected your critical faculties,' said Spicer.

'You mean my intelligence?'

'Since you bring the matter up, yes.'

'It's quite a problem to know what to give you, Spicer, since you won't drink coffee or tea any more, and seem to have gone off so many foods. Now even bacon.'

'These days my system rejects both stimulants and animal foods. I'm sorry if it's an inconvenience.'

'Spicer, are you seeing someone else?'

'How do you mean "seeing"?'

'Having an affair with another woman.'

'Annette, you're more than enough for any man to cope with. I would hardly have energy for another. You exhaust me. First the sniping, then the nagging, now come the accusations, the jealousy. I think we'll find it shows up.'

'Shows up where? In my astrological chart? The one done for the morning, not the evening? Is she working on it even now? Are you having an affair with an astrologer? Is that it? Because someone somewhere's trying to turn you against me. That's all it can be.'

Spicer began to laugh. He ate one square of bacon sandwich, and drank half the chocolate drink. He enjoyed the first, but not the second. Then he ate the rest of the sandwich.

'I am so hungry,' he explained, 'I have to give in. Dearest Annette,' he said, 'I am not having an affair with anyone. Are you?'

'Of course not,' said Annette. 'I'm pregnant.'

'Is that the only reason you're not having an affair with anyone?' asked Spicer.

'Of course not,' said Annette. 'I love you.'

'I love you too, very much, Annette,' said Spicer. 'And I'd do nothing to hurt you. Your suspicions are without a rational base. I've told you I'm changing, and in many ways. Please just try and accept it. But there are other reasons for a man changing, apart from him having a mistress! Perhaps he begins to be open to his own soul. I am not the same person you married, any more than you are the same person I married.'

'You keep saying that,' said Annette, 'and it doesn't sound like you saying it, although it comes out of your mouth. Your beautiful mouth I love so much.'

'Where are the children?' asked Spicer.

'Susan's watching a video and Jason's playing on his computer,' said Annette.

'You're so caught up with yourself and your fantasies,' said Spicer. 'You're letting this whole family go to pieces. I know it's not your fault. Do you think perhaps you need treatment?'

'What sort of treatment?' asked Annette. 'Do you mean for my head?'

'Yes, Annette, I do,' said Spicer.

'Therapy?'

'Yes,' said Spicer.

'But you're so against therapy,' said Annette.

'When did I say that?'

'I don't know, Spicer. Way back when, I suppose.'

'I can't remember ever being against it,' said Spicer. 'I think you must have imagined it, or thought that because you thought something, I thought it too. Somehow we have to get you less inner-directed, more outer-directed: more separated-out from me.'

'Who would I go and see?'

'You have to be very careful,' said Spicer. 'There are all kinds of quacks and charlatans about. And we have to keep you away from the psychiatrists: we don't want you filled up with pills when you're expecting a baby.'

'*We're* expecting a baby, Spicer, not just me.'

'Please don't start, Annette,' said Spicer.

'Sorry,' said Annette.

'That's okay,' said Spicer. 'I know you do your best. I'll have a word with Marion. She's in therapy.'

'Marion? Ernie's girlfriend? But she seems so balanced.'

'That's because she's in therapy,' said Spicer, 'I expect.'

'How do you know she's in therapy?'

'Annette, for God's sake —'

'I only asked how you knew, Spicer. I wasn't suggesting anything.'

'I should hope not,' said Spicer. 'Marion of all people! Marion is more than happy with your publisher friend. He has all the money anyone could want, and provides her with the life she needs. She and I were talking about it at the opera, while you were chattering about dustjackets with Ernie. But there is an area of Marion's life which she's had to suppress; she goes to therapy in order to be put back in touch with her inner self; the part Ernie Gromback denies her. Her soul. Okay?'

'Of course it's okay, Spicer,' said Annette. 'I'm sorry.'

'I suppose you can't help it,' said Spicer. 'I think we'll find you have a Mars/Pluto aspect which is at the root of your possessiveness. It certainly causes a lot of trouble. Shall we nudge the children out of their rooms and all play Monopoly? Try and have some kind of ordinary family life? There may be some areas of it left we can work on. Get back to normal somehow.'

'You were late home tonight. I rang the office but it was on answerphone. I do need reassuring, Spicer. I know I shouldn't, but I do. I don't want to weep onto the Monopoly board and upset everyone, or give away Mayfair by mistake.'

'Darling Annette,' said Spicer. 'At least you can still make me laugh. I was selling bin-ends to Humphrey Watts and his wife Eleanor who live round the corner in the Mews. There are still some people left who don't mind having less than six bottles of the same wine, just as there are still some who don't mind mixing and matching the china at a dinner party, but in these days of recession a man has to seek them out. You have to go to them; they don't come to you. Why, what did you think I was doing?

28

Laying a lady astrologer at a propitious time? That's better. You laugh too. I do love you, Annette.'

'Hi, Gilda,' said Annette. 'I'm so tired, I can't think why. We all played Monopoly last night and I lost. I had houses on all the wrong squares. Spicer had Mayfair and Park Lane. He always does. I went to bed early and fell asleep before Spicer came up. Did you notice the moon?'

'Not particularly,' said Gilda.

'It was such a bright night last night. It shone through the window on to the bed. I held up my hand in the light and it shone right through my hand: it was blue and translucent. Spooky.'

'Are you okay?' asked Gilda.

'I was only telling you because you're a friend,' said Annette. 'I'm sorry.'

'I tell Steve that kind of thing,' said Gilda, 'but I suppose it's not the kind of thing you'd tell Spicer.'

'No,' said Annette. 'You can get very lonely being married. The word "corpse" came into my mind when I looked at my hand but I put it out again. It seemed unlucky.'

'Annette,' said Gilda, 'we may be only just in time. I've found someone wonderful for you to see.'

'See? You mean a therapist?' asked Annette. 'But I feel okay now. Honestly. I just get in a state with Spicer sometimes. It's being pregnant. It'll be over soon.'

'You need some support, Annette,' said Gilda. 'Steve says you have a lot to cope with.'

'I thought Spicer was the one having the trouble coping with me,' said Annette.

'On the other hand,' said Gilda. 'If you're going for Spicer's sake it might not work. You're supposed to want therapy for yourself: that's what Eleanor says. Do you know Humphrey and Eleanor Watts?'

'I've met them once or twice,' said Annette. 'They live in the Mews. Spicer sells them bin-ends.'

'Really? How odd. They always seem the kind to buy wine by the case. Anyway, Eleanor was on the phone this morning about the street party – how people do muscle in: it's not going to be just us and a Bella Crescent party; now all the Bellas are going to be involved: Mews, Road, Street, Lane, as well as the Crescent. What was I saying?'

'Therapists,' said Annette.

'I'm just rambling, sorry' said Gilda. 'I'm nervous. It seems such a responsibility recommending a therapist. Supposing they give you the wrong advice? It would all be my fault.'

'Apparently they don't exactly give advice. They resolve your inner problems,' said Annette.

'What inner problems?'

'You were the one who suggested therapy, Gilda,' said Annette. 'And now even Spicer says it's a good idea, so I suppose I must have these inner problems, whatever they are. How does Eleanor Watts come to know about therapists? She doesn't seem the kind.'

'It's very fashionable, all of a sudden. Eleanor goes to one in Hampstead. They're mostly in Hampstead: there's a real shortage of them down here. Someone ought to fill in the gap in the market. Nice large houses, too big just for families, just right for clinics.'

'This house is just right for my family. I love it,' said Annette. 'It isn't too large at all.'

'Don't change the subject, Annette,' said Gilda. 'Eleanor's man is called Dr Herman Marks. He's very famous. He writes books on the power of touch. One of his patients has just left, so you're in luck: he has space for another. But you'll have to act fast. Eleanor says she'll mention you to him. She seemed very keen for you to go, I don't know why. Well, I do. Eleanor lives in the Mews. People in the Crescent have bigger houses than people in the Mews, so Eleanor sees a way of upgrading herself, if only by association. She wants you and her to share a therapist. That's the way her mind works.'

'Then this Dr Marks doesn't seem to have done her much good,' said Annette.

'Think how much worse she might be without him,' said Gilda.

'So now Eleanor Watts knows I'm mad,' said Annette. 'Honestly, Gilda! Well, I suppose I'd better at least make an appointment. Eleanor buys our bin-ends, I see her therapist. That's the way the world goes round. And at least it's a man. It would be nice to talk to a man, not always women.'

'Thank you very much, Annette!'
'I didn't mean you, Gilda, you know I didn't. I don't know what I'd do without you.'

'Spicer,' said Annette, 'I seem to have found a therapist. So don't ask anyone else for names. I don't want everyone knowing how nuts I am.'
'You're a bit late,' said Spicer. 'I asked your friend Ernie's Marion to put forward a few names. She recommends anyone affiliated to the AAP, the Association of Astrological Psychotherapists.'
'She would be into all that gobbledegook,' said Annette. 'I thought you said be careful of quacks?'
'Don't mock what you don't know about,' said Spicer. 'The AAP is affiliated to AJAP, the Association of Jungian and Allied Psychotherapists, extremely serious people. Who have you found?'
'A Dr Herman Marks in Hampstead,' said Annette.
Spicer was silent for a little. Then he said, 'If that's the way the cookie crumbles, that's the way it crumbles.'

'There's very little to say,' said Annette, 'and I'm sorry for wasting your time. I'm sure there are others far worse off than me. It's just I've been happily married for ten years and now I've become pregnant I find myself catching my husband out in every little thing; I'm even beginning to think he might be having an affair. I know he isn't, but the thought just somehow sticks around and he's getting fed up with the way I behave.' Dr Marks laughed: it was a gentle and surprisingly seductive laugh. Annette wondered what it would be like to be engulfed and enfolded by this man, and if there was a Mrs Marks, and what kind of person she would be.
'Quite probably,' said Dr Marks, 'that is a simple matter of projection. You have had an affair, or two, or three, during the course of your relationship with Spicer: now you are pregnant and feel helpless, and your guilt, your unresolved shadow-side, comes back to persecute you.'
'You can do something about me, then?'
'My analysis makes sense to you?'
'Yes.'

'Then I imagine a cure will easily be found. By cure I mean understanding, peace of mind. You are not a demonstrative person, I can see that. But then you are English: it is not surprising or in itself a cause for concern, as it would be, say, for a Mediterranean woman.'

'How do you know I am not a demonstrative person? Other people think I am. My husband Spicer says I go round touching people far too much.'

'You huddle away from me. Touch my hand. What does that make you feel?'

'Trapped,' she replied. 'Well, you grabbed it. Please let go. You're hurting.'

'Trapped,' he repeated. 'We will work with that, since it's the best we can do.'

'Well?' asked Gilda. 'How did it go? Is he attractive?'

'I don't know,' said Annette. 'He was like a great lump of granite, sitting in a winged chair by the fire. He overflowed its edges.'

'That doesn't sound like granite,' said Gilda.

'You asked what he was like. I'm doing my best. He was about sixty. His face was hairy, as if greenish grey shrubs were growing out of a mountain side. They came out all over his face; from his nostrils, his ears, over his eyes, out of his scalp where they at least pretended to be head hair, not foliage.'

'You're making this up,' said Gilda.

'I'm not,' said Annette. 'He's just a man with a lot of facial hair. He has a fleshy nose and his mouth's crooked. I thought perhaps he'd had a stroke. He spoke mid-European: the kind that's designed to make you feel foolish. He had an old watch on a chain which he swung to and fro.'

'It sounds a nightmare,' said Gilda.

'Every now and then he scratched his chin and flakes of skin scattered on to his trousers. The trousers were tweed, so you couldn't see the flakes when they landed.'

'And you took this person seriously?' asked Gilda.

'He asked me to touch his hand and I did. He twisted it and grabbed my wrist. His hands had liver spots and were horribly strong. I still have marks: I reckon they'll be bruises tomorrow.'

'Was he helpful?'

'How do I know? I might be in a worse state if I hadn't been to see him. He doesn't seem to have a gender: he's too foreign. Sometimes I think he's making a pass: at other times I think how stupid and vulgar of me to think any such thing: there is a kind of attraction but it's not a male–female thing. He is just a very powerful person.'

'But he did make you feel better?'

'I think so. I did some confessing. And that was only the first session. It was rather like lancing a boil.'

'Confessions? What about?'

'Well, you know. Various things. A person.'

'Who?'

'I'm not going to tell you who, Gilda. It's all over now.'

'While you were married?'

'Yes.'

'Did you have a fling with Ernie Gromback?'

'Of course I didn't, Gilda. You're insane. Far too close to home.'

'I just wondered.'

'Nobody you know and nobody you'll ever know,' said Annette. 'It was in the summer, when Spicer was away in France and everything was just stupid. You know how I hated Spicer going away without me: you know how I miss him: how lonely and edgy I get. Sex grounds me, that's all. It wasn't love, anything like that: it was just sex.'

'In the first place,' said Gilda, 'I don't know how you had the nerve. And in the second place I don't know how you were stupid enough to tell Dr Herman Marks. Supposing he tells Eleanor Watts and she tells her husband and he tells Spicer over a drunken bin-end?'

'But what you tell a therapist is completely confidential,' said Annette. 'They're like priests.'

'I hope you're right,' said Gilda.

'Anyway,' said Annette, 'I could always just deny everything.'

'Is this Dr Marks married?' asked Gilda.

'I think so. There were two brass plates on the door: Dr Herman Marks and Dr Rhea Marks. She had so many letters after her name! MBBS, MRC, AJAP, AHTN. I remember those. My father had the first two. I used to polish the brass plate outside our door. Dr Rhea had far more letters than Dr Herman did. I wondered if that made him jealous, and then I thought, no, they're therapists. They'll have been so analysed-out themselves, they wouldn't have an unreasonable emotion left in them. I expect they're blissfully happy. Except he does do rather a lot of hugging and touching. I wouldn't like it if I were her. When he stood up he was at least six foot five, and his arms were like a gorilla's. He put them round me.'

'Wasn't that horrible?'

'No. It was like being embraced by a cross between a father and a bear. It makes you feel safe and drowsy. When he's hugged all the air out of you he lets you go. But thank God he didn't mention astrology. Gilda, do you know anyone who's into astrology?'

'Ernie Gromback's Marion talks about star signs non-stop.'

'Ah.'

'But I don't think Spicer's having an affair with Marion,' said Gilda.

'Neither do I,' said Annette. 'He loves me too much. I've made a real effort not to be paranoid, and I reckon I'm succeeding.'

'Annette,' said Spicer that night, 'the fact is that I do not want to hear about Dr Herman Marks: what he said to you, or you said to him. You have to keep some areas of yourself apart from me, the way I do with you. We are separate people. You just descend upon me hook, line and sinker: you squash me into the ground.'

'It's true,' said Annette, as lightly as she could, 'that I've put on a lot of weight lately, but most of it is the baby. Our baby.' But it was Tuesday night. Spicer had returned at 7.02 and was not in the mood for jokes. 'And anyway,' she said, 'I thought marriage was about togetherness.'

'Your vocabulary,' said Spicer, 'comes straight out of a woman's magazine. Togetherness!'

'You know what I mean,' said Annette.

'I don't,' said Spicer. 'Explain it to me.'

Annette declined, saying she would wait until Spicer was better; Spicer said there was nothing wrong with him, only with her; her demands were unreasonable, but she was so afflicted in the seventh house it was not surprising. She had had an unhappy childhood and was taking it out on Spicer.

'But, Spicer darling –' said Annette.

'Don't call me darling: it rings false.'

'But, Spicer, your childhood was far unhappier than mine.'

'This is not a competition, Annette. And it is no laughing matter.'

'If I'm laughing it's because this is silly,' said Annette. 'In the childhood-tragedy stakes you win hands down, Spicer. I still have both my parents: you lost your father when you were four and your mother went insane and rushed round screaming till they shut her up.'

'Annette,' said Spicer, 'sometimes your insensitivity takes my breath away.'

'I'm sorry, Spicer. I was trying not to be too heavy about it, that's all.'

'Your mother is still most certainly around,' said Spicer, 'and hasn't yet done you the favour of dying. How you hate her, poor woman.'

'What is the matter with you?' asked Annette. 'I don't hate my mother at all.'

'I've heard you say so many a time, Annette.'

'Sometimes she annoys me in the way mothers do, Spicer,' said Annette, 'and I may have said things against her – and confided them in you because you are my husband – but I love my mother, I don't hate her.'

'I don't think you know what you say or how you feel,' said Spicer. 'Your Neptune is afflicted by Pluto and you live in a state of perpetual confusion. We have found out a great deal about you in the last few weeks. Now we have the correct time of your birth, all kinds of things become clear,' and he went into the study to read.

'Dad! Is everything all right?'

'Just fine, Annette. A friendly call. How're things with you?'

'Fine. Any changes back home?'

'Everything much as usual,' said Giles Thomas, Annette's father. 'Your mother wants new carpets. Do you think we need new carpets? They are getting shabby.'

'If it was me I'd take away the carpets and polish the floorboards, and have rugs.'

'Wouldn't that create dust?'

'Yes, it would, Dad,' said Annette. 'But you could take Mum away for a week while it settled.'

'I couldn't afford that if we had new carpets. Interest rates are down again. People rejoice when interest rates go down: they don't think what it's like for retired people who live on fixed incomes.'

'But you're managing?'

'Of course we're managing, sweetheart. Don't worry about us. How's the baby?'

'Flourishing,' said Annette. 'So am I.'

'Spicer?'

'Just fine. Reading at the moment, in the study.'

'So what are you doing?' asked her father.

'Trying to focus on the Europa Myth. This producer friend of Gilda's is trying to link the failure of the GATT talks with Europa's rape by Jupiter in the form of a bull; the bull being the US.'

'Does it work?'

'I'm doing my best to make the connection. It's just that being pregnant makes you keep falling asleep. Dad, what was I like when I was a little girl?'

'You were the sweetest thing, Annette. The light of all our lives. Bright as a button, chattered all day. You were an only child and a late one; you were worth waiting for. Why? What's the matter? Is Spicer being difficult?'

'Of course not,' said Annette. 'It's just sometimes nice to hear, and I know you'll always say it.'

'Because men can react strangely when their wives are pregnant,' said Giles Thomas. 'I loved your mother dearly, but even I –'

'Yes, I know about that, Dad,' said Annette.

'So keep an eye on him,' said Giles Thomas. 'Boys will be boys, but there are limits.'

Annette went into the study.

'Spicer,' she said. 'We have been together for ten years. I would have thought you'd have known what I was like by now. Why do you need an astrological chart to tell you? And who is this "we" you keep talking about which is not you and me?'

'None of it is anything to do with you,' said Spicer.

'But it is,' said Annette. 'Is this other person a woman?'

'The gender of the other person is immaterial,' said Spicer, 'since they are a skilled professional. You're a feminist; you should be the first to agree.'

'An astrologer is a professional?'

'Of course,' said Spicer.

'And my chart is bad news?'

'Yes,' said Spicer. 'In so far as it relates to mine.'

'Then it is to do with me,' said Annette. 'If you believe this nonsense.'

'Annette,' said Spicer, 'I am trying to read.'

'In what way is my chart bad news?'

'You are badly afflicted in both the Fourth and Seventh houses. The house of childhood and the house of marriage. The unhappy, lonely child of elderly parents: a mother badly treated by a faithless husband: we know all that to be true, don't we.'

'It hardly registered like that, Spicer,' said Annette.

'Your Pluto being afflicted by your Neptune,' said Spicer, 'you're so confused, hardly anything registers. Look at us. Your total lack of sensitivity.'

'Spicer, what is the matter? Please!'

'Don't upset yourself. You're so excitable, these days. I thought pregnancy was meant to calm women down. The matter is that your moon in the First is quincunx your moon in the Seventh; you simply have no idea how to be a wife. Well, the unhappy daughter seldom has.'

'I am a good wife, Spicer. And a good mother.'

'Really? Do good wives nag? Are they obsessively jealous? Do they break plates and burn books? Do they blab the secrets of the marriage bed to all and sundry? You have wonderful qualities, Annette, and I love you dearly, but let us not suppose you are without faults. As for being a good mother, you have a kind heart and a good nature but your idea of cooking is a bacon sandwich. Your idea of child-rearing is to let the kids watch TV all day. They

are increasingly withdrawn and disturbed. It's quite a worry.'
'If it's all written in the stars, Spicer,' said Annette, 'there's
nothing we can do about it, so why worry? I have to have an
afflicted whatever it is to show up in Susan's and Jason's
star-charts as a persecuting mother. And my parents had to be
what they were, in order to prove my affliction.'
'Everything's interconnected, Annette,' said Spicer. 'I'm
surprised you don't recognise that.'
'How can I recognise anything if it's written in my star-chart that
I won't? And how can anything surprise you about me now you
know what I'm like before we even begin?'
'Annette, you are becoming upset about nothing at all. Our
compatibility-chart shows up problems, that's all I'm trying to
say. I'm tired. I say things I don't mean because you provoke
me. I wish you wouldn't say "star-chart"; you do it to mock
and deride. The proper description is natal-chart. Now please,
Annette, leave me alone.'
'Well, Spicer,' said Annette, 'if it makes you feel better, I'll be
down to the nearest fortune-teller the moment I can.'
'You are impossible,' said Spicer. 'There's the phone. How any
woman can spend so much time on the phone beats me.'

'Annette?'
'Ernie!'
'You busy?'
'No. Just talking to Spicer.'
'I hope he's saying nice things,' said Ernie Gromback. 'Is he in
the room?'
'No, Ernie, he isn't,' said Annette. 'He's in the study and I'm in
the hall. But it makes no difference. I won't say anything to you
I wouldn't say if he was by my side.'
'That's what worries me about you, Annette,' said Ernie. 'You
won't. He is in your head. I thought you were looking peaky the
other night.'
'I thought I was looking rather beautiful,' said Annette.
'You are always beautiful, Annette,' said Ernie Gromback. 'But
you were distracted. Distracted people are not productive. I need
my writers to be productive.'

'So this is a business call?'

'Of course,' said Ernie Gromback. 'I have had an offer from a German publisher who wants to do *Lucifette Fallen*.'

'That's wonderful,' said Annette. 'Will there be much money?'

'Very little,' said her publisher. 'It's a first novel, a foreign sale, and translation costs are high. But I thought it might cheer you up to know.'

'I'm perfectly cheerful as it is,' said Annette. 'Do you know anything about astrology?'

'As little as possible,' said Ernie Gromback. 'But everyone's into it. Marion's writing a book on the nature of Sagittarians. I'm a Sagittarian. I talk too much and am faithless. I think of you a lot, Annette.'

'Goodbye, Ernie,' said Annette.

'Goodbye, Annette,' said Ernie.

'Who was that?' asked Spicer. 'Your lesbian friend?'

'It was Ernie Gromback,' said Annette.

'What did he want?'

'He's sold *Lucifette Fallen* to the Germans,' said Annette.

'Trust the Germans,' said Spicer. 'And trust that little runt to disturb a peaceful evening. That last dig of yours, Annette, about fortune-telling? Shall we go back to that? Astrology is nothing to do with fortune-telling. It is a wonderfully useful diagnostic and therapeutic tool, in the hands of intuitive and sensitive people. And thank God there are some around.'

'And I'm still not to know the name or gender of this wonderful and sensitive person,' asked Annette, 'who means so much to you?' 'I've been advised to tell you as little as possible,' said Spicer. 'Though in fact she may want to see you sometime.'

'She,' said Annette. 'I knew it. You're having an affair with her.'

'I knew you'd be like this,' said Spicer. 'No wonder I put off telling you. She's my therapist.'

'Your therapist? You have a therapist? You?'

'There is nothing sexual in my relationship with her,' said Spicer.

'I should bloody hope not,' cried Annette. 'And why does this astrologer-therapist want to see me, and why should I go, and

why do you want one in the first place, Spicer? What's the matter
with you?'

'The matter is, Annette,' said Spicer, 'that because of scenes like
this, and the perpetual stress of the rows you precipitate, my
blood-pressure has become dangerously raised, and I am in
danger of falling dead with a heart-attack or stroke.'

'Your blood-pressure? But you're too young!'

'Stress can kill at any age,' said Spicer.

'But this is dreadful! What does Dr Solstice say? Is it going to be
okay?'

'I'm not seeing Dr Solstice. I'm seeing a homeopath.'

'I don't believe this,' said Annette.

'I shouldn't have confided in you,' said Spicer. 'I might have
known this is how you'd react. No sympathy, no understanding:
nothing except hysteria.'

'Spicer, you have my every sympathy. I'm just terribly worried.
You don't believe in alternative medicine. Who on earth
recommended it? Your therapist? This astrologer?'

'Well, yes,' said Spicer.

'And who recommended the therapist?'

'Marion,' said Spicer.

'Spicer!' cried Annette. 'Marion's an idiot. You know she is!'

'I knew it wasn't wise to tell you,' said Spicer. 'My therapist said
you'd react like this. If I so much as talk to another woman you
curl up with spite and jealousy. Therapy and homeopathy helped
Marion's asthma when conventional medicine failed. I started
getting headaches, my vision was blurred. I took Marion's advice;
that's all there was to it. I don't want to live on doctor's pills for
the rest of my life.'

'But what is this homeopath doing for you, Spicer?' asked Annette.
'Is it working? That's all that matters. I'm sorry, I didn't mean
to raise my voice. I was just taken by surprise.'

'She's given me drops,' said Spicer, 'which I place on my tongue
every morning and every evening.'

'She?'

'Annette, leave off! I can feel my blood-pressure rising already.
Half the human race is female.'

'I'm sorry.'

'Try not to make me choleric,' said Spicer. 'It'll kill me.'

'Choleric's a funny word,' said Annette. 'Where did you get it from? I suppose it's a homeopathic term. Kind of medieval. Are the drops working?'

'My blood-pressure is down, yes, though scenes like this don't help.'

'It isn't a scene. It's just me reacting. What sort of drops? What's in them?'

'I don't know,' said Spicer. 'All I know is you have to make sure they get to the tongue without first coming in contact with any other part of the body, or they don't work so well.'

'Like sex without foreplay,' said Annette. 'A shock to the system.'

'Quite so,' said Spicer.

'Could be good, could be bad,' said Annette.

'Let's go to bed and find out,' said Spicer. 'I'm glad that's out in the open. I'm glad I've got it over. Now let's get back to normal.'

'Is making love good for blood-pressure?' asked Annette.

'Best possible thing,' said Spicer.

'I suppose it will give me time to let all this sink in,' said Annette. 'Think things through.'

'The important thing for you, Annette,' said Spicer, 'is not to think too much. Just accept. Come upstairs.'

The phone rang.

'Don't answer that,' said Spicer.

'I won't,' said Annette.

'Pay attention to me,' said Spicer.

'I will,' said Annette, and they went upstairs to the bedroom, and the phone went on ringing.

'Wait till I take my drops,' said Spicer.

'I will,' said Annette. 'Spicer, I suppose the therapist and the homeopath aren't the same person?'

'Let's say they're part of the same gestalt,' said Spicer. 'Annette, will you help me? My eyes cross if I try to do it myself. Thank you.'

'What's a gestalt?' asked Annette.

'A German word for a whole made up of parts which you could separate out but on the whole would be better not to,' Spicer said.

'So they could be the same?'

'Actually, yes they are. She is both healer and astrologer. Now don't make a fuss.'

'She's not making a lot of money out of you?'

'My God,' said Spicer, 'a man's health is not to be measured in monetary terms.'

'Of course not,' said Annette.

'Nor is his mind, or his soul.'

'Sweetheart,' said Annette, 'I love your tongue, I love your teeth, I love your mouth, I love all of you. How often do you see her?'

'Four times a week at the moment,' said Spicer, 'while the crisis lasts.'

'Oh,' said Annette.

'The nicer you are to me the sooner the crisis will be over,' Spicer said.

'Of course,' said Annette. 'I wish you'd tell me her name.'

'Let it be, Annette,' said Spicer.

'I can always sleep in the spare room,' said Annette.

'I wouldn't put it past you,' said Spicer. 'You are inconsistent enough. I can't rely on you for anything.'

'Other people find me perfectly consistent and reliable,' said Annette.

'Other people, other people!' said Spicer. 'I don't like your habit of appealing to these convenient witnesses. What other people?'

'I'm sorry,' said Annette.

'Your apologies are accepted,' said Spicer. 'Rest assured my therapist/astrologer/homeopath has conventional medical qualifications and I am in excellent hands; it's just that at the moment I'd rather be in yours. The great thing about you being pregnant is that your breasts are finally a proper size.'

'Yes, but there's this bump beneath them,' said Annette.

'I'll forget it,' said Spicer, 'if you will. Put on your white pleated silk nightgown. I like so to take it off. You are so beautiful, even with your bump.'

'I'm not sure the white nightie will fit over the bump,' said Annette. 'But I'm willing to try.'

'Don't talk all the time, darling. Stop thinking. Just *be*.'

'Can I just say one more thing?'

'If it's neither critical nor reproachful,' said Spicer.

'I wish you'd told me earlier you were going to see a therapist,' Annette said.

'I have told you,' said Spicer.

'But isn't it just what Aileen did?'

'That's a silly comparison,' said Spicer. 'Aileen wanted to end the marriage. I want the opposite for ours. I want to live in peace and tranquillity.'

'Help me put the nightie on,' said Annette. 'Just a little tug at the back. I love your hands, Spicer. I always have.'

'I love all of you, Annette,' said Spicer. 'You're like the sea; I love to drown in you. But like the seas you have your moods: sometimes you can be dangerous. So I must learn to navigate you. Is that comfortable?'

'Well, not totally any more,' said Annette. 'You are quite heavy on the bump.'

'Turn on your side, then. Is that better?'

'Well, yes, but then I can't see you,' said Annette. 'I like to see you: the expression of your face. I like to watch you loving me.'

'But by liking to see me we have to stay very decorous, very missionary, Annette.'

'Something's lost, something's gained,' said Annette. 'I'll turn on my side. Not too hard, not too violent, please. I wouldn't want you to shake the baby loose –'

'Babies are well locked in,' said Spicer. 'Nature sees to it. Other women don't make this fuss. Don't make me feel guilty or none of this will work.'

'Sorry, Spicer,' said Annette. 'If I bring my knees up – wonderful, wonderful – you've always been wonderful like nothing else, no one else.'

'Then why can't you be more secure in me?'

'I am, I am,' said Annette. 'I shouldn't have spoken the way I did to Gilda: I didn't mean to be disloyal.'

'You speak far too much to Gilda,' said Spicer.

'I'll try not to in future,' said Annette.

'Gilda isn't a real friend: she just wants someone to gossip about.'

'I expect so.'

'The way you go on about me,' said Spicer, 'makes me wonder about you. You are sure it is my baby?'

'Of course I am, Spicer.'

'Because I have to have you all to myself,' said Spicer. 'I couldn't bear to share you.'

'Only you, Spicer, only ever you.'

'Not like Aileen.'

'Never, never like Aileen,' said Annette. 'Spicer, not so rough: Spicer, whatever you like – but you are tearing my best nightdress.'

'It's too tight over the bump; why did you wear it? Please don't talk, it distracts me – turn over, talk into the pillow if you have to –'

'I don't want to turn over,' said Annette.

'Why not? I love every bit of you, every part of you,' said Spicer.

'I want to be able to say that too,' said Annette. 'To your face, not to a pillow.'

'Do as I say,' said Spicer.

'Oh very well,' said Annette.

'I love you,' said Spicer into his wife's ear. 'So much love must be good for the baby. It couldn't possibly harm it: that's what Rhea says. There, I've told you. Dr Rhea Marks, my therapist. Annette, I'm coming, I can't help it, you moved so suddenly – come with me – please –'

'I am, I am. There.'

'There. Oh my God. I love you, Annette.'

Spicer brought Annette some orange juice and sat in the blue basket chair by the bed.

'You were faking, weren't you,' said Spicer.

'I was not,' said Annette.

'Yes you were. I can always tell.'

'I'd quite like to go to sleep now, Spicer,' said Annette.

'You never talk when I want to talk,' said Spicer. 'You always talk when I'd rather you didn't.'

'I expect I'm afflicted in my planets. Ask Dr Rhea Marks. She'll tell you all about it.'

'Sulky, sulky!' said Spicer. 'Rhea told me it would happen.

Spouses feel resentful if an outsider, as they see it, comes into the marriage. But of course it isn't like that.'

'Isn't it?'

'Good God no,' said Spicer. 'Is your seeing Dr Herman Marks coming between you and me? No. The opposite is true. Weren't we together just now? You were wonderful. He's already dispersed some of the frigidity.'

'But I've never been frigid,' said Annette. 'What do you mean?'

'Lilith is cold,' said Spicer. 'Lilith is the devourer of children, the hater of men. Lilith stops women coming. See Dr Herman as Saturn: only Saturn can deal with Lilith.'

'What are you talking about, Spicer? You're frightening me.'

'You mustn't be frightened,' said Spicer. 'I'm coming back into bed. We have to drive Lilith out. You were faking.'

'I was not so, Spicer,' said Annette. 'I want to go to sleep. Please. I'm pregnant.'

'Spoilsport. Talk to me.'

'Very well,' said Annette. 'Is Dr Rhea young and attractive? Or is she the female equivalent of her husband?'

'She's kind of in the middle,' said Spicer. 'I do not have a sexual relationship with her. Okay? And I've never even met her husband. It seems such a waste for the baby to have your breasts.'

'It won't be for long,' said Annette. 'Then you can have them back. Do you see her in the house in Maresfield Gardens?'

'Yes. But it's on a lease from the AJA. They have to move out soon.'

'The AJA?' asked Annette.

'The Association of Jungian Analysts,' said Spicer. 'Very reputable, very respectable. She was well recommended. I'm not a fool.'

'If you go to the same house, how come you haven't met her husband?' asked Annette.

'I like your knees,' said Spicer. 'I've always liked your knees. Part them just a little. If I haven't met her husband it's because anti-synchronicity is almost as strong a force in the universe as synchronicity.'

'I must say,' said Annette, 'this is rather like being in bed with a stranger. I've never heard you talk like this.'

'All the more exciting,' said Spicer. 'We have layer upon layer with which to encounter each other. You are so hot between your legs since you've been pregnant. It's almost worth it.'

'I suppose Dr Herman and Dr Rhea won't get together to discuss our cases?' asked Annette.

'I wouldn't think so,' said Spicer. 'It wouldn't be ethical. Why, have you got something to hide?'

'No,' said Annette.

'That's just as well,' said Spicer. 'I'm coming in you now.'

'Gilda?'

'What is it, Annette? It's very early to ring.'

'I'm sorry,' said Annette. 'But I have to tell someone.'

'Could it possibly wait, Annette? Because I'm having breakfast with Steve, and he doesn't like me on the phone when he's in the house.'

'Oh very well,' said Annette. 'Don't worry. It can wait. It's probably better if I don't tell you. Spicer's coming out of the bathroom now, anyway, so I can't talk either. If you and me were earning more than peanuts and Steve and Spicer were house-husbands would we be the way they are about using the phone?'

'I don't think so,' said Gilda.

'I don't think so either,' said Annette. 'Bye.'

'Is something the matter, Spicer?' asked Annette.

'For God's sake, Annette,' said Spicer. 'I am sitting in my dressing gown, drinking orange juice and reading the morning paper like any other husband. What should be the matter?'

'You don't look at me, you don't speak to me. You're angry.'

'I am not in the least angry. I will put down my paper. Speak to me, I will speak back.'

'When you thought I was born in the evening, did I seem a nicer person?' asked Annette.

'Let us say you had fewer life problems,' said Spicer. 'And so did I. The evening sun was cuspate. But your morning sun remains firmly in Virgo; it hasn't even begun to move over into Libra.'

'I see,' said Annette. 'Is that bad?'

'Nothing in astrology is bad in itself,' said Spicer. 'But Virgos have a problem with their sexuality. They hold back. Librans are more giving. They don't have to fake.'

'Good Lord,' said Annette. 'Who'd have thought it!'

'Which of course is not a source of grief for the Virgo,' said Spicer, 'on the contrary, but can be to the Sun-Aquarian who marries her.'

'I really wish,' said Annette, 'my mother had kept her legs closed a little longer, at least until evening.'

'Try not to be so insensitive,' said Spicer.

'I'm sorry,' said Annette. 'Besides the sun in the wrong place, what else?'

'For God's sake,' said Spicer, 'I'm trying to explain that nothing in astrology is "wrong". No one is to blame. It is just useful to locate the problem areas. We now find your moon is square my Neptune, and my Neptune's in my seventh house, which does suggest marital upsets.'

'But you're to blame as much as me if it's your Neptune, not mine.'

'You're simply trying to provoke me, Annette. You are being stupid on purpose.'

'I'm sorry,' said Annette. 'I just don't seem able to get my head round astrology.'

'It's not an easy subject. It took Rhea years to get her degree.'

'Her *degree*?' enquired Annette. 'Who on earth gives degrees in astrology?'

'There are very reputable associations in existence which supervise training and issue qualifications,' said Spicer. 'It's a growing field.'

'You're telling me!' said Annette. 'Anyway, I'm put very firmly in my place. Tell me, if I'm so stupid and insensitive, how do I get to hold down a job of work and get a novel published?'

'Your job of work,' said Spicer, 'brings in a little pin money. You do it in your spare time. It's Gilda's work anyway: you just do the overflow. As for you being the artistic and creative one in the family,' said Spicer, 'that's another of your fantasies. Your idea of art is a novel called *Lucifette Fallen*, which you manage to get published by a dwarf who thinks he'll get cheap wine from me in return.'

'I never claimed to be artistic or creative, Spicer,' said Annette. 'I never even mentioned the words. I'm a researcher by nature. You're the imaginative one. And the title was your idea, and I'm sure Ernie Gromback doesn't want his wine cheap. Why should he? He's rich enough.'

'Everyone wants their wine cheap. When I said call the bloody book *Lucifette Fallen* I was joking. You took me seriously and went ahead with it. I could hardly believe it.'

'You were being ironic? And you let me go ahead? Laughing at me?' wept Annette.

'One thing I have learned from Rhea Marks,' said Spicer, 'is that it is best to allow people to take the consequences of their actions. For one spouse to intervene to protect the other is in the long run counterproductive. Marriage doesn't mean that life learning stops. Though Sun-Virgoans do all they can to make it so.'

Annette went upstairs to the bathroom and vomited. Spicer followed her.

'Are you okay, Annette?' he asked. 'It's important for us to get these feelings out into the open: we have to speak the truth to each other. It is one of the things that Dr Rhea stresses.'

'Please go away and let me be ill in peace,' said Annette.

'Now why does that sound so familiar? Of course, Aileen! How a man does repeat the same mistake! Aileen was a Virgo too.'

'Please don't compare me with Aileen,' said Annette. 'I keep getting a terrible headache, Spicer. Something's going wrong with the baby.'

'I'm the one who's ill,' said Spicer. 'But Virgoans do love to compete. If there was anything wrong with you they'd have picked it up at the Clinic. That's why you go.'

'I haven't been to the Clinic for three Tuesdays in a row.'

'You pretend to care about this baby,' said Spicer, 'but at best you're ambivalent. That's why you don't go to the Clinic. I feel quite drained after my conversations with you. Rhea says this is because you represent the suffocated and suffocating mother. First Aileen, now you.'

48

'Spicer,' said Annette, 'I am doing my best to make this relationship work.'

'Are you?' asked Spicer. 'I really wonder. Your problems conceiving? An unconscious rejection of the baby: hatred of the husband? That's what it feels like to me.'

'I'm going back to bed,' said Annette. 'I feel really ill.'

'And I'm going to work,' said Spicer. 'Present you with a little truth, Annette, and your reaction is to sulk. It's the children I'm sorry for. But not having had the experience of a happy childhood, how can you hope to recreate it for your own children? At least you're in therapy: there may be some hope for the rest of us: otherwise God help us.'

'Oh God, Gilda.'

'Now what's the matter?'

'I've just had a very strange dream,' said Annette.

'But it's the middle of the morning,' said Gilda.

'The morning sickness was so bad I was exhausted and went back to bed,' said Annette.

'You've hardly been morning sick at all so far,' said Gilda, 'and it's far too late to start now.'

'Well, I had a row with Spicer and I was. Not exactly a row: just home-truth time. He's seeing a therapist: she's the one who's been turning him on to astrology.'

'So that's it,' said Gilda. 'At least it's not a mistress. They do say treatment stirs things up. That's why he's been so moody.'

'She's also a homeopath. She's mending his mind, casting his star chart, and mine, and giving him drops for high blood-pressure.'

'Steve said something about Spicer's blood-pressure,' said Gilda.

'I expect it's all all right. But it can't be nice having another woman helping out in quite so many respects.'

'It isn't,' said Annette.

'Are the drops working?' asked Gilda.

'Spicer says so,' said Annette.

'That's something,' said Gilda. 'But you have to be careful, Annette. Therapists tends to think all illness is caused by stress, and stress is caused by the spouse, so to cure the patient get rid of the spouse.'

'I think you're rather over-simplifying matters,' said Annette.

'I'd never let Steve go to a therapist,' said Gilda. 'For therapist read the rapist. The rapist of dreams and weddings.'

'Spicer does what he wants,' said Annette.

'You can say that again,' said Gilda. 'What was your dream?'

'I dreamt I was having a row with Spicer and he bit me on the shoulder.'

'Like a vampire?' asked Gilda.

'More like a love bite,' said Annette. 'It hurt and I woke up. Oh, how extraordinary!'

'What's extraordinary?' asked Gilda.

'I do have a love bite on my shoulder and it is hurting. Spicer must have done it last night. Sorry, Gilda.'

'That's okay,' said Gilda. 'Any time. But is quite so much sex good for the baby? See you at the Clinic tonight. Now do you mind if I get on with buttering my toast?'

'Hello, Annette.'

'Hello, Mum.'

'All well?'

'Everything's fine.'

'What did they say at the Clinic?'

'Everything's running to plan.'

'Because I thought on Monday your wrists were a little puffy. Did they say anything about that?'

'They picked it up,' lied Annette. 'They're very careful. They decided any puffiness was well within normal limits. Now don't worry, Mum: everything will be just fine.'

'And how's Susan? Are you spending enough time with her? She isn't still sulking in her room? You should take her out and about. No reason why mothers and daughters shouldn't be friends. You don't want her to feel neglected even before the new baby comes along.'

'I'm very conscious of the danger, Mum. But Susan's a very self-sustaining girl. And she has a lot of friends up and down the Crescent.'

'And Jason? I mustn't forget little Jason. He does tend to keep himself to himself rather, I've noticed. Not the most sociable little chap.'

'He has a new friend, Tommy by name. They shut themselves in his room and play video games.'

'Tommy? What sort of boy?'

'Really nice,' said Annette. 'Peaceful.'

'It all sounds a little convenient, Annette. It isn't good to let these intense one-to-one relations develop between children.'

'I don't think it's all that intense,' said Annette.

'How do you know?' asked her mother. 'If the pair of them shut themselves into his room? And do you check the games? They can be really unpleasant, I hear. But it's the fashionable way to bring up children, I suppose. The hands-off method. How's dear Spicer? He did seem a little stressed last time I saw him – you shouldn't let him be so rude to you. But he did ring me up in the afternoon, and was sweet to me. Really affectionate. He's a good man, Annette. I hope you value him properly. A good husband's hard to find.'

'I know that, Mum.'

'Because men can get a little stressed when their wives are pregnant. When I was carrying you your father had an affair.'

'Yes, I know that too, Mum.'

'Our marriage limped along after that: we managed but things were never really the same. Of course you children never got to know. Your father and myself were careful to present a united front. And I wouldn't bring any of this up, Annette, except I do worry for you and Spicer, and I wouldn't want to happen to you what happened to me.'

'Honestly, Mum, Monday lunch was just a fluke,' said Annette. 'You can't expect Spicer to be the life and soul of the party all the time. It was really stupid of me to forget he doesn't drink coffee any more.'

'You shouldn't drink coffee either, Annette,' said her mother. 'It's bad for the baby. It isn't good of you. Sometimes you surprise me by your selfishness. But you were like that even as a child: what Annette wants, Annette has to have. If Spicer's stopped drinking coffee, it's probably to set you an example.'

'I expect that's what it is, Mum,' agreed Annette. 'Honestly, we're just fine. Don't worry.'

'Annette, why haven't you called me?'

'Oh hello, Gilda. I've been busy, I expect.'

'Because you weren't at the Clinic,' said Gilda.

'I know,' said Annette. 'I felt kind of depleted. I didn't want to be somehow examined and found wanting.'

'You sound really low.'

'I'm just fine.'

'No, you're not,' said Gilda. 'I can tell from your voice.'

'Gilda, you won't tell anyone what I told you last time? You do understand it's confidential?'

'Of course I fucking understand it's fucking confidential. What's the matter with you?'

'Don't be so emotional,' said Annette.

'You are so *English*,' said Gilda.

'You're English too.'

'But I don't feel it,' said Gilda. 'I was born an outsider. You always want to be an insider. You like to be accepted.'

'Gilda, I don't know why I didn't ring you before. It's a great relief talking to you. You make me laugh. I just kind of get muddled in my head all the time.'

'That's being pregnant,' said Gilda. 'It will get better.'

'Dr Herman Marks says I'm very English. I always thought it was a compliment, but apparently in a woman it means cut off, repressed. I had the oddest dream about him: we were waiting for a whole lot of vague people to leave his consulting room so we could make love. But we never quite got there. You know how these dreams are. I'm not really in therapy, either: I've only been to see him once. All the touching and hugging somehow got him into my head: but he's disgusting, really.'

'When are you going again?' asked Gilda.

'This afternoon. Gilda, I shouldn't tell you. I meant not to. Everything gets so gossipy.'

'Thanks a million, Annette.'

'I don't mean you gossip – oh God, everything with you gets so involved.'

'Steve says that too. He says it's my lesbian past. He is quite convinced I have a lesbian past, and I expect he has told Spicer. That kind of thing quite turns men on. All I did when I was fifteen was share a bed with a prefect who touched me all over, most beautifully, and I won't say I didn't like it because I did. Okay? Shall we now forget my being over-emotional, etcetera, etcetera?'

'Sometimes I'm glad I'm a repressed English woman, Gilda,' said Annette. 'And you won't tell Steve what I said about you know what, because what's happened, which I didn't mean to tell you, is that that therapist Spicer has been going to see is Herman Marks's wife, a Dr Rhea Marks, the one with all the letters after her name. They share consulting rooms.'

'Oh my God, Annette,' said Gilda.

'You don't think this phone is bugged?'

'No.'

'Because I saw a TV programme about private detectives,' said Annette, 'and it's the easiest thing in the world to bug telephones.'

'Who would want to do such a thing?' asked Gilda.

'Spicer, of course,' said Annette.

'Annette, Spicer is right, you've gone nuts.'

'You mean Spicer told Steve I'd gone nuts?' asked Annette.

'Not exactly,' said Gilda.

'It's as if I'm not standing on the proper ground,' said Annette, 'but on a rug, and people keep snatching it from under my feet.'

'Don't cry, Annette. Shall I come round?'

'No, you'd better not,' said Annette.

'Why not? Wouldn't Spicer like it, because of my lesbian past?'

'I'm so muddled, Gilda,' said Annette.

'I can tell. What time are you seeing this Dr Herman Marks again? Because the sooner the better.'

'It just seems so peculiar,' said Annette, 'that I'm going to the husband, and Spicer's going to the wife. And Spicer knowing but doing nothing to stop me. Is it ethical?'

'I don't see much wrong with it,' said Gilda.

'Not in itself,' said Annette. 'But wouldn't they be tempted to talk to one another about their patients?'

'It does happen,' said Gilda gloomily. 'All London knows about

53

Ernie Gromback's herpes because a gossip columnist happened to be sitting in a restaurant at the next table to a group of therapists discussing case histories, with names. But I'm sure the Doctors Marks aren't like that. They're original Hampstead types, from the sound of them, and old-fashionedly professional. So no one except themselves would understand the jargon they spoke. What do you think she looks like?'

'She didn't seem to make much impression on Spicer,' said Annette. 'It doesn't sound exactly sexy: a New Age homeopathic therapist astrologer. But I suppose one never knows. What I can't stand is Spicer being so gullible. He never used to be. I hold Dr Rhea Marks responsible for sapping his intellect.'

'Annette,' said Gilda, 'if you take my advice, you won't speak against his therapist, or he'll side with her against you.'

'But I'm his wife.'

'For a man to be close to his therapist might be worse than his having a mistress. An affair without sex. A meeting of minds. What could you do about it? Nothing. There are no laws against it; nobody to socially disapprove; nobody to cut dead in the street.'

'I do see,' said Annette, 'that I might have a real problem.'

'Is that Dr Herman Marks?' said Annette over the phone. 'This is Mrs Horrocks speaking. I have an appointment with you this afternoon but if you don't mind I think I'll cancel. I'm not feeling very well.'

'All the more reason to come and see me,' said Dr Herman Marks. 'A young woman in the full flood of pregnancy should be the happiest, healthiest creature in the world. If such a person is ill, the distress seeps out from the mind, not the body. I will see you at three this afternoon. I went to some trouble making space for you, as you will understand. There are many calls upon my time from people in serious need.'

'Believe me, I understand that.'

'As we arranged, Mrs Horrocks. Annette. So I'll see you at three, as we planned.'

'Yes, Dr Marks.'

*

54

At 2.52 Annette knocked on the door of the Doctors Marks, and was admitted by a woman in her mid-thirties. She had a sweet face and a gentle, welcoming smile. Her lashes were colourless, her eyes protruded, her face was without make-up, her clothes indeterminate dove-grey, and her mousy hair was pulled back in a bun. Her movements were graceful and her demeanour was peaceful.

'I will show you into my husband's surgery, Mrs Horrocks,' said Dr Rhea Marks. 'Although you are a few minutes early.' Her voice was agreeably soft, low and tentative. 'We do like patients to arrive at the appointed time.'

'It is difficult to time one's arrival to the dot,' said Annette, 'traffic being what it is, and random.'

'Patients sometimes just park and sit in their cars outside and wait,' said Dr Rhea Marks, 'and take the opportunity to relax, or meditate if they are in touch with their inner being, until the proper time.'

'I came by public transport,' said Annette.

'What a nuisance for you!' said Dr Marks sympathetically.

Annette sat in the leather chair facing Dr Herman Marks's desk. The Persian carpet was worn. The room was hot and the ceiling yellow from cigarette smoke. She fell asleep.

'Oh, Dr Marks, you startled me!'

'Do please call me Herman. Otherwise I might mistake myself for my wife and that would never do. Two Doctors Marks in one house! When I married, my wife was my student; the merest miss. Now she outstrips me in everything, including doctorates. You were asleep, my dear. How flattering. How at home you must feel!'

'Well, I'm awake now, Dr Marks. If you don't mind, I won't call you Herman. It seems so informal.'

'You are very nervous today, I can tell. In a very English mood,' said Dr Herman.

'I told you I was not feeling very well,' said Annette.

'And how does this mysterious "not well" affect you?'

'I have a permanent headache,' said Annette. 'There seems to be

55

a kind of space in my head where things aren't connecting.'

'You put it very well,' said Dr Herman. 'Things "not connecting". Well, we will help if we can. Do you often get these headaches?'

'No.'

'But you have today. I wonder why?'

'I'm not getting enough sleep,' said Annette. 'And when I do sleep I get dreams which wake me up. Or else it's the baby kicking. I don't know.'

'And I figure in these dreams?'

'Well, yes, come to think of it.'

'In what way?' asked Dr Herman. He bent towards her. The hairs in his nostrils were black, thick and curly. There was grey in his head hair but not in his nostrils.

'Do we have to go into all this?'

'I think perhaps we do,' said Dr Herman. 'And in some detail. You must learn to trust me; not to hold back. There is no blame in our sexual fantasies. You have already trusted me with many confidences. I really would prefer you to call me Herman. See me as a father: be a good daughter: call me what I ask.'

'I could call you Doctor Herman,' said Annette.

'Thank you, Annette,' said Dr Herman. 'That is a satisfactory compromise. Many of your troubles stem from yourself as the daughter of a perhaps too loving father.'

'That simply is not the case,' said Annette. 'He seemed to love me just about right. Still does.'

'These memories are often buried,' said Dr Herman. 'It does not mean they are not there, simply that you have overlaid them. See what has just happened? I instructed you to call me Herman: at first you refuse: then you change your mind and obey, from which I deduce that you see me as the father, you oblige me with your obedience. You were unwilling; but how easily I am able to override you.'

'I just wanted you to stop going on about it,' said Annette.

'You just wanted the father to stop,' said Dr Herman. 'How often do we not hear that story?'

'Now hang on a minute,' said Annette.

'I think you protest too much, Annette. You identify me with your father; then you dream of me in intimate terms: now what are we to make of that? It was almost the first thing you told me. Practically bursting out of your lips.'

'Actually, I've got too bad a headache to make much of anything, Dr Marks. Dr Herman. But I can promise you I was not the victim of child abuse at the hands of my father.'

'At the hands of your father? Or something worse than hands?'

'Do you have any aspirin?' asked Annette.

'Perhaps we should take your blood-pressure,' said Dr Herman. 'If you are having headaches. Just stand here beside me. There is no need to be nervous of physical contact. I am not your father in the real world, though in your dreams you fantasise that I am.'

'I can go to my own doctor to have my blood-pressure taken. Really, I'd rather.'

'But will you? Since you are avoiding treatment for both yourself and your baby?'

'How do you know I'm avoiding treatment?'

'You see! I am right. You are ambivalent about your baby. So others must look after it! Roll up your sleeve, please: I will wrap this black collar round your arm. The sleeve higher, please. It won't roll up any further? Then I think you should take your blouse off altogether. When I have taken your blood-pressure, I will need to listen to your heart anyway. Don't be prudish. I am a medical doctor. I have seen many a bare bosom in my time, even younger and prettier than yours – what are you ashamed of?'

'Gilda,' wept Annette, 'please come and help me.'

'Where are you? What's the matter?'

'I'm in a phone box at Finchley Road station.'

'What's happened?'

'Gilda, it's terrible. Awful. I'm in such a state.'

'Shall I get hold of Spicer?'

'No, just you. Quickly, please.'

'Oh, thank you, Gilda. You are so kind,' said Annette.

'Just lie and soak in the bath, Annette. It will stop you trembling. Are you hurt anywhere? He didn't actually rape you?'

57

'Oh no, no,' said Annette. 'Of course not. His wife was in the house.'

'Well, what?'

'First he made me stand there without anything at all on top –'

'Not even your bra? Most doctors let you keep your bra on when they take your blood-pressure.'

'He forgot about my blood-pressure as soon as my blouse was off. He kept saying he wanted to listen to my heart,' said Annette. 'Then he complained about the little wired metal rose in the centre of my bra: he said it was interfering with the electronics of his stethoscope, so would I take the bra off, and I felt stupid not wanting to, as if I was seeing sexual implications when there weren't any. What made me think I was so attractive anyway: pregnant women aren't exactly fanciable by all and sundry, are they? A breast's a breast in a medical context. So I took the bra off, but then he said there was something wrong with his stethoscope after all, and I just had to stand there while he found another, not sure whether I was meant to put my bra back on. There comes a moment when modesty is almost more suggestive than anything else. Then he did listen to my heart, and to my back while I coughed. He said my heart was okay. So what else was new! Then he felt my nipples, and said they were very engorged, and not very attractive, and my husband could hardly like them in that state. Then he pinched them; first one, then the other; he told me to see if they'd retract –'

'Why didn't you just kick him in the balls and run?'

'I was kind of paralysed. It was so hard to believe. I thought it might be genuine, some kind of middle-European nipple test. How was I to know? He told me he was just making sure they were healthy,' said Annette. 'That it was extra-oestrogen not malignancy which was smudging them.'

'So you just stood there?'

'I was so taken by surprise,' said Annette. 'He seemed to be suggesting the reason I had marital difficulties was because Spicer must find me unattractive.'

'What marital difficulties?' asked Gilda.

'I have no idea. It was just somehow assumed I had them,' said Annette. 'And I thought perhaps he's right. Perhaps Spicer doesn't fancy me any more. Then I thought no, that's absurd, the way Spicer's been carrying on lately: if I'm tired it's because of Spicer. So I fought back, Gilda. I said why are you trying to humiliate me? And do you know what he said? He said because the more I identified him with my father the better. He said he had to rework the trauma and then I'd be cured.'

'Oh dear God,' said Gilda.

'And I was still puzzling over that when he began to palpate my breasts – you know how the nurse does it at the Clinic, checking for lumps so you don't have to have the mammogram and be slammed up between those metal plates – by that time he was standing behind me. And I somehow came to, and said what are you doing: is that really necessary? He just snapped that it was, because pregnant women can get a galloping form of breast cancer, did I know that, so I had to be checked. I couldn't work out whether he was a doctor, my father or this horrible man with black hairs coming out of his nostrils. Then those long, long arms were hugging me from behind: the way he'd done the week before, but now he was talking this junk about undoing the trauma; about how I had to love the touch of the father in adult life, as I had learned to loathe it in infancy, and this long, hard thing was pressing into my back, so I shrieked and turned round and hit his face, and grabbed my clothes and ran. I suppose that counts as an indecent assault but who'd ever believe me? He'd just deny it and say it was therapy. His wife was in the hall, arranging roses, can you believe? Dr Rhea Marks. The one Spicer so adores. I bet she'd been listening in. I pushed past her and let myself out of the front door, and she just stared after me. I had to stop to put on my shirt, can you believe it? In the street? Then I ran on down to the station and called you. I don't think anyone saw me. Are my nipples really so horrible?'

'They look quite ordinary to me,' said Gilda, 'though they have kind of spread, I suppose. Some women at the Clinic have far worse. Theirs are kind of chocolate brown, yours are coffee.'

'That's something,' said Annette. 'I suppose.'

'You don't think you imagined it?' Gilda asked. 'Women do fantasise about doctors.'

'Of course I didn't imagine it,' said Annette. 'Would I imagine phrases like the homeopathy of humiliation? The rebirth of response? I'd be ashamed even to make them up.'

'I don't know, Annette. It does seem unlikely, but then so does being assaulted by a therapist. The human brain is very strange, especially when it's pregnant.'

'Whose side are you on?'

'Yours. I was just theorising,' said Gilda. 'For all we know, what Dr Herman Marks was doing is a perfectly accepted form of therapy. It sounds reasonable to me. Sexual rehabilitation via the therapist. A cure for child abuse trauma. Identify the therapist with the father, relive the original experience as an adult, and bingo.'

'It sounds disgusting to me,' said Annette, 'especially as I wasn't traumatised as a child.'

'That's what you say. But supposing this doctor is right, and you've buried the memory? And now he's cured you anyway. You'd never know. Well, if it's orgasms, orgasms, orgasms from now on in, I suppose you will. Are you going to tell Spicer?'

'I don't think he's going to want to know,' said Annette.

'I can always tell Steve,' said Gilda. 'And Steve will go round and beat Dr Herman Marks up. He would if it happened to me.'

'Spicer will only think I led the doctor on,' said Annette. 'Spicer will only blame me. Or he'll say I was fantasising. Perhaps I was? But what was I doing at Finchley Road station trembling and my bra in my pocket if it didn't happen?'

'It's a hot day,' said Gilda. 'Your bra might have got too tight and you just took it off.'

'I'd never have taken off my bra just because it was hot,' said Annette. 'My breasts have got so big they bounced all the way down the hill. I hated that. Of course it really happened.'

'I'll bring you some champagne,' said Gilda.

'Well, just a glass. More would be bad for baby,' said Annette.

'What was your blood-pressure,' asked Gilda, 'as a matter of interest?'

'He never got round to taking it,' said Annette. 'And the other reason I can't tell Spicer is because you're right: he'd be more anxious to protect Dr Rhea Marks than he would me. If he didn't believe me he'd be angry because I was causing unpleasantness:

if he did believe me he might decide to rescue Dr Rhea Marks from Dr Herman. She wasn't exactly pretty: just sort of helpless, and she has a very little voice, with which she puts you in your place. And I can just see her gazing up at Spicer with her pale pop eyes, and flattering him by talking about his soul.'

'I suppose not many people talk to wine merchants about their souls,' said Gilda.

'Probably not,' said Annette. 'I'd better get dry and go home, and face whatever happens next.'

'Annette?'

'Oh hi, Spicer.'

'You were a long time answering,' said Spicer on the phone. 'Have you just come in?'

'Yes,' said Annette.

'Where were you?' asked Spicer. 'Out gadding with your beloved Gilda? I had your friend Ernie on the phone. He was trying to get hold of you. You didn't even put the answerphone on.'

'I forgot,' said Annette.

'If you forget, there's very little point in owning one, wouldn't you think?'

'I was out seeing my therapist,' said Annette. 'I got nervy.'

' "My therapist"! I knew it would happen,' said Spicer. 'You have joined the ranks of the ladies-in-treatment. Now at last my Annette can hold her head up in the cafés and coffee shops! She will be equal in the beauty parlours and the hair salons. Oh to be a lady of leisure and the doors of the soul held open wide.'

'You're very lyrical, Spicer, considering it was your idea I went in the first place.'

'I think you misremember it, Annette. You misremember so much.'

'Anyway, Spicer, you go to a therapist too.'

'It's hardly the same,' said Spicer.

'I don't understand why not,' said Annette. 'Unless it's different for men.'

'You're very sharp and edgy today, Annette,' said Spicer. 'Let me put it like this: men, unlike women, seldom seek therapy for

trivial reasons. Rhea Marks is a Jungian: a transcendentalist.
Herman Marks, her husband, is an eclectic: a behaviourist. I am
seeking treatment from the first, you from the second. How did
you get on with him this time?'

'Not very well, actually,' said Annette. 'I don't think I like him
very much. In fact I think I'll stop seeing him.'

'Oh dear, oh dear,' said Spicer. 'Oh, the whims and fancies. First
I will, then I won't. You do find it difficult to persist in anything,
Annette. Not even our baby's welfare has done anything to steady
you down.'

'For God's sake, Spicer –'

'If you're going to be unpleasant there's very little point in ringing
you.'

The phone buzzed. Spicer had cut her off. Annette switched the
yellow button over to save the battery. She sat down. She could
see her ankles: they were indeed puffy. She took off her shoes.
The phone rang again.

'Spicer?'

'No, Mrs Horrocks,' said Wendy. 'It's me. Mr Horrocks said to
say he's sorry he had to go and asked me to tell you to call Mr
Gromback at once. Apparently Oprah Winfrey are interested and
Mr Gromback needs a yes or no from you as soon as possible.'

'Oprah Winfrey? You mean the TV show?'

'Yes. She's over here doing a series on literary women worldwide.'

'But that's extraordinary. Why should they want me?'

'I don't know why, Mrs Horrocks. Mr Horrocks just asked you
to call Mr Gromback. Isn't it exciting!'

'I suppose so. Can I speak to Spicer?'

'He's in a meeting. I always watch Oprah Winfrey if ever I'm ill
which is hardly ever. Mr Horrocks says he doesn't know who in
God's name she is, but I bet he does. Well, everyone does. Must
go!'

'Ernie?'

'Thank God you called back, Annette,' said Ernie Gromback.
'Where have you been? Where do you housewives get to? I was
worried. You're meant to be resting.'

'As it happens,' said Annette, 'I was out being indecently assaulted by a mad therapist.'

'There's a lot of it about,' said Ernie Gromback. 'Anyone can do a weekend course and set up in business. Or not even bother with the course. Marion's thinking of setting herself up as a counsellor.'

'She's not!'

'She threatens to,' said Ernie. 'But enough about Marion, are you okay?'

'Just about,' said Annette.

'Not traumatised?'

'No,' said Annette. 'I don't think so. It was a long way this side of rape.'

'Spicer didn't say anything about it,' said Ernie, suspiciously.

'Spicer doesn't know.'

'Funny kind of relationship you and Spicer have,' said Ernie Gromback.

'It's a very good relationship,' said Annette, automatically. 'We're very close and we love each other very much.'

'Now that's settled,' said Ernie, after a short pause, 'Oprah Winfrey wants you to be on her show next week. Literary schmiterary, but she'll shift a book or two.'

'But, Ernie –'

'Look, publishing's hit hard times. This is a first novel. You turn down Oprah Winfrey, you do Gromback Partners a bad turn. And yourself. I have a feeling you need all the good turns you can get.'

'But why would anyone be interested in a book called *Lucifette Fallen*?'

'Some researcher picked up an early review. "The archetype of the matrimonial row: God and Lucifette, sub-title Lilith in her new appearance".'

'Why haven't I seen this review?' asked Annette

'Because it came out in some nutty New Age journal,' said Ernie Gromback. 'Winfrey must have got hold of a proof copy. Probably by way of Marion. Marion's into the New Age: she goes to a self-discovery group: so do all sorts of TV people. Drives me nuts. I'm the only rational man left in the universe; everyone else has gone Carl Gustav. Personally, I'd rather put my faith in a rabbi, but even they are gazing into crystals these days and telling their fortunes by the stars.'

'*Lucifette Fallen* is nothing to do with the stars,' said Annette. 'It's all cosmos, darling,' said Ernie. 'All cosmos. At any rate I'm glad they think it is. There's money in the New Age.'

'Can you be more precise about the magazine?' asked Annette.

'I'll put it in the post to you,' said Ernie Gromback. '*Jungian Eclectics, Astrologian Psychonuts*, I can't remember. So I'll ask the Oprah Winfrey people to get back to you as soon as possible. That's decided?'

'But Ernie,' said Annette. 'I don't think Spicer would like me going on a chat show. We never look at things like that on TV.'

'Does Spicer want you to earn any money out of this book or not?'

'Well frankly, Ernie,' said Annette, 'possibly Spicer doesn't. And possibly I don't, because I can see trouble ahead, and family is more important to me than anything else, and I love Spicer, as you know.'

'Perhaps it's because you're pregnant,' said Ernie Gromback, 'that you're slightly out of your mind.'

'I am so not,' said Annette. 'I've waited so long to have this baby, and I mean it to be born into a happy, settled family. Now you know all that, Ernie.'

'I suppose this baby of yours is Spicer's? It isn't mine?'

'Ernie!' protested Annette.

'Well, Annette?' asked Ernie Gromback. 'It's a reasonable question.'

'Babies have a gestation period of nine months,' said Annette. 'The last and indeed the only time you and I had any association of a carnal nature was two years and one month ago.'

'You make it sound rather bleak,' said Ernie, 'but at least you've been counting. So have I, if you want to know. And I wish Spicer would be better to you, but what can I say? Do this one small thing for me, Annette, since you won't do anything else – appear on the Oprah Winfrey Show, in the full flower of lovely motherhood, tribute to Gromback's knack for picking talent. Literary talent, that is.'

'But what angle are they going to take?' enquired Annette. 'I'll have no control over any of it. Supposing my mother sees the

programme, and thinks *Lucifette Fallen* is all about her and my
Dad. Which it is. Oh God, Ernie, couldn't I just unwrite this
novel? And it has such an embarrassing title.'

'The title works, Annette,' said Ernie Gromback. 'I rather
doubted it would but since *Astrojunk* has picked it up you were
spot on in your judgement. So you're going to say yes to Oprah
Winfrey?'

'I'll think about it, Ernie,' said Annette. 'I'm going to look
dreadfully pregnant and I've had such a terrible day.'

'Husbands are for telling about terrible days,' said Ernie
Gromback. 'Keep it for Spicer, since that's the way you want it.
When exactly are you having this baby?'

'On Christmas Day,' said Annette.

'Ah, a little goat,' said Ernie.

'What?'

'A little Capricorn,' he said. 'Marion has me well-trained. I'm on
the cusp between Scorpio and Sagittarius, did you know that?
Wildly attractive but a sting in the tail! Marion's a Gemini. We
were born for each other; but Scorpios simply have to scuttle from
out of their rocks from time to time to see what they're missing.
Marion knew that when she took me in. Perhaps in the spring,
when your waist has returned, and you're a world-famous author,
I could scuttle past your door and you would look out from your
Virgoan isolation –'

'Ernie, I have to go,' said Annette.

'But never forget the sting in the tail,' said Ernie Gromback.
'Oprah Winfrey?'

'Oprah Winfrey, Ernie,' said Annette sadly. 'I can see I have no
option.'

'Not really, no,' said Mr Gromback of Gromback, Little & Peach:
Gromback since 1982, Little since 1921, and Peach since 1810,
and doing nicely, even in this year of recession.

'Annette,' said Spicer, 'I'm trying to read.'

'But you haven't had your supper, Spicer,' said Annette. 'Straight
in the door, hardly a word to anyone, and into your study. Aren't
you hungry?' The evening sun shone in the window and made all
things gold.

'I had some fruit,' said Spicer. 'That's all I need.'

'Don't get too thin,' said Annette. 'Your shoulders are so broad and nice as they are. What are you reading?'

'Not a book I think you'd understand,' said Spicer.

'*Cutting Free from Hurtful Ties*, by Chalice Wellspring,' Annette read over Spicer's shoulder. 'Am I one of the ties that hurt? Does that include wives?'

'Annette,' said Spicer, 'the book is a study of the internalised negative figures that can sabotage everything that a man attempts to do. The inner enemies. If you wish to take on the role of enemy in my life there is no way I can prevent you. But I will then have to do my best to escape you. You certainly represent something phenomenal in my life – last night in my dreams I was Jonah inside the whale; the seas were tumultuous, terrifying.'

'I was the whale?' asked Annette.

'Annette, please just go away and leave me in peace, for God's sake! If you see yourself as the whale, that's your problem. Most women would have realised they were the sea. Get on with your own life. It's busy enough, to all accounts.'

'No. I won't go away,' said Annette. 'I'm your wife. I want to know. I have a right to know. Okay, so I'm this inner enemy, just suppose. What does the book tell you to do about it?'

'Invoke the High C,' said Spicer. 'Now you won't understand that, you'll just laugh, as the ignorant and antagonistic do. The Inner Enemy all too often takes the form of the seducer, the doubter, the one who mocks. Not surprising you're prepared to hold your husband and family up to ridicule by appearing on a TV show in an advanced state of pregnancy.'

'I'm not laughing, Spicer,' said Annette, 'or mocking. If you are cutting the ties that link you to me, if you are detaching yourself from me, then this is very painful for me indeed. Don't you understand that? That it hurts?'

'How you centre everything upon yourself,' said Spicer. 'You are hopelessly egocentric. A man can be tied to many things, from drink to drugs to rubber fetishes to money, let alone wives. Good Lord, Annette, can't a man even read a book someone's recommended without your coming over all paranoid?'

'Who recommended this book?' asked Annette. 'Dr Rhea Marks?'

'Yes,' said Spicer. 'She did. As it happens.'

'I went to see Dr Rhea Marks's husband today,' said Annette, before she could stop herself, 'and he indecently assaulted me. Perhaps he does that to all his patients. Perhaps Dr Rhea's decided to get rid of pathetic old Herman Marks and Spicer Horrocks would do very nicely thank you. Wine merchant in prime of life, energetic in bed, merely persuade him to cut the ties that hurt, and voilà!'

'Perhaps I'd better ring your mother,' said Spicer.

'Why?'

'Because you're insane,' said Spicer. 'Your mother may know better than me how to deal with you when you're in this frame of mind. I frankly have no idea what to do for the best.'

'You could close the book and talk to me,' said Annette.

'Very well,' said Spicer. 'I can see I have no choice. But it doesn't endear you to me. Now, can we take these things one at a time? First, Dr Herman Marks indecently assaulted you? Really? In what way?'

'I don't even want to say – You are so out of sympathy with me,' said Annette.

'You can't make these accusations and then just leave them in the air,' said Spicer. 'People get into real trouble doing that. You need to be more careful, Annette.'

'Don't bully me like this.'

'What form did this assault take?' Spicer asked.

'He made me undress,' said Annette.

'Made you? Really? How does someone make someone else undress?' asked Spicer. 'Tell me!'

'On pretext of a medical examination,' said Annette.

'Annette, he is a doctor, and you are pregnant,' observed her husband.

'Forget it,' said Annette. 'Let's just say I had to run out of his room half-naked and then out of the house, past his wife.'

'Oh dear God,' said Spicer. 'Poor Rhea. This madwoman running out of her husband's consulting room, shrieking rape. Is this what pregnancy does to women? First obsessive jealousy, then accusations, now fantasies of sexual molestation?'

'I knew you wouldn't believe me,' sobbed Annette. 'You always side with my enemies.'

'Enemies? A middle-aged middle-class housewife with enemies?' enquired Spicer. 'Only if she's a paranoiac. Now shall we get back to your earlier statement? That Dr Rhea Marks has decided to get rid of her husband and selected me as a substitute? You do see that this can only be the product of a distressed mind?'

'I know it sounds stupid, Spicer, and I'm sorry,' said Annette, 'but why else is she trying to break up our relationship? How can you believe all the nonsense she speaks? She's the one who's destructive, not me. She feeds into your vanity, she flatters you. Something's going on I don't understand. Perhaps she procures patients for her husband.'

'You have to stop making these allegations, Annette, or you'll end up in prison,' said Spicer. 'And the more you insult Dr Rhea Marks, who is extremely helpful, supportive and positive, the more difficult things will get between you and me. So please, for God's sake, stop. Let me make you a cup of tea. You distress yourself so.'

'But things between us aren't difficult, Spicer,' said Annette, as she sipped her tea and dabbed her eyes. 'Or they weren't before you started going to see Dr Rhea Marks.'

'Not for you, perhaps,' said Spicer. 'What about me? Could you really believe the rows, the scenes, make me happy? I was becoming ill, Annette,' said Spicer. 'The stress of being married to you was showing. My blood-pressure was up. I could have had a stroke, a heart-attack, any minute: thank God I got to Dr Rhea in time. I'll always be indebted to Marion for getting me to her.'

'If you're really ill, and not just a hypochondriac, go to a proper doctor,' said Annette. 'Get your blood-pressure lowered by pills. Or get someone else to measure it, who isn't taking your money.'

'Is that your only response? No concern, no love; just to suggest doctor's pills which always do more damage than they do good. You should hear Dr Rhea on the subject. She's turned her back on the orthodox medical establishment. She's seen too much of it. Now don't start crying again. I spoke to Rhea today,' said Spicer. 'She feels she needs to see you, in the hope of bringing you to some understanding of just how drastic my situation is. Just how ill I am: how careful you have to be.'

'I'm too stunned to cry any more,' said Annette. 'Why should I see someone who obviously has such a low opinion of me? Who reads my star-chart and says it's shit? I suppose yours is the cat's whiskers.'

'It certainly isn't afflicted in the way yours is. My planets cluster in air signs. Yours are mostly earth, and in the bottom half of your chart. Well, there's nothing wrong with that. It just means I am intuitive and imaginative, while you are practical. We balance each other, more or less.'

'But I drag you down?' cried Annette sadly. 'The top-heavy end of the see-saw.'

'I didn't say that,' said Spicer. 'But I do think we should go together to see Dr Marks. She'll have a thing or two to say to you. I'll keep you out of Dr Herman's way, if only for his sake.'

'Very well, Spicer,' said Annette. 'Make the appointment.'

'Gilda,' said Annette. It was 2.10 on a Friday afternoon.

'Hi, Annette,' said Gilda. 'Why are you whispering?'

'Because I'm in Dr Herman's room using his phone. It's okay. He's gone to Austria, or somewhere, for a conference. Spicer's upstairs with Dr Rhea. On the way he said I was very brave to see her, considering what she knew about me.'

'That wasn't very nice of him, Annette,' said Gilda.

'He's in a funny mood,' said Annette. 'Dr Rhea opened the door sort of excited to see me, I don't know why. You just get a feeling. She was on some kind of power trip. Then she wiped the smile off her face and said I was to wait while she saw Spicer for twenty minutes, then she'd see me for twenty minutes, then both of us together, and she showed me in here to wait. There's a chart on the wall of how to search the breast for lumps.'

'Didn't you ask her why she wanted to see you?' enquired Gilda.

'Yes, I did,' said Annette. 'I was quite bold. I said to her the minute we were in the door, what are we in, some kind of marriage therapy?'

'What did she say?' asked Gilda.

'She just said oh we don't like to call it that, and led Spicer

69

upstairs. She's wearing a kind of pleated navy blue dress with a white collar. It's perfectly horrible; the kind of thing a nun would wear on her afternoon off. And an old yellowy cardigan.'

'What are you wearing?'

'Tights and my old Calvin Klein mustardy top. I'm trying to look serious. Spiritual, even.'

'What's Dr Herman's room like? Apart from the breasts. Does it give you the shivers?'

'There's a big wing chair, a greasy patch either side where his head touches it. The ceiling's yellow from cigarette smoke. There are locked bookcases.'

'It would give you the creeps,' said Gilda, 'in the circumstances.'

'I think perhaps I did imagine what I thought happened,' said Annette.

'But you said he had an erection and it pressed into your back,' said Gilda.

'It could have been a pipe in his pocket or a slide rule or something,' said Annette. 'He was behind me. It might have been some kind of crystal device these nutters use to heal you, I don't know.'

'I think the simplest explanation is best,' said Gilda.

'But it felt long,' said Annette. 'Too long. Mind you, it did occur to me that's the kind of length it would have seemed if I was a child and he was a grown man.'

'You mean your father?' asked Gilda.

'I simply cannot believe any such thing about my father,' said Annette, 'but perhaps an uncle. Who's to say?'

'So either way,' said Gilda, 'Dr Herman's let off the hook. Either you imagined it, or if you didn't it's a legitimate therapy and you'll end up sexually liberated.'

'Yes,' said Annette.

'You never struck me as sexually unliberated,' said Gilda. 'In fact I remember things from our student days when you were decidedly liberated.'

'Just shut up about those,' said Annette.

'And you were trembling and crying in that telephone box,' said Gilda.

'I think they call that abreaction,' said Annette.

'They're brainwashing you,' said Gilda.

'I just want to live happily ever after with Spicer,' said Annette, 'and if I have to turn my head inside out it's worth it. I've got to go now. Spicer's coming downstairs. Gilda, I'm petrified. I don't know why. I just get intimidated by doctors.'

'Well now,' said Dr Marks cheerily, 'what do you want to tell me about your relationship with your husband?'

'I thought you were going to tell me about it,' said Annette. 'That's why you wanted to see me.'

'It would help me if you told me how you saw it first,' said Dr Rhea.

'He seems upset at the moment,' said Annette. 'I don't know why, and he blames me for everything that goes wrong, and he's giving me a really hard time. But I'm sure we can work through it. Marriages go through bad patches and come out the other side, don't they? We've been happy before and we will be again. I'm pregnant and not at my best. I expect I imagine things that don't happen: Spicer says I do. Everything will just click back into place as soon as the baby's born. Spicer and I need each other, always have. Until we met both our lives were messy. After we met we got things together. I stopped raving, Spicer stopped drinking. It was love at first sight. We met at a party and went home together and never left each other's side thereafter. Though we both had to get unmarried to third parties to do it. We still call each other on the phone every day. Well, Spicer calls me. He doesn't much like me calling him because he can be busy: it interrupts the flow of money-making thought, he says. And the children are in private schools; so the money has to flow. We try and give them stability. Spicer and I hate being apart. He has to go away in the summers to France, to see the vineyards: then we both feel desperate, lonely. We're just intertwined. We're so lucky to love each other. Lots of couples aren't like that. By ourselves Spicer and I are nothing: together we add up to something. Well, a lot. Friends rely on us; our families; Spicer's aunts: we're central to so many people, you've no idea. Things have just got to work out.' Annette fell silent.

'Ah,' said Dr Rhea Marks, and she got up and stared out of the window. 'You must realise, Mrs Horrocks,' said Dr Rhea presently, 'that Spicer would get on perfectly well without you. After all, he has his own friends, his own work, his own interests, his own income.'

'Oh!' said Annette, and she giggled.

'And no doubt the same applies to you,' said Dr Rhea.

'Do you really think so?' asked Annette, and she giggled some more.

'Spouses are often far less dependent upon each other than they imagine,' said Dr Rhea. 'The close relationship can turn destructive; in response it is not unusual for one partner to develop an image of themselves as dependent.'

'My feeling more dependent than usual is nothing to do with being pregnant?' asked Annette.

'Oh no,' said Dr Rhea. 'Your feelings of dependence are to do with your attachment to the child: a reflection of embryonic dependency, which is becoming a basis for your unconscious and conscious maternal solicitude.'

'Well, thank you very much,' said Annette.

'You are more light-hearted than your chart suggests,' said Dr Rhea. 'You giggle a lot.'

'Nerves,' said Annette. 'What you say is quite shocking to me, but I'll try and take it seriously.'

'Of course, Spicer, being male, experiences the primordial mysteries directly and indirectly as provocative: a force that sets him in motion and impels him towards change. It is a matter of indifference whether the transformation of the male is caused by positive or negative fascination.'

'I'm not altogether indifferent,' remarked Annette, 'to changes in Spicer.'

'But of course in Spicer we notice the emergence of something soul-like – the anima – from the Archetypal Feminine, the unconscious, represented by yourself; so the relation of the ego to the unconscious changes. What you describe as a bad patch, Mrs Horrocks. It may be more profound than this.'

'That sounds bad,' said Annette.

'The transformative character fascinates but does not obliterate. It sets the personality in motion, produces change and ultimately transformation. The process is fraught with danger, even mortal peril. Spicer will fight for the preservation of his ego: you the Feminine are determined to retain his ego as your mate.'

'I see. Well, I don't really, but I expect we'll weather it,' said Annette. 'Can't Spicer come in and join us? I'm beginning to miss him.'

Dr Rhea thought for a moment. 'Spicer tells me you have been suffering from sexual fantasies of a markedly destructive nature.'

'He told you this?' asked Annette.

'He is open with me, of course,' said Dr Rhea. 'Don't reproach yourself. The spontaneous processes of the collective unconscious are at their most demonstrable in mental disorder.'

'Mental disorder? Are you telling me I'm nuts?'

'My dear,' said Dr Rhea, 'don't be distressed. Of course not, or only as the world will see it. You are simply open at the moment to the elementary character of the Archetypal Feminine. The affected individual doesn't in reality have visions, they occur as an autonomous natural process. You will have these visions: you will communicate them to your husband; the structure of the transformative character, that is to say Spicer, already relates to a personality embracing the spontaneity of consciousness, that is to say yourself. It is a fascinating phenomenon, Mrs Horrocks.'

'Good,' said Annette. She polished her nail with her thumb. Her fingers were quite stiff and swollen.

'Spicer's dreams indicate the degree of transformation. The Western symbol group of the Terrible Mothers – night, abyss, sea, watery depths, snake, dragon, whale – all the symbols colour one another and merge. Devouring water, rending earth womb, abyss of death, hostile snake of night and death, whale, sea – all aspects of the negative unconscious; which lives in the nocturnal darkness beneath the world of man and threatens catastrophe.'

'Poor Spicer,' said Annette. 'Though I wish you wouldn't call him Spicer, and me Mrs Horrocks. It smacks of possession. He is my husband. He has been dreaming of whales, as it happens.'

'It's understandable that you are resistant. Spouses often are. You fear the anima in Spicer, he the anima in you. You to him are like the enchantress who turns men into beasts. He sees himself as Odysseus, the successful suitor; you as Circe invited to share your bed. But danger is all around: to be changed into a pig is the fate of those who displease Circe: your anima is negative, your intention to poison his male consciousness, as he sees it, like Circe to endanger it by intoxication –'

'Is that why he's gone off drink?'

'You have a frivolity, Mrs Horrocks, that isn't altogether helpful to your own cause. You are putting up barriers to understanding. Very well, I will speak in language you understand.'

'What is my own cause?' asked Annette.

'To keep your husband, Mrs Horrocks.'

'I don't think I am in any danger of losing him,' said Annette.

'Tell me, do you have children?'

'No. But we are not thinking about me, we are thinking about you.'

'I'm thinking quite hard about you,' said Annette. 'You'd be surprised.'

'You may not realise quite how ill your husband is. He collapsed and nearly died in this very room on his first visit to me.'

'He didn't mention it to me,' said Annette.

'Perhaps he thought he wouldn't receive much sympathy. Your husband's view is that there is so great an unconscious hostility to him that you welcome his illness, indeed have brought it about.'

'Your view or Spicer's view? His illness or the one you've put into his head?'

'And please try not to be hostile to me. I am here to help you both if I can. My concern is primarily with Spicer: he is my patient and therefore my responsibility, as you are not. But because of your relationship you and he are interlinked. That is why I needed to see you.'

'And my star-chart isn't sufficient to tell you all about me?'

'It can tell me a lot but not everything,' said Dr Rhea.

'I see,' said Annette. 'And Spicer can get on very well without me. That's the conclusion you've reached.'

'Spicer and I have discussed it between us, and yes, we have more or less come to that conclusion,' said Dr Rhea. 'Spicer is not the man he was when you met him. We all change: you as well.'

'Don't tell me what is perfectly obvious, Dr Marks,' said Annette.

'And when Spicer so nearly died, or so you say, how exactly did you save him?'

'I am medically trained, as is my husband. We were able to revive Spicer with an appropriate remedy. A natural stimulant.'

'You didn't think to call an ambulance?' asked Annette.

'There was no need,' said Dr Rhea. 'The danger was over. Hospitals do more damage than most people realise. The body is a self-healing entity. Statistics show that heart-attack victims, simply left to themselves, have a better survival rate than those who are rushed off to hospital. It is the journey which kills, and powerful drugs introduced into a system already under stress. I am a qualified medical doctor, Mrs Horrocks; I do know what I'm talking about. Now I understand your hostility to me: most spouses profoundly resent the therapist: so don't see yourself as unusual. The spouse sees therapy as an interference in the life of the marriage: but sometimes a therapist will intervene to help a marriage survive which would otherwise fail, if the therapist judges that is the best option. You feel threatened: of course you do: I understand that.'

'I don't feel threatened,' said Annette. 'I am threatened. And not even free to ask a second opinion. Are you telling me I'm the cause of Spicer's alleged heart-attack? And telling that to Spicer too?'

'Why "alleged"? Why are you so resistant to the idea of his illness?'

'Because he hasn't been to see our doctor.'

'He has changed his doctor, Mrs Horrocks. I am his doctor, and his counsellor.'

'Don't forget astrologer. Got him all ways, haven't you?'

'You have a very treacherous Mercury, Mrs Horrocks. You present yourself as a doubting Thomas, the fool who mocks, the enemy of the self. A great deal of negative energy can shelter behind mirth. You have an afflicted Mercury in the Tenth house.'

'So it's just stress that's harming Spicer's heart; not a history of drinking, or smoking, or genetics, anything like that? Not even a negative Mercury? Just stress, that is to say me?'

'The spouse,' said Dr Rhea, 'is in most cases the primary source of stress.'

'So Spicer's illness is my fault?'

'We are not talking about blame, Mrs Horrocks,' said Dr Rhea.

'You don't like me very much, do you?' observed Annette. 'Or is it just that you love rocking the foundation of other people's lives?'

'On the contrary, I am surprised I like you so much,' said Dr Rhea, 'even though you are temporarily so hostile to me.'

'It'll all be in my star-chart,' said Annette. 'I wonder what your motives are in doing this to me? Are you jealous because I'm pregnant? Or because I've written a book? Perhaps you're a would-be novelist? Perhaps you've tried and you can't so you sit there earning a living by writing living fictions: altering the narrative of other people's lives: changing it in their heads: writing your scenario about Spicer getting on perfectly well without me. For God's sake, Spicer and I would both be lost without the other! We have a very special, very solid relationship.'

'It has been deteriorating for years,' said Dr Rhea. 'But you haven't perceived it.'

The baby gave Annette a blow beneath the ribs. It had woken up.

'But this is appalling,' said Gilda to Annette. They were lunching at Antoine's. Gilda picked at a roast pepper pâté, Annette at a tomato and feta cheese salad.

'At first I thought it was funny,' said Annette, 'and then I saw it was appalling. When she called Spicer in, having totally devastated me, I said, as lightly as I could, "according to Dr Rhea here the next step for us is divorce." Spicer said no one said anything about divorce: divorce is just a scrap of paper, and Dr Rhea said I am glad Mrs Horrocks can take it so lightly: a separating out would in the circumstances perhaps be advisable. To which I said, well in my mind you're either together or apart; it's only eggs get separated out.'

'You shouldn't have been so flippant,' said Gilda. 'She'll really have it in for you now.'

'But at least Spicer said he'd like to give us another try: if I could be sexually more responsive it would help, and she talked about the generative earth and the phallic penetration of the primeval hill, which was consciousness rising out of the unconsciousness, the foundation of the diurnal ego.'

'Was she talking about him buggering you? It sounds like it,' said Gilda.

'I have no idea. I hope not,' said Annette. 'But I daresay that's how Spicer registered it.'

'Why do you hope not?' asked Gilda.

'Because, forget the diurnal ego, all he's doing when he buggers me is confirming the shit-like nature of my existence,' said Annette. 'Rubbishing me.'

'Hush,' said Gilda. 'Not so loud. I don't see why you have to see buggery like that. I quite enjoy it.'

'Well I do see it like that,' said Annette, 'and that's that. The non-maternal end of me, as it were. The reluctant hole. Unnatural love. The slippage into pleasure/pain, into death not life, into grunts not murmurs, into silence. Then Dr Rhea gave us this stuff about the uroboric primeval serpent, and the luminous principle, and I agreed to give it another try, as expected to.'

'What, the marriage?'

'By that time "the marriage",' said Annette, 'seemed to be a kind of luminous principle in itself, not just a word which described Spicer and me living together. And I was the one who was somehow burrowing under it, wearing it away, with dark archetypal flood water and I had to be stopped.'

'But Spicer isn't doing anything wrong?'

'No. Spicer is just emerging like a moth out of a chrysalis of unknowing.'

'And Spicer takes all this seriously?' asked Gilda.

'I told you she has sapped his intelligence in some peculiar way,' said Annette. 'But what was most nightmarish was the way his loyalty seemed to be towards her, not me. And his saying I was sexually suffocating and he was an unhappily married man.'

'He's trying to punish you,' said Gilda. 'He doesn't mean it.'

'But why should he want to punish me?' asked Annette.

'For the same reason she's doing what she is. Because you can make things where there was nothing before. You're having a baby and you've written a book and they're screaming with envy in their souls, the pair of them. And he's frightened of death, and if he has to ditch you to save his life, he will.'

'It does seem to boil down to all that,' said Annette. 'But what can I do about any of it? Too late! I was born the way I was, and it served Spicer very well for ten years: now this!'

Annette pushed away her plate. Gilda asked for duck and red cabbage.

'What was your feeling?' asked Gilda. 'What was the sub-text? Is she trying to make or break the marriage?'

Annette thought for a little. 'To break it,' she said. 'As Spicer and I left, an exciting thought seemed to come to her. She waved her hands in the air. She had serpent rings on her fingers. She said that since the majority of Spicer's planets were in the creative and romantic constellation and mine were in the active, the relationship was all but impossible. "Thank you so much, Dr Marks," I said, and she quickly amended it to "needs a great deal of work". So let us just say that she hopes it doesn't work, so she can be vindicated in her belief in astrology.'

'I wish you'd eat more,' said Gilda.

'I've lost my appetite,' said Annette.

Gilda ordered toffee pudding for herself and a black coffee for Annette.

'Annette,' said Spicer, 'there is a side of me you simply don't understand.'

'I'm trying to understand it, Spicer,' said Annette. 'What's the time?' she asked.

'Two-thirty,' said Spicer.

'Afternoon or night?' asked Annette.

'Night,' said Spicer. 'Have you been taking sleeping pills?'

'Of course I haven't,' said Annette. 'They'd be bad for the baby.'

'I don't know how you can sleep while there's so much going on.'

Spicer turned off the ceiling light and turned on the bedside lamp.

'Did you say something?' asked Spicer.

'No,' said Annette.

'It sounded to me rather like "it's because I'm so earthy and practical."'

78

'I wouldn't be so smart-alecky, Spicer,' said Annette. 'I just sort of groaned, I think.'

'I hope so,' said Spicer, 'because I can do without the wisecracks. Especially at this time of night.'

'Spicer,' said Annette, 'if it's two-thirty in the morning, where have you been?'

'Walking, thinking, dealing with my shadow-side.'

'Is that the whale?' asked Annette. 'Sorry, I was joking. You must mean the uroboric primal principle.'

'I wish you wouldn't talk about what you don't understand, Annette.'

'I'm sorry. Can you tell me what uroboric means?'

'The uroboros is the circular snake biting its tail,' Spicer said.

'I see,' said Annette.

'I don't think you do,' said Spicer. 'It's the symbol of the psychic state of the beginning. I am a creative man, Annette.'

'Of course you are, my darling,' said Annette.

'A romantic.'

'I know, my sweet,' said Annette.

'My conscious ego takes on the female role, just as yours does the masculine. That's the case for everyone.'

'So?' asked Annette. 'What's the problem?'

'There are power struggles going on inside me. In the creative, romantic male the mother archetype in the collective unconscious tries to take over, so I find myself fascinated by certain things. I can't help it.'

'What sort of thing, Spicer?' asked Annette.

'It's known as uroboric incest,' said Spicer. 'I believe.'

'Dr Rhea tells you all this?'

'Yes. It's dangerous, perilous, Annette,' said Spicer. 'It can lead to madness, or death. God, I wish I were married to someone who understood me.'

'Just come to bed, Spicer. You seem terribly distressed about nothing.'

'You're so dangerous to me, Annette.'

'I don't feel dangerous, Spicer,' said Annette.

'I think I'll sleep in the spare room,' said Spicer.

*

'Annette,' said Spicer.

'What's the time, Spicer?' asked Annette

'I don't know,' said Spicer. 'But it's not quite dark and not quite light. I couldn't sleep. Move over so I can get into bed. You are so beautifully warm and soft. Female.'

'I should hope so,' said Annette.

'But in that very fact lies the threat. How can I locate my anima when you've stolen it all?'

'Spicer,' said Annette, 'couldn't you just stop seeing Dr Rhea Marks?'

'It's natural for you to feel threatened,' said Spicer. 'She told me you would be. I think she's right about us separating out. At least for a time.'

'But why?'

'Because I am going on a journey, and you're incapable of keeping me company.'

'A spiritual journey?'

'Yes,' said Spicer.

'I see,' said Annette, 'towards the oneness, the wholeness, the ineffable light.'

'Don't mock,' said Spicer.

'I suppose Dr Rhea Marks would keep you very good company on this inner journey? Having first pointed out the way.'

'I should have stayed in the spare room,' said Spicer. 'You're beginning again.'

'If you want to go and live somewhere else, Spicer,' said Annette, 'please do. Go and meditate to your heart's content, or should I say soul? And I'll have the three kids, or would you do Jason the honour of taking him with you? Though I suppose he'd get in the way of your soul's development. And we just part, do we? A property settlement? All that?'

'Annette, you're leaping ahead. Of course I don't want us to part permanently. I'm only suggesting a temporary separation, while I sort things out. And how could there be a property settlement? There's no property to settle.'

'There's the house,' said Annette.

'It's in my name, sweetheart,' Spicer said.

'Don't sweetheart me,' said Annette.

'If it upsets you so we won't even contemplate it,' said Spicer. 'Don't sob like that. Here, let me hold you close. I won't leave you. I'll never leave you.'

'Oh Spicer, don't frighten me so,' she wept. 'And how could you talk about our sex life to Rhea Marks? It's so disloyal.'

'So that's what's upsetting you,' said Spicer. 'You talked about it to Gilda, why shouldn't I talk about it to Rhea?'

'I wish you wouldn't call her Rhea. Kiss my eyes to stop me crying.'

'There,' said Spicer. 'That's your eyes. Now your ears.'

'Please no,' said Annette. 'It makes me feel I'm going deaf.'

'You can't let go,' said Spicer. 'Why can't you just let go? If you'd let go I wouldn't be in the state I am.'

'I'm sorry, Spicer. If only I knew what you meant,' said Annette.

'Do it to me,' said Spicer. 'Put your tongue in my ear.'

'There might be wax in there,' said Annette.

'Oh God,' said Spicer, 'why did I marry so repressed a woman?'

'It's in your stars, I expect,' said Annette. 'No, Spicer, I don't mean to make you angry. I'll do whatever you like.'

'But I want you to want it,' said Spicer. 'You're not wearing your nightie.'

'None of them fit any more,' said Annette. 'They're uncomfortable.'

'The bump's grown,' said Spicer. 'I can't get near you. Come on top of me.'

'No.'

'Why not?'

'My breasts are swollen,' said Annette. 'You might feel overwhelmed: whatever it was you complained of to Dr Rhea. Your anima being taken over. Archetypes creeping out of my you know where. Swept away by floods. And my nipples are blotchy and you might see too much of them and go off me. Dr Herman hated the sight of them.'

'I don't mind. It's only temporary. Isn't it?' asked Spicer.

'I don't know. They didn't go like this with Susan,' said Annette. 'I worry dreadfully.'

'Now you are putting me off. I shouldn't really be doing this, anyway.'

'Why not?'

'I need to be in control. I went to the spare room. You lured me out. Now you've got the better of me,' said Spicer.

'How do you mean I've got the better of you? How did I lure you?'

'It's so seductive. Giving in to needing you, you needing me. Eve with the apple. Sex,' said Spicer.

'It isn't just sex, Spicer. It's love. Isn't it?'

'It's a diversion from important things,' said Spicer. 'It's a distraction.'

'But I'm your wife, you're meant to,' said Annette. 'I need you. Put your hand here.'

'You're so wonderful,' said Spicer. 'I can feel you needing me. Come on top of me.'

'All right,' said Annette. 'But I'm such a funny shape.'

'It's the shape we made by doing this,' said Spicer. 'It's our punishment and our justification.'

'I've had my punishment and I don't need any justification,' said Annette.

'Stop talking,' said Spicer, so Annette did.

'Now turn over,' he said. 'That's enough of that.'

'You won't see her again, will you?' Annette asked. 'Please stop seeing Dr Rhea, please come back to me properly, all of you.'

'I don't want to think about it,' said Spicer. 'Not at the moment. Rhea's unimportant. Lean your forehead against the pillow; then you're at the proper angle. That's wonderful. I'm not hurting the baby?'

'No. Just gently, though.'

'You don't let me do this usually, from behind,' he said. 'Why not?'

'Because it lacks dignity,' said Annette.

'Sex isn't dignified,' said Spicer.

'It ought to be,' said Annette. 'Since it produces children with souls.'

'Rhea says we should try speaking less when making love,' said Spicer. 'Then it might work better.'

'Isn't this working? It seems to be working for me.'

'But it won't for long enough,' said Spicer. 'We ought to be able to go on for hours.'

'Who says?' asked Annette. 'Dr Rhea Marks?'

'I can't hear you,' said Spicer. 'Your voice is muffled by the pillow.'

'It probably wasn't important,' said Annette.

'If you can't say anything nice,' said Spicer, 'don't say anything at all.'

'Let me turn over so I can see your eyes,' said Annette, 'and the shape of your lips when you talk.'

'I'll think about it,' said Spicer. 'I'd rather just move the pillow.'

'If you want me to stop talking you could turn me over and kiss me,' said Annette.

'I don't like kissing,' said Spicer. 'Mouths are for toothpaste and toothbrushes.'

'I blame the dentists,' said Annette. 'They're in our mouths, and the gynaecologists are in our cunts, and the epidemiologists are after our cocks – yours, that is – and the surgeons are after our hearts, and now the therapists are after our souls. I wish they'd leave us alone.'

'How about the Pope?' asked Spicer.

'He just wants the human race to outbreed the professionals,' said Annette, 'so there are so many mouths, cunts, cocks, hearts and souls in the world no one can possibly decipher them, and they flow undiscussed to God. I'm on his side.'

'And the TV people? The media?'

'They're looting our lives for narrative,' said Annette. 'Please be careful of the baby. It's somewhere in there.'

'It's walls and walls away from me,' said Spicer. 'Nature looks after that, or I wouldn't be doing this. The tendency would have been bred out. You're very hot in there, though. Hotter than usual.'

'I'm sorry,' said Annette.

'I like it,' said Spicer. 'Let's hot it up some more.'

'Please not so hard,' said Annette. 'You've changed the angle somehow.'

'So you told the Oprah Winfrey Show to bugger off?' said Spicer.

'I tried to, but Ernie Gromback put the pressure on so I said I'd do it.'

'Bitch,' said Spicer, and all the spirit went out of him.

'Please come back inside me, Spicer,' said Annette. 'I miss you.'

'How can I?' asked Spicer. 'See what you've done to me? I have a soft banana instead of a cock.'

'I'm sorry,' said Annette. 'I didn't mean to. What's wrong with Oprah Winfrey? It's a special about literature and life, not the kind where husbands and wives appear together for everyone to jeer at.'

'Bad enough having our lives looted for a novella,' said Spicer, 'without you talking about it on TV. For God's sake don't start crying. Sex for us always ends up like this. You crying, me incapable.'

'But it doesn't,' said Annette. 'It never has before. Or only once or twice in all our ten years. You remember everything wrongly.'

'I don't know what's the matter with you,' said Spicer. 'Why do you do it to me?'

'Can't we just go to sleep?' said Annette.

'I don't feel like sleep,' said Spicer. 'You've made sure of that.'

'But you need dreams to report to Rhea Marks,' said Annette. 'How can you dream if you don't sleep?'

'You're so cunning,' said Spicer. 'You don't like me seeing Dr Rhea Marks so you steal my potency.'

'You mean you're Samson and I'm Delilah,' said Annette, 'and when I mention the Oprah Winfrey Show I'm cutting your hair?'

'Yes,' said Spicer. 'But I'm not defeated yet, though you'd like me to be. Now I'm going to bring the temple down around your ears. Turn over onto your front.'

'Please don't,' said Annette.

'I have to find my shadow-side,' said Spicer, 'and confront it. See, I'm strong again.'

'But why?' asked Annette. 'Why are you doing this?'

'Because I must find my anima within your animus. Because I need dark, difficult depths. Because you are the cleft in the hill and I am the tree. Because if this is the only way I can, this is the way I will.'

'But Spicer, there it's too small and it hurts and I hate it.'
'Too bad. If it's the only way it works for me, what else can we do? Now just shut up. You don't want to wake the children. At least I hope you don't. Dr Rhea isn't too sure.'

'Divorce him,' said Gilda.
'It isn't as bad as that,' said Annette.
'It sounds like marital rape to me,' said Gilda. 'Sodomy without consent.'
'You could get to like it,' said Annette. 'You could be trained to like it. But you wouldn't like yourself for liking it, if it wasn't your idea in the first place.'
'Take him to court, prosecute.'
'Gilda, what's the matter with you? Yesterday you were telling me to lie back and enjoy it. Poor Spicer. He's upset about me doing Oprah Winfrey. It was my fault. I just wasn't tactful.'
'You mean upsetting and hurting you is what turns him on?'
'It isn't like that, Gilda. I think it was because I wouldn't let him do what he wanted that he went to see Dr Rhea Marks in the first place. The blood-pressure's just an excuse. If he was really ill he'd go and see a proper doctor.'
'So him seeing Dr Rhea is your fault too? You drove him to it?'
'No one's talking about fault,' said Annette. 'I shouldn't have told you.'
'If Spicer's talking about your sex life to another woman,' said Gilda, 'then it's all up for grabs.'
'A therapist doesn't count as another woman,' said Annette.
'You reckon not?'
'I don't think he's sleeping with her,' said Annette.
'But it's occurred to you?'
'Yes,' said Annette, 'of course. But she's much too holy, much too prissy. And Spicer would keep her existence secret if he was. Wouldn't he?'
'You reckon?' asked Gilda.
'I just don't know,' said Annette. 'If she was, she wouldn't have had the nerve to ask to see me. She'd be too guilty.'
'In the name of healing, people do extraordinary things,' said

Gilda. 'Perhaps she wanted to take a look at the opposition. And therapists don't feel guilt. They justify everything.'

'Anyway she'd be struck off,' said Annette. 'It wouldn't be ethical.'

'Struck off from what?' asked Gilda. 'Some association which formed itself last year? Which invented its own ethics the week before last?'

'Gilda, what's the matter with you? You sound really upset.'

'Steve's joined a group called Fathers As Equal Parents,' said Gilda.

'They have a card up on the board at the Clinic. What's the matter with it? I wish Spicer joined things like that.'

'He wants me to have the baby the Leboyer way, in water, and I don't want to: I'd be frightened the baby would drown, and I say to Steve surely what I want goes, but he says no, why should it if he's going to be an equal parent, so we're arguing all the time.'

'Oh Gilda, I'm sorry. I was relying on you to be happy so I could be unhappy at you.'

'Well,' said Gilda, 'it's not as hard as all that and at least I'm not married to a monster.'

'Spicer isn't a monster,' said Annette. 'He's Spicer my beloved husband; it's just he's in therapy and the therapist's got it in for me.'

'Is he seeing her today?' asked Gilda. 'How often do you think he sees her?'

'I don't know. He said four times a week while the crisis lasts. But perhaps the crisis is over? At least this morning he left the house happy and friendly. I can hardly walk but he's okay.'

'Well,' said Gilda, 'we all have our ways of fighting back. I must go now. I'm meeting Steve for lunch.'

'I have Mr Horrocks on the phone for you,' said Wendy. It was three o'clock. Annette had her feet up on the sofa. 'Or I will have in a moment. He's just signing some papers in the other office. Could you try persuading him to let us have our coffee machine back? It made dreadful coffee but at least it was coffee. Now he keeps trying to get us to drink herbal teas. Mr Horrocks can do as he likes, but why should he impose his views on us? If we want to kill ourselves with caffeine that's our business, not his. Here he is.'

'Hello, Annette,' said Spicer.

'Hello, Spicer,' said Annette. 'Wendy sounds very lively.'

'We're all in a good mood today,' said Spicer. 'What are you doing?'

'I have my feet up on the sofa. I'm sewing proper name-tags on all Jason's sports gear. It keeps going astray at school.'

'I love thinking of you sitting there at home, being domestic. I thought we could go and see a show tonight. Kids and all –'

'Oh Spicer, how wonderful!'

'I've had Wendy check it out. We can get tickets for *Buddy*.'

'But that's rock and roll. You'll hate it.'

'The kids will love it. That's the main thing. I can't impose my tastes on others all the time.'

'Does that mean you'll give the staff back their coffee machine?'

'Probably. It's only gone for cleaning. But it does them good to live in suspense a little. Keeps them on their toes.'

'I see,' said Annette.

'How are you feeling, sweetheart?' asked Spicer, settling in to talk.

'I'm just fine, Spicer.'

'I knew you would be. I'm glad we got all that out of our systems. We're going to make a go of things, aren't we, Annette.'

'Of course, Spicer. I never doubted it.'

'Dr Rhea has been a great help to me. It upset me when you got so paranoid about her. It made me feel you didn't really love me.'

'I do love you, Spicer.'

'Dr Rhea really liked you, Annette. She says if it helps to get you back in balance, and I can handle it, then I can postpone treatment for a month or so, until after the baby's born. But you would need to go back to Dr Herman: one of us has to be working towards equilibrium.'

'But I thought Dr Herman was away?'

'He came back unexpectedly. Rhea can make the appointment.'

'The trouble is, Spicer, I think it was seeing Dr Herman which so upset my equilibrium.'

'Rhea thinks it will be difficult for you to go through the parturition process unless you come to terms with your own tendency to sexual fantasy. That was quite an episode to which you subjected us all.'

'Yes, I know. I'm sorry. Did you see Dr Rhea this morning?'

'Yes,' said Spicer.

'Did you tell her about last night?'

'Annette, don't begin again. Please.'

'I'm sorry, Spicer,' said Annette.

'So, what do you say about Dr Herman?' asked Spicer.

'I would rather wait to see him until after the baby's born, Spicer. But I promise to see him after.'

'Okay,' said Spicer. 'It's a deal. We'll both give the therapists a rest. Just you and me; the mountain and the tree. It's an early show tonight. We'll be back by nine. I'll bring back some champagne. Shall we have one of our special suppers, to celebrate?'

'What are we celebrating, Spicer?'

'Oh God, darling, everything.'

'My book?'

'Annette, don't provoke.'

'Sorry, sorry. We'll leave the book out of it. An accidental outcrop on the mountain, not true female creativity: not proper soil for the tree.'

'You're learning, my sweetheart. I really liked your analogy to Samson and Delilah. It quite turned me on. I think Wendy's coming back. We'll have to stop now. Tell you what, Annette –'

'What, Spicer?'

'Steak would be going too far, but we could have lamb cutlets for supper.'

'Red meat, Spicer! How wicked – how wonderful –'

'Bye, my sweetheart,' said Spicer.

'Is that you, Annette?'

'Yes. Who's that?'

'It's Marion. You know, Ernie's Marion. That's how people know me, I don't understand why. Perhaps it's because I'm so much younger than him. No one takes me seriously. I have a crystal which is supposed to help with that kind of thing. A rose crystal. It increases self-esteem.'

'Does it really?'

'It's meant to, but you're supposed to leave crystals overnight in running water in the full moon if they're really going to work, and whenever I remember the full moon's always been and gone. I used to wash them in the little lead fountain in Queen Elizabeth's Rose Garden, but because there's an official drought they've had to shut it down, and I don't think tap water works. Anyway, my self-esteem isn't up to much at the moment.'

'I'm really sorry, Marion.'

'That's not why I'm calling, though. It's just I was doing your Tarot cards and they came up with all these frightful things. First the Tower – all that red and black, with all those bodies falling from it; then that awful card with the man lying flat on his front with seven swords skewering him through; and then I turned up Death, though everyone says that really means life; I can't think why. So I just thought I'd call and say please be careful, Annette: stepping out into traffic, that kind of thing. None of it means anything: just do be careful.'

'Marion, why on earth were you doing my Tarot cards?'

'Well, Ernie and I had a row, and he told me he'd had affairs with all his lady authors under forty and I asked if that included you and he said yes, and after that he denied it, so I didn't know what to think. You're supposed to be able to find out the truth from the cards, so I consulted them. One has a right to the truth.'

'I certainly haven't had an affair with Ernie, Marion,' said Annette, 'nor would I ever. I'm happily married to Spicer.'

'Spicer comes and talks to me sometimes, Annette.'

'Does he?' asked Annette. 'What do you mean, talks?'

'Just talk, Annette. He knows I get lonely and the office is just round the corner from us. And Ernie is away so often, off with all his lady authors under forty for all I know, and Spicer and you have your troubles, and he needs to talk about them. Everyone has to have someone to talk to. But I do get kind of worried sometimes in case you'd mind. Women should stick together. I feel better, already. There's nothing in it. I love *Lucifette Fallen*. What a brilliant title. Ernie gave me a proof copy to read. Is it really about your family life? Your mother and father? It must have been really gruelling. Poor you. I'm always sorry for the children in this kind of thing.'

'Aren't we all,' said Annette.

'I gave the book to this friend of mine,' said Marion. 'An astrologer, to see what she thought of it. She did this review for *New Astrology*. I'll send it on to you.'

'Dr Rhea Marks?'

'Yes. How did you know? God, she's brilliant. She has proper medical qualifications along with everything else.'

'And then the Oprah Winfrey Show picked it up,' said Annette.

'Did they? That's wonderful!' said Marion. 'So you're going to be a TV star! No wonder we're all so jealous. Things just fall into your lap.'

'Marion, it was through you that Spicer got to see Dr Marks?'

'It was me who recommended her, yes,' said Marion.

'Does Spicer still come round to talk to you, Marion?' asked Annette.

'Not since he started seeing Dr Marks. I rather wish I hadn't mentioned her,' said Marion.

'So now you're doing the cards and wishing me a road accident,' said Annette.

'How could you say anything so awful, Annette?' said Marion. 'It isn't like that at all. It was only the once with Spicer; after that it was just talk: I've just felt so guilty: it will never happen again, I promise. I love Ernie with all my heart; I just wish he had more soul, he was open, you know? And I'm sure Spicer loves you, Annette. He kept saying so. He said you had sexual problems. It was hard for him. I just wanted to help. It'll never happen again.'

'Okay, Marion, okay,' said Annette. 'What's past is past. Spicer and I are starting again; we've all been through a bad patch. Thank you for calling. Really.'

'Only do be careful,' said Marion, 'stepping into the road. Those cards were really dreadful. And don't be angry with me, Annette. I can't bear it.'

Annette banged down the phone.

*

'On our sides is nice, really nice,' said Spicer. 'Worth being pregnant for. Why didn't we do this before, you missionary you. But turn over on your face now. That's right. I didn't use vaseline the other night; I should have. Perhaps I was angry. Yes, perhaps I was. I wanted to hurt. I don't know. I love you. I've given up everything for you, Annette. When I say I love you your insides do such wonderful things. Bring your knees further up now, so I can move up easily from there to here; that's it: what an easy slippage it is, meant by the Maker. You're not comfy, I can tell. If I take the pillow from under your face and put it below your breasts above your bump. Keep your head on the side so you can breathe – there, that's glorious for me – is it comfy for you?'

'Yes, Spicer. You seem to know such a lot about doing it like this. Is this what Marion taught you? Spicer, please don't go! I only asked – I thought you'd find it exciting, thinking of her as if she were here too. Isn't this how your mind works? Where are you going? Don't leave me like this, now. It's so humiliating. Spicer? It's not even as if you can't. You can but you won't. Spicer?'

'This is appalling,' said Gilda.

'After that Spicer just went to the spare room. I cried all night. I heard him leave at about six in the morning.'

'You can't go on like this,' said Gilda. 'You'll have to go to your mother's.'

'That's defeat,' said Annette. 'That's going back to where you were before you began. It's just so up and down with Spicer and me at the moment.'

'You can say that again,' said Gilda. 'But drifting downwards all the time. The major drift is to rock bottom, Annette.'

'I don't want to think that,' said Annette. 'Don't say it. It isn't true. Yesterday we all went to a show. The kids loved it. So did I. Spicer pretended to, for our sakes. We were just a normal, happy family, on an outing. For twelve whole hours I was so happy, Gilda. I was so confident. Not even Marion calling and saying what she did could really shake me.'

'Spicer and Marion! I still can't believe it.'

'It was only the once,' said Annette.

'Oh yes?'

'Spicer does end up in bed sometimes with other women if he's had too much to drink or taken too much coke,' said Annette. 'I don't like it but I have to accept it: it doesn't mean anything: it's me he loves.'

'Oh yes,' said Gilda.

'It's because I'm so bad at sex,' said Annette. 'It's a kind of disability. You can't blame Spicer. Sex just doesn't come naturally to me, the way it does to other women. I say the wrong thing or do the wrong thing at the wrong moment and spoil everything. You don't mind anything Steve does to you, do you?'

'Steve isn't Spicer. Steve wants me to be happy,' said Gilda. 'He doesn't care what I do or say or when. It makes no difference. And he's given in about Leboyer.'

'I'm so glad,' said Annette. 'I'm dreadful. All I do is talk about myself. That's another thing Spicer has to put up with. I'm so self-centred.'

'I'd talk about myself if I were you,' said Gilda.

'I can't let go in bed, I expect that's the trouble,' said Annette. 'I can't stop thinking. I keep wondering if the cat's been put out or what's for breakfast.'

'Then perhaps it's Spicer who isn't very good at it.'

'No, it's me,' said Annette. 'I can't blame Spicer. Sex makes my mind active. All the energy flies into my head. I hardly ever have orgasms. There, I've told you. I'm so upset, Gilda.'

'I know,' said Gilda. 'I can tell.'

'I was trying to play it Spicer's way,' wept Annette. 'Or I wouldn't have even mentioned Marion. How was I to know he'd react like that? Only six words: "Is this what Marion taught you?" and your whole life falls to pieces.'

'I reckon Spicer's playing games with you, Annette,' said Gilda. 'He's nice for a bit just in order to be nasty. He does it on purpose. He reads you. He presses a button. He knows how you'll react and he does it deliberately.'

'But why should he, Gilda?' asked Annette.

'Because he's a sadist,' said Gilda. 'It's how he gets his kicks. And you're a masochist. Or you wouldn't put up with it. As for Marion, she's perfectly capable of making the whole thing up just to upset you.'

'Why should she do that?' asked Annette.

'I don't know, Annette,' said Gilda. 'Perhaps Marion's found out about you and Ernie and is getting her own back.'

'Oh God,' said Annette.

'There! Caught you!' said Gilda. 'I knew I was right about you and Ernie. Why did you deny it in the first place? I'm your friend. It was that time Spicer was at the Bordeaux Wine Feste, wasn't it? Did you get herpes?'

'No, I did not. That's just a disgusting rumour. Industrial espionage probably, put about by other publishers who hate him making money and not being a gentleman. Please, please, keep it to yourself, Gilda. So Spicer could have thought it was just me being paranoid again, by mentioning Marion? That's why he acted the way he did?'

'It's perfectly possible, but how would I know?'

'Poor Spicer,' said Annette.

'I wouldn't go as far as that, Annette. Just divorce the bastard.'

'But I love him.'

'I have to go now,' said Gilda. 'Steve's got the engine running. He sends his love, by the way. Bye, Annette. Look after yourself. Call me tomorrow. I worry about you.'

'Bye, Gilda. Thanks.'

'Spicer,' said Annette.

'Wendy,' said Spicer to his secretary, but so that Annette could hear, 'I did ask you not to put calls through to the office. It's too bad. Annette, I'm really very busy. Please, please just leave me alone for once.'

'But Spicer, I have to talk.'

'Annette,' said Spicer, 'I am trying to keep this business afloat. We are in a recession. Try to help, not hinder.'

'I can't bear it when you leave in the morning without saying goodbye.'

'Why don't you go and stay with your mother for a while?'

'You know I mentioned Marion last night,' said Annette, 'and it seemed to upset you so much?'

'I have no idea what you're talking about, Annette,' said Spicer.

'It's just that Marion rang me up –'

'For God's sake,' said Spicer. 'I'm so busy, and here comes the hysteria again. Obsessive sexual jealousy. I'll be late tonight.'

'Why?'

'Don't crowd me, Annette,' said Spicer. 'As it happens, I'm seeing Dr Rhea after work. She found time for me. I wish I didn't have to see her. But since you refuse to see Dr Herman, I have no choice: the tensions get too great: I can't cope with you without help.'

'I didn't say I wouldn't see Dr Herman,' said Annette. 'I just wanted to wait until after the baby was born.'

'For all I know you've invented this baby,' said Spicer. 'It's a hysterical pregnancy which gives you an excuse and an outlet for your hostility to men and your destructiveness towards yourself.'

'But the baby showed up on the scan, Spicer,' said Annette. 'How can it be a hysterical pregnancy? Perhaps you didn't want it to be a girl, perhaps that's it?'

'Annette,' said Spicer, 'I am way beyond worrying about this baby's gender, I just worry for all our sanity. You ought to think seriously about going to stay with your mother.'

'How could I? What about the children?'

'Jason and Susan? They're hardly children any more,' said Spicer. 'They've had to grow up too fast. I can get someone to come in a couple of hours a day after school easily enough, to fill in the time before I get back. They're not accustomed to much mothering, God knows. The Pizza & Video generation. Prime candidates. Now this next one turns up for another round of punishment.'

'Oh, Spicer –' said Annette.

'What?'

'You sound so cold,' said Annette, 'and hateful.'

'Oh Annette,' said Spicer, 'you do so little to warm me up, and the hate flows from you, not from me. Is this all for Wendy's benefit?'

'Of course not.'

'Because I have a new telephone system, and from now on calls on this number come over the speaker in Wendy's room and are recorded.'

'Why didn't you tell me? Don't you have a private number?'

'I don't think I can trust you with it, Annette,' said Spicer. 'Not with you in the mood you are.'

'Hello, child,' said Annette's mother Judy.

'Why hello, Mum,' said Annette. 'How are things with you?'

'Just fine, sweetheart,' said Judy. 'And you?'

'Just fine, Mum,' said Annette.

'Now don't say that, Annette,' said Judy. 'I know they're not because dear Spicer rang and he said things were definitely not right with you. He is so concerned. I'd worry much less about you if you would only tell me what was really going on, instead of pretending everything's okay when it isn't.'

'What was Spicer concerned about?'

'Don't sound like that, Annette,' said Judy. 'You're lucky to have a husband who cares. So many don't. Spicer asked me to talk to you: apparently he's having some kind of therapy and you've developed an obsessional aversion to whoever it is he goes to see. Is this so?'

'You could see it like that,' said Annette.

'Because it's not very helpful of you, dear,' said Judy. 'Not that I'm in favour of shrinks, they do encourage introspection so, but if Spicer wants to be in the swing of things I suppose he should be allowed. I don't see why you should object. It only causes trouble.'

'It's all a bit complicated, Mum,' said Annette.

'But you're all right? In yourself?'

'Yes of course,' said Annette.

'Because Spicer seemed to think you wanted to come and stay with me and Dad for a while.'

'It might be a little difficult to arrange,' said Annette.

'That's what I told Spicer,' said Judy. 'I don't think it's a good idea at all; you can't just leave Susan and Jason on their own, and you need to be near the hospital.'

'Yes, I know,' said Annette.

'I don't really know what Spicer was thinking of, suggesting it,' said Judy. 'Men are so impractical. They seem to think women just have to wave a wand and it's done. Your father and I lead very quiet lives; you know how he likes his routine. I must warn you, Annette, it is simply not a good idea for a wife to leave a husband alone if she can help it. Spicer's bound to get into trouble. He is a very sexy man.'

'Yes, he is, Mum,' said Annette. 'You're quite right.'

'And a good man is hard to find,' said Judy. 'Annette –'

'Yes, Mum?'

'Did Spicer actually get round to putting the house in your joint names, dear?'

'I don't think so,' said Annette. 'I'd have known, wouldn't I? I'd have had to have signed something?'

'Because he was going to do that as security for the loan your father gave him,' said Judy. 'This whole family is so vague and trusting. And Spicer hasn't made any repayments lately and your father doesn't like to press him, it's so un-family, and he rather wondered if you'd bring the matter up with Spicer. You married him after all, and it was because of you your father made the loan, and though the whole world seems to rejoice when interest rates go down, I'm sure your father and I don't. It's what we live off. And a whole chunk of capital is tied up in Spicer's business.'

'I'm sure it's all okay, Mum,' said Annette. 'Spicer knows what he's doing.'

'That's what worries me,' said Judy. 'Men do tend to. Annette, I don't like saying this, but whatever you do, don't leave the matrimonial home.'

'Why would I want to do a thing like that?' asked Annette.

'Because I feel uneasy, Annette,' said Judy. 'Why does Spicer want you out of the way? Has he found someone else? Is that what the matter is? Men do get very odd when their wives are pregnant.'

'Don't ill-wish me, Mother,' said Annette.

'That's a perfectly horrible thing to say, Annette,' said her mother.

'Please don't you get upset, Mum,' said Annette. 'It didn't mean anything. I was joking.'

'I lie awake worrying about you, and all I get in return is this kind of insult. Of course I'm not ill-wishing you. How can you think such a thing?'

'Sorry, sorry, sorry,' said Annette. Her headache had returned.

*

'Olive Green speaking. How can I help you?'

'I'd like to make an appointment to see Dr Solstice, please,' asked Annette, on the phone to the Health Centre.

'Who's speaking?'

'Mrs Horrocks. Annette Horrocks.'

'In future,' said the receptionist, 'please try and contact the appointment desk before nine A.M.'

'I thought that was just for house calls,' said Annette.

'Not any more,' said Olive Green. 'By nine A.M. we've usually filled our books for the day. We run a busy and efficient service here, Mrs Horrocks.'

'I don't doubt it,' said Annette. 'I just need to come in and see Dr Solstice now.'

'Now? Dr Solstice is fully booked until next Friday afternoon. He's very busy.'

'Jesus Christ!' said Annette.

'There is no need to be abusive,' said Olive Green.

'I wasn't,' said Annette. 'I'm sorry.'

'According to our computer records you've missed three Clinic appointments without explanation,' said Olive Green. 'So I am unable to fix an appointment anyway, unless you send a formal letter of request.'

'That's insane,' said Annette.

'I don't like your attitude, Mrs Horrocks,' said Olive Green, 'and I don't make the rules. But what's the point of making appointments for you if you don't mean to keep them?'

'I don't want to get into an argument with you,' said Annette, 'and I'm sorry I've upset you somehow, but I'm seven months pregnant and I don't think I'm very well and I need to see someone today.'

'If it's an emergency,' said the receptionist, 'we suggest you go to Casualty at the Royal Free hospital. Otherwise your best plan is to attend tomorrow's Clinic. You can't not turn up there and then demand special attention from the doctor just on a whim.'

'I'm not demanding,' said Annette. 'It's not a whim. I just need to see a doctor, for fuck's sake.'

'Please try not to be so aggressive,' said Olive Green.

'Why? Will it go on my notes?' asked Annette.

'It already has,' said Olive Green. 'Swearing always does. We have to put up with a lot, but we don't have to put up with this.' And she put the phone down.

'It's been a dreadful day, Gilda. Spicer was so horrible on the phone I could have died; my mother ill-wished me and when I tried to get an appointment with the doctor it just ended up with me having a row with this person on the appointment desk.'

'That will be Olive Green,' said Gilda. 'She's always like that. You have to creep and crawl and beg for help before she relents and lets you see someone. Then she's the one dispensing charity: it's the only way she has of being kind. Why do you want to see a doctor?'

'I just get headaches all the time,' said Annette.

'Personally, I blame Spicer,' said Gilda.

'I expect it has a lot to do with it,' said Annette. 'He's had a new phone system put in, so if I ring him the calls are public. You've no idea how hurtful that is.'

'You shouldn't be hurt,' said Gilda. 'He's just got one of the new systems that records everything automatically.'

'How do you know that?' asked Annette.

'Steve told me,' said Gilda.

'I see,' said Annette.

'No need to say "I see" in that tone of voice,' said Gilda. 'Are you feeling okay? Spicer told Steve you were insane, suffering from a paranoid episode. I told Steve there was nothing insane about it: the proper response to Spicer is paranoia. Do you want me to come round?'

'No. I'm okay,' said Annette. 'Susan's cooking us supper. Jason's sulking in his room because I made him throw away a marijuana plant he was growing on his windowsill. At this very minute Spicer's seeing Dr Rhea.'

'I thought you said he'd given up seeing her,' said Gilda.

'He's changed his mind,' said Annette. 'He says he can't cope with me without help from her.'

'That figures,' said Gilda. 'It's how you train dogs. You're quixotic. They never know what to expect next, a kick or a pat, so they end up fawning and licking every boot that comes along.'

'But I haven't given in about Oprah Winfrey,' said Annette.
'I won't. And that's what it's all about, I'm sure. Or most of
it.'
'You look for one thing in a marriage going wrong,' said Gilda,
'you look for another: you can never quite be sure. If I were you,
I'd go and see this Dr Rhea Marks on your own and just tell her
to leave Spicer alone. She's spoiling your marriage and damaging
your health.'
'I'm frightened of her,' said Annette. 'I only have to think about
her and I get a headache.'
'Or issue Spicer an ultimatum,' said Gilda. '"Her or me".'
'Ultimatums are dangerous,' said Annette. 'Supposing he chooses
her? No, I just have to sit it out until the baby's born. My
mother's always saying men behave in a peculiar way when their
wives are pregnant.'
'That's because your father had an affair when she was pregnant
with you,' said Gilda.
'Fancy you remembering that, Gilda!' said Annette. 'I'm touched.
You're a really good friend to me.'
'I try to be, Annette,' said Gilda. 'Look, there's something I have
to say to you. About Spicer.'
'What?' asked Annette.
'It was a long time ago,' said Gilda.
'I don't want to hear this,' said Annette.
'I think you ought to know. It was when he was having this thing
with Marion,' said Gilda.
'You knew about that?' asked Annette.
'Yes,' said Gilda.
'Then why didn't you tell me?'
'Because it's so difficult. You know that perfectly well,' said Gilda.
'And anyway, I had my suspicions about you and Ernie
Gromback, and I thought Spicer was probably just evening things
up a little. It was just all too complicated. And Spicer's so
charming, and you and I weren't such good friends then.'
'Please just tell me, Gilda,' said Annette. 'I don't want to hear
your excuses. What happened?'
'Nothing happened,' said Gilda.
'Liar,' said Annette.

'It didn't,' said Gilda. 'I promise. Spicer just wanted me to make up a threesome with him and Marion.'

'I can't believe that! Was he drunk, or on drugs, or what?'

'It was only a phone call, Annette,' said Gilda. 'I didn't know him well enough to tell if he was on anything.'

'And where was I?' asked Annette.

'I think your father was ill,' said Gilda.

'And did you?' asked Annette. 'A threesome? Oh, Gilda!'

'Of course I didn't. I was with Steve by then anyway,' said Gilda.

'But why should he think you would?' asked Annette. 'Why should he call you?'

'Because Marion told Spicer about her and me ending up in bed together after some stupid drunken party. I'd had so much of this and that I couldn't tell male from female, and things happened that shouldn't have. Marion's like that. Anything for kicks. Of course she's into celibacy now, or says she is, for Ernie's benefit.'

'Oh God, I don't want to know any of this,' said Annette. 'I just want to have some kind of decent home to bring my baby into.'

'I feel better now I've told you,' said Gilda. 'Please don't say anything to Steve.'

'I just want to forget the whole thing. If you said no, who do you think said yes? Eleanor Watts?'

'It isn't beyond the bounds of probability,' said Gilda. 'Just because she looks like a horse doesn't mean she doesn't enjoy an orgy. Annette, it was at least ten years ago and we were all a lot younger. I'll come round tomorrow and we'll talk more, shall we? Spicer does love you, Annette. He just has a lot of sexual energy but he's not very good at sex so he has to experiment,' said Gilda. 'I'm only speculating. And anyway, according to Steve, Spicer's trying to reform. That's why he's been seeing this therapist: for your sake.'

'Is that what Spicer told Steve, or what Steve thinks for himself?' asked Annette. 'Or what you're all just saying to make me feel better?'

'What Spicer told Steve,' said Gilda. 'Spicer wants to make a go of the marriage: he's trying to settle down sexually. I didn't know how much you knew about what Spicer gets up to. Now I know about you and Ernie Gromback I reckon there's no point in you not knowing everything I know. Some marriages depend upon fidelity: some don't. Mine and Steve's does. Yours and Spicer's doesn't.'

'It does so,' said Annette.

'You took Marion quite calmly,' said Gilda. 'I'd have gone mad.'

'I just feel so depressed,' said Annette. 'I'm going to bed. Susan's making cheeseburgers. I can't face them. She slices the onion really thick.'

'Spicer.'

'What is it, Annette? I'm reading. I thought you'd gone to bed.'

'I went to bed early,' said Annette. 'At eight o'clock. What time did you get in?'

'Around midnight,' said Spicer.

'I didn't put any fruit out for you. I'm sorry. There's some in the fridge I bought specially. Shall I fetch it?'

'That's okay, Annette. I ate out.'

'It isn't very warm in here,' said Annette. 'You've opened the windows.'

'This temperature suits me,' said Spicer. 'You keep the house hotter than I really like.'

'Isn't it too dark to read? You're using candles.'

'Candles are natural, Annette,' said Spicer. 'Electricity is cold and harsh.'

'What are you reading?' asked Annette.

'A book called *Healers of Olympus. Theotherapy: The Magic of the Gods Symbols and Practice*. You wouldn't be interested.'

'Did Dr Rhea give it to you?' asked Annette.

'Please, Annette, go back to bed, go to sleep,' said Spicer. 'I'm not doing you any harm. I'm just sitting in my study and reading by candlelight. I wish you very well. I'll sleep in the spare room so as not to disturb you.'

'I was coming round this morning, Annette,' said Gilda on the phone, 'but there's a new washer-drier being delivered. Steve bought it for a surprise. Now I've got to wait in for the man.'

'That's okay. Have you heard of Theotherapy, Gilda?'

'I can't say I have, Annette.'

'It's archetypal psychology,' said Annette. 'Jungian.'

'You've already left me behind,' said Gilda.

'Symbols are primitive analogues that speak to the unconscious,' said Annette. 'I've been reading this book. Actually it's rather more complicated than that. To quote Gustav Jung himself, they're also ideas corresponding to the highest intuition produced by consciousness. Archetypes get to us all, Gilda. They're what we know without knowing.'

'Is it Spicer's book?' asked Gilda.

'Yes,' said Annette. 'He said he'd sleep in the spare room, but he didn't. He read till about five when he slipped in beside me. He was very cold. I think he just wanted to get warm. I was sorry for him. I don't know why. He says if my reactions are screwy it's because I have the moon in Aquarius. He seemed inclined to forgive me for my existence. Poor Spicer. I wish he were happier. A threesome with you and Marion and him won't make him happy: I can see it might relieve some inner pain, but how horrible to have the pain in the first place.'

'The threesome didn't happen, Annette,' said Gilda. 'Believe me.'

'I believe you, Gilda,' said Annette. 'I feel quite calm this morning. I think probably I'm good and he's bad. But at least he's trying to be good. I stretched out my hand and touched him. You know how men will be in bed, careful not to touch you but wanting your warmth?'

'I can't say I do, Annette,' said Gilda. 'I don't know men like that.'

'Lucky old you,' said Annette. 'In the early days we'd lie entwined, facing each other; I'd have my knee between his legs. That hardly ever happens now. Of course I've always had to wait for him to make sexual overtures to me; he's always had to initiate lovemaking. If I make the first move he'll turn over and go to sleep, or turn on the light and start reading, so I've learned not to. But last night I just touched him because I was so sorry for him. He winced. He just shrank away from me. It was worse than if he had hit me.'

'You don't have to tell me all this, Annette,' said Gilda.

'I'm sorry, Gilda,' said Annette. 'It's too personal, isn't it, sorrow?

Even more personal than threesomes. Let's get back to Theotherapy. Oh look, it's inscribed inside the front cover: "To Spicer – a special gift, from Dr Rhea Marks".'

'Are you crying, Annette?'

'No. I feel quite calm,' said Annette.

'It could have said "To darling Spicer with love from Rhea",' said Gilda.

'Quite so,' said Annette. 'It's the "special" I don't like. There's a pencil mark down the side of page eighty-one. Spicer never marks books. He hates the children doing it, or me. So we've learned not to. I expect Dr Rhea did the marking. He wouldn't think to reproach her. The passage marked is about the goddess Hera, Gilda. Otherwise Juno. I suppose the first is Greek, the second Roman. It says "Attributes: Fatal softness, gullibility, dependence: ill treatment by husband: shame, embarrassment, bickering: scheming; meddling: intrigue: lying; insane jealousy: use of sex as a weapon . . ." Gilda, what's going on? A little further on it says: "Therapies: bathing in moonlight, running water, wearing of bangles, bracelets and anklets." I am suddenly so sleepy, Gilda, I am just going to lie down and sleep. I can't go on talking.'

'I wish I could help more, Annette.'

'We used to be happy, Spicer and me,' said Annette. 'Really happy. But he seems not even to remember that any more: it's as if someone were stealing all our good past: replacing it with something dreary and dreadful. But how can that be? I have to go to sleep.'

'Annette, darling, you took ages to answer the phone.'

'I was asleep, Spicer.'

'Sleep is the best thing for you,' said Spicer. 'You've been looking so tired! Good news. The British Rail deal has come through at last. All signed and sealed. Horrocks Wine Imports out of the woods.'

'I didn't know Horrocks and Sons Wine Imports were in the woods,' said Annette.

'I didn't like to worry you with it, darling,' said Spicer. 'It's all been touch and go, financially, over the last couple of months. If

I've been behaving out of character, that's all it's been. I've been under a strain.'

'Spicer, I wish you'd told me,' said Annette. 'I thought I was causing the strain, but all the time it was only business worries! How wonderful –'

'"Only business worries" is a rather mild way of describing near-bankruptcy, Annette,' said Spicer. 'You've no idea how close to ruin we were. How it distressed me, the thought of letting the family down: you, Susan, Jason, the baby, all of you!'

'You would only have let us down in a material sense, Spicer,' said Annette. 'We wouldn't have thought you loved us any less. You have been behaving rather strangely, Spicer.'

'In what way, strange?' asked Spicer. 'I'm sorry you see it like that!'

'I don't see it any way, I'm just so pleased to have you back,' said Annette. 'Your voice is altogether different –'

'The BR contract means me spending quite a few months in France each year,' said Spicer. 'I'll have to go over in January, February. I'm sorry about that. The baby will be so new I'll hate to miss a day. My loss. Shall we go out to lunch to celebrate? One o'clock? Can you make it?'

'I've let myself get into such a mess,' said Annette.

'Stick your hair under the tap,' said Spicer.

'My eyes are swollen –' said Annette.

'Why? Does pregnancy do that?' asked Spicer.

'Seems to,' said Annette.

'We'll have champagne and lobster,' said Spicer.

'I'm not sure about lobster,' said Annette. 'Salmon would be good.'

'You can't not like lobster all of a sudden,' said Spicer.

'My digestion's a bit queasy,' said Annette. 'But it's only temporary.'

'I should hope so,' said Spicer. 'You're my-lobster-and-champagne girl. Don't let new motherhood change you too much. So it's meet me for lunch, sweetheart, and put all our troubles behind us and start again.'

'Oh, Spicer! Oh, darling!'

*

104

'Gilda, it's Annette. Gilda, everything's explained. Spicer nearly went bankrupt. That's why he's been so dreadful. He'll give up therapy now, I know he will. It's only when the material world fails that the spiritual one seems so exciting.'

'Annette,' said Gilda. 'I can't bear to hear you sounding so happy.'

'Why?'

'Because it's too sudden,' said Gilda.

'We're having a celebration lunch, Gilda. Just him and me. Everything's just fine. I'm sorry to have been such a pain. I have to go. I can't find the hairdryer anywhere.'

'Happy birthday, Annette!'

'Happy birthday!'

'Many happy returns of the day –'

'Here's to you, Annette!'

'Many happy whatsits.'

'Why, Spicer! And Ernie and Marion – and Eleanor and Humphrey! Good heavens, it's my birthday! I'd quite forgotten!'

'Trust Annette to forget her own birthday!'

'Champagne, Annette? We opened it,' said Spicer. 'You are rather late. I said one. It's one-twenty –'

'Spicer, I'm sorry. It's just when you say one it's always one-thirty –' said Annette, 'so in my head I was going to be early . . .'

'It's party time again! My beautiful wife. Isn't she lovely, isn't she perfect, in spite of her bump!' said Spicer. 'In spite of her being the vaguest person in the world. Forgetting her own birthday!'

'Because of her bump,' said Eleanor, 'not in spite of. It's not the neatest bump in the world, it's true. It is kind of all-pervasive. Round the back as well as in the front.'

'I'd marry Annette tomorrow if I wasn't married already,' said Humphrey. 'I love every single bumpy bit of her.'

'That's only because to live with Annette is to live in the Crescent,' said Eleanor, 'and that is your major ambition in life. You say it's mine but everyone knows it's yours.'

'Hump would have to move me out first,' said Spicer. 'And if I ever move out of that house it will be feet first so I'm afraid we're talking about murder.'

'I did your Tarot cards again this morning, Annette,' said Marion. 'Here's the computer printout. Happy Birthday! You can get a Tarot programme now. It chooses your cards at random. Jungian Synchronicity. You should read the great Carl Gustav's intro to the *I Ching*. All part of the flow, the ebb and the flow. Isn't that so, Spicer? Your cards were brilliant, Annette. Death upside down. That means new life, new hope, rebirth.'

'And I've got Annette a couple more chat shows,' said Ernie, and a *Guardian* interview. It looks as if this book of hers is going to make quite a splash, even without the Oprah Winfrey intervention!'

'I may not be feeling up to any of it,' said Annette. 'I'll let you know.'

'Annette will decidedly not be feeling up to it,' said Spicer. 'Here comes the lobster thermidor. I ordered for everyone inasmuch as it's a working weekday: we've all got to get back to work, except of course the birthday girl, who can sleep all day and often does. We have so very much to celebrate, Annette and myself: haven't we, darling? Here are my birthday gifts to you, Annette, with all my very, very, very, very, very special love. One present for every very. Annette, the love of Spicer's life. The only one.'

'Thank you, Spicer,' said Annette. 'That was a really lovely speech.'

'Start opening your presents now,' said Spicer. 'Nothing messier than lobster thermidor when the claw crackers start cracking.'

'What pretty little packages,' said Marion. 'What can they be? Five little flat circles, so prettily wrapped! Are those mandalas on the paper?'

'Mandalas, Marion?' asked Ernie. 'The things you know. Marion is into the occult. She's had a pyramid made above her bed to focus the energy but it's the energy of dreams that concerns her, nothing else.'

'Sex is a waste of time, Ernie,' said Marion. 'It stands between a soul and its dreams.'

'Bangles, bracelets and of solid gold, Spicer? You are so extravagant –' said Eleanor, 'and only recently you were talking bin-ends and desperation.'

'I went down to Bond Street this morning and bought them,' said Spicer. 'Between one meeting and the next. I wanted something very special for Annette, on this very special day.'

'But what's the gold chain for, Spicer?' asked Eleanor.

'It's an anklet chain,' said Marion. 'So pretty!'

'Spicer, how glamorous, how thoughtful, just what I want. I simply love the bracelets,' said Annette, 'but the anklet will have to wait till after the baby. My ankles are so puffy! Look at them! I couldn't bend down to get it on, let alone take it off, but I can put the bracelets on now. Just!'

'Baby wrists,' said Spicer. 'I love them. Let me put them on. Not too tight?'

'Just nicely firm,' said Annette.

'Now you look positively Indian!' said Marion. 'Properly docile. Not wild-eyed and academic at all. Ernie, will you buy me some bracelets?'

'No, I will not,' said Ernie. 'I'll give you some anti-New Age books to make you think.'

'I'll jangle wherever I go,' said Annette, 'from now on. And wherever I go I'll think of you, Spicer. Thank you, my darling husband. I am so happy.'

'Eat up your lobster,' said Spicer.

'Gilda?'

'Hi, Annette,' said Gilda. 'I'm in the bath. Can you hear it? I have a phone in the bathroom now. Steve bought it for me, so you and I could talk more comfortably. Steve worries about you. So now I can lie in the warm water, which always relaxes me, and watch my tummy rippling. Ooh, there he goes. A foot or an elbow. Some people can tell which: I never can. The Clinic says he'll be on time. You didn't go again. They say the head's engaged. I like being pregnant: I never thought I would. Being helpless is so sensuous. I don't look forward to the birth one bit. How was the kiss-and-make-up lunch?'

'I told Spicer I didn't want lobster but he just went ahead and ordered it.'

'I expect he just forgot.'

'Yes,' said Annette. 'I expect so. But now I have indigestion. And it wasn't tête-à-tête at all. There were other people.'

'Spicer's sociable by nature,' said Gilda. 'We all know that.'

'Why didn't he ask you and Steve? He asked everyone else.'

'I've no idea,' said Gilda, after a little pause. 'Do you think I've offended him in some way?'

'It's easy to do,' said Annette. 'Quite often nowadays it happens all by itself. It was my birthday and he gave me gold bracelets.'

'Oh my God, I forgot your birthday!' cried Gilda. 'I'm so sorry, Annette.'

'I forgot it too,' said Annette, 'what with one thing and another.'

'That is just terrible!'

'Spicer remembered,' said Annette. 'That was something. But I wish he hadn't given me the bracelets.'

'Sometimes I feel quite sorry for Spicer,' said Gilda. 'Not often, just sometimes. It does seem difficult for him to do anything right. It sounds a really nice present to me.'

'If you remember,' said Annette, 'the therapy for the goddess Hera is bangles, bracelets and anklets. Turn to the relevant page and there's another passage marked by Dr Rhea in the book on Theotherapy: it says Hera is endowed with all the positive characteristics of a good wife and mother, but is at the same time so prone to feelings of jealousy that she is prepared to sacrifice everything she believes in – even her own life, if need be – in an attempt to establish what she believes to be her own rights. Consequently, her married life tends to be dogged by ever-growing crisis.'

'So?' asked Gilda.

'So, Gilda,' said Annette, 'having got nowhere with horoscopes, Dr Rhea is now attacking me with Theotherapy. She's just near enough the truth to do me down in Spicer's eyes. I'm not an unreasonably jealous person, am I?'

'Not considering the way Spicer behaves, no,' said Gilda.

'But she will somehow persuade Spicer I am,' said Annette. 'She's re-setting his tuning, as people do with radio sets. So all he hears is what she says he'll hear. But why is she doing this to me? He's not going to stop seeing her, not if he went out this morning and bought me bangles, bracelets and anklets. The bracelets are really tight round my wrist. The skin is already rubbing. It's the curse of Dr Rhea Marks and I'm walking round with it on my body.'

'I think you'd better go and see her, Annette,' said Gilda. 'Not just for your sake, but for Susan and Jason and the baby too. You are getting really obsessive.'

'Yes, I know,' said Annette. 'I will. Now I've washed my hair, I feel stronger.'

'By all means come and chat to me, Mrs Horrocks,' said Dr Rhea on the phone. 'Just you, or Spicer too?'

'Just me,' said Annette. 'If you're going to call Spicer Spicer perhaps you'd better call me Annette.'

'Well, no, Mrs Horrocks. Spicer is my patient, and we believe in a degree of informality in treatment. You are the spouse, and formality is in order. These are the ethics of the situation. You are an interested but not primarily involved party to the counsellor–client relationship.'

'I'm his wife,' said Annette.

'I am very well aware of that, Mrs Horrocks,' said Dr Rhea. 'Shall we say five on Friday week?'

'I would rather come and see you today,' said Annette.

'Oh dear,' said Dr Rhea. 'As bad as that?'

'It would just be more convenient today,' said Annette.

'As it happens, I do have a cancellation,' said Dr Rhea. 'One today.'

'Thank you.'

'Not any earlier, Mrs Horrocks,' said Dr Rhea. 'We still have the builders in and my husband is using his consulting room so there is no waiting room available. I'm sure you understand. I'm sorry.'

'I get the message,' said Annette.

'No message is intended,' said Dr Rhea. 'I am simply stating that we have the builders in.'

'One o'clock then, Dr Marks,' said Annette.

'I look forward to it,' said Dr Rhea Marks.

'Perhaps you would answer one or two questions, Dr Rhea,' said Annette.

'I would be happy to,' said Dr Rhea, 'so long as the answers don't breach the confidentiality which exists between Spicer and myself.'

'But he's my husband,' said Annette.

'You keep saying that. Spouses don't own one another. He is your husband. Very well. He is my patient. Likewise, very well. I am sorry you have seen fit to discontinue your treatment with my husband. It would have been very helpful to you, and indeed to Spicer, if you'd gone on with it. Spicer has had a lot to cope with lately.'

'I know,' said Annette. 'So have I.'

'Perhaps you don't realise to what extent Spicer is in crisis,' said Dr Rhea, 'or how your own matrimonial jealousies exacerbate the situation and exactly how important it is for you to see Dr Herman. I do suggest twice a week, at least.'

'Well, I'm not going to,' said Annette, 'and that's that. I don't have money to throw away. And what situation are you talking about?'

'Both Lilith and Saturn eat their children,' said Dr Rhea. 'Now I put that very bluntly, in terms of the archetype, but I think you are intelligent enough to understand. In Spicer a malefic Saturn struggles to assert himself. It's unwise to underestimate Saturn.'

'I'll try not to,' said Annette.

'The pull of Saturn is into deadness, inertia and unconsciousness. Into depression, in fact.'

'Spicer isn't depressed. He's funny, clever, lively – or was till he came to see you.'

'You protest too much, my dear,' said Dr Rhea. 'In any case we are talking about a creative depression, which contains within its core unbridled life energy, but which can be stultified if the shadow-side remains unrecognised. Then we have all the ingredients for a human tragedy.'

'I think I'd rather you called me Mrs Horrocks than my dear,' said Annette.

'It's quite natural for you to be angry with me,' said Dr Rhea. 'Believe me, I understand and sympathise, but it doesn't alter the situation. The work against nature, against the endless mechanical cycle of reincarnation, is necessary work against Saturn and towards creativity. Every effort Spicer makes to escape his habitual nature, his conditioning, environment, habits, duties, parents, spouse is an effort to escape the devouring jaws of Saturn. And I, as his therapist, am duty-bound to help him. It is a perilous venture for both of us.'

'So you are helping him escape me?' asked Annette. 'His spouse? Is that what you mean? I quite certainly heard you say that.'

'Only in so far as you represent Lilith,' said Dr Rhea. 'And inevitably you must.'

'And who the fuck is Lilith?' enquired Annette.

'Lilith is the Black Gall; she is under the rulership of Saturn; she is the melancholy of the deepest realm of death, poverty, darkness, tears, complaints and hunger. She is the screech owl. The destructive force that works against the flow of harmony that should exist between men and women.'

'Oh, thanks,' said Annette.

'I don't want to feel I am wasting my time here,' said Dr Rhea.

'I'm sorry,' said Annette. 'Please go on.'

'Spicer stands on the brink of a very great journey,' said Dr Rhea. 'He is a very special person: a profound artist: destined for spiritual greatness. Only Saturn and Lilith hold him back from his appointed task. Once he's free of these principles, once he has faced and incorporated his shadow-self – I have never met one so strong, Mrs Horrocks – Spicer will shake free from the material world. He will cut the ties that bind. You understand what in your culture you describe as someone who is a mystic, I take it?'

'It's your culture as well, Dr Rhea, but tell me more.'

'The Buddha, in the blunt Christian term, is a mystic. A great spiritual leader. The Buddha left wife and family behind when he had grown out of them, could see beyond them, and set off on his mission in the world.'

'And that's what Spicer's going to do?' asked Annette. 'If you have your way? If I don't see your husband and somehow stop it? Be a Buddha?'

'It's nothing to do with what I want,' said Dr Rhea. 'It's there in Spicer's chart. I am just the instrument of his liberation from the material world.'

'I hope you can stand up and say this in a court of law,' said Annette. 'It may well end up there.'

'I think basic Jungian thought is now well accepted in most courts,' said Dr Rhea. 'Certainly the counsellors and social workers are acquainted with the language of the archetype: many are trained in astrology, too. The ASAP is affiliated to the ATCCT.'

'What's that?'

'The Association for the Training of Court Counsellors and Therapists.'

'You have wormed yourself in everywhere with all your nuttiness,' said Annette. 'And seem to be dragging the whole world along with you. You'll be ducking witches next: pricking people to find out if they're child abusers.'

'Interesting that you should say that,' said Dr Rhea. 'That child abuse is what comes to your mind.'

'What you're really saying to me,' said Annette, 'is that if I don't have therapy from your husband you'll break up my marriage. You're blackmailing me.'

'Poor Spicer,' said Dr Rhea. 'I thought he exaggerated, but he doesn't. Lilith is very, very strong in you. But Spicer is strong too. He's breaking free.'

'Spicer took me out to lunch yesterday,' said Annette. 'We had lobster and champagne. He didn't seem all that spiritual to me. I think he lays a lot of it on for your benefit. It's how he entertains himself.'

'I think he only took a little of the fish, Mrs Horrocks, and sipped the champagne, to keep you in countenance. Strange you forgot your own birthday. Or perhaps you wanted to. Fight against fate all you want, Mrs Horrocks, be as rude to me as you like, really it makes no difference: the spiritual change has begun in Spicer and will continue in spite of all your efforts to hold him back. You'll have noticed the change in his diet. His body now rejects red meat, alcohol, craves natural foods. It's a sure sign of spirituality. You'll find stops and starts in Spicer's progress. Of course you will. He'll suffer from what I like to call the hot flushes of the soul. His sexuality may become suddenly more intense, alternating with periods of abstinence, melancholy. He will turn himself back for a time into a family man, or someone preoccupied with business, but the process towards oneness, once begun, is inexorable. Spicer is leaving you, Mrs Horrocks, and the material world.'

'Dr Rhea,' said Annette, 'I'm sorry if I've spoken out of turn at all. As you say, it's natural for me to be angry. This all comes as rather a shock. But please, for my sake, the family's sake, could you stop encouraging Spicer in all this? Not flatter him by talking about his spirituality, his creativity? He's just a wine merchant, with a wife and two children and a baby on the way: no one special, just himself, which has always been good enough for me, and him. The consequences of his breaking up the home are so terrible for so many people. Couldn't you somehow include all them in the area of your responsibility? Because we're all going to suffer terribly if Spicer goes on like this. Please search your conscience, to see if you can't find a way within it not to break up this marriage. Not tell lies to Spicer, not as strong as that – just stay quiet about his spiritual destiny, as you see it?'

Dr Marks thought for a little.

'In all conscience,' she said, 'I can't. My responsibility is to my patient, not to his family and associates. As I say, these are the ethics of my profession. Your husband approached me for help of his own free will, and I must give it to him. That, and only that, is my duty.'

'Even if helping him actively makes so many people unhappy?'

'In my experience families adjust very quickly,' said Dr Rhea. 'Sometimes material details can be a problem, but in this case they're minor. I have encouraged Spicer to talk to you about them, but I'm afraid he keeps putting it off. The Lilith in you is so quickly aroused. I think Spicer finds it quite frightening: you frequently alarm him, Mrs Horrocks, with what he sees as sexual insatiability.'

'What about my baby, who according to you must do without a father?'

'Every child has a father,' said Dr Rhea. 'I'm sorry you seem so out of sympathy with your husband. Don't you care about his welfare at all? I don't think you've ever grasped how ill he was until he came to see me: how unhappy his childhood was.'

'We all have unhappy childhoods. So what? Didn't you?'

Annette saw Dr Rhea Marks's face flicker: the colourless lashes lowered over the pale, prominent eyes.

'I was the child of an unsupported mother,' said Dr Rhea Marks.

'Is this your plan for all newborn babies?' said Annette. 'That, like you, they'll end up with no father?'

'Try not to be so excitable,' said Dr Rhea. 'It's bad for the baby. I understand your ambivalence towards your coming child but try to control it.'

'Do your patients often set out on this journey of theirs,' asked Annette, 'and leave their spouses behind?'

'Quite often, Mrs Horrocks, yes,' said Dr Rhea.

'That doesn't seem strange to you?'

'Not at all,' said Dr Rhea. 'Men who stand on the brink of spiritual revelation do naturally gravitate towards me. We like to call it synchronicity.'

'You don't put it into their heads?' asked Annette. 'This leaving of spouses? You don't have your own agenda, hidden or otherwise?'

'This is bizarre,' said Dr Rhea Marks. She rose from her chair and went to the window and contemplated the trees. The legs that emerged from the long skirt were slim and her ankles were pretty.

'And perhaps your plan for all pregnant women,' said Annette, 'is that they'll end up alone, and repeat your mother's story? You're not so much helping the men as attacking the women, and have found an ideal way of doing it. Power mad, like the teachers and the doctors. Now the therapists too. I think you just want other women to end up lonely.'

'We don't talk about loneliness,' said Dr Rhea, smugly. 'We prefer to talk about aloneness.'

'I bet you do,' said Annette. 'But you're all right, aren't you? You're safe enough. Not much chance of your old man going on a spiritual journey. He's too busy palpating breasts, the disgusting old pervert, and sticking his cock into his female patients, and you collude. You even procure. I expect he prefers the pregnant.'

Dr Marks picked up the internal phone and dialled.

'Herman, could you come in a minute? I have Mrs Horrocks in my surgery. She's being abusive.'

*

'Gilda, thank God you waited,' said Annette. 'Get me away from here quickly. I can't get the seat belt on; I'm sorry. Is there some way you can turn the alarm off? Hang on, I'll try and move the seat forward. No, that's hopeless. I can't fold myself in half any more. You have such a neat little bump: I'm just overall, all-purpose vast. No, I'm okay. Really. Not even particularly upset; I expect that will come later. I was in there with her for ages, wasn't I? It felt like it. Things were shapeless; what she said was random; the conversation was without form: like me, pregnant all over the place: what she's about to give birth to is some great lump of evil. It doesn't mean Dr Rhea's necessarily bad: she may just be rather stupid and likes to have power, and has found a way of using it; I suppose that could add up to evil. But no, I don't think so. Evil is something which attaches from outside: you can't use it as a description; it's a thing in itself and she's going to give birth to it. Did you know that Rhea was Saturn's wife? I wonder if she was born that; more likely it was Doris Legge. Can't you turn that alarm off? Take out a fuse or something, Gilda. Wedge a match in there. Bloody Volvos, always doing things you don't want for your own good: if it's not the lights, it's the fasten-seat belt buzz. Thanks, that's better. No, I don't want coffee. Let's go straight home. Those lights were red, Gilda. God, you're an awful driver. It's just as well we're in a Volvo, the four of us. Gilda and baby Henry, Annette and baby Gillian. These bangles are beginning to cut into my wrist. My hands have got so puffy. Do you think they'd cut bangles off at the Fire Station? Shall we go there? Rhea Marks has entered into this marriage as a third party. She's half-way between a mistress and a voyeur. Perhaps Spicer just has this appetite for threesomes. Spicer and me and baby makes three. I was never absolutely certain I wanted this baby; Spicer and Aileen plus Jason never made it. You start off anti the first wife, don't you: you think she didn't understand him: you think she was cold, heartless, stupid, faithless: she must have been. In the end you see she was just another woman, trying to cope.

'I hit Rhea Marks on the chest. She told me Spicer was leaving me to go on a spiritual journey: she told me there were just a few material details left to clear up: God knows what Spicer's told her: they chat twin souls, I suppose, and mutual creativity. She's just the kind of woman who longs to write a novel. She always had the last word: you know how therapists do. If you're angry they say they understand your anger: if you do anything at all, they tell you to stop acting out. I found myself saying dreadful things to her. I accused her of procuring, God knows what. When Herman came in, I hit her. I pummelled her chest; she said stop acting out, you are no longer a child: and he came from behind me and said "Daddy's here – stop hitting Mommy!", and put his arms round me and pulled me away, and his fingers dug into my breasts for longer than he need have, and he just held me at a distance from her, and she smiled at me sweetly and forgivingly. I'd have a fuller, happier life once Spicer was gone, she said; I was now a media personality and a successful writer, and I must stand on my own feet; that I wasn't the woman Spicer had married: that people's life paths sometimes split and went in different ways, and some more guff about Lilith and Saturn. So I swore and spat a bit more, and they turned me out and thank God you were still waiting in the car.'

'Annette?' said Gilda.

'Yes, Gilda?'

'Do you really want to go to the Fire Station to get the bracelets off?'

'Yes, I do,' said Annette. 'They hurt like hell.'

'I'm not sure you handled the session very well,' said Gilda.

'Why not?' asked Annette. 'Why shouldn't I call her names? And him. They're filth.'

'Because you don't want them telling Spicer about Ernie Gromback, etcetera, do you?'

'I'd just deny it,' said Annette. 'Look at these weals coming up on my wrist. Not just are the bangles cutting into the flesh, I'm sensitive to the metal. Spicer probably got them from her and they've been soaking in some magic potion. Her husband's piss, probably. Or hers. I bet they're into Golden Showers.'

'Calm down, Annette. This can't be good for the baby. Shouldn't I take you to Spicer?'

'No. The Fire Station. At once.'

'I just don't like the feel of this,' said Gilda. 'Not at all. You don't want people like the Markses as enemies.'

'They're not much cop as friends,' said Annette. 'What do I care? What can they do?'

'You remember what I said about Spicer asking me to join him and Marion?' said Gilda.

'Yes, I do, Gilda,' said Annette.

'I'll swear there was a Fire Station somewhere down here,' said Gilda. 'Where's it gone? Well, I did.'

'Oh, did you,' said Annette.

'Don't sound so dull and drear, darling,' said Gilda. 'It was a long time ago. Spicer and I, well, sometimes when you were out, or at a party when you were in the kitchen, we'd have a quickie under the coats; it just got to be a habit. Actually, Annette, it was always a quickie because that's how Spicer is. I hate the way you think you're so bad in bed, Annette, because actually it's Spicer. He has no natural instinct for sex. If you lie there thinking about what's for breakfast, it's because he's trying to remember the sex manual. It was Spicer and me asked Marion in: not Spicer and Marion asking me. When Steve and I got together that was the end of it: and by that time Spicer had got more interested in Marion than in me. That's the problem with threesomes: they end up with a different twosome: so that was the end between me and Spicer. I won't say I was hurt, but I took offence.'

'They've closed the Fire Station,' said Annette. 'Look, it's a garden centre now. Perhaps it's just as well or I'd have asked them to cut my throat.'

'Mrs Horrocks?'

'Yes? Who's that?'

'I'm sorry, have I disturbed you?'

'No. I'm just a bit sleepy. A friend gave me some stuff to take called Easy Night. I took rather a lot. Who am I talking to?'

'I'm so sorry, didn't I say? This is Amelia Hardy of the Oprah Winfrey Show. I'm the researcher. I wondered if we could have a brief conversation about tomorrow?'

'Tomorrow? I thought it was months ahead.'

'We did write to you.'

'I haven't been opening all my letters lately.'

'That's your privilege as a creative artist,' said Amelia Hardy. 'Never mind, tomorrow it is, your publisher okayed it, and we're all set up and ready to go, if I can just have this brief conversation with you first.'

'Actually, could I call you back in half an hour?' asked Annette.

'I'll call you at – what's the time now; three-fifteen? In the afternoon. At four o'clock precisely. Will you be there?'

'Yes, of course,' said Amelia Hardy. 'I'll wait for your call.'

'Just fine! I expect the Easy Night will have worn off a little by then,' Annette said.

'Shall we make it four-thirty? I take Easy Night sometimes myself. I swear by it, but it is quite strong.'

'Wendy, can I speak to Spicer? It's urgent.'

'He's in a meeting, Mrs Horrocks.'

'Can you get him out of it?'

'I don't think I'd better try. The meeting's with British Rail,' said Wendy. 'You know we have this great big deal going through: it's really saved our bacon. I've got Jason and Susan here. Susan, do you want to talk to Mum?'

'Hi, Mum!'

'What are you doing in the office?' asked Annette. 'I thought you were both upstairs in your rooms.'

'Dad's taking us to a puppet show in Islington,' said Susan. 'Jason wanted to go to London Dungeon and I wanted to go to the zoo, but Dad said scenes of torture were unsuitable and the zoo was an abomination, so there's only puppets left. If we'd known, we'd have stayed home.'

'Why didn't you tell me?'

'We tried to but you were asleep,' said Susan. 'Dad just rang and said hi, let's go, so we went.'

'Why are you calling him Dad all of a sudden, not Spicer?'

'He says he wants me to. It makes us feel like more of a family. But I keep forgetting. Spicer – I mean, Dad – said it would get us out from under your feet, give you time to rest if you needed rest. Was that okay? It didn't seem right leaving you but you

were so fast asleep. You looked so pretty and peaceful. You hadn't
been crying or anything?'

'No.'

'I wondered,' said Susan. 'I suppose when you're pregnant you're
meant to get puffy all over. You looked like a kind of mushroom.'

'Thank you, Susan,' said Annette. 'I reckon I'm okay. What sort
of puppet theatre?'

'I don't know,' said Susan. 'Rainbow Childline something or
other. I'm not looking forward to it. It'll be meant for much
younger kids: it will be full of tree spirits and stuff; understanding
each other and what to do when your parents start touching you
up. Jason will make puking sounds all the way through. But it's
always nice going out with Dad. Doesn't often happen.'

'We all went to *Buddy* the other day,' said Annette.

'Buddy Holly's stone age,' observed Susan. 'We're more back into
Angry Medieval, Sounds of the Suburbs stuff. But it was a nice
try. Thanks, parent.'

'Can I speak to Jason?' asked Annette.

'Probably not,' said Susan. 'He's trying out the graphics on
Wendy's PC.'

'Give him my love.'

'He sends it back,' said Susan. 'You don't have to worry, Mum.
Jason isn't withdrawn. He just likes computers. Why, hi, Dr
Marks. Dad's still busy with British Rail, but he shouldn't be a
minute. Bye, Mum, must go now.'

'Wendy!'

'Yes, Mrs Horrocks.'

'Who exactly have you got in your office?'

'Susan, Jason and this other lady who's just come in,' said Wendy,
sotto voce. 'I haven't seen her before. She looks harmless enough.'

'I want to speak to her,' said Annette.

'Are you sure you want to?' asked Wendy. 'You sound a bit
strange. Hang on, I'll go through to the other office.'

'Are you there, Mrs Horrocks?'

'Yes, I am, Wendy.'

'I've been a bit worried,' said Wendy, 'because I think it's the woman he keeps speaking to on the phone, and meeting for lunch, and what with you being pregnant it doesn't seem fair: and now if he's taking the kids out mid-afternoon, and he actually cancelled a meeting, and she's turned up in person – well, I don't like it, Mrs Horrocks. I know it's none of my business, but you've always been really nice to me. I'm sure there's nothing to it: she looks really quiet and perfectly sweet and very serious, and she's a doctor so she must be responsible. Your kids are yawning already, but even so – here comes Mr Horrocks, out of his meeting. Mr Horrocks, please speak to Mrs Horrocks. No, don't make faces at me, do it now.'

'Hi, Annette –'

'Hello, Spicer,' said Annette. 'So, you're taking the kids out?'

'You were too fast asleep to even answer the phone.'

'And Dr Rhea Marks is going too?'

'My, what a lot you seem to know, sitting up there in the safety of Bella Crescent. Yes, Annette, Dr Rhea Marks is coming with us. She wants to observe the children a little: see if there are signs of precocious behaviour, that kind of thing: we thought just an ordinary family outing would be a good background for it.'

'I don't understand,' said Annette.

'Let's face it,' said Spicer. 'You have become rather seriously disturbed, Annette. The Markses practically had to get the police today, to have you removed from their offices. You were violent. You really can't go on behaving like that. But I don't want to talk about it on the phone. I for one don't want the kids to overhear.'

'So you, Dr Rhea Marks and the children are going to the theatre together,' said Annette, 'leaving me behind at home, that's what it amounts to?'

'You are such a child, Annette,' said Spicer. 'You don't seem to understand the seriousness of your own situation. Dr Herman Marks thinks it's unwise for you to be alone with the children too much. In his judgement your fantasy life is too strong to be ignored; it might slip, might already have slipped, over into real life, particularly in relation to Jason, who's your stepchild. Annette, none of this is your fault; don't think I blame you. But Jason's obsession with video games and 18-rated films just isn't natural. I have to protect the children.'

'By leaving them?' asked Annette. 'Dr Rhea Marks says you plan to leave us to pursue your spiritual journey, so what is this sudden concern for the children? It sounds rather hypocritical to me.'

'You have obviously misinterpreted what Dr Rhea said,' said Spicer. 'It's part of the negative pattern. You're having a very difficult pregnancy, which means that we all are. Most certainly I see the way ahead to the light, but I could hardly leave my family in the state it is: I love you, Annette, in spite of everything. What kind of man would I be if I just abandoned you? Not much cop on the wheel of life. I'd fall right off, right through to the cockroaches. Laughing?'

'Trying to,' said Annette.

'Take another slug of Easy Night. Gilda rang me. She was really worried about you. Go back to sleep, sweetheart. See you later. We'll bring back fish and chips.'

'And Dr Rhea Marks? Will she come over too for fish and chips?'

'I shouldn't think so,' said Spicer. 'You've terrified her out of her wits. Annette, I'm not exactly looking forward to Rainbow Puppeteers. Don't make matters even worse than you've made them already.'

'Sorry, Spicer. Is this call being broadcast through the office?'

'Yes,' said Spicer, 'come to think of it. But you're a media personality. It shouldn't worry you.'

'Mrs Horrocks?'

'Yes?'

'This is the Oprah Winfrey Show. Amelia speaking.'

'Oh, hi.'

'We mean to record tomorrow and hold over and screen for our New Year show. We like to do things live but even Oprah has to have a holiday sometimes. Can I just say how much I loved *Lucifette Fallen*? Of course the timing is good for you – Ernie Gromback tells me he's scheduled publication to fit in with our transmission. Isn't he a charmer?'

'Oh yes,' said Annette.

'We're building the programme around the domestic row,' said Amelia. 'We reckon God and Lucifer had the first one: brilliant of you to have seen that Lucifer was female. After that it was

Jupiter and Juno. What can the rest of us poor mortals do in the face of the archetype? We have our pet psychotherapist to help us see through the dark to the light. That's the bit we'd like you to read from *Lucifette Fallen*: on page eight of the proof copy. I must say your publisher whizzed it round to us. The para beginning "Where darkness becomes light" – down to "What can a child do but repeat the experience?" And then sit next to Oprah and chat a bit about your own experiences and what drove you to write the novel.'

'I'm sorry – I've lost you. I'm still a bit sleepy –'

'You are very central to the show, Mrs Horrocks,' said Amelia. 'Have you had experience of TV before?'

'No,' said Annette.

'Welcome to the real world,' said Amelia.

'Gilda, hi. What is going on here? I'm not taking any of that stuff of yours ever again. I'm only just beginning to wake up. First there was you saying you had an affair with Spicer – I must have dreamt that: then there was the thing about Spicer taking the kids out with Dr Rhea Marks, that's completely unbelievable. And then there was this conversation about archetypes and *Lucifette Fallen* with a TV company. It can't be true. TV is the antithesis of the archetype. What's the time, Gilda? I feel too languid to get up and look at the clock.'

'It's nine twenty-one,' said Gilda, 'in the evening. Steve and I have just had supper and are settling in to watch TV. Careful what you say. He's in the next room. He likes me to watch the News with him.'

'Nine twenty-one? In the evening? Then where are Spicer and the kids?'

'Probably still out with Dr Rhea Marks,' said Gilda.

'Are you trying to tell me,' asked Annette, 'that those conversations actually happened?'

'Yes,' said Gilda. 'Well, the one with me certainly did.'

'And you used to go to bed with Spicer?'

'It wasn't often the bed, it was usually the sofa,' said Gilda.

'The sofa I'm lying on now?' asked Annette.

'You've had it covered since,' said Gilda. 'I was glad when you did. It made me feel better. Shall we just forget that and get on to what's important?'

'You and Spicer are both fairly important to me, Gilda,' said Annette.

'I trusted you with the information in order to help you,' said Gilda. 'I don't want you letting Spicer know you know, because Spicer can be vindictive. He might tell Steve and then I'll have to say it's all Spicer's fantasy, and honestly I haven't the energy for any of this at the moment, Annette, I'm pregnant, so just shut up, okay?'

'Okay,' said Annette. 'It's not what I want everyone to know, either.'

'Now what does worry me is if Spicer said to you the things you say he did, then something not very nice is going on. You are being told that if you don't back off about Dr Herman Marks assaulting you they'll start accusing you of child abuse, and they're the therapists and they'll win.'

'That's absurd,' said Annette. 'Why should they do a thing like that?'

'Think about it,' said Gilda. 'It happens a lot these days. And be glad there seems to be some kind of bargain being struck. They could just charge in there and get your kids taken away.'

'How could they possibly do a thing like that, without proof, without evidence? You're being bizarre,' said Annette.

'If I were you,' said Gilda, 'I'd shut up and be sweet as pie about the pair of them until the baby is born, and just hope they fade out of Spicer's life. The AJA trains the counsellors who train the social workers, and if they say child abuse, you've had it. If Jason so much as looks up Susan's skirt that's it.'

'Sometimes Jason helps me with the ironing,' said Annette. 'He irons Susan's knickers because I can't see the point in ironing them. Jason says I just screw them up: he doesn't like it.'

'Well, there you are. Condemned already. Unnaturally sexually precocious and "screw" is a pun, isn't it.'

'That's ridiculous.'

'Think about it,' said Gilda. 'Okay, Steve, I'm coming.'

'Sweet as pie,' said Annette. 'That's me. Don't worry.'

*

'Hi, Mum!'

'Hi, Susan. Hi, Jason. How was the show?'

'Spooky,' said Susan. 'I don't want to know about all that stuff. I'm sick of having it rammed down my throat.'

'What do they think we are?' said Jason. 'Children?'

'Where's Dad?'

'He dropped us off and took Dr Rhea home and said he'd get fish and chips on the way back.'

'Did you like Dr Rhea?'

'She was okay,' said Susan. 'But she kept asking questions and pretending she wasn't.'

'She smiles all the time,' said Jason, 'but she isn't really. Who is she, anyway?'

'A friend of Daddy's,' said Annette.

'What does he want friends for?' asked Susan. 'He's got you. What sort of doctor is she, anyway?'

'A head doctor,' said Annette.

'Why? Is one of us mad?' asked Susan. 'It's probably Dad, taking us to a show like that.'

'She made us drink caffeine-free coke,' said Jason. 'She can go and take a leap at herself.'

'Annette?'

'Hello, Spicer.'

'You always take so long getting to the phone,' said Spicer. 'I nearly gave up. I'm speaking from a call box. Look, all the fish and chip places in London seem to be closed. And I promised the children.'

'Don't worry,' said Annette. 'They'll survive. They can have an omelette. They're very tired anyway. They loved the show, Spicer. And they really liked Dr Marks.'

'Good,' said Spicer. 'I just can't understand your antagonism to her. Or all this stuff about her unfortunate husband. It makes things really difficult for me.'

'I feel more settled in my head now, Spicer,' said Annette. 'The rush of hormones when you're pregnant can do all kinds of things. It says in my *Before the Birth* book that in the sixth month women sometimes get very sexy; they even find themselves reading pornography.'

'Good God, do they really?'

'Yes,' said Annette. 'So I expect it was just that kind of energy gone sour: I kind of imagined things that just weren't happening. I'm ever so sorry, Spicer,' said Annette.

'I might ask you to put that in writing when I come home,' said Spicer.

'Which bit, Spicer?' asked Annette. 'About it not happening or about being sorry?'

'Either or both, darling,' said Spicer. 'Or none at all so long as it's all clear in our heads. Actually, Rhea can be a bit of a pain: all this stuff about transitional crisis. Anyway, I'm on my way home, fish and chipless. Shall I buy some champagne?'

'I thought you were off alcohol?'

'Well, you can go too far, can't you? And champagne's different,' said Spicer. 'It doesn't count.'

'Brilliant!' said Annette. 'Did Rhea think the kids were okay?'

'Tell you when I get back,' said Spicer. 'Shall I bring you an interesting video?'

'What sort of video?'

'A sixth month of pregnancy video.'

'Oh, Spicer! How exciting. You are in a good mood. Come home quickly. You'll find me sweet as pie.'

'Spicer,' said Annette. 'The price tag's still on the bottle. £120. It's insane.'

The children had gone to bed. The fire was lit.

'Don't wet-blanket, Annette,' said Spicer. 'So's our telephone bill insane. You talk too much to Gilda.'

'Sorry,' said Annette.

'What do you find to talk to her about?'

'Just babies,' said Annette. 'Childbirth. Washing machines. Domestic detail.'

'And, Annette –'

'What, Spicer?'

'You're married to a wine merchant.'

'I know that, darling,' said Annette. 'And a very successful one.'

'To a wine merchant,' said Spicer, 'all bottles are cheap at the price. £120 is not insane.'

'Sorry, Spicer,' said Annette. 'I'm the one who's insane.'

'Funny one,' said Spicer forgivingly.

'It's lovely having you here beside me in such a good mood,' said Annette.

'I have been worried,' said Spicer. 'To be frank. Anxious, even.'

'About money, you mean?'

'No, about you and what peculiar things were going on in your head, and whether it was okay to leave you with the kids,' said Spicer. 'That's why I wanted Rhea to see them.'

'I see,' said Annette.

'I've been doing my best,' said Spicer. 'Family outings and so forth. But you've been really distracted.'

'In what way has it shown itself, darling?' asked Annette.

'How long since you cooked a proper meal?' asked Spicer. 'You don't eat dinner any more.'

'That doesn't mean the kids have to be doomed to frozen TV chicken platters,' said Spicer. 'But, according to Rhea, the kids are just fine.'

'I'm so glad she thought so,' said Annette. 'I really trust her judgement. A warning shot over the bows does no one any harm.'

'Rhea's very well qualified,' said Spicer. 'A wise woman, in both the Jungian and the worldly sense. Highly respected in her profession. Her word goes in a court of law. Not many laughs, though, on an afternoon out. I really missed you, Annette. And the play was dire. Embarrassing.'

'I'm sorry you didn't enjoy it,' said Annette.

'Life can't be all wine and roses,' said Spicer.

'There's the soul as well,' agreed Annette.

'There's a time and place for the soul,' said Spicer. 'Shall I put on the video?'

'Anything you say, darling. Anything that makes you happy.'

'That makes *us* happy,' said Spicer.

'That makes us happy,' repeated Annette.

'Ernie Gromback called this morning,' said Spicer. 'He couldn't raise you at home. He seemed to think you were doing the Oprah

Winfrey Show. I told him you weren't, you didn't want to be
gawped at by the whole world.'

'I wouldn't dream of doing the Oprah Winfrey Show,' said
Annette. 'They're bound to worm things out into the open one
would rather keep to oneself. Family's more important than fame.
Fame's vulgar.'

'Annette, you haven't even finished one glass. I've had three.'

'I'm not saying it's acid; champagne can't be acid at £120,' said
Annette. 'It's just that being pregnant makes it give me
indigestion.'

'The whole point about champagne is you have to drink the whole
bottle,' said Spicer.

'Yes. Otherwise it goes flat,' agreed Annette, staring at the screen.

'If I drink the whole bottle on my own I'll go flat,' said Spicer.
'You don't want that, so help me out.'

'Of course, Spicer,' said Annette, and took another glass of
champagne.

'Why are you shutting your eyes?' asked Spicer. 'This is a good
bit.'

'I expect it is,' said Annette, 'but I don't think I want to look at
it.'

'Prude!' said Spicer. 'Perhaps Dr Herman Marks was right about
you. Perhaps you need treatment more urgently than any of us
realise?'

'I've opened my eyes,' said Annette. 'I'm just fine.'

'I'll put it on pause so you can tell what's going on,' said Spicer.

'Thank you, Spicer,' said Annette. 'That's very thoughtful of you.
Doesn't it hurt? Two men at the same time like that?'

'That's a silly question.'

'I'm sorry. I thought you wanted my comments.'

'God, Annette, you are hopeless. In answer to your question, not
if she relaxes, not if she enjoys it, no, it doesn't hurt.'

'But I suppose if it does hurt just a little bit,' said Annette, 'she
enjoys it a bit more.'

'Yes. Exactly. Everyone does,' said Spicer.

'Well, I'm really glad for the human race,' said Annette, 'that it's
evolved the way it has.'

'Next you'll be saying the one behind her reminds you of Dr
Herman Marks,' observed Spicer.
'He's not in the least like Dr Herman Marks,' said Annette.
'I was only joking,' said Spicer. 'Why do you have to take
everything so seriously? You're sure the kids are asleep? We
wouldn't want them to come in and find us watching this.'
'No, we certainly wouldn't.'
'You in your sixth month and liking porno all of a sudden.'
'I didn't say that exactly, Spicer,' said Annette.
'I certainly heard you say it,' said Spicer.
'Well, if you heard it, I said it,' said Annette. 'I have no excuses
to offer. It's perfectly clear that anything I say about Herman
Marks was just me making trouble.'
'But why should you have wanted to make trouble?' asked Spicer.
'I was jealous about you seeing so much of Dr Rhea Marks,' said
Annette.
'At last you admit it!' said Spicer.
'I want to make it up to you now, Spicer,' said Annette. 'To show
how sorry I am. Jealousy is a truly pathetic emotion.'
'I've had enough of Pause,' said Spicer. 'Let's put it on Play.'
'It's quite on-turning,' said Annette. 'You can't help it in the
end.'
'Thank God for that,' said Spicer. 'You're becoming human at
last. See how the woman's enjoying it? Even more than the men?
She's not faking. You can tell. Now, you relax. At least there's
only one of me. That should suit you.'
'Couldn't we go upstairs? Do we have to do it on the sofa?'
'Oh for God's sake, Annette!'
'Sorry, Spicer,' said Annette. 'We'll stay here.'
'You are so inhibited,' said Spicer. 'But perhaps that's why I love
you. I as Zeus the seducer-lover-divine, you as Danaë.'
'Just call me sweet-as-pie,' said Annette, 'and I'll answer to it.'
'Those bracelets are practically sinking into your arm. You can't
have got fatter since yesterday.'
'Water retention,' said Annette.
'Don't be so unglamorous,' said Spicer. 'Don't they hurt?'
'Yes,' said Annette.
'I quite like the thought of that,' said Spicer. 'Turn over.'

'Dr Rhea told me you were leaving me,' said Annette.

'I'm beginning to think Dr Rhea's nuts,' said Spicer.

'But did you tell her that?'

'I tell her all kinds of things she wants to hear,' said Spicer. 'From dreams I invent to scenarios of the future.'

'But why?'

'Because I'm easily bored,' said Spicer. 'And she drones on and I like to get her to change the subject, or at least the archetype.'

'But why do you go to her?'

'Because I'm in a transitional crisis, because I need to liberate my Perseus from my Polydectes, and slay Medusa, the poisonous feminine, or look at it another way, cast off Medusa and escape Lilith; or simply be the tree, the trunk, the pillar, the stake, the anti-natural which penetrates the cleft hill. Does that hurt?'

'Yes.'

'It's meant to,' said Spicer. 'Just a bit. Isn't this good?'

'Yes,' said Annette. 'Just call me Tweetie-pie. Each to their own myth. Personally, I choose Disney.'

'Annette?'

'Hello, Mum.'

'Did you speak to Spicer about your father's money?'

'No, I didn't,' said Annette. 'Spicer has had business worries. They're over now. I'm sure the repayments will start flowing any minute. Don't worry about it.'

'Don't you know anything about Spicer's business affairs?'

'Not much, actually. Look, Mum, I've got a headache: please, can't this wait?'

'I don't think so, Annette,' said Judy. 'I was awake all night worrying. Spicer's such a charmer, but do we really know him?'

'Probably not, Mum,' said Annette. 'Men are always full of surprises. Wives can be married to bigamists and not know it till both families meet up at the funeral. Rapists and serial killers likewise.'

'I'm not suggesting Spicer is a bigamist, a rapist or a serial killer, Annette,' said Judy. 'Don't misrepresent me. I'm very fond of Spicer. I have to be. He's going to be the father of one of my grandchildren. I want everything to go well for you both. You can always come and stay with me, Annette. You know that. This is always your home.'

'Thanks, Mum,' said Annette. 'But things are looking okay. Just fine.'

'I'm glad to hear that, Annette, because something's just occurred to me. You remember yours and Spicer's wedding?'

'Of course I do,' said Annette.

'It wasn't a legal ceremony, was it? You were going to have that later. Did you?'

'It was a wonderful wedding party. A marquee in the garden: all those roses, and songs.'

'It was all very charming, Annette, but it wasn't legal. Your divorce hadn't come through.'

'A scrap of paper,' said Annette.

'Your voice has gone very quiet.'

'You're right, Mum. I don't think Spicer ever did put the house in joint ownership and we didn't actually get to the Registry Office. They're such dismal places. Births, deaths, marriages all lumped together and you have to book up so far ahead and either Spicer or me were always busy, and it just kind of drifted off into "one day we'll get round to it." But it's okay, Mum. It doesn't make any difference. I'm a common-law wife.'

'There's no such thing, Annette. A woman has some legal rights once there's a baby of the unwed union, but none at all if there isn't. She has just the same status as a friend who's happened to live in all those years, and enjoyed the perks while she was at it.'

'But I am having a baby, Mum, so there's no worry.'

'I don't mean to upset you, puss,' said Judy, 'but you do need reminding of practicalities sometimes. Your father's been looking it all up.'

'Dad hates Spicer, Mum,' said Annette. 'Of course he's been looking it up.'

'He doesn't hate Spicer,' said Judy. 'Not at all. He finds him as charming as I do. We're just both the worrying kind. You are our only daughter. Now don't get upset and start lashing out at us because we're in the way. I'm going to put the phone down now, puss, so you can get a hold of yourself.'

'I'm perfectly in control of myself, Mum,' said Annette.

'Goodbye, Annette,' said Judy. 'Love to Spicer. And I mean that. And look after yourself.'

'Goodbye, Mum.'

'Annette, are you okay?' asked Gilda. 'There was another child abuse case on the news last night. I sometimes wonder what my own father was like. He died when I was three. If you don't remember it, is it there in your psyche, traumatising you for ever? Or do you have to remember it for it to damage you? The things they never tell you; it's worse than AIDS. Annette, are you there?'

'I'm here, Gilda.'

'Annette, I spent most of the morning on my hands and knees scrubbing the kitchen floor,' said Gilda. 'Scrubbing! Does that mean I'm going to have this baby soon?'

'Probably,' said Annette. 'It's the nest-building instinct. You make things clean.'

'I hate being taken over like this,' said Gilda. 'I'm terrified. Supposing I split?'

'You do split,' said Annette. 'They sew you up afterwards. Or else they cut you open neatly before you begin.'

'They don't say that at the Clinic, or did I miss it? It's all about holding your birth-partner's hand.'

'That's why I don't go much to the Clinic. I don't want to hold my birth-partner's hand, I want gas-and-air and an epidural and a nurse I've never met who's never heard of an archetype.'

'What's the matter?' asked Gilda.

'Do you remember when Spicer and I got married?'

'Yes.'

'Well, we didn't,' Annette said.

'It was a wonderful wedding,' said Gilda. 'A marquee and champagne and a band, but none of us got asked to the ceremony itself, I do remember that. We felt demoted to second-class friends. I went right off you and that was the real reason I had that stupid thing with Spicer. I keep trying to think of reasons. I feel so bad about it, Annette. I'm superstitious. If I have a clear conscience, I'll have an easy birth. So I keep confessing to everyone. It's insane. I know it's insane but I can't help it.'

'There was a hold-up to my decree and we'd done all the

organising, so we went ahead with the reception. And then we just never got round to getting married. It didn't seem to matter.'

'Get married now,' said Gilda. 'Suggest it to Spicer. How can you get divorced if you're not married?'

'Now seems a little edgy, Gilda,' said Annette. 'Though I'm being as sweet as pie, I really am. And it's working. He's running down Dr Rhea himself: I don't have to do it.'

'Oh God, Annette, is it worth it?' asked Gilda. 'I'm getting contractions. They don't hurt; my belly just goes hard as a board. I rather like it. Do you think men feel like this when they have an erection? Purposeful and out of control at the same time?'

'I expect so,' said Annette. 'I wonder if Spicer realises about the house and us not being married?'

'Of course he does, darling,' said Gilda. 'He's a very successful businessman.'

'Not all that successful,' said Annette. 'If it wasn't for British Rail we'd be bankrupt; poor Spicer was just about to put everything in my name.'

'Who told you that? Spicer? Steve says he has so much salted away it's unbelievable,' Gilda said. 'Annette, I can't talk any longer, I'm going to lie in the bath.'

'Don't do that,' said Annette, 'because if the waters break you might not notice.'

'Annette?'

'Who is it?'

'It's me. It's Ernie. Where are you? Why did you take so long answering?'

'I went back to bed,' said Annette. 'I was tired.'

'But you're okay? I worry about you.'

'Thank you, Ernie. I just didn't get much sleep last night, one way and another. And I had to grope for the phone. Somewhere on the floor in the bedclothes. I'm sorry.'

'It sounds a wild scene,' said Ernie Gromback.

'It was rather.'

'Should you be doing this kind of thing?' asked Ernie Gromback. 'You being so pregnant?'

'I'm told it's natural,' said Annette. 'And if it's natural it must be good, or else the patriarchal spirit will triumph, and Eve will be wrenched once more out of Adam's rib.'

'You're rambling, Annette.'

'Am I? Sorry.'

'You sound like Marion on a bad day,' said Ernie Gromback. 'I want to run off with you and look after you.'

'What do you need, Ernie? Why did you call?'

'Don't be like that, Annette,' said Ernie Gromback. 'It's eleven o'clock: you're meant to be at my office seeing the Oprah Winfrey researcher at half-past, and you're not even out of bed.'

'I didn't know we had a meeting,' said Annette.

'Didn't Spicer give you the message last night?'

'He must have forgotten,' said Annette. 'We got rather tied up. Ernie, I'm not going to do Oprah Winfrey.'

'Why not? Because Spicer doesn't want you to?'

'I suppose so,' said Annette.

'You can't let him do this to you,' said her publisher.

'There seems to be rather a lot at stake,' said Annette. 'More than you'd imagine.'

'What I need like a hole in the head,' said Ernie, 'is a first novelist in a time of recession turning down the Oprah Winfrey Show. Do you want my entire business to go down the drain?'

'If it's my marriage, or what passes for my marriage, or your business,' said Annette, 'I'd rather it was your business down the drain. I need the roof over my head.'

'Do you have a marriage there worth saving?' asked Ernie.

'It's not just me,' said Annette. 'It's Susan, Jason, my parents, our friends, the house, the garden, everything. I have to have time to think.'

'You've been brainwashed,' said Ernie Gromback. 'The man's a monster.'

'He's the man I love,' said Annette. 'You just say that because you want me to do Oprah Winfrey and make money for you.'

'It's money for you,' said Ernie Gromback. 'Fiction is your way to independence. That's why Spicer doesn't pass on messages.'

'I'm so tired, Ernie, and I keep getting pains,' said Annette. 'I expect it's indigestion. I drank too much champagne last night.'

'Who gave you champagne in your condition?'

'Spicer says champagne doesn't count as alcohol,' said Annette. 'It wasn't too much in ordinary terms, Ernie, just too much because I'm pregnant.'

'And Spicer doesn't think of that.'

'He's a man,' said Annette.

'I'm a man too,' said Ernie. 'I wouldn't do that. I'd know how to look after you. I know a lot of things. I know Spicer didn't give you my message. I know Spicer has been seeing a lot of Marion. I know it's hopeless to try and do business with friends. When Spicer gave me your manuscript I should have run a mile. Get your clothes on and come down here at once, or Spicer will have won.'

'But I'm so tired,' said Annette.

'Of course you are,' said Ernie. 'Spicer made you tired.'

'It wasn't calculated, Ernie,' said Annette.

'No? When did Spicer ever not calculate anything? I'm coming round to fetch you. I'm going to bring you back to my office, where you can put your feet up. Then you go on to the studio. What are you going to wear?'

'I haven't got anything to wear.'

'Borrow something from someone,' said Ernie Gromback. 'Spicer gave me that manuscript because he expected me to turn it down. It wasn't my kind of book. He knew that.'

'Then why didn't you?'

'Because it was really good.'

'Gilda.'

'Hello, Annette,' said Gilda. 'I feel okay again. A false alarm. I did have a bath. Now I'm busy decorating the crib. Steve's home: he bought all these ghastly things from a car boot sale. White satin ribbons and stuff.'

'Have you got anything I can wear for the Oprah Winfrey Show?'

'What sort of thing did you have in mind?' asked Gilda. 'Spicer's going to be furious.'

'Too bad,' said Annette. 'Anyway, Spicer won't know. I'll be home by seven, before Spicer gets back. He has an appointment with Dr Rhea at six-thirty. The last one, he says. I was right to do a tweetie-pie, it really worked. Disney wins against Mount

Olympus. Spicer and me are on course, truly on course. I just want to be on the Oprah Winfrey Show. They're not screening it till January, when Spicer will be in France. He'll never even see it.'

'I do have that blue sort of spotted shift,' said Gilda. 'Armani.'

'Shows too much arm,' said Annette.

'Wear it with a jacket,' said Gilda. 'What about your hair?'

'I'll do it under the shower now,' said Annette.

'Someone's bound to tell Spicer,' said Gilda. 'You won't get away with it.'

'Oh, shut up,' said Annette. 'There's no possible way I can know what to do for the best so I'll do what I want.'

'Good thinking,' said Gilda. 'What the hell.'

'What the hell, Gilda, what the hell. In my mother's good days she used to quote from *archy and mehitabel*. Archy was a cockroach, Mehitabel was a cat. They typed each other letters on the office typewriter: they couldn't manage the upper case. Mehitabel used to sign off: "what the hell, archie, what the hell." So that's what I'm signing off to you, Gilda: what the hell, gilda, what the hell.'

'Do you know where you are?'

'I think so. Who are you?'

'I'm Doctor McGregor, casualty officer. Who are you?'

'I don't know you,' said Annette. 'You have really nice straight teeth.'

'Thank you. Try and understand what I'm saying.'

'Why can't I?'

'You're still feeling the effect of the anaesthetic. Now, what is your name?'

'Annette.'

'That's a very pretty name,' said Dr McGregor. 'Could we have a second one? And an address? Even the luxury of a next-of-kin?'

'What's it got to do with you?' asked Annette.

'We like to know these things,' said Dr McGregor. 'You are in hospital, Annette. You collapsed in a taxi you'd picked up in the street. You didn't have a handbag with you. Just some loose change in your pocket. So you're a mystery to us.'

'That's not my fault. I couldn't find my bag and I was in a hurry.'

'Good. If you can remember that, can you tell us your second name?'

'Shan't.'

'Where are you? Can you remember that?'

'In hospital.'

'Good girl. We're admitting you. We're waiting for a bed in gynae.'

'That's nice,' said Annette.

'We need to find your husband.'

'Do I have one?' asked Annette.

'We had to cut off a wedding ring when you were under the anaesthetic. And some bangles. I hope you don't mind. There was a nasty mess beneath them.'

'I wish I could remember more,' said Annette.

'Don't worry. It will come back. You're very thin, but well-dressed. Designer clothes, nurse said. We don't see many of those.'

'Thin? I'm enormous,' said Annette. 'Vast like a mountain, like a cleft hill, like Lilith, like Medusa; I'm about to flood the world.'

'Oh Christ, she's gone again,' said Dr McGregor. 'It may not be just the anaesthetic. She may be disturbed.'

'She's in some kind of therapy,' said the nurse. 'We were doing that stuff in Bereavement Counselling. I'm new in this hospital. What's the deal on foetus disposal? Incinerator?'

'At seven months? Coffins, memorial service and counselling,' said Dr McGregor. 'We do things properly here.'

'You mean my baby's dead?' asked Annette.

'Don't try and sit up,' said Dr McGregor. 'You'll find it difficult for a couple of days. You had an emergency caesarian. You were haemorrhaging. A flamboyant toxaemia: you're lucky to be alive. Why did no one pick it up? This is what our entire antenatal service exists for. The baby didn't make it. We couldn't pick up a foetal heartbeat. I'm sorry. She had probably been dead for a couple of days. This is no way to break this kind of thing to anyone. That was why I needed to find your husband. You do have a husband?'

'Listen, and you hear your own heartbeat. Listen hard enough and it'll tell you the story of your life. Whether it's comedy or tragedy depends only upon where you stop, at a good bit or a bad bit. But the heart doesn't let you stop,' said Annette on to the tape machine Dr McGregor gave her. 'It just goes on and on, carrying its owner along with it, past the definite conclusion its owner longs to have. My resentment at this is nothing to do with suicidal inclinations: just the desire for proper endings and understandings, proper tyings-up, in real life as well as fiction. Not that you care about my mind, Dr McGregor; your area is my body. One of the rules of writing feature films, or so Ernie Gromback told me, is that if everything's looking just fine three fifths of the way through, the next two fifths must be devoted to making everything go sour. If all is black and sad three fifths in, thereafter you move relentlessly towards your happy ending. If I could see losing the baby as three fifths of the way in, I could then look forward to happiness. Or was the three fifths point when Wendy startled me with "Oh, born on Christmas Day, a little Capricorn, a little goat." And the five fifths when the new casualty nurse said "What's the deal on foetus disposal here?" It felt like five fifths at the time but the heart goes on beating, and before you know you're carried on into some other film, quite possibly three fifths of the way through and sitting up and paying attention again, wondering what's going to happen next. The plural of foetus is foeti but catch a nurse, anyone, knowing that and acting upon it. People in hospitals have more sense than to be sticklers. She came up and apologised later. She'd thought I was unconscious but I'd just had my eyes closed.'

'You could try contacting your friends on the telephone,' said Dr

McGregor. 'I'm no therapist, but shouldn't you be sticking to the point? I'm a busy man.'

'Just give me another tape,' said Annette. 'You are under no obligation to listen. Indeed, I hope you won't. I don't want to speak to my friends. I can't be sure who they are, not even Gilda. And I don't feel like saying "I'm just fine." Not yet. But it's true that from spending so much time on the phone I have become accustomed to understanding my own life through my ears: so I need the tape. Call it aural predelection if you like, and it may well have to do with overhearing the rows between my mother and my father as a child: listening through doors: working out patterns. I used the patterns in *Lucifette Fallen*, a novel I wrote, Dr McGregor. A stupid and pretentious title for a rather neat, too controlled, short novel. But you are obviously too busy to listen to all that.'

'The girl from Oprah Winfrey was furious when she heard I was in hospital,' observed Annette to her tape recorder, 'and had lost the baby. "Now what am I going to do?" she said. "Annette Horrocks was to be the centre of the show. And I've had to come all the way into town for nothing." Ernie Gromback wrote to tell me about it: Ernie seems to be the only person left in the world able and willing to write a letter. I've had no visitors. It's not their fault, I know, but it doesn't stop me feeling deserted. If I have visitors, if anyone from the outside world comes near, my blood-pressure zooms up. Dr McGregor's getting it under control, Staff Nurse says: they drip various drugs plus antibiotics into my arm. As well as toxaemia I had septicaemia, its source of origin, where the skin had broken beneath one of the bracelets. The nurses bring me three-times-daily messages from Spicer: of the I'm-thinking-of-you,-darling, get-better-soon kind, but they somehow lack conviction. I can't quite feel Spicer's real, though I send loving messages out again. Poor Spicer: his baby too, his idea becoming my flesh. It's just hard to feel and think "poor Spicer".'

'I had a Bereavement Counselling session: a young woman called Anya told me the sense that Spicer wasn't real could only be a function of the drugs I was being given. Such medicines poisoned the mind, she said: she disapproved of them. She described herself as an holistic healer. When the drugs stopped, she told me, I'd bring Spicer to life again, and have proper sympathy with him. She made me visualise a flight of white marble stairs and at the top a place where I had been happy. She held my hand and persuaded me to climb, in my mind, a step at a time towards this goal. I obliged, though I felt embarrassed. It was unfortunate that the place at the top was a McDonald's: Anya thought I was mocking her when I said so: I wasn't. I just remembered taking Susan and Jason out to the cinema one day, and we ended up at McDonald's, and we were all, for some reason, pleasantly and simply content, stealing each other's French Fries. In my "visualisation", as she called it, the man behind the counter was large, strong and surrounded by a brilliant white light: he had a face which looked as if it had been hewn out of a piece of wood. I imagined I was seeing Jesus, but I didn't tell Anya that: I didn't know her well, but enough to tell she wouldn't want Jesus described as a fast-food counter-hand. It was my vision not hers, anyway, and the paramedics being under instruction not to excite me, when I mentioned McDonald's she smiled stiffly and brought the session to a rather sudden end, which I'm sure she wasn't meant to. She left me with instructions to visualise a mandala; which I gathered looks rather like a pie-chart with four divisions in different colours, representing intuition, intellect, sensation and emotion. The trick is, apparently, to get the colours evenly balanced in your mind, and hold them there for two minutes. Then you become less "stressed". I did try. Really. I don't want to be a mocker. Spicer hates mockers. Cynicism, he once told me, is sneering at your own soul. I don't want to do that.'

'If you don't mind,' said Dr McGregor, 'since we are under instruction to work with non-orthodox healers when practicable, to save the cost of expensive drugs, we'll give hypnotherapy a go. A pleasant young man has just joined the team. His name is Peter. I will send him along to you.'

'Hypnotism!' said Annette, and the bleepers on her blood-pressure monitor began to sound. He switched them off.

*

'Well?' asked Dr McGregor on his rounds the next day. 'What happened? It didn't go too well, I hear.'

'Listen to it on the tape,' said Annette, turning her head into the pillow, 'if you're really interested and not just being polite. It's all there.'

Dr McGregor took the tape away.

'This Peter, this person from the fringes, was slight and sweet and had soft thick wavy hair, nut-brown, and a baby face. It was, as I feared, Peter, Peter Pan, Pan the Goat God. Rhea had got into my head. So I expected him to bring out a pipe and start playing it to me, and found myself looking down to see if he had cloven hooves. He didn't: he had brown shoes, rather worn but much polished. So perhaps he was a Peter Pan after all. He told me that if I would allow myself to be put in a light hypnotic trance he would locate the psychological trauma which, according to him, was sending the blood pounding so through my veins and keeping my blood-pressure high. This account of my condition seemed to me to beg many questions: I asked him if he had any medical training and he said no: but he'd studied psychology at college and found he "had a knack for hypnotism." Even the most orthodox practitioners had begun to view many forms of illness as internalised behavioural problems – which had always been obvious so far as facial tics, stammers, addictions and so forth were concerned – and hypnotherapy was proving a useful, inexpensive, effective and non-toxic form of treatment in many cases: in particular the lowering of blood-pressure. I then asked him what he would do with the psychological trauma once he located it in me, and he said if appropriate he would re-lay the memory so it ceased to be traumatic.'

'"Tell me more, Peter," I said, "tell me more," thinking of the way Spicer now recalled the matter of the bacon sandwiches, and he replied that actually, though the re-laying of memory was considered okay in the States, it was still seen as unethical in Europe. I was fortunate that the hospital I was in had a management team imported from the US, and so long as a treatment worked, didn't bother too much with the detail of how or why it worked. How, I asked, did he do this locating?'

'"A traumatic memory," Peter said, "could be located by regressing the patient – a victim of, say, child abuse – to the period of its occurrence, recalling the episode in its fresh form and re-tuning it, as it were, persuading the child/adult that the fear, self-loathing and sense of guilt experienced was inappropriate and by bolstering accompanying feelings of affection, response and gratitude, even creating them if necessary. The memory, dusted down and polished up, would then be re-laid in the adult mind as something that could be coped with – still unpleasant, perhaps, but no longer traumatic. A whole range of behavioural problems could quickly and cheaply be dispersed by Re-lay Hypnotherapy."'

'I only report what Peter Pan told me, though I can't quite believe it. An isolated instance perhaps, but you surely couldn't wipe away an entire childhood's wretchedness by simply persuading the victim to forget it? Surely memory would re-emerge through its coating of forgetfulness? Old stains beneath new wallpaper? I asked him if you could re-lay pleasant memories with nasty ones, turn a pleasant seaside outing into a horrid one, a good sexual experience into something oppressive and smothering: by restructuring a past, turn a wife against a husband, a husband against a wife, and he said oh yes, he assumed so, but who would bother?'

'"Does this apply to everyone?" I asked. "Can everyone be hypnotised?" and he said one in a hundred perhaps not, and so you could get any woman into bed with you, bar the one in a hundred, by persuading her that you were the most attractive man in the world, and Peter Pan said, well yes, most women, eighty in a hundred. But he, though he admitted he had been tempted, would never do anything like that. Common wisdom held that you couldn't get anyone to do anything under hypnosis that went against their conscience, because they would snap out of the trance at once. But with a little ingenuity any hypnotist could alter the perspective in which that conscience worked – the mildest person would take an axe to a door if told a child was dying behind it, the most honest would rob a bank if persuaded a nation would perish otherwise. A truly loyal wife could find herself in a situation in which disloyalty was the only appropriate answer: if the hypnotherapist is the Chief of Police say, and the husband about to be put to torture, then what can the wife do but oblige the Chief of Police to keep the husband safe?

'"I think," I said, "I'm the one in a hundred," and he asked me to fasten my hands together above my head and told me I couldn't separate them, but I could and did, and he laughed and said I was indeed the one in a hundred, but he'd enjoyed our chat. The blood-pressure machine began to put out warning bleeps; Nurse McKenzie, who has red hair and freckles, and reminds me of Wendy, asked him to leave. Nurse McKenzie sat beside me for a while and told me of a newly-married friend of hers who went to a hypnotherapist to be cured of over-eating and ended up having sex on the sofa with him and being charged double, which post-hypnotic suggestion made her pay without argument. On the other hand, her friend had lost weight and didn't regret any of it. Whatever knock-out drops they've added to my drip are beginning to take effect. I'm drifting off again.'

'Well, hypnotherapy didn't work,' said Dr McGregor, visiting Annette in the Special Care Unit to which she had been moved. 'I had a quick listen to the tape. I don't think Peter will stay on the team for long. Obviously the sleazy end of alternative medicine.'

'How can you have a quick listen to a tape?' asked Annette. 'You either listen or you don't. I have another one here for you to ignore.' Dr McGregor took it away.

'I try not to think about Dr Rhea or Dr Herman Marks because my blood-pressure goes sky-high if I do. Thieves, murderers, perverts, devourers of babies! Destroyers of true love. Lilith and Saturn. In mythology Rhea is Saturn's wife. In Spicer's book on Theotherapy – Spicer sent it to me here in hospital, unasked: what can this mean? The title page with Rhea's dedication written in was missing, but a few more passages had been marked. These were the ones relating to the goddess Rhea. If I keep an eye on the blood-pressure monitor I can sometimes direct my will and organise my mind – I can't describe it in any other way – to keep the level steady. But I can't, alas, focus in this way and read at the same time. Perhaps that's the reason I read so little? I risk glances at the pages from time to time.'

' "Over-eagerness to promulgate divine mysteries", I read, "of the goddess Rhea. Shamanism, the grandmotherly guardian of much secret love: the woman who smothers those around her with an excess of love. The less love she gets the more she gives. Her problems are severest around mid-winter." Good. We're moving into the cold, dark months. "Before Hellenic masculinisation – by which we mean the imposition of the Greek Gods upon the earlier pagan ones – Rhea was the Universal Great Mother Goddess and ruled supreme, needing no protective consort." She can manage well enough without Saturn, in other words. Just my luck to fall foul of the Great Mother Goddess Cow. Other people's husbands end up with ordinary therapists. Perhaps what Spicer was doing to me with the tree and the cleft hill business was nothing other than Hellenic masculinisation? The rendering male of the female. Eleanor Watts wouldn't want to move into Bella Crescent if she understood how the archetypes roared up and down it, sucking us all in, whirling us around with their almighty backdraught.'

'Still my blood-pressure won't go down. It's been worse since Peter's visit. I might die of a stroke, they carefully don't say. I've been moved into a SC Unit, Special Care, but not yet IC, Intensive Care.'

'Gilda has had her baby, in the maternity ward below this one. A healthy baby boy, both are doing fine. Gilda came to stand in the ward doorway this morning and wave at me. She was wearing a bright blue wrap which, together with her red hair, by virtue of some reflected halo effect made her shimmer within a mauve aura. Blue and red make mauve, or is it purple? Gilda didn't have her baby with her. I was sorry not to have a glimpse of him. Gilda was being tactful. But really she didn't need to be. Her baby was a little bit mine, as mine had been a little bit hers, and I was proud for her. So it's okay. Really. There was never a friend as good as Gilda in the whole history of the world, and if anyone's to have a baby when I don't, it had better be her.'

'I think Mrs Horrocks can be moved to Light Care,' said Dr McGregor. 'She seems to be much improved. Now how do we account for that?'

'I'll leave you a tape to explain it,' said Annette, 'though you won't believe it.'

'This afternoon I got really tired of the drips and tubes and being wired up and couldn't stand the business of screens and bedpans for a single minute longer, and when the nurses were elsewhere I plucked off terminals, cuffs, leads and unhooked drips and got out of bed and went to the ward bathroom: I was very weak, and almost sorry for my poor little feet – they were quite translucent against the white tiled floor. I remembered my feet as having been firm, strong and solid. Well, everything changes. I stood beneath the shower and let the water run over my hair, my face, my shoulders, breasts, and too-flat stomach, the thin loins. There wasn't a towel so I had to go back to my bed still dripping. Nurses McKenzie and Smiley dried me down – their instructions not to excite me warring with their natural desire to kick my ankles hard – and got me back into bed and re-wired me. The blood-pressure cuff round my forearm went into its automatic tightening phase: the diagnostic readouts settled at pulse-rate 70, and BP 120 over 80. Perfect. Nurse McKenzie dealt the screen a sharp blow with a ruler: the numbers quivered but stayed steady. Nurse Smiley switched off the whole machine and switched it on again, which sometimes did the trick. The cuff took another reading. Pulse 75, BP 125 over 85. The extra fives were no doubt the product of my reaction to what I could only describe as McKenzie's and Smiley's condition of doubt. Staff Nurse came to admire; then Sister: it was twelve hours before the Registrar turned up, but hospitals are so full of bad news there's not much time for the good. In a couple of days I can go home.'

*

'Thus it became apparent to me that running water – described in Spicer's book on Theotherapy as being the best cure for Hera's problems, along with moonlight, bracelets and bangles – had done its bit, though the bracelets and bangles, being false gifts, poisoned offerings, had almost killed me. All it took was a shower. Why I had so resisted being Hera – typified by slyness, softness, gullibility, shame, embarrassment, jealousy, use of sex as weapon and so forth – I couldn't imagine. If we're all just a mixture of adjectives, one representative goddess is as good as another, so long as Saturn's ravenous wife Rhea doesn't have her hand in it. Which of course she had.'

'I'm now downgraded from Special Care to Light Care, where all they do is feed me up, and I'm allowed to make phone calls except the phone is out of order. "What's the name of this ward?" I ask a nurse, reporting the fault. "Olympus", she says. "We're part-funded in here by the sports' firm. We have to rely in this hospital on business sponsors."
'I can all but see Pegasus, trapped in Medusa's sick body for so long, bursting through from the end of my bed, breaking free, spreading his white wings in the sky above Mount Olympus, dissolving into nothingness, bearing my soul away for safe-keeping. Now Spicer can be real again.'

'Two visitors to see you,' said Nurse McKenzie, who is also being allowed a rest in Light Care. 'If you're okay with these two, we'll let the others in.'
'Hi, Mum,' said Susan.
'Hi, Annette,' said Jason.
'We're sorry about the baby,' said Susan. 'When are you coming out?'
'Probably about a week,' said Annette. 'How've you been?'
'It's been okay,' said Susan. 'But Gran won't let us have our meals in our rooms.'
'And Grandad takes us out to find fossils in cliffs,' said Jason, 'which is boring.'
'And we have to get a taxi to school,' said Susan, 'and people see.'

'Though we get him to drop us on the corner so they don't,' said Jason.

'And I haven't had a pizza for five weeks since you came in here,' said Susan.

'And the games disc on my computer's corrupted and Gran says she can't afford a new one,' said Jason. 'So I've nothing to do.'

'Do you mean to say,' said Annette, 'you haven't been at home? Spicer hasn't been looking after you? You've been at my mum's?'

'Spicer hasn't been very well either,' said Susan. 'There's some kind of trouble at the office. He says he may have to go bankrupt. Something to do with British Rail.'

'I've set the bleeper warning at 160 over 110,' said Nurse McKenzie. 'If you get to that the kids will have to leave. Try not to upset your mother more than you have to.'

'I'm not upsetting her,' said Susan. 'She's our mother. We're bringing her up to date. And Jason can't upset her because he's concentrating on his Game Boy.'

'I'm up to level six,' said Jason.

'Did Spicer say when he'd be in to see me?' asked Annette.

'He's coming this evening,' said Susan. 'He said to send his love. They'll only let in two visitors at a time, so he said we should come first.'

'How does he seem?' asked Annette.

'Just the same,' said Susan. 'Are you two getting divorced?'

'Of course not,' said Annette. 'Why should we?'

'Perhaps you ought to,' said Susan. 'You look quite different in here. Much younger. Your face had got a funny sort of fixed expression on it, as if you were expecting someone to hit you all the time.'

'Don't be silly,' said Annette.

'Gran's got it in for Spicer too,' said Susan. 'She says he owes her a lot of money. She goes on and on about it. I wish they'd let you out of here so you could get home and sort things out.'

'It isn't very nice at Gran's,' said Jason.

'I thought you were too busy with your Game Boy to listen,' said Susan. 'If I say anything to you, you tell me you can't hear. So why is it different now all of a sudden?'

'I hear all kinds of things you don't know about,' said Jason. 'Life at Bella Crescent is just one long primal scene. Shit, now I've blown it. Back to level five.'

'You'd better go now, kids,' said Nurse McKenzie. 'Your mother's bleeper's going. If this is what the children do, what's going to happen when the husband arrives?'

'Hello, darling,' said Spicer.

'Oh, Spicer,' said Annette. 'It's been so long! I've missed you so. Our poor baby – I'm so sorry.'

'It wasn't your fault,' said Spicer. 'The sooner you're out of here the better.'

'They say I should stay another couple of days.'

'It's probably the hospital itself that's making you ill,' said Spicer. 'If the taxi driver hadn't brought you in, but taken you home, none of this might have happened.'

'I don't think it was quite like that, Spicer,' said Annette.

'What do any of us know?' asked Spicer. 'Only what the doctors see fit to tell us. But what's done is done. Now we pick up the pieces.'

'Susan said there was trouble at work,' said Annette.

'Don't worry your head,' said Spicer. 'Just a hiccup. You look really pretty, Annette. Perfectly healthy. Glowing, in fact.'

'It's because I'm so happy to see you,' said Annette.

'Why don't you discharge yourself?' asked Spicer. 'Come home now?'

'They've been so good to me here, I don't like to do that,' said Annette.

'You don't want to come home to me?'

'Of course I do, Spicer.'

'Dr Herman said you would probably quickly develop a dependency on the hospital, the authority figure: the substitute father. It seems to be in danger of happening,' observed Spicer.

'I just don't want to get ill again, Spicer,' said Annette.

'All the more reason to get out of here and into therapy as quickly as possible,' Spicer said.

'Therapy follows you to hospital, Spicer; you've no idea,' said Annette. 'It sweeps over you: a great tidal wave of it.'

'Not much has changed, Annette,' said Spicer. 'You can't avoid the smart retort. Your book has had a few early reviews. Everyone says how smart it is, you'll be glad to hear.'

'I think the doctor was hoping to discuss things with you, Spicer, before I went home.'

'We have our own doctor,' said Spicer.

'Dr Rhea? Still Dr Rhea?' asked Annette.

'Of course,' said Spicer. 'She's a great support. You and I need to talk about your reaction to her. It's of course projection. It's to do with your affair with Ernie Gromback. I understand, Annette. There's no need to deny it. I was upset at the time but I'm over that. Enforced monogamy is absurd. And you're a child, so far as your sexuality is concerned. Dr Herman says this is the problem with the sexually abused child: maturity is seldom reached.'

'And he told Dr Rhea and she told you,' said Annette. 'So much for them. They're rubbish.'

'Shall we avoid the gossip,' said Spicer, 'and get back to important matters? Who cares who fucked who one dark night? I certainly don't. Your anger with your mother is finally explicable. She failed to protect you from your father –'

'My father did not abuse me,' said Annette. 'I am not angry with my mother.'

'While you continue to block out the truth you will continue to make my life a misery,' Spicer said.

'If you truly think that about my father,' said Annette, 'why have you sent my daughter and your own son to live with him?'

'Shall we get back to Ernie Gromback etcetera, Annette?' asked Spicer. 'Your casual infidelities? I think you should have told me, but perhaps you were too ashamed? At least my relationship with Marion was not an act of degradation, but based on common interest and a shared spirituality. I wish you could have chosen someone less physically unattractive than Gromback. But I suppose that's part of the syndrome.'

'I think perhaps you'd better leave,' said Nurse McKenzie. 'I've seen Mrs Horrocks in all kinds of states, but not hyperventilating and in tears. She's lost her baby: she needs comforting, not whatever it is you're doing, Mr Horrocks.'

'She didn't lose *her* baby, she lost *our* baby,' said Spicer. 'She didn't even lose it: she threw it away. You don't understand how disturbed my wife is. Or indeed how powerful. She didn't have to take an instrument to herself, as she's done many a time in the past: she simply had to will the poor creature's destruction. Dr Rhea predicted it, Annette. She told me your ambivalence towards Gillian, a girlchild, would affect the foetus, and in all probability lead to stillbirth. It's been the source of so much distress: the Lilith in you so strong. Lilith-Annette, destroyer of man's virility, sapper of male strength, strangler of babies.'

'I'll fetch Security,' said Nurse McKenzie. 'The man's mad. And truly nasty.'

'No,' said Annette. 'I'm discharging myself. Stop the bleepers, set me free of all these wires.'

'Gilda?'

'Annette? Where are you speaking from? The hospital?'

'No,' said Annette. 'I discharged myself.'

'Where are you?'

'I'm at home, locked in my bedroom,' said Annette.

'Is the key on the inside,' asked Gilda, 'or the outside?'

'The inside,' said Annette. 'Spicer drove me home. I came straight in, ran upstairs into this room and locked the door. He banged a bit and then went away.'

'That's all right,' said Gilda. 'Well, it's better. Not exactly good, though. How do you feel?'

'Okay,' Annette said. 'In fact I'm fine.'

'What happened?' asked Gilda.

'Spicer wanted me to discharge myself, so I did,' said Annette.

'He's irresponsible,' said Gilda. 'He's a monster, but what's new?'

'I know that now,' said Annette. 'I called his bluff, that's all. Spicer knows about Ernie Gromback.'

'Oh God,' said Gilda. 'Well, it was bound to happen. So much for confidentiality. Marion has left Ernie Gromback. She said he was too worldly for her. Where's Spicer now?'

'I don't know,' said Annette. 'It's terribly quiet out there. What do I do now?'

'Wait for the enemy powers to gather,' said Gilda. 'I'm sure they will.'

'How's the baby?' asked Annette.

'Divine,' said Gilda, 'but I won't say so if it upsets you.'

'It doesn't upset me,' said Annette. 'It cheers me up no end.'

'How long do you think he's known about Ernie Gromback?'

'Probably from the day I told Herman Marks,' said Annette. 'God, I was naive.'

'Steve says Spicer is what the Americans call a mind-fucker,' said Gilda. 'Hang on, I have to fetch the baby . . . you still there, Annette?'

'Yes,' said Annette. 'Of course I am. You are my only contact with the real world. What's that gurgling noise?'

'It's the baby feeding,' said Gilda. 'I'm lying on the bed. Do you mind?'

'No,' said Annette. 'I've just found something under Spicer's pillow that's really interesting.'

'What?' asked Gilda.

'I'll tell you when I understand it better,' said Annette. 'I'm glad you're feeding the baby yourself. I thought perhaps you wouldn't. They added something yet more to my drip to dry up my milk. I should have gone to the Clinic, though. I do blame myself for that, terribly.'

'There were lots of people around you,' said Gilda, 'certainly me, who should have got you there. While everyone was thinking about the state of other people's heads, the body was in trouble. I blame the therapists.'

'God, how I blame the therapists!' said Annette. 'I can hear the front door. It's Spicer and someone coming back. I'll ring you later, Gilda. All is becoming clear.'

'Annette,' said Spicer, 'I've brought Dr Rhea and Dr Herman to reason with you. Why don't you open the door so we can talk?'

'No,' said Annette.

'Please,' said Spicer.

'I'm not leaving this house, Spicer. You are. Go and live with your friends the Doctors Marks.'

'It's my house,' said Spicer, 'and you have no claim on it. We are not legally married. So anything I let you have is out of my goodwill. You had better make sure you keep it. I suggest you open the door.'

'Okay,' said Annette. 'First round to you.'

'There's no need to get so upset,' said Spicer. 'I spoke what was in my head rather brutally, I do admit that, but at least it's out and we can work on it. I was very upset about the loss of the baby.'

'Hello, Dr Rhea,' said Annette. 'How are things?'

'This is a very distressing situation,' said Dr Rhea.

'Hello, Dr Herman,' said Annette. 'How's the wanking?'

'We are recording this,' said Dr Herman, 'so be careful.'

'Second round to you,' said Annette. 'But I do have a trump card.'

'What's that?' asked Spicer.

'Never you mind,' said Annette. 'Carry on with your observations.'

'You would do better to return to your parents' home,' said Dr Herman, 'at least for a time, and come to terms with your childhood trauma. There is a great inner peace resultant from eventual reconciliation with the damaging parent.'

'This is my home,' said Annette. 'I'm not leaving it. Spicer is.'

'It's my home in law,' said Spicer.

'We'll see what a court has to say about that,' said Annette.

'It's not as if we had any children together,' said Spicer.

'You saw to that, Mrs Horrocks,' said Dr Rhea, 'I am sorry to say. Refusing medical and psychological care while pregnant! In the US women get put in prison for that. The right of the foetus predominates.'

'That law is not here yet,' said Annette, 'though I can see it coming.'

'You're not even my wife,' said Spicer. 'You're just a mistress. You sponged off me for years.'

'Spicer doesn't love you,' said Dr Rhea. 'It's a long time since he loved you.'

'He did love me,' said Annette. 'Why did he want us to have a baby if he didn't love me? He loved me until you put it into his head that he didn't.'

'What is this word love,' said Dr Rhea. 'I don't understand its meaning.'

'It's the best part of a person,' said Annette. 'Take it away and the worst is left. All I have of Spicer now is the worst; all there's left of him is dregs. You two dismantled him in six months. That's all it took. Nothing to do with therapy, with healing. You wanted his body, his soul, his money, his house. I was in the way, and unfortunately for you, the one in a hundred. So you got Spicer to get rid of me, to drive me out.'

'You're insane,' said Spicer. 'Paranoid. But then you always were.'

'Dr Rhea is a hypnotherapist,' said Annette. 'That's what AHTM means. The Association of Hypnotherapists in Medicine.'

'So?' said Spicer.

'As well as therapist, healer, counsellor, astrologer, homeopath, she is a hypnotist as well. She is in every part of you. She has your soul.'

'At last our Annette believes in the soul,' said Spicer. 'That's something achieved.'

'All they've left of you is dregs, husband,' said Annette. 'But it doesn't devalue what went before. Even if you don't remember it, I do.'

'You always adored me,' said Spicer, 'that's true enough, but I always rather despised you. I needed someone to look after Jason so I took you on. I should have known it was a mistake.'

'You believe that because Dr Rhea and Dr Herman made you believe it, not because it's true. We're together because we fell in love.'

'Ah, such romantic fantasy!' breathed Dr Herman. 'Such Englishness!'

'Let her wear herself out,' said Dr Rhea. 'She soon will.'

'Spicer,' said Annette, 'they've made you forget all the good memories of you and me together; they've taken them out, re-laid them, re-placed them. They even got to the bacon sandwiches. You can't even have those as a pleasant memory, in case you remember you loved me.'

'What are you raving about? Bacon sandwiches? Pork's disgusting,' said Spicer.

'When you think of our time together, Spicer,' said Annette, 'you associate it with trouble, boredom and the need to escape. You even believe I render you impotent.'

'You do,' said Spicer.

'Where once you thought of your Annette, you now think of Lilith, who is dangerous and destructive. Spicer, you couldn't even remember having met Dr Herman, though of course you had. God knows what else they wanted you for. Well, I do know, but never mind that.'

'What are you raving about?' asked Spicer. 'Just get out of my house. You have no right here. Take your personal possessions and go: stop persecuting me.'

'I've given you up, Spicer,' said Annette. 'I could call in my friend Peter Pan and have your memories relocated and re-laid properly and truthfully, but I don't like you any more, let alone love you. I don't believe anyone can make a human being talk and behave the way you do to me, unless there's a large slice of that human being wants to. Dr Rhea can set up whatever scenario she likes in your mind – the reasons other than sheer forgetfulness that you didn't put half the house in my name, the reasons other than idleness that we never got properly married – it makes no difference. There is every excuse for you, but I don't accept them. I want to be free of you.'

'When you're finally out of here,' said Spicer, 'Dr Rhea and Dr Herman are to set up their surgery in this house. There's no room for you, or the kids.'

'I thought as much,' said Annette. 'The Drs Marks' Hampstead house is leased to them by the AJA, the Association of Jungian Analysts, or the British Psychodrama Association or the Association of Sexual and Marital Therapists or whatever comparatively respectable association you care to name, and the Drs Marks have been struck off and turned out, quite rightly, so they think they'll try further down the hill, where there's quite a shortage of therapists and a gap in the market to fill, and ours is a nice house, isn't it? Or was. We were happy here, Spicer, you and me, but you won't remember that.'

'What a fantasist she is,' said Dr Herman. 'You know she made the most extraordinary sexual advances to me?'

'Poor thing,' said Dr Rhea. 'She has been abusing her children. The boy more or less told me so.'

'You'd better get out, Annette,' said Spicer, 'or things will turn really sour for you. Dr Rhea and Dr Herman are good people: you are a very nasty piece of work.'

'Spicer,' said Annette, 'I would like you to look at this polaroid photograph I found beneath the pillow of our marital bed.'

'Why should I?' asked Spicer. 'What trickery is this?'

'It is a photograph,' said Annette, 'of you, Dr Rhea and Dr Herman engaged in sexual intercourse in this very room. Troilism. Dr Rhea in the middle. Do you have any memory of this? Look closely, Spicer. You can see the faces quite clearly.'

'I don't understand,' said Spicer. 'What is this? Oh dear God!'

'It is a photograph,' said Dr Rhea, 'my dear Spicer, of you and me standing in Highgate Cemetery, next to the bust of poor old Karl Marx.'

'So it is,' said Spicer. 'You have a very sick mind, Annette, full of the most distressing sexual fantasy. Now please just leave, before we throw you out. You are such rubbish, such a soulless person. Here today, gone tomorrow. There is no place for you here. You have always made me profoundly unhappy.'

'Oh well,' said Annette. 'I suppose I had better go. I just wanted to be sure I understood the situation properly. Saturn and his loathsome wife, their lease expired on Mount Olympus, taking refuge where they can, spreading destruction and the end of love wherever they set foot.'

'I understand your anger,' said Dr Rhea. 'It is perfectly natural. When relationships break down, it is the unfortunate therapist who always gets the blame.'

'Gilda?'

'Oh God, Annette, is that you? We've been so worried!'

'What about?'

'It's been more than three weeks! No one's heard from you. Where are you?'

'I told Spicer where I was. I called him. I left a phone number. I'm sure I did.'

'Well, he didn't tell us. All he said was that you'd walked out on him and the kids, and gone off with Ernie Gromback and he didn't know where you were. We called Ernie and he sounded really surprised and said he hadn't heard from you either; he wished to God he had. So we called Spicer back and Spicer said he'd been trying to save your face, you'd left him because he was in financial difficulties and ill, and perhaps you were with your mother. Are you okay, Annette?'

'I was until you started telling me this, Gilda.'

'Shall I stop? Is it very painful?'

'It's okay. You can go on.'

'Your voice sounds quite strong, so I will. You need to know. I got through to your mother, who said she had the kids, but she had no idea where you were. Spicer had told her you'd aborted the baby to go off with a lover, and though your mother didn't believe that, your father was inclined to. You'd better get in touch with your parents, Annette. They sounded rather miffed. Well, I suppose they would, if the kids have just been dumped on them. Spicer told your mum and dad he was too ill to have them back; his doctors had advised him to sell up his business. The stress was too great, what with you killing his baby and then walking out on him. I got Steve to call Spicer but all Spicer said was that you'd been having an affair with Ernie Gromback all these years, and that's why poor Marion had walked out on Ernie. Spicer said you were the destructive goddess Kali and then he hung up. Are you okay?'

'Not as okay as I was five minutes ago, Gilda.'

'Of course I don't believe any of it, Annette.'

'Good. I'll try not to. But it's hard. I've believed everything Spicer said for ten years. If husbands say dreadful things about you, why should they be lying? If you've shared a bed for so long and been close and companionable and in and out of each other, wouldn't the other know?'

'I guess they just sometimes turn, Annette. And the closer they've been the more they want to damage you in other people's eyes, to justify the turning.'

'But why should Spicer want to hurt me? Wasn't losing the baby enough? I haven't hurt him. I'm just trying to hang on in here, Gilda, and survive.'

'Where are you, Annette?'

'Never mind. I thought I was getting better but I'm not. I must go and pick some more flowers.'

'Pick flowers? Like Ophelia?'

'A bit. Rosemary grows round here. Rosemary for remembrance. The whole place is scented. I hadn't realised it flowered. Blue and tiny flowers, and very pretty. I put them round the shrine.'

'What shrine are you talking about, Annette? Are you in some kind of religious centre?'

'Good heavens, no. I have a photograph as a talisman, that's all, in my bedroom. I've built a shrine around it. I surround it with flowers. I worship it as objective truth.'

'What sort of photograph, Annette?'

'I'm pretty sure it isn't of Karl Marx's grave.'

'Do you have someone with you, Annette? You're not on your own?'

'I'm not with Ernie Gromback. I'd notice a thing like that.'

'Are you in your right mind, Annette? Are you in some kind of nuthouse?'

'No. I'm just staying with friends till I feel better.'

'But you're okay? I hope I haven't upset you.'

'It comes in waves. This kind of conversation makes my head sink and sink right under the water, so I guess I'll stop now. I'm not as strong as I thought.'

'Annette, tell me where you are, please don't just hang up –'

'Oh God, Steve, that was Annette and she just hung up and didn't leave a number. Yes, I suppose I was tactless. But that's what Spicer's saying about her. The trouble is, Steve, she loves him. Supposing she decides to go back to him? She needs to know the truth. She needs to know what a bastard he is.'

'Can I speak to Spicer, please, Wendy? This is Gilda Ellis. Annette's friend.'

'Is Mrs Horrocks okay, Mrs Ellis? I worry for her. I know I

shouldn't, what she did was unforgivable, but she was always so nice to me. Secretaries and wives don't necessarily get on. She made a real effort and I liked to think it worked well between us.'

'What is Mrs Horrocks meant to have done, Wendy?'

'Terminating a foetus at that late stage! I'm a pro-lifer. A dreadful thing to do! She'd even given the poor little girl a name. Gillian. Mr Horrocks has been so upset about it. Mrs Horrocks put her career before her family, before everything: apparently she couldn't bear to be seen pregnant on a TV screen. She said it was bad for business. And we're all to lose our jobs, and no redundancy money because of the bankruptcy. Mr Horrocks doesn't seem to know what he's doing any more, now that Mrs Horrocks has walked out on him. What a time to choose! We've got this great big order: why is he declaring bankruptcy? Strange, isn't it. Everything seems so normal and happy, and then one day it all just shatters to bits. It almost makes you believe in astrology. Some kind of transit in the heavens; stars getting too close for comfort; all you can do is sit it out and try to do the right thing, and hope it passes without dragging you with it. But I can't chatter on like this. I'll put you through.'

'Hello, Spicer.'

'Is that you, Gilda? I'm very busy.'

'Spicer, I heard from Annette. I forgot to get her number. She said you had it.'

'I don't know what kind of sick game you and she are playing now, Gilda, but whatever it is, it won't work. The truth is out now. You were in on her affair with Ernie Gromback. Must have been quite a turn-on for the pair of you, sniggering at me from the corners of rooms. Forever whispering and giggling, running up telephone bills, the pair of you, for me to pay. Mr Stupid! Mr Cuckold, the universal provider. What does Annette want from me now? Money? Tell her from me I don't pay women who murder unborn children and sexually molest the others –'

'Spicer –'

But Spicer put the phone down.

*

'Gilda?'

'Annette, before you say a thing, please give me your phone number.'

'I will later. It's okay, I'm better now. I won't hang up.'

'Where are you?'

'Does it matter?'

'Describe the room you're in,' said Gilda.

'It's in Yorkshire, I think. It's a square room with whitewashed walls and the telephone's fixed to the wall. It's an old-fashioned one with a dial. It takes for ever for the dial to rattle back after every number. I'm standing at the window looking at some moors and some grey stone walls. I can count twelve sheep. Did you know most grazing animals have to eat for twenty-two hours out of twenty-four to get enough nourishment to survive? I'm really glad I'm not a sheep.'

'So am I, Annette.'

'If you, as a human, eat slices of sheep,' said Annette, 'you can get your daily nutritional requirements in about ten minutes, because they've done all that work and all that focusing. If you're a vegetarian it can take a whole half-an-hour munching away: you're getting the value of mere photosynthesis. There's a three-piece-suite here with big yellow flowers on it, and an Axminster carpet in purple and red, and a blue spotted lamp shade. Nothing goes very well together but I'm not complaining. If I stretch the telephone cord I can sit on the arm of the chair, just about. There! It's really good to be on-line again, as it were. Things are looking up.'

'Why do you only think you're in Yorkshire? How come you don't know?'

'Because I reckon I'm 208 miles more or less north of Watford, which would be about Yorkshire, wouldn't it?'

'I could look it up in an atlas if you wanted, Annette.'

'You don't have to humour me, Gilda. I'm not insane. I have been, I think. And I had this nasty wound in my neck but it's healing now. At any rate Henry and Buttercup say it is. It's round the side so it's really difficult to see in a mirror. It certainly feels better.'

'Who are Henry and Buttercup, Annette?'

'They're the ones I'm staying with. The ones who picked me out of the ditch.'

'A ditch, Annette? What were you doing in a ditch?'

'Crawling about. What one does in ditches. Henry and Buttercup are quite old. He must be eighty-five, she's ninety-something; quite a bit older than him. I don't think these gaps in ages matter much, do you? He has more rheumatism than she does. I don't think she was christened Buttercup, but that's what everyone calls her. Not that everyone is very numerous round here. I'm talking about the postman, the doctor, the milkman and the man who came to dip the sheep. Sheep have to be dipped annually for scabies by law, but the stuff the Ministry give you to dip them in can really poison you if you so much as breathe the fumes in. Henry says the Ministry care more about sheep than they do about people, but a department has to do what a department has to do. Henry is a very uncondemning person. He sees people on the whole helpless in the face of circumstances. They need to be forgiven, even Spicer.'

'That seems to be going a bit far. You were telling me about the ditch, Annette. Is it on an A road or a B road?'

'You're trying to find out where I am, aren't you, Gilda?'

'Yes, I am, Annette.'

'If I just give you a telephone number, will you stop?'

'Yes, Annette.'

'It's on the B 3210, and the telephone number is 0886 435281. Okay? Have you got a pen?'

'Steve just handed me one.'

'Steve's not listening in on the extension, Gilda?'

'No, he's not, Annette.'

'I believe you, because you're my friend, even though you did sleep with Spicer. So Steve had better not be on the extension, had he, or you'll be in trouble. It's better when I talk to you than when I just think about you.'

'Don't brood, Annette. I've said and said I'm sorry. And Steve knows.'

'As I say, it comes in waves. I can feel one coming on now. It's a pit in the stomach.'

'Tell me more about the ditch. Please.'

'I'm using Henry and Buttercup's phone. They can't afford luxuries, and I haven't any money. Perhaps you'd better call me back?'

But when Gilda called the number Annette had given her, all she got was a continuous bleep.

'Spicer, are you in there?' Steve called through the letter box of the Horrocks' house in Bella Crescent, since no one had answered his knocking and his ringing. 'I know you are, because you just opened the door to Marion. She got out of the taxi ahead of me, and pretended not to see me. We need Annette's number, nothing more. Give it to us and we'll go away and leave you in peace.'

'What makes you think I have Annette's number?' asked Spicer cheerfully, opening his study window, sitting on the sill. He wore an Indian cotton dressing gown, striped red and yellow.

'Annette says she gave it to you.'

'Annette is a liar,' said Spicer. 'Hadn't you heard about her secret affair with Ernie Gromback? It's been going on for years. What did Annette care about what she was doing to poor Marion? Annette's ruthless. I suited Annette while I was well and could oblige her, physically and financially, but now I'm ill and bankrupt and have to sell the house, she's just buggered off. Marion comes round to nurse me. That's all there is to her and me. We're not exactly a number. Christ, someone has to be nice to me after all I've been through.'

'You look quite well to me, Spicer.'

'That's the high blood-pressure – it produces a flush. I'm told I could have a stroke at any moment.'

'Don't you worry at all about Annette, Spicer?'

'Worry about Annette? As well worry about a piranha fish. She dropped that baby without turning a hair. Dropped it dead, of course, as suited her purposes.'

'Gilda speaks to Annette on the phone. She says Annette doesn't sound too good,' said Steve.

'Don't be taken in by Annette,' said Spicer. 'She had the nerve to call me the other day, pretending to be in tears, begging me to have her back. I didn't believe a word of it. Gilda had put her up to something, I could tell.'

'Spicer, I don't think you're in your right mind.'

'Never been more in it, old chap,' said Spicer from his windowsill. 'They're two of a kind, Annette and Gilda, a monstrous conspiracy of women. Take my advice, Steve – get rid of Gilda the first opportunity you've got. She's foisted that baby on you. I could tell you things about Gilda which would surprise you, a nice fella like you.'

'I expect you could, Spicer. On a more realistic level, have you actually sold this house?'

'Are you spying for Annette? What's going on here? I'm not a material person. I'm not interested in money. I'm not selling this house. I am giving it away by deed of gift, before the official Receivers get their filthy hands on it.'

'So who are you giving it to, Spicer? Not Annette, I take it?'

'Are you joking? Give it to the woman who drove my poor wife out of her own house, rendered my son Jason a virtual orphan and then took sexual and emotional advantage of him? Why should I give her my house? No, I'm making it over to a couple of people I trust. Not many of those around.'

'Then he slammed the window shut,' said Steve to Gilda, 'and as he moved away his dressing gown fell open and I'll swear he had an enormous erection.'

'Don't tell me,' said Gilda, 'or my milk will dry up. Was Marion in the room with him?'

'I have no idea,' said Steve. 'My feeling is he just gets off on abusing Annette.'

'I suppose that could be a tribute to his love for her,' said Gilda, cautiously, 'which will emerge again when this mental illness, or whatever it is, has passed over the pair of them. Because he must be mad, mustn't he?'

'For a nasty piece of work read mad,' said Steve. 'For mad read a nasty piece of work. Who knows?'

'Life's easier to bear,' observed Gilda, 'if you can write off a sector of the populace as mad: that is, not pertaining to the race of the proper people, the nice kind ones. Then you don't have to think any more about any possible resemblance between you and them. You're sane, they're mad. Finis.'

They fell silent.

'Perhaps Spicer's right about Annette,' observed Steve in due course. 'Perhaps Spicer is to be pitied more than Annette.'

'I don't think so,' said Gilda. The baby cried in the next room. Steve went to fetch him, and Gilda unbuttoned her blouse, and they sat close together while she fed him, as if by so doing they could keep the world out.

'Hi, Gilda.'

'Annette, you gave me a wrong number. I tried to ring back but it was unobtainable.'

'What number did you try?'

'0886 435281.'

'You must have written it down wrong. I told you 0846. Have you got that?'

'Yes.'

'You can test it if you like, when I ring off.'

'I don't trust you. I'd rather you gave me your address so Steve and I can come and fetch you.'

'I don't think I can quite cope with that yet. Anyway where would I go? I don't have a home any more. Spicer's hijacked it.'

'You can stay with us. Or you could just walk back in, and say hi, Spicer, I'm back home. If anyone's going to leave, you are. Or, Hi Spicer, why don't we set up home together again?'

'It just doesn't feel as if I could do that, Gilda. If you're rejected by a man, your instinct is to stay in the gutter: you're disallowed the home. Besides, Marion's there. And I have no legal rights.'

'I think perhaps you ought to get back in there, Annette. Spicer seems to be giving the house away.'

'Don't tell me. To the therapists, just to hurt me more.'

'I suppose so, Annette. To a couple of people he trusts, he says. At the very least, you need to get your stuff out of it.'

'But there's almost nothing in the house that's mine, apart from some clothes. I've lost a couple of stone so I reckon they'd look really weird on me now. Spicer bought the car and the stereo and stuff like that: my earnings paid for holidays and food and loo paper and it was always me who filled up the tank. So I've nothing to show at all for those ten years, not even by way of possessions.

I don't like talking about it, Gilda. It makes my neck start hurting
again.'

'What's the matter with your neck?' asked Gilda.

'I cut it on a bit of metal when I fell into the ditch.'

'This ditch. How did you get into it?'

'It's a kind of black pit, not just a simple ditch, Gilda. It takes
forever to get out of it. The sides are slippery. There's mud and
blood everywhere. I always knew there was bound to be a gap;
but in my head I'd sanitised it into The Gap, you know, the chain
store, all the clothes neat, clean, folded and properly catalogued,
and the same wherever you are in the world, not in the least like
the gap really is.'

'What are you talking about, Annette?'

'Do you think Spicer's seeing Marion, Gilda?'

'Yes, I think he is.'

'Sleeping in my bed, casting her disgusting Tarot cards on my
dining table, cooking at my stove, using up my soap, her hand
on Spicer's cock; she's so stupid, Gilda, why does he prefer her
to me?'

'Perhaps that's why, Annette. Because she's stupid. Or to get
back at Ernie Gromback. I have no idea. Forget it, forget him,
or else just walk back in.'

'He's forgotten me. He's blocked me out. And the Marks team –
the Grouchos and the Harpos, the Lenins or the Stalins, now the
therapists, what's the difference? – will own the house and set up
surgery, and all the freaks and nutters in the world will walk up
my steps and ring my bell and take off their clothes and cavort
in my rooms, and Herman's hands will palpate two thousand
breasts and Rhea's soft voice will destroy a thousand marriages,
and the negative archetypes will swoop and whistle and scream
down the Crescent, and bow the trees down because I'm not there
to ward them off. You know Spicer and I conceived Gillian in the
back garden? We made love to the scent of night jasmine under the
racing moon, before we had any idea how damaging the transits of
the moon could be, when he loved me as much as I loved him.'

'Stop it, Annette. You're upsetting yourself.'

'I am not upsetting myself. It is being done to me. Head over
heels down into the pit again, slipped through the gap, the waves

breaking over me again. I'm going to have to go now, Gilda. Do be careful of the gap. You know how the guards call out on certain stations of the London Underground, "Mind the gap! Mind the gap!" What can this possibly be, this "gap", foreigners wonder, looking round for some little scuttling thing you're supposed to look after? When what's meant is "notice the space between the straight line of the carriage and the curve of the platform and don't slip down it". The true gap is the space between the world as it ought to be, and the world as it is; between what you think love and marriage and babies is going to be and what it turns out to be, and its proper name is Disappointment. Anyone can fall into it, Gilda. It's horrible down here. Bloody and pulsating; mean, spiteful and full of hate; grabbing and sucking down and grasping. Disappointment is the mother of all nasty emotions. You want the world to be perfect and it isn't. It drives you to terrible deeds. You can't see properly down here because your eyes are misty. You think it's tears have done it and feel sorry for yourself, but it isn't; your vision is cloudy because you're growing a cataract of rage, a kind of second eyelid. The white skin across the eye cats reveal to you when they're sick. You never knew it was there: you just stroked its shiny fur and trusted and hoped for the best, but all the time the cat's worms were travelling to its brain, and by the time you notice it's too late to help. It's having fits.'

'Can't we come and fetch you, Annette?'

'No. Once you're in the black pit you've got to get out of it yourself. There's a route somewhere. I'll find it somehow. You've got to blink away the rage so you can see clearly: the trouble is the rage is the only way you know how to survive. And you keep stumbling over wreckage. I keep thinking I've found the way out, and I even get my hands on the edge to pull myself out but there's Spicer's great black boots, tramping and stamping and kicking me down into the pit again. He circles it for ever. I'm falling, Gilda, even as I speak. He's such a shit, isn't he?'

'Yes.'

'Not worth loving. No special relationship, ever. Just him laughing at me behind my back, mocking me, wondering how to get rid of me. If I learn to despise him, will I stop loving him? Is that the way?'

'I don't know, Annette.'

'The pompous shit, the sleazeball – I'll call him names. I'll practise and see if that works. I'm going now, Gilda. Goodbye. Buttercup's just come in.'

'Gilda?'

'Hello, Ernie.'

'I can't stand this not knowing,' said Ernie Gromback. 'Someone has to find Annette. My PR people are going crazy. Now she's not available, all the media big guns want her for their shows. I can't hold up publication for ever. Besides which, I'm worried about her. What a bastard Spicer is. The only good thing to be said about him is he's taken Marion off my hands just in time for her Macrobiotic Vegan phase. All she'll eat then is grapes and brown rice. I want all the clues you have, Gilda.'

'208 miles north-ish of Watford, twelve sheep, a moor, rosemary, a dial telephone, a shepherd with a breathing problem owing to ingesting Ministry chemicals, a bedroom with a shrine to a photograph in it, a front room which sounds peculiarly horrible, and an elderly pair called Henry and Buttercup. That's it.'

'I'll get my people on to it.'

'Oh, Ernie, you sound so rich, effective and powerful.'

'Are you mocking me, Gilda?'

'No, I'm not, Ernie.'

'Why would Annette be so certain of the exact mileage, when she's so vague about everything else?'

'I kind of don't want to ask her that, Ernie.'

'Why not?'

'I don't know. I'm afraid of the answer.'

'Can you accept a reverse charge call, please, from a call box?'

'Where's the call box?'

'Yorkshire.'

'Okay, okay. Put her through.'

'Gilda?'

'Hi, Annette. How are things?'

'Better. I was telling you about this ditch.'

'The black pit of the soul. I'm having a real problem with my milk, thanks to you.'

'I'm sorry. I've forgotten all that old stuff. I'm back in the real world. It was just a perfectly ordinary ditch and I was just very lucky Henry and Buttercup happened to pass by in their old Ford Prefect. Or I might have been there all night and died from loss of blood and/or hypothermia. That's what the doctor said. Though I don't know. I was half out of the ditch when their lights caught me, something shapeless and struggling in the mud. Brave of them to stop. One of their headlights goes off at an angle, like someone with a cast in their eye, otherwise I wouldn't have been seen. They picked me up, washed me down, stitched me up, and here I am, cold-turkeying on Spicer, tied to the mast to stop me going back to burn the house down, cut out the crotch of his trousers, scratch the side of his car with a coin, get the Markses three months in prison under Section 4 of the Vagrancy Act – using a fortune-telling device, namely a horoscope, to discompose one of Her Majesty's subjects, and that's what you can get, three months – tar and feather Marion, all the things I knew would help me out of the pit, only Henry and Buttercup tell me it's another false exit, all I'll see silhouetted when I look up to the sun will be Spicer's boots, Spicer's smiling face. They're right.'

'You're still not really better. You said you'd lost two stone. That's a worry. You must be almost not there.'

'I can't think why. We live on chops, potatoes, and lardy cake.'

'How horrible.'

'It helps break the pattern.'

'You're not on drugs, Annette?'

'I'm addicted to Spicer, that's why Henry and Buttercup tied me to the mast. I am hooked on my own punishment.'

'Punishment for what, Annette?'

'For being a victim. Blame the sinned-against for the sin, blame the victim for the crime. See how Spicer blames me! Dear Spicer, please forgive me for the hurt you have done me. Dear Spicer, forgive me for the death of the baby you killed. Spicer, cruel master, let me lick your boots, let me fawn upon you; take me back; if I can't have your kindness, let me have your cruelty.'

'Annette, that is disgusting.'

'I know. I am entropied, degraded. Did my father really believe I aborted the baby? Went off with a lover? Or was that just what my mother said he believed?'

'Your mother said it.'

'Then we can discountenance it. She has never forgiven him for his affairs. Neither have I. If he wanted anyone but her, why didn't he have me? Did you speak to the children?'

'No.'

'Please do. Tell them to hang on in there. Say I'll be in touch very shortly.'

'Okay. You are getting better, Annette. I can hear it in your voice. How's the pit?'

'The shit and the mud seem to be drying up. It would make good fertiliser. But I still can't find the path out. Any number of false starts, but you keep slipping back and you know Spicer's roaming up there anyway. Shall I tell you how I got to be in here?'

'Yes please, Annette.'

'Well. I got out of hospital and went home and found the photograph of the Doctors Marks and Spicer naked and doing God knows what to each other, in the name of therapy no doubt, and got thrown out. I had the evidence of my own eyes but it still wasn't good enough. I started walking north. I don't know why, except the further north you get in this hemisphere the colder it gets, so it seemed a fitting direction. All kinds of people stopped to offer lifts, so I accepted them. Why not? None of them were going far, that was the problem. A woman gave me her jumper, a man gave me sandwiches. Two young people tried to take me to a doctor. I suppose I looked very strange. I shivered a lot. I got as far as the big service station at Watford, where I took the initiative and started hitching. I probably should have just let what happened, happen. A lorry driver picked me up. He was young and goodlooking and had tattoos on his arm. They were brown and bare and muscly. It was kind of domestic in the cab. A rug on the seat; some artificial flowers in a silver vase he'd won in a raffle; a photograph of his mother's cat stuck in the rearview mirror. He said he'd take me as far as I wanted if I'd have sex with him once every fifty miles, that was his fee for lady hitchhikers. I said yes, okay.'

'Annette!'

'Well, why not? He was very warm and soft to the touch. I can't explain it. Spicer was always so contained and somehow chilly, even in performance. Straight trade seemed better to me. We got fifty miles and stopped in a layby, and another fifty, and another and another, and then he wanted to again after only another five miles, and I said that wasn't in the deal and began to get angry. Why had he been so precise if he was going to do this? It was dark by then. He left the main road and went off into the countryside, bump, bump along tiny roads, in a temper, and I got frightened, which was stupid because what could he do which he hadn't done already – but I was passionate in defence of the deal. It is the only way I can describe it. It seemed a matter of life and death to me that he should stick to the bargain and to him that the sex should be more than the bargain.'

'What a disgusting person,' said Gilda.

'No, Gilda, you don't understand. He wanted me to love him, not just to use him, and he was disappointed.'

'You are out of your mind. Well, what's new?' said Gilda bitterly.

'There's such a wonderful smell of rosemary up here. I can see for miles and miles, through the squares of glass in this telephone box. The sky's like the kind of colour wash they make children do in Rudolph Steiner schools, but latticed. Water colours on wet paper. Susan went to a Steiner school once, till she got so bored I took her out. "Rosemary and rue; these keep Seeming and savour all the winter long:" That's just after Exit Pursued By Bear in *The Winter's Tale*. Jason was in that. He was very good. Even Spicer said so.'

'English oil of rosemary is infinitely superior to the stuff you get from France or Spain,' said Gilda, 'because of the colder climate, but we never bother to produce it here. Quite a marketing problem for the EC. You worked on a programme with me, Annette. Don't you remember?'

'Just about. But it isn't the green-leaved rosemary that grows round here, the stuff you use to get the oil, it's the silver and gold kind, with little blue flowers, that just grows. Anne of Cleves wore a wreath of it at her wedding. Was she one of the wives who was beheaded or one of the ones who survived?'

'I'd have to look it up, Annette.'

'Don't bother. Anyway, here we were, this truck driver and I, fighting, and he just opened the cab door and pushed me out, all the way down to the ground, and I rolled into this muddy ditch. It was raining. He got out and looked at me down in my ditch and said I was lucky he hadn't raped me and strangled me, and drove off. I didn't think I was particularly lucky; I daresay that was what I'd wanted. So there I was in this ditch, exhausted and without my knickers, which can chill you down a lot, and it was raining, and my neck was hurting and bleeding. I found later there was this great cut in it. I had to have a tetanus jab. He shouldn't have left me there, should he? Do you think he was worse than Spicer, or better?'

'Annette,' said Gilda, 'truck drivers are expected to be brutes. Terrible things happen to girls on the road. That's why good girls don't hitch. But Spicer is meant to be civilised, and you are his wife. Spicer is worse than the truck drivers.'

'But I might have been fighting him in some way I didn't understand and he did, so what he did was reasonable?'

'No.'

'Thank you, Gilda. And I don't suppose they're exactly in competition for worst place, anyway. One must just be grateful for not being raped or murdered, physically or spiritually. I'll have to go soon. There's someone wanting to use this phone box. How extraordinary! It's so isolated up here. Moors to the right of you, moors to the left of you, just this footpath and this phone box in the middle of nowhere, and the smell of rosemary. I couldn't resist calling you. I hope you don't mind me reversing the charges. I thought we could talk for ever. And now there's someone else here. Another person. A man. He doesn't seem threatening. I can go on a little, I guess. I'll turn my head and pretend I haven't seen him. Where was I? Another photograph. In the paper the other day. An old atrocity picture, dating back to the forties. The newspaper reprinted it, with apologies to their readers' sensitivities, in an attempt to explain contemporary times in Yugoslavia. You don't want to look, you have to. This photograph was of a young man, alive and well and handsome, except he is being held down by three other young men, looking perfectly cheerful, and a fourth is sawing through his neck with an ordinary wood saw. He's trying to keep his head in its proper position and there's a look of total surprise on his face – he's taken aback –'

'Please don't, Annette –'

'I only mention it because Henry and Buttercup observed that people get so civilised they don't dare do that kind of thing to you physically, they'll do it to you mentally. We're all Serbs and Croats and Bosnians at heart. Spicer's been sawing through the inside of my head, not the outside, that's all. People like to do to each other the most gruesome thing they can possibly think of. Sawing people's heads off is quite funny, in its way. Separating the conscious, aware part from the automatically twitching part. There! That's the way to do it, that's final, that's the end of disappointment. Do you a good turn. Spicer hurts me. I twitch. Get to the spinal column, and he can put a stop to all that and feel good again. Only Spicer didn't quite manage. I'd laid my head on the block but I got it out in time. Hardly his fault at all. My neck's healed. Are you crying?'

'Yes. I thought you were out of the pit. You're not.'

'You don't have to get out of it, Gilda. There isn't any route out. You just clean it up a bit, grow a few flowers and ask everyone in. Gilda, he's tapping on the glass, he's getting really angry. I have to go. Oh dear God, it's Ernie. What is Ernie Gromback doing out there in a suit and tie and shiny shoes? He looks absurd.'

'Ernie,' said Annette, six months later. They were picking up the children from school.

'What is it, my dear?' said Ernie.

'Shall we just drive down Bella Crescent, past the house?'

'Are you sure you want to?' asked Ernie.

'Yes, please,' said Annette. 'Tell you what, I'll shut my eyes till we're there, then I'll open them for a second, take in what I see, close them again, and you drive like hell out of there.'

'We don't want to be late for Susan and Jason,' said Ernie. 'We don't have much time to spare.'

'You just don't want me to see Spicer again in case I fancy him,' said Annette. 'Fall back under his spell.'

'You are so right,' said Ernie Gromback.

'Don't worry about it,' said Annette. 'It was in another country, and the Spicer I knew is dead. A simulacrum walks around in his place. How can you love a simulacrum?'

'A pity about the property though,' said Ernie. 'To be cheated out of it like that.'

'Never mind,' said Annette, 'I could put it all into a novel.'

'Nobody would believe it,' said Ernie. 'Don't even think of it.'

'I've changed my mind,' said Annette. 'Let's go straight to the school. I don't want to drive down Bella Crescent, after all. I know what I would see. The house in a kind of seedy disrepair; its porch somehow shrunk in stature; the steps crumbling; two plates outside the door, with a fresh set of bogus initials on them. Spicer looking out of a top window: a kind of poodle for their pleasure, and Marion too perhaps. The windows will be foggy from a haze of incense, marijuana and the quality of the minds within. There will be a trail of trusting people to the door, looking for someone to believe in, anyone: so what if families split, and in the name of love and peace, malice abounds. You wouldn't want to see that, and neither would I. It might put my blood-pressure up, and that would be bad for our baby. I reckon we'd better forswear the experience, keep what belongs to the past in the past.'

'I reckon so too,' said Ernie Gromback, and turned the car, and they went to pick up the children.

'Ernie,' said Annette, as they parked the car outside the school gates. 'Do me a favour?'

'Anything,' said Ernie.

'Take a look at the photograph.'

'What, again?'

'Please,' said Annette. 'Do you see a bust of Karl Marx in it?'

'No,' said Ernie. 'I don't.'

'That's okay then,' said Annette.

'Put it away in case the children see it,' said Ernie. 'Let's try for a little respectability round here. Thank God it's a polaroid, and already fading.'